EDUCATING KELLY PAYNE

PAYNE

HAZEL WARD

Hope St Press

1

THERE WILL BE CONSEQUENCES

Kelly rang the doorbell. She had a key but hadn't used it since her dad had moved his woman in. That was what, three years ago? Something along those lines. Kelly had already moved out by then because she'd seen how things were going, and because this house had stopped being home well before then.

A head appeared at the window. She thought it was Dan, but she couldn't be sure. The net curtain made it hard to tell which of her two little brothers it was, although they weren't that little anymore. At thirteen and fifteen, they were bigger than her.

A minute later Dan opened the front door. 'We're not supposed to answer, but as it's you.'

She followed him into the living room. Someone had gone overboard with the Christmas decorations. That woman, probably. Dan flopped down onto the settee next to Conor, her youngest brother, and picked up a gamepad. Straight away, his head was back in the game.

Kelly glanced around. No sign of any adults. 'You two on your own?'

Dan kept his eye on the TV. 'Mum and Dad have gone shopping.'

'Carol and Dad,' she corrected him. No way was that woman their mum.

'Yeah, whatever.'

Kelly looked around the room. There was a new Christmas tree in the corner. One of those plastic ones that was supposed to look real. They must have got rid of her mum's old one. That would be Carol's doing.

Her phone rang. It was Craig, her so-called boyfriend. 'Where are yer?'

'At my dad's.'

'Could've left a message. I woke up and you were gone.'

'I told you last night.'

'There's no milk.'

'Just go to the shop, Craig.'

Over on the settee, Dan and Conor were glued to the telly. She might as well not be here. Anyway, she didn't want to be around when her dad and Carol got back.

'I'm just leaving. I'll pick some up on the way.'

Kelly put a couple of presents under the tree and took the ones with her name on them, along with a card. 'I've left presents for you.'

Dan's head twitched. That was probably the closest to a thank you she was going to get.

Conor did the same, but managed: 'Cool.'

She rolled her eyes, but they didn't notice. Obviously. 'Merry Christmas.' No answer. 'You'll get eye strain.' That was something her nan said. Jesus. She was only just nineteen and was already turning into an old woman.

On the way back to Craig's flat she stopped off at the Tesco

Express, which was busier than usual, with it being Christmas Eve. She just about had enough money for two turkey ready meals, a loaf, a grab-bag of crisps, the milk, and a can of squirty cream. There were some mince pies and chocolates in the flat that she'd brought back from the foodbank she helped in, so that was Christmas Day sorted.

As soon as she opened the door to the flat she heard the sound of *Call of Duty: Black Ops*. Craig was never off that game. Sure enough, he was plonked on the settee, the gamepad in his hands. 'Did you get the milk?'

She went over to the little table in front of him. There was a bowl of dry Shreddies on there, next to a full ashtray and a plate with what was left of last night's dinner cemented to it – gungy red chicken and dried-hard noodles. It turned her stomach. She stuck the milk in his face.

He twisted his neck around her and carried on playing. 'Pour it in for us, will yer?'

Kelly slammed the milk down on the table. 'Do it yerself.'

Craig threw the gamepad down. 'What? You're so arsey, you know.'

That didn't even deserve an answer. She sometimes wondered if there was any difference between Craig and her brothers. Except there was, obviously. For one, Craig was twice as old as them. For another, she was supposed to be his girlfriend. Not his big sister, and definitely not his mother.

Kelly put the shopping away and flicked the kettle on. 'Do you want tea?'

'Nah, I'm going out.'

'But I've only just got back.'

He shoved a spoonful of Shreddies in his mouth. 'Not my fault. I've gorra go and see Jay.'

'Is Letitia gonna be there?'

'Of course she is. He's three. It's not like he can wait there for me on his own, is it?'

Kelly knew that. It wasn't like she begrudged Craig seeing his kid. It was Letitia, the ex that never went away, that bothered her. Letitia bothered Kelly more than she was prepared to admit. Mainly because she wasn't one hundred per cent sure Letitia was still Craig's ex. She had a feeling he was still seeing her.

'When will you be back?'

'Dunno. I'm seeing me mates after.' A piece of Shreddie fell out of his mouth onto his chin. He wiped it away and it fell to the floor.

'Where? I could meet you.'

'Won't know 'til later.' He pushed another spoonful in.

'Craig! It's Christmas Eve. Are you seriously gonna leave me here, all on my own?'

'Fine. I'll give you a bell or something, later.'

She didn't believe him. 'You'd better. Because if you don't, the consequences will be dire.'

He snorted, sending more half-chewed Shreddies across the room. 'You what? The consequences will be dire? You bin taking lessons from that posh friend of yours? She bin telling you what to say, has she?'

Kelly stood up to her full height, which wasn't very high at all. 'I don't need no friend to tell me what to say. I'm warning you. If you leave me here alone, all day and night and come back pissed, or stoned, or whatever, there will be consequences. And they will be dire.'

Craig took three steps towards her. She held her breath while he weighed her up. Then he picked up a big box wrapped in cheap Christmas paper and turned away. 'I'll see you later.'

She let her breath slip slowly out when she was sure he'd left the flat. Consequences will be dire? What the hell made her say that? Stupid question. Anger made her say it. Anger that had been boiling up for the last two days, ever since the foodbank. It had been the final one before Christmas and it had been totally mad, and totally brilliant. Totally full-on Christmas. Afterwards, all the volunteers had gone out for a meal. It was the best time she'd had since she was a little kid. Then she'd got home to this shithole, Craig off his face and sulking because he'd expected her back earlier. The bubble burst, and she'd been winding herself up ever since. All the same, she had no idea why she'd said those exact words, except that she liked the sound of them. Craig had been right. They had come from her new friend, Annette – or the posh one, as he usually called her. Kelly preferred to call her Net. She'd heard Net say those very words once, and had to Google them to find out what they meant. Something really bad, apparently.

She tried to imagine what Net was doing now. Whatever it was, it was probably really fabulous. She probably wasn't alone in a stinking flat with nothing but the telly for company.

The presents she'd brought from her dad's caught Kelly's eye. There was no tree to leave them under, so she put them on the floor by the TV, ready for the morning. She opened the card:

'Dear Kelly,

Merry Christmas and a happy New Year. Hoping 2018 will be a good one for you.

All our love,

Dad and Carol xx'

· · ·

The writing inside was Carol's. Typical. Her dad couldn't even be bothered to write her card. And talk about gushy. It made Kelly want to spew. On the plus side, there were two ten pound notes in there. That would come in handy, being as she'd maxed out on Christmas presents.

Kelly took her tea over to the settee. The milk was still on the table. She pushed the half-eaten bowl of Shreddies, the ashtray and dirty plate to the far corner. What was she doing here? Why did she put up with this crap? She blew on her tea. Because she had nowhere else to go. That's why.

2

BACK IN THE FUTURE

Kelly was so bored. 2022 was less than a week old and she was already bored of it. There was nothing on the telly and, for some reason, she couldn't get that last Christmas with Craig out of her head. No idea why. It was four years ago and it wasn't exactly a standout Christmas. Not the right kind of standout anyway. They'd split up a few months later and she'd made a point of not thinking about him since, so it was funny that he was back on her mind tonight. Must be the boredom.

Kelly wasn't one of those people that made New Year's resolutions but if she was, it would be to make this year a bit less boring. A bit less home alone with no one but the dogs for company.

Also, if she was that kind of person. Which she wasn't. But, if she was, she'd probably make it a year to find some-one. He wouldn't have to be great-looking or anything. Just nice. Someone nice who didn't make her feel like she had to apologise for being her. Someone like Will Grey maybe. Not Will himself. He was her bestie, her brother from another mother – her friend, Netta, actually. He was a no-go zone.

For all sorts of reasons, but mainly because he had a girl-friend. The lovely Belle.

Kelly switched off the TV, pulled her knees up to her chest, closed her eyes and listened to the quiet in the house. It was a nice sort of quiet. A warm quiet. She loved this house. It belonged to Netta. Kelly had moved in here when she'd left Craig and from day one it had felt like home. It was the only place she didn't mind being alone in, luckily, because it was just her and the dogs tonight. Again. Everyone else was out.

Kelly yawned. She was ready for bed. She let the dogs out and waited on the back step for them. Maud came in first. She never hung around on a cold night. Betty took a bit longer. Probably got distracted by a falling leaf or some-thing. It didn't take much where Betty was concerned. When they were both finally in, Kelly locked up and switched off the downstairs lights.

She'd nearly reached the stairs in the hall when she heard muffled voices coming from the front garden. Netta wasn't due back. She was staying with her lover-man, Frank, tonight. Frank only lived next door, so there was always the chance they might pop over. But it wasn't Netta. It was Will. Kelly recognised his shape through the stained glass window. Normally she'd have opened the door for him, but not tonight. Belle was with him. Of course she was. She was always with him. She'd practically moved in as soon as they got back from uni for the holidays. Belle, with her long blonde hair and her pretty face. She was probably in a nice dress and wearing the kind of make-up that made her look even prettier and more natural. Kelly was in a pair of stupid Christmas pyjamas and one of Will's old jumpers, and hadn't bothered with make-up since New Year's Eve.

She was trying to work out if she could get upstairs

before the door opened, and before Will had a chance to see how crap she was compared to Belle. Then the key turned in the lock. *Shit.* She shot into the study on the other side of the staircase, and pushed the door until it was nearly shut.

The front door closed behind Will and Belle. From the other side of the study door, Kelly could tell they sounded drunk. Not falling down drunk, but definitely a bit giggly, and the more they tried to keep quiet, the gigglier they got. Most likely they'd go straight up to bed and she could come out of hiding.

Kelly's bum was beginning to ache. She'd been sitting on the wooden floor in the study for at least half an hour, listening through a crack in the door. Will and Belle were still in the living room, talking. Bloody talking. Why didn't they do what normal people did when they were wasted and just fall asleep dribbling? It's not like they were even talking about drunk stuff, like the number of Hula Hoops you could wear on one finger, or how many cheesy Wotsits you could stuff into your mouth in one go. That kind of stuff. They were talking proper intellectual shit. That was the thing about clever people. They couldn't even get pissed properly.

Suddenly, it went quiet. Finally, they were going to bed. Or were they? What was that sound? Were they? Was that? No. Really? Not on the leather sofa? Oh my God! They were actually doing it. Ugh! That was so, finger down the throat, disgusting. Kelly shuddered. She was totally grossed out. And she was freezing. But there was no way she could go into the hall now.

There was a little settee at the back of the study. Kelly tiptoed over and curled up on it. At least the dogs hadn't given her away. They were probably too busy watching those two, at it. Jesus. She was disgusted all over again. She yawned and shivered at the same time. If she wasn't so cold, she'd go to sleep.

Kelly woke up, still freezing cold. She must have dozed off after all. The house was quiet again. That pair had obviously finished. The study was still dark, but not as dark as it had been when she'd closed her eyes. She could make out the books on the shelves that covered the opposite wall now. She'd never counted them, but there had to be hundreds. They'd belonged to Edie Pinsent, the old lady who lived in the house before Netta. Kelly wondered how many Edie had actually read. Probably quite a few, judging by the diaries Edie had left behind when she died. How amazing was that? Kelly hadn't read a single book since school. Before that, if she was honest. She hadn't really read one since she was twelve, when her mum died. Not proper books anyway. She'd read some of Edie's diaries. They were much more interesting than proper books.

She went over to the shelves and let her eyes follow a line of big, fat books, stopping at the biggest and fattest. She shone her phone on it to see the title. *Concise Oxford English Dictionary*. Oh, it was just a dictionary. Disappointing. She wasn't sure what concise meant though. She'd have a look in it later and find out. Right now she really wanted to go to bed.

Kelly crept across the hall for a sneaky peek through a small gap in the living room door. Betty's furry nose poked through the gap. Kelly patted the dog's head and pushed the door open a little. Belle and Will were asleep in each other's arms, on the sofa. They still had their clothes on. One thing to be grateful for. Kelly couldn't take her eyes off them.

They were quite alike in looks really. They had so much in common as well. They were perfect for each other.

She noticed Maud was watching her from the armchair. Maud knew, even if no one else did. Maud understood everything. The only thing Kelly understood was that she needed to stop loving Will Grey.

3

WET SOFAS AND SOGGY ARSES

Netta woke up in Frank's bed. No surprise there, since she'd climbed into it last night and cuddled under the duvet with him. They'd been too tired for anything other than that. The evening had started quietly enough with a meal in town, but they'd decided to call into Frank's favourite pub, The Hope and Anchor, afterwards and found a party in full swing. According to Adrian, the owner, it was someone's birthday, although no one knew whose exactly. They'd joined Frank's friends and stayed for much too long, finally crawling home in the early hours rather worse for wear. Consequently, Netta was feeling more than a little shabby this morning.

Frank came in with a tray of tea and toast. 'Breakfast, milady?'

'That is perfect. You really are Mr Wonderful, you know.'

He put the tray down on the bedside table and got back into bed. 'I do. Kiss me, woman, before we fill our faces with jammy toast.'

'Be quick then, I'm starving and I need tea.'

They kissed. He pulled away first. 'Right, that's enough of that. Pass me my tea. I've a desperate thirst on me. Next time I suggest stopping off at the Hope and Anchor on party night, remind me I'm too old for that kind of thing.'

'The Hope and Anchor has a party night?'

'Did you not know? Every night's a party night at the Hope and Anchor. Adrian's a big one for the glitter ball.'

Frank's phone rang. It was his daughter, Robyn. He washed his toast down with a mouthful of tea and answered it. 'Hello, Rob. How are yer?'

Netta slipped out of bed and went to the bathroom.

Fully washed and dressed, she returned to the bedroom. Frank was still on the phone to Robyn. Netta gave him a peck on the cheek and whispered: 'See you later. Give her my love.'

It took all of two minutes to reach her house. It was one of the benefits of living next door to your partner. Netta let herself in through the front door. It was still early and she was expecting everyone to be asleep. Kelly and Will weren't early risers and neither was Belle, who was bound to be staying over. Netta's daughter, Liza, was best at getting up at a respectable hour, but she'd been at her dad's house for the last two days.

There'd been a time when Liza and her dad had been thick as thieves but lately, it was all Liza could do to spend a night at Colin's. As far as Netta knew, it was mostly because his partner, Arianne, drove Liza up the wall. She'd only stayed this time because Colin's parents were visiting, and she didn't want to upset them.

It was a surprise to find Kelly on her knees in the lounge with a bowl of soapy water. Closer inspection revealed that she was washing down the old leather sofa. Netta leaned against the door frame. 'Morning. Somebody had an accident?'

Kelly's face was flushed. 'Yeah, Betty knocked my tea over it.'

'Ah well, don't worry. It all adds to the character. What did you get up to last night?'

'Nothing much. Just watched telly with Betty and Maud.'

Netta nodded. She wished Kelly had some friends of her own. It was a constant worry. 'Anything good on?'

'Nah, not really.'

'When did Will and Belle get back?'

'Dunno. After I went to bed.'

'I don't suppose we'll see them until lunchtime then.'

'They've already gone out. Liza messaged to say her dad was bringing her back and he might come in. Will didn't want to be around. With him not talking to his dad and all that.'

It wasn't a statement that required comment. Will hadn't spoken to his father for several years, and he didn't seem to be in a rush to change that. The question was, why was Colin coming inside? If Liza had messaged Will specifically, maybe it was to warn him that Colin wanted to speak to him. Netta's speculation was cut short when Colin's car pulled up outside. Her mood sank as quickly as a just cooked soufflé. If only Liza had messaged her too. She could have hidden out at Frank's until the coast was clear.

She let them in while Kelly emptied the bowl of water. They had bags of Christmas presents with them, presumably from Colin's family.

'You're looking great.' Colin gave her his most charming smile. It was one she'd seen many times over the years, when he was trying to be matey with someone. It wasn't one he usually blessed her with, until today.

'Thanks.' She said it with as much sincerity as she could muster. She was doing her best to put on a good show for Liza's sake.

Liza's eyebrows twitched upwards. 'Dad thought he'd come in and say hello.'

'Oh! Hello!' Before she could stop herself, Netta flew into an involuntary jazz hands expression. This really was quite awkward.

'Hello.' Colin's charming smile had become more rigid and grimacing. 'I was hoping Will might be here. Still in bed, is he?'

Netta matched his smile with something similar. 'He's out I'm afraid.'

'Out?' He looked like he didn't believe her. All the same, he followed Liza into the lounge.

Kelly stood in front of the fireplace, arms folded. 'Yeah, you just missed them.' There was a touch of mockery in her tone that was bound to rub him up the wrong way.

Colin gave Kelly a cursory glance. 'Them?'

'Will and Belle,' said Netta.

'Ah, the elusive Belle.'

'She ain't that elusive. She's here all the fucking time,' said Kelly.

Liza sniggered. It set Kelly off too. Colin laughed along with them, to let them know he was in on the joke. He wasn't, of course, but he probably knew that.

Liza took a glossy book from one of her bags and opened it out on the coffee table. 'Kel, this book my aunt got me is full of the coolest art.'

She and Kelly knelt down to look at it.

Colin did a theatrical eye roll. It was his forte, something he liked to do just before hitting the sarcasm button. 'Honestly, Lize, not everyone's interested in that sort of stuff, you know.'

Liza kept her eyes on the pages. 'We're good.'

'Really, Liza?' He seemed determined to push on. 'I doubt it would mean anything to Kelly.' And there it was. Sarcasm button well and truly pressed.

Kelly sat back on her heels. 'I'm going upstairs. We'll look at this later, Lize, yeah?' She got up and stood in front of Colin, eyeballed him for a minute and sucked air through her teeth. He blinked, like a man who was already regretting pressing that button. She might have been small but, my God, Kelly could be scary.

Liza waited for Kelly to go upstairs before opening her mouth. 'Unacceptable, Dad.'

Colin shrugged. 'Sorry, darling, I'm not with you.'

'Yeah, really. I'd better make sure Kelly's all right.' She shot him a withering look. 'See yer.'

With Liza gone, Colin turned to Netta and blew out his cheeks. 'What was all that about?'

'I think we both know what it was about, don't we?'

He stuck his bottom lip out. 'Nope. You're going to have to enlighten me. I mean, I was just trying to point out that it wasn't the sort of thing Kelly would be interested in.'

Netta gritted her teeth. 'Why wouldn't she be interested in it?'

'Well, because … you know.'

'No, I don't know.'

'Well, she's hardly the sharpest crayon in the box, is she?'

'And you'd know that, would you? You've met Kelly, what, three or four times? And yet you've already decided that she doesn't match up to your superior intellect.'

'Steady on, that's not what I meant. But actually, I know more about Kelly than you think, given that Liza talks about her all the time. And now that you've brought it up, I'm a little worried about the influence she wields over our daughter.'

So that's what this was all about. Liza and Kelly were bonding and he was jealous. She might have known he hadn't wanted to patch things up with Will. It was just an excuse to get inside so that he could lob in a grenade and cause friction. It was a bit obvious by Colin's standards though. He must be losing his touch. 'There's no need to worry. Being with Kelly has done Liza nothing but good. Besides, she knows her own mind. She's quite capable of weeding out the wrong type of influence.'

'You think so, do you? Talked about it, have you?' He kept his voice low and precise to make sure no one else could hear him. It was a trick he used when they were still living together. It was always so much more menacing in those days. 'I knew this was going to happen. I could have put money on it. I can see it now. The two of you filling her head with all sorts of nonsense about me. Just like you did with Will.'

Netta suppressed her laughter with a snort. 'Sorry to disappoint you, Colin, but we hardly ever talk about you. You're just not that important. Or interesting.'

He opened his mouth and closed it again. Maybe it was the shock of hearing that he was neither important, nor interesting. He dropped down to the sofa and immediately shot up again. 'What the…This seat is soaking wet!'

'Oh really? Sorry about that.'

He felt the backside of his jeans. 'Shit! I'm supposed to be going food shopping. How can I walk around M&S with a soggy arse? I don't suppose you have something to dry it with?'

'What, like a hairdryer?'

'Yes, that would do it.'

'No. Sorry.'

He glared at her, then went to the bottom of the stairs. 'Liza. Honey. I'm going now.'

There was no reply.

'I'll call you.'

Still no reply.

He turned to Netta. 'Maybe I should go up.'

Netta shook her head. 'I don't think so, Colin. In fact, I think you'd better fuck off and take your soggy arse with you.'

4

BETTY MILKS THE GUILT BISCUITS

Kelly lay on her bed, staring up at the ceiling. She, Liza and Netta had painted the room last year. The walls were soft yellow, the colour of pale butter, and the ceiling was as blue as the sky on a summer's day, with a couple of white wispy clouds dotted here and there. Shooting out of one corner were three faint strands of yellow, like the sun was just reaching out to her. It nearly always made Kelly feel warm and fuzzy.

It had been Liza's idea to paint it like this. Kelly had been feeling a bit depressed and Liza thought it would cheer her up. Kelly's nan had died the year before and it had caught up with her. Freaky really. One minute she was going along okay, thinking she'd got over things and the next, she wobbled.

Liza appeared in front of the open door. Kelly was expecting her: she'd heard the floorboards creaking on the landing a few minutes earlier. Liza must have been listening at the top of the stairs. 'Okay if I come in?'

'Sure.' Kelly shuffled over to make some room.

Liza looked up at the ceiling. 'You all right?'

'Yeah, course. Just a bit tired. Didn't get much sleep last night.'

'Will and Belle?'

Kelly smiled. 'Sort of.'

'Sorry about my dad. He can be a real prick sometimes.'

'No need for you to say sorry. It's not your fault.'

'I guess not. But I want to. Could you hear what he was saying?'

'Yep.' She'd heard every word. She'd deliberately left the door open for that purpose. Although, why she'd done that she couldn't say, because the last thing she needed was some smarmy arse shitebag spelling out what she already knew.

'He does that stupid low voice because he thinks we can't hear him, but actually, it makes it easier to hear than if he talked like a normal person. Don't let him get to you. He's an unbelievable snob. So are Gran and Grandad. Honestly, I do love them and everything but they are so up themselves. Nothing like Nanny Geraldine and Grandad Arthur. Also, I think Dad's threatened by you. He can't deal with strong women. Plus, I think he's jealous that you, me and Mum get on so well. You should see the look on his face every time I talk about you. It's so pathetic.'

The sun suddenly split the clouds outside and burst through the bedroom window, across the ceiling to meet the painted rays. It made Kelly feel sunny too. 'They look like they're shimmering, don't they?'

'Yeah. It's amazing. I think I might do my ceiling like this. Will you help me?'

'Yeah, course.'

'I think he's gone now. Shall we go back down?'

Netta was in the kitchen when they got downstairs. She was

messing with Frank's machine. She'd bought it for Frank a few years ago and, although it lived in their kitchen and everyone used it, they still called it Frank's machine.

Netta poured milk into the jug that they kept especially for frothy coffees. 'Who fancies a cappuccino?'

Both Kelly and Liza raised a hand. Liza fetched the book from the living room and Kelly grabbed a tin of biscuits from the dresser.

'Why is the sofa wet?' asked Liza.

'I had to wash it. Betty knocked my tea over,' said Kelly.

Betty cocked her head to one side and whined. Kelly felt bad about blaming her, but what else could she do? She gave the dog a biscuit when she thought the others weren't looking.

She sat with Liza at the kitchen table. Kelly knew nothing about art but she liked looking at the pictures with Liza. What Colin the Prick didn't get was that you could still appreciate something like that, even if you were thick.

Netta sat with them. It was nice, the three of them together. Kelly told herself it didn't matter that Colin the Prick thought she was ignorant and not good enough to be friends with his daughter. It wasn't like his opinion counted for anything. It wasn't like she cared.

Will and Belle came in, all pink and rosy from the fresh January air.

Will grinned at Liza. 'I take it he's gone?'

'Yep.' Liza pointed to the living room. 'There are presents in there from Gran and Grandad. They weren't very happy about not seeing you again.'

'I'll mail them or something.'

Liza tutted. 'You're such a coward, Will.'

'Yeah, yeah. I know.' He went into the living room. 'Why is the sofa wet?'

'Kelly washed it,' said Netta.

Kelly's cheeks went hot. 'Betty knocked some tea over.' She slipped another guilt biscuit to Betty.

Will came back into the kitchen and glanced at Kelly, then at Belle. 'Oh right. I'll just take my presents upstairs.'

Belle ran after him. 'I'll come with you.'

Netta went upstairs too. Kelly and Liza went back to reading the book.

'I think Betty wants another biscuit,' said Liza.

Betty gave Kelly a haughty look, as if to say: 'Shall I tell them or will you?' Bloody dog was really milking it. Kelly gave her one final biscuit.

Liza lowered her voice. 'Was it really Betty?'

Kelly shook her head.

'Will and Belle?' whispered Liza.

Kelly nodded.

'On the sofa?'

Kelly nodded again.

Liza screwed up her nose. 'Eeww!'

5

THE GOODBYE

Will was going back to university in York tomorrow and Netta wanted their last family dinner to be a special one, so she'd pulled out all the stops to make it nice. She put the finishing touches on the big, wooden kitchen table. The Christmas tablecloth that had once belonged to her grandmother, Ada Wilde, was having its final outing before being packed away until December. The candlesticks, the good cutlery, the glasses, and chinaware had been Edie's, her house's former owner.

'The table looks gorgeous, Mum. So vintage.' Liza took a photo of it on her phone. 'I'll send it to Nan. She'll love it. Shame they couldn't come.'

'They've got something on. They'll be here in the morning.' Her parents' social calendar had grown in the last year. You could say it had blossomed. Or maybe that was her mum who was a changed woman after going through therapy just over a year ago.

Kelly called from the lounge to say Will was back from dropping Belle home in Netta's car. She was spending the night with her own family before going back to Leeds. If

Netta was honest, it was a bit of a relief. She liked Belle, but she had been here pretty much twenty-four-seven during the holidays which Netta didn't mind really. It was more that it had a rather negative effect on Kelly and since she and Liza were keeping a close eye on Kelly's moods, it left them both a bit tense. Talking of which, she hadn't quite got to the bottom of this morning's wet sofa incident. She suspected poor Betty was carrying the can for someone, or something, else. Something she was probably better off not knowing about.

Frank came in through the back door. He was wearing a red-checked shirt that Robyn had given him for Christmas. It suited his Irish colouring and steel-grey hair. He looked good in it. Pretty damn sexy, actually. It was easy to forget what a handsome man he was when you were busy with everyone else.

Netta lit the candles and dimmed the lights, and Frank poured the wine. It was all very grown-up. Her children weren't children anymore. Will was twenty-one, and Liza was nineteen. She was at university as well now. Fine Art. Surprisingly, she'd chosen to do her degree in Birmingham. Netta had expected her to move away, but Liza was happy where she was. It was sensible really. Why leave when you could live rent free at home? Especially when you had two artists in the family to mentor you – Frank and, when he wasn't behaving like a complete dickhead, Colin.

The only one she was worried about was Kelly, who wasn't actually her child but felt like she was. Kelly was getting quieter. Some people might say that was a good thing, but Netta didn't agree. Over the last year Kelly had lost her sparkle, and Netta wasn't sure what to do about that.

Frank, interrupted Netta's thoughts: 'I spoke to Robyn earlier, Kelly. She's going to call you tomorrow evening.'

From Netta's point of view, Robyn was the one bright light on Kelly's horizon. They got on fantastically. The only problem was Robyn lived in Edinburgh. A lovely city, but a long way from Birmingham. At least she'd been able to make it here for Christmas.

'She said she really enjoyed Christmas after being stuck up there on her own with the boyfriend last year. It's nice for her to be part of a bigger family. Christmases were usually quiet affairs before you lot moved in next door. Unless we went over to Ireland, which we rarely did.'

'Is that supposed to be a compliment?' said Kelly.

'It is. Do me a favour, will you? When you speak to her, try to find out how things really are. I've a feeling it's not going so well with her and Nick, but she won't tell me.'

'Frank, mate, if she won't tell you, there are two likely reasons. One, there's nothing to tell.' Kelly put one finger up. 'Two, she doesn't want you to know.' She put a second finger up and looked very much like she was telling Frank where to go.

Frank took a sip of wine. 'Thank you, Kelly, for that piece of insight. Strange as it may seem, both of those possibilities did occur to me, which is why I'm asking you to find out. I worry about her.'

'I get that. Tell you what, Frank. I'll ask her and if she wants me to, I'll tell you.'

'Thank you.' Frank refilled their wine glasses. 'Let's have a toast. To the year ahead. I have a feeling 2022 is going to be a good one.'

They raised their glasses. Yes, it was all very grown-up indeed.

. . .

They were all up early in the morning which was just as well because Netta's parents were there soon after. Her mum looked stylish and glamorous in a fashionable navy jumpsuit. Netta felt positively dowdy next to her. She made a mental note about New Year's resolutions and smartening herself up.

Her parents brought their dog, Minnie, daughter of Maud and sister to Betty and Frank's dog, Fred. When Frank came over with Fred, the young dogs went wild.

Ignoring the dog pandemonium, Netta's mum gave her a bag that contained enough food to keep them going on a week-long expedition. 'I've made you a packed lunch for the journey.' For all her recent glamour, it was reassuring to know that underneath it all, her mum was still her mum.

'Thanks, Mum. You know it's just me and Will going, don't you?'

'Yes, but you'll be making two journeys, Nettie, and Will's a grown man now.'

Well that explained it then. Netta and her dad exchanged a look. He gave her a sly wink but he was too slow.

'I saw that, Arthur Wilde, you cheeky monkey.' Her Mum poked him playfully in the ribs.

He laughed. 'You got me, Gee. Caught in the act.'

'Proper pair of lovebirds, aren't they?' whispered Kelly.

Before Netta could answer, Will was doing the rounds of hugs and kisses. It was time to get on the road.

'See you soon, I guess.' Kelly was poker-faced. It was hard to tell what was going on behind that well-practised expression.

He gave Liza a final hug and turned to Kelly. 'Look after yourself, yeah? Pick up when I call.'

Kelly rolled her eyes. 'Yes, Dad.'

'Sorry. I just wanna be sure you're okay. We're mates, aren't we?'

Kelly put her arms around him. 'Always.'

'We'd better get going,' said Netta.

Will pushed himself away from Kelly. It was only then that Netta noticed Kelly's eyes.

6

READ A BOOK

Kelly was pissed off. That shitting sofa was still damp. Why did she do it? It wasn't like it was actually needed. And could she have made it any more obvious? Every time Will looked at her now, all she could think was that he knew she'd been spying on them.

If that wasn't bad enough, she'd made herself look like a complete twat by nearly crying when he left. Crying! What the fuck? He must have seen it too, otherwise why would he be telling her to look after herself, like there was something wrong with her. Netta definitely had. She'd probably spend the whole drive to York and back, trying to work out what had caused it, and all of next month pitying her. Kelly hated being pitied, and she hated pitying herself. It was weak. Which is why she was really, really pissed off. Because right now, she was being unbelievably weak.

Then there was that stuff Colin the Prick said, and what he meant by it. Kelly knew she was thick. She didn't need him spelling it out. Of all the things she'd had to put up with in the last few days, that was the one that was really getting to her. Will was gone, Robyn was gone, and she was a thick, weak twat. Fucking awesome. Welcome to 2022.

Arthur clapped his hands together in the way old people did when they were about to do something. Kelly made a bet with herself that 'Right' would be next word to come out of his mouth.

'Right, I'm popping to the allotment while I'm here. Anyone want to come and give me a hand?'

One point to Kelly. At least she wasn't completely and utterly stupid.

'Sorry, I can't. I promised to see my friend Jade before she goes back to uni,' said Liza.

'I'll come with you, Arthur,' said Frank.

Geraldine helped Arthur with his coat. 'You go with Frank, love. Kelly and me will take the dogs for a walk.' She eyeballed Kelly. 'Don't give me that look, young lady. A bit of fresh air will do you good.'

'I expect you're sorry to see Will go back,' said Geraldine.

'Yeah, I suppose,' said Kelly, as if she hadn't already thought about it a hundred times that day.

They'd reached the park and the three young dogs were a bit hyper. Maud wasn't with them. She wasn't one for park walks.

'Not Belle though?'

'No. She's all right. It's just a bit much with her being around all the time. Liza feels the same.'

'I can imagine. What about you, love. How are you?' Geraldine had this spooky ability to pick up on the little things that gave you away, no matter how much you tried to hide it.

'I'm okay.' Kelly picked up a stick and threw it for the dogs.

Geraldine watched them run after it. 'Where were we? Oh yes. You were about to tell me how you are.'

'I already said I was okay.'

'You did, but that's not what you meant, is it? Tell me to mind my own business if you like, but something's not right with you. You seem a bit down. And I don't think it's just because Will's gone back, or because Belle outstayed her welcome.'

'It's nothing.'

Geraldine gave her a look that basically told her they both knew she was lying. You literally could not get anything past her.

'Okay, okay. I am a bit down at the moment. You're right.'

'I usually am.'

'All right, fucking Obi-Wan Kenobi, you got me.'

'Mind your language please. Do you want to tell me about it? I might be able to help.'

'Nah, it's stupid. You'll only laugh.'

'In that case you better had tell me. I haven't had a good laugh in ages.' Geraldine had that twinkle in her eye that she got when she knew she was being mischievous.

'I'm sick of being thick.' Kelly mumbled it, because just saying it sounded stupid.

Geraldine tutted. 'You're not thick.'

'I am. I missed a lot of school after my mum died. I don't know anything.'

'That's not the same thing, Kelly. You're a clever young woman who hasn't had the benefit of a good education.'

'Sorry, Gez, but that's just a nice way of saying I'm

thick. And I'm sick of people thinking I'm thick. I live in a house full of clever people and I'm the token idiot.'

Geraldine's mouth curled up at the ends.

'I told you you'd laugh.'

'I'm not laughing, love. It just amuses me that you see yourself as a token anything. What's brought this on? No one in Netta's house thinks you're thick.'

'Maybe not, but at least one person thinks I am.'

'Who? Who thinks that?'

'That shitebag Netta used to be married to. Colin. He said some stuff when he came round yesterday. Liza says it's because he's threatened by me. I can't see it myself. I reckon he just thinks I'm not good, or clever enough to be friends with his daughter.'

'I wouldn't pay any attention to Colin Grey. He's a vile, manipulative snake who takes great pleasure in wrecking people's lives,' said Geraldine. 'Liza's probably right. Everything threatens Colin. I'm sure that's the reason he spends all his time trying to control people. Arthur and I despise him. Don't tell Liza that though. We have to pretend to be neutral. He is her dad, after all. Don't tell Will either. I know he hasn't spoken to Colin since he found out what an absolute swine he was to Netta, but they might reconcile at some point in the future.'

'I won't. I know what he's like as well which pisses me off even more, because I let him get to me. I feel stupid enough as it is. I don't need him to make it worse.'

'Oh my poor girl.' Geraldine clapped her hands together. Kelly knew what was coming next. Geraldine didn't disappoint: 'Right, what can we do to put a stop to this nonsense?'

There was only one thing that was going to do that but

it was asking for the impossible. Kelly knew it and Gez probably did too. 'Make me intelligent.'

'I've told you, you already are. I think what you actually
want is an education.'

An education? Maybe that was it. But Kelly had never
been much good at learning. Look how badly school had
gone for her. 'You mean like college and that? I don't know,
I'd have to think about it.'

'Not college necessarily. When I had to leave school at
fifteen, I thought that was the end of my education and it
made me feel worthless and inferior. But Arthur's mum,
Ada, gave me books to read and took me to all sorts of
cultural places. Eventually, I went to night school and
learned bookkeeping too, but my education really began
when I met Ada. You might want to go to college or university, but make that decision when you feel better about
yourself. In the meantime, why not start small? Read a
book.'

'A book?' Was that the best Geraldine could come up
with?

'Yes. A proper book, mind you. Jane Austen, George
Eliot. Maybe one of the Brontë sisters. There are loads of
them in that study. I've seen them.'

'Too many big words.'

'Writing yourself off already?'

'No. Sounds boring, that's all.'

'How do you know if you don't try it? Unless that is,
you're afraid to try in case you fail?'

Kelly was cornered. If she refused she'd basically be
admitting she was scared of books. Bloody Geraldine. 'All
right. I'll try one book.'

'Good. I'll help you pick one out when we get back. And
if you come across a word you don't know, look it up in a

dictionary and learn it. If you like, we can discuss the book as you go along. I used to do that with Ada.'

'Hmm. That your way of checking up on me?'

'Nonsense. It just makes it more fun.'

Kelly wasn't sure about that. Her idea of fun and Geraldine's idea of fun were very, very different. Still, she'd accepted the challenge now.

'Perhaps we could go to some museums, or something. That would be nice,' said Geraldine.

'Maybe. We'll see. Just one question. What does inferior mean?'

'Look it up in a dictionary.' Geraldine looked very pleased with herself.

Kelly tutted loudly. She was not impressed.

'Inferior: Lower in rank, status or quality.'

Kelly closed the *Concise Oxford English Dictionary* and put it back on the shelf. 'So which of those three things did you feel?'

'Oh all three,' said Geraldine. 'But quality most of all, I think. I felt stupid and less worthy when I compared myself to other people. Even Arthur which is silly really. He's very intelligent but I can run rings around him when I want to. You're the same. Everyone's always saying how smart you are.'

'Really?'

'Yes, really. That's a good dictionary you've got there. Relatively new. Was it here when Netta moved in?'

'I think so. There are others but they're falling apart.'

Geraldine looked inside. '2006 edition. Edie must have fancied a newer one.'

'What does concise mean?'

'Why are you asking me? Look it up.' Geraldine pointed at the dictionary.

Kelly sighed. 'Please don't tell me it's for my own good.'

'Okay then I won't. Read it out.'

'It says it means giving information clearly and in few words.'

'There you go then. That's two new words you've learned already. Let's choose a book. How about Jane Austen? You can't go wrong with her. *Pride and Prejudice*. Everybody loves that one. Have you read it?'

Kelly shrugged.

'Maybe you've seen the TV show. Mr Darcy? You must have seen the bit where Elizabeth Bennet comes across him in his wet shirt?'

'Er, no.'

'A long white shirt it was. Very white. A bit see-through. Caused quite a stir at the time.'

'Sorry, Gez. Must have been good though, being as you've got that faraway look in your eye. Does Arthur know about you and this Darcy dude?'

Geraldine winked at her. 'No, and don't you tell him either.'

'All right. As long as you do the same for me. Don't tell anyone I'm reading. I don't want them knowing. Not yet anyway.'

'Okay, love. It'll be our secret. But you shouldn't be embarrassed about it. There's nothing wrong with getting an education.'

7

MR DARCY'S A NOB

'Are things any better between you and Nick?' Kelly was in bed, FaceTiming Robyn. Well not in bed exactly but she was under the duvet. There was only one bad thing about this house – the heating was rubbish which made it freezing in winter.

'Not really,' said Robyn. 'I thought Christmas would have given us some space but it's made things worse. I hate being in the flat when he's here. He's out tonight and it's so nice.'

'Sounds a bit shit. Do you think–'

'We'll break up? Maybe. Probably. I dunno. It feels like it's over but we can't say the words.'

'Your dad's asked me to find out what's going on with you, by the way. I haven't told him I already know.'

'Oh crap. I didn't say anything to him because I didn't want to worry him.'

'Too late. What do you want me to say? I can tell him to mind his own business if you want.'

Robyn laughed. 'You would as well, wouldn't you? Just

say me and Nick are working through some issues and I'll
tell him if he needs to start worrying.'

'Okay. If you want to talk or anything though, I'm here.'

'Thanks. It's good to have a friend who's just mine and
not Nick's as well. I've got a couple of my own up here, but
most of them are joint friends. Actually, they're Nick's
friends really. Anyway, changing the subject, how're things
with Will?'

'He's gone back today. Netta's given him a lift. I almost
lost it and cried when he was leaving. In front of everyone.'

'Shit! Are you all right now?'

'Yeah. It was just a bit humiliating.'

'Did anyone else notice?'

'Netta might have. Not sure about the others. No one
else knows except you. I really need to get him out of my
head.'

'You need a cure,' said Robyn.

'Yeah. A magic potion.'

'Or another man.'

'Huh, fat chance. Oh, meant to say, Geraldine's got me
reading a book. She thinks I need educating.'

'Interesting. Why?' Robyn clipped up her long red hair
onto the top of head as she spoke. It showed off her elegant
neck and beautiful features perfectly.

'My own fault for saying I thought I was thick. That was
her answer. I like your hair up like that, by the way.'

'Cheers. You're definitely not thick. Anyone can see that.
Any particular book?'

'*Pride and Prejudice*. Have you heard of it?'

'Yeah. Good choice. You might find the language a bit
old-fashioned but you'll get used to it. Mr Darcy, though.
He'd make you forget Will.'

. . .

Robyn had hung up half an hour ago and Kelly was still in bed with Betty and Maud next to her. She ran her hands along their rough coats and thought about the man she always thought about when she was alone.

Kelly hadn't meant to fall for Will. In fact, the first time she saw him, she'd thought he was a posho prick. But then he moved in with them and got under her skin. In the beginning it was the kind of love you had for a best friend, or a brother. But that had changed over time. Not that she'd noticed straight away. It was Belle that made Kelly realise her feelings had changed. She felt sick the first time he brought Belle home. That's when she understood, she properly loved Will Grey. But there was no point loving him like that, was there? Because he was in love with Belle.

She opened up one of the drawers next to the bed. There was just enough room inside for the reading book and the dictionary. She took out *Pride and Prejudice*. The cover was hard and solid. It looked well old, and had the same musty smell the study used to have, before they cleared out the papers and diaries that Edie had stashed in there.

Kelly opened it and held it up to her nose to catch a whiff, then wished she hadn't. She threw it on the bed before she gagged. Maud stuck her nose on it, sneezed and left a trail of dog snot all over the pages.

'Great. Thanks for that, Maud.' She wiped it with a tissue, but that just smeared the snot across the page. She picked the book up between her thumb and fingers to check the damage. Not too bad. She could probably dry it.

Kelly turned the hairdryer on. The pages fluttered with the blast of air. Something fell out of them and landed on the floor. It was an old card. On one side was a black and white photo of some ancient buildings. Ruins. There were some words printed in one corner:

'*Roma – Arco di Tito*'.

Other than a few French words remembered from school, she couldn't speak foreign languages, but it was easy to guess that Roma was Rome. What were those things called in the front of the picture? She tried to remember what else she'd learned. Columns. Roman columns. That was it. 'Not so thick after all, eh?'

On the other side of the card were more printed foreign words. Italian, probably. The rest was blank, except for one handwritten sentence:

'*Rome, 1956 – The Spinster Society's first outing.*'

It was Edie's writing. Kelly had read enough of her diaries to recognise it, but The Spinster Society gave it away. It was the name Edie and her friends had given themselves.

Oh my God! She had to show Netta and Liza. They'd think it was amazing. Even though none of them had known Edie, they were really into all the stuff she left behind. Just touching this card made Kelly's fingers tingle. She was absolutely buzzing. What a brilliant find. She couldn't wait for Netta and Liza to get home.

The buzz lasted for as long as it took to remember that she didn't want anyone to know she was reading. Bollocks. She could only tell Geraldine and Robyn. They'd be interested but it wouldn't mean the same to them. She'd have to keep it a secret for now. Wait and see how she got on with the book. Maybe she'd tell them when she'd read it. That would be a double surprise for them.

Kelly looked at the card again. Imagine going to Rome back then. It would have been much harder than it was now, especially for three single women. Edie really had been a trailblazer. She gave the book a shake, in case there were any more in there. None came out. Edie must have been using it as a bookmark. Well, if it was good enough for

Edie... She settled back in the bed, pulled the duvet up and started to read.

After the first chapter, Kelly was ready to stick it back on the shelf and forget all about *Pride and Prejudice*. The sentences were all wrong and they talked funny. It was only Edie's card that stopped her. Although it had been couple of years since she'd read the diaries, she could remember all the things Edie did before she went on that holiday. It had been her first trip abroad after some really dark times. All the heartache Edie had experienced up till then, and she was still looking for new challenges. If Edie could do all of that, the least she could do was read a book.

She took a deep breath and went back to the beginning. This time, she read more slowly and used the dictionary when she needed to. She just reached the end of the third chapter when she heard someone coming in. She tapped out a message to Geraldine:

'*Started. Three chapters done. Getting used to the weird language. Mr Darcy a bit of a nob so far. Love Mrs Bennet. She's so funny. Reminds me of you.*'

A message came back a few minutes later:

'*Three chapters is good. Not sure I like being compared to Mrs B but yes, she is funny. Wait and see on Mr D. Looking forward to a proper chat about it when we see each other again.*'

'Hey, Kel. You and the dogs in there?' It was Liza.

Kelly jumped. She marked her place with the card and closed the book. 'Yeah, yeah. Give me a minute.'

She put the books back in their hiding place and went to check her face in the mirror. Her cheeks were pink from the warmth of the duvet and her eyes didn't look quite so lifeless as they normally did, but there were no obvious signs she'd been educating herself.

The dogs were waiting at the door. Kelly opened it and

followed them out. Netta would be back from York soon. Everything was back to normal. Except for one small change. She was a reader now.

8

EDIE'S TRAIL

'I've finished *Pride and Prejudice*.' Kelly placed her elbows on the table and picked up her cup with both hands. She was copying a girl in a film she'd watched with Liza. It was French but they'd printed the words in English at the bottom of the screen, so it was okay. The girl in the film was small and skinny with short hair, just like her. When she'd held the cup to her mouth like that, Kelly thought it was just so sophisticated.

'*Sophisticated: Showing worldly experience and knowledge of fashion and culture. Appealing to sophisticated people*'.

She did know what sophisticated meant, but she looked it up in the dictionary to be absolutely sure. She'd repeated the words until she knew the meaning off by heart. It was a new thing she'd started doing. At first it was to understand what Jane Austen was going on about, but she got really into it after a while. Now, she was learning a new word most days. If she didn't come across one when she was reading, she just opened the dictionary at any old page and picked one out. Amazingly, she was good at memorising them.

She was with Geraldine, in Gez's number one choice of

café. It was done out all retro, like the coffee bars she used to go to with Arthur when they were young. Kelly had been here so many times with Geraldine, she could probably name most of the tunes they played. The one that was on now was 'Here Comes the Night'. Kelly liked it. She liked a lot of those old tunes.

'Who was your favourite character?' said Geraldine.

'Elizabeth. She was really sassy and she saw right through the bullshit. Well, most of it. That Wickham fooled her with his good looks and charm, but she realised he was a tool eventually. I liked Mrs Bennet as well, but I was wrong about her being like you. You're far more sensible and sophisticated than Mrs B.' Kelly took another sophisticated sip on her coffee, pleased with herself to have been able to slip her latest new word in.

'I should think so too. What about Mr Darcy? What did you think of him in the end?'

'Definitely up himself until Lizzie told him where to get off but yeah, I get the whole Mr Darcy romantic hero thing. I didn't see anything about a wet shirt though.'

'No that was just the TV show. We should watch it.' Gez had that faraway look in her eye again.

Kelly didn't want to know what was going on in that mind of hers. She was in her seventies, for fuck's sake. She should be thinking about fruit cake and daytime quiz shows, not hot, brooding men with their nipples poking through clingy wet shirts. 'You know you're outrageous, don't you? Whatever would Arthur say?'

Geraldine chuckled. She was in one of her mischievous moods again. Kelly loved being with her when she was like this. It made her realise how lucky she was to have Geraldine as a stand-in nan. Gez had offered to be it on the day

Kelly's real nan died. She'd said it to comfort her but whether she'd meant it or not, that's what Gez had become.

Geraldine pushed her fork into a slice of tiramisu. It was the café's speciality. 'What are you going to read next?'

'Dunno. I'll have a look when the others are out.'

'You'll carry on then?'

'Definitely. Prepare to be shocked. I like reading.'

'Well, blow me down.' Gez had a very sarky look on her face.

'I've got something to show you.' Kelly passed over the card she'd found. 'It was in the book. It was Edie's. She's written on the back.'

Geraldine looked at the picture and turned it over to read the writing. 'It's a postcard. I don't suppose you've sent many of them. We used to send them every time we went on holiday before mobile phones were invented. This is lovely. Have you shown it to Netta?'

Kelly shook her head. 'I will do though. When I'm ready.'

'Italy must have been such a contrast to dreary old England in those days.'

'Mmm, very sophisticated.'

Geraldine's mouth was twitching.

'What?'

'Somebody's been at the dictionary again.' If anyone else had said that… But this was Gez and she wasn't being snarky or anything.

Kelly grinned at her stand-in nan. 'So?'

'So, I think it's blummin' wonderful, and I hope you do too.'

'Gez, I've read one book and learned a couple of new words. Let's not get too excited.'

'Stuff that. Let's absolutely get excited. You've earned it.'

It was Monday night. Two days since Kelly had seen Geraldine, and there'd been no chance of secretly picking up another book because someone was always in the house. Kelly was alone in the living room. She was pretending to watch TV but really she was thinking about Edie's postcard, wandering if there were any more hidden among the books in the study.

Netta stuck her head round the door. 'I'm popping over to Frank's. Won't be long.'

At last a chance. Liza had already gone over there an hour ago to ask Frank about some coursework. Netta probably wanted to make sure Lize wasn't taking too many liberties. Frank taught part-time at a college and painted the rest of the time, so giving an extra evening lesson might not have been his idea of a rest. He didn't seem to mind though. He was all right like that.

As soon as she thought Netta was safely inside Frank's house, Kelly switched off the TV and ran upstairs to grab *Pride and Prejudice*. In a few minutes, she was back down in the study, scanning the shelves for more Jane Austen books. One called *Emma* looked interesting. She gave it a shake. Nothing came out. There were two more by Jane Austen. Kelly tried them. The first was as empty as *Emma*, but another card fell out of the second when she shook it. It was called *Mansfield Park*. That was the one then. Her next read.

She heard Frank's front door closing and shoved the books back on the shelf, switched off the light, and raced to the living room. She just about had time to switch the telly back on before Netta and Liza came in. Her heart was thumping and, in spite of the house's rubbish heating, she was hot. All this sneaking around was great for keeping warm.

In the middle of the night when she was certain everyone else was asleep, Kelly crept downstairs.

Betty was nowhere to be seen. She'd be flat out on Liza's bed. In the living room, Maud was curled up in her favourite armchair. She jumped off and followed Kelly into the study.

Kelly switched on a desk lamp and looked for *Mansfield Park*. It was too late to read it now. She'd start it tomorrow night when she was in bed. Tomorrow was a foodbank day. They'd be rushed off their feet, so it'd be a good excuse for an early night. There'd be time then to have a proper look at that postcard. She'd kept hold of the other one to show Netta when the time came, and written down where she'd found it. At the weekend, she'd buy a notebook and make proper notes on which books the cards had come from. Now that she'd found two, she was hoping there'd be more. That was going to be another new challenge. Every time she finished a book, she'd look for another with a postcard. She was going to follow Edie's reading trail and see where it took her.

Maud came closer, her eyes on the book. She'd been Edie's dog once. Kelly wondered if she still remembered her. She held the book out for Maud to sniff. The little dog groaned and wagged her tail. Kelly put her finger to her lips. 'Shh. Our secret.'

9

CONSEQUENCES REMEMBERED

Kelly and Netta pulled into the car park at the foodbank. They volunteered here on Tuesdays and Fridays. When she'd first started coming here, Kelly hadn't been very popular, on account of her being a bit of a gobshite. Everybody hated her except Netta, who she'd hit it off with straight away – to everyone's amazement, including her own – and Neil, who was way too nice to hate anyone. She'd calmed down a lot since then, and the other volunteers didn't seem to mind her now.

They went in through one of the double doors that would be properly opened at eleven, for the clients. Neil was already there. He was always early for everything. Him, Kelly and Netta had a jam and pickles business that they ran out of a kitchen on an industrial estate, not far from the foodbank. Neil was nearly always the first one there and the last one to leave.

Kelly gave him a nod. 'All right, Mr I Don't Need Sleep?'

He winked at her. 'Morning, Ms I Don't Need Charm.'

'Yeah well, in spite of what you might think, Neil, you ain't exactly charm personified yourself, you know.'

'*Personify: 1. Represent a quality or concept by a figure in a physical form. 2. Attribute a personal nature or human characteristics to.*'

She'd learned that new word two weeks ago and had been looking for an opportunity to drop it into a conversation.

Neil's hands shot to his heart. 'I'm offended. I'll have to work harder to make you succumb to my bewitchery.'

Succumb? Bewitchery? That was two more words to look up. It would have been good to come back with something that cut him dead, but since she hadn't got a clue what he was talking about, she pretended to ignore him. Her watertight smart-arse plan had backfired. Trust Neil.

It was Kelly's turn to help in the café today. It wasn't like a proper café because customers got their food for free. Normally, they only did sandwiches, cakes and biscuits but lately, some of the volunteers had been making hot food as well. Neil was the main one. He was a mad keen cook. The foodbank was in a church hall and the vicar was okay with them using the kitchen to do it. He even came to help some days. He was here today with his wife. She'd made soup and Neil had made veggie stew. Kelly, who had made nothing, was on serving duty.

Neil was sitting at one of the tables taking somebody's details and explaining how everything worked. They did that when people came here for the first time. Kelly was busy serving and wasn't paying attention to him, until he was right on top of her. 'There's a client over there says he knows you. Wanted to say hello.'

The old man he'd been talking to looked a bit unsure.

Maybe he thought she wouldn't remember him. Of course she did. If it hadn't been for him, she'd have probably ended up in hospital that last Christmas with Craig. She turned to the vicar. 'Take over for me will you, Rev?'

She grabbed two cups of tea and a slice of cake and went over. 'All right, Vince? It's been a while. I brought you some cake. It's good. Homemade.'

The old man smiled. 'Hello, Kelly. I thought it was you but I wasn't certain. I had to check with the fella. You look different. You've filled out a bit.'

Kelly laughed. 'I expect that's because I'm eating proper food now. Not living on crisps. How's Una? Is she still going strong?'

'Oh yes. We both managed to get through all that Covid business safe and sound. We're moving soon. One of them sheltered flats. Ground floor. It'll be better for Una. The money should stretch a bit further as well. Shouldn't need to come to a place like this then.'

Kelly touched his hand. 'Don't you worry about coming here, Vince. We get all sorts. People you'd think'd have plenty of money. Everyone's having problems. Glad you're moving though. I always felt sorry for you living next door to Craig. Still there, is he?'

'He is, I'm sorry to say. He's a bit quieter than he used to be, but he's still got a mouth on him.'

'Once a wanker, always a wanker, eh? I've got to get back to my station. It's lovely to see you though. Give my love to Una. If you give me your new address, I'll come and visit.'

Consequences will be dire. That was all she could think of for the rest of the day. Christmas Eve 2017. Crazy how she hadn't thought about it in ages, and then this year it was twice in the space of a month.

'I'm warning you. If you leave me here alone all day and night and come back pissed or stoned, or whatever, there will be consequences. And they will be dire.'

She still had no idea why she'd said that, because it was guaranteed to wind Craig up. There had definitely been consequences. And they had been dire. Or at least they would have been if Vince hadn't stepped in.

As soon as it had come out of her mouth, she knew Craig would leave her on her own all day and night, even if he hadn't planned to before. Just because she'd told him not to. That was the kind of nasty bastard he was. And guess what? He'd done exactly that. She'd given him a few hours and then messaged him. The message was, of course, ignored and so were her calls. So she'd carried on messaging every hour. She'd even called his horrible fucking mother who'd just laughed at her.

By the time he did finally get home, it was technically Christmas Day. Kelly had been so mad she'd been ready to dish out her dire consequences, until she saw the way he looked at her. He'd been out of his head on beer, whisky and something else. She hadn't asked what. Drugs frightened her. They made her think of death. Craig was always taking something, either to add an edge or to take the edge off. There was always an excuse. He never ran out of excuses.

Straight away, he'd started shouting his mouth off about dire fucking consequences and what he was going to do to that snotty bitch friend of hers. It was disgusting.

Kelly had tried to go to bed but he'd grabbed hold of her in the hall. She'd thought about dodging past him to get out of the flat. She could have run to her nan's, or her dad's.

Better that than being there. But he was in the way. His fists kept opening and closing like he was flexing them. She'd kept her mouth shut, fearful of giving him a reason to use them. Dire consequences.

Suddenly, there'd been banging on the door. Neither of them had moved. The banging had carried on until it couldn't be ignored.

Craig had ripped the door open. 'Fuckin' what?'

It had been Vince, in his slippers and dressing gown, a nice old guy who did no harm to anyone. 'You okay Kelly, love?'

Kelly was scared for herself but she'd been more scared for Vince. 'I'm fine, Vince. Sorry for the noise.' She'd inched closer to the door in case there was a chance of getting past Craig, but he'd shoved her backwards and sent her bouncing off the wall.

'No you're not. I think you'd better come out of there.' Vince had held his hand out for her, but Craig was in the way.

He'd jabbed Vince in the chest. 'Fuck off yer nosey old bastard.'

Vince had toppled back slightly then righted himself. 'I'm going nowhere without Kelly.'

'Just go home, Vince. Please,' she'd screamed.

The next minute, Craig had grabbed the old man's dressing gown. Then he'd stopped, his fist hovering in mid-air. The door of the flat opposite Vince's had opened and three guys were in the hall.

One of them put himself between Craig and Vince. 'Need some help, Vince?' He was a big guy, a body builder. With one movement he'd knocked Craig out of the way and taken her arm. 'Come on, Kelly.'

'That's my girlfriend,' Craig had whined.

'Out of my way, prick.'

Craig might have been stoned but he wasn't stupid. He'd backed off.

Kelly had spent the rest of that night at Vince and Una's. The next morning, she went back to Craig. She didn't know what else to do. He'd sobered up by then but he was in a right mood. He'd said he was going to his mum's and she'd better be gone when he got back. Happy Christmas.

She'd called Netta, or Annette, as she was then. Of course she did. Who else could she talk to? Netta had taken her over to Neil and Chris's place. She and Paula, from the foodbank, were staying there. They'd all accepted her, no questions asked. They even had some presents for her. It had been the greatest day.

Unfortunately, she messed it up by falling for Craig's lies and going back with him on Boxing Day to that dirty, stinking flat and that sad little life. One thing was for sure, Craig was no Mr Darcy. He was more of a Wickham. Except he wasn't that good-looking and he wasn't charming.

With thoughts of Craig still at the back of her mind, Kelly made her excuses early that night and got into bed with *Mansfield Park*. The new postcard was in colour, but it was faded and not very natural. It was a photo of a wide road with some old cars on it. At one end was a big stone arch and beyond that there was water, maybe a river, with some buildings on the other side. The name of the place was Cours Victor Hugo and Bourgogne Gate. Edie had written on the back again:

'Bordeaux, 1959 – with Roberto.'

Kelly remembered that Roberto was usually called Bob.

Edie had been with him for a few years. She'd loved him but she let him go because she couldn't give him what he wanted. Edie was kind of amazing like that.

Bordeaux sounded familiar too. Then she remembered where she knew it from. They made wine there. Netta and Frank liked it.

Kelly sank back into her pillow and looked up at her blue ceiling with its rays of sun and little clouds. The skies were probably like that in Bordeaux. She saw herself in a French café, ordering a glass of Bordeaux wine. She'd be wearing sunglasses. Obviously. And one of those stripy tops like Geraldine sometimes wore. Breton. That was it. She'd be sophisticated as fuck.

She slid down the bed and as she drifted towards her dreams, she had a smile on her face. But then Craig popped into her head again, his crazy, stoned eyes glaring at her. Before she could get rid of him, Colin Grey was there too, with a sneery, snidey face on him. 'Kelly wouldn't be interested in that sort of thing,' he said in a weeny whiney little voice.

Kelly shuddered. It woke her up from her half-sleep. Go to Bordeaux? Sophisticated? As if.

10

A FELLOW BOOKWORM

It was a good job she wasn't a virgin. If she had been, this would have been a real fucking let down. Her first time with Marcus and it was in a park, behind some bushes. Very fucking romantic. Not that her actual first time ever had been that great, but at least she didn't have stinging nettles up her arse. At least Craig had the decency to take her to his flat. She'd say that much about him. Even if he was a first-class shitebag.

A first-class shitebag. That was one of her mum's favourite descriptions. She was always calling people that. If her mum had been around when Craig came on the scene, she'd have probably taken one look at him and said: 'What are you doing with that first-class shitebag? You can do a lot better than that.' She'd have been right too. It just took Kelly a long time to work it out. It's not that easy when you have to do these things for yourself.

Posho was another of her mum's favourites. She'd have definitely said Marcus was a posho. Shitebags and poshos. There must have been some in-between classifications, but Kelly couldn't think of them right now. Too many other distractions, like how many creepy crawlies were trying to get inside her bra.

Marcus made a loud noise when he came. Loud enough to alert the fucking authorities. There were probably wild animals running for cover right now. At least he was finished. He rolled off and leaned back on the ground. 'That was great. Really something.'

Was it? Kelly could only think about Elizabeth Bennet and Mr Darcy. She couldn't imagine them doing it on the damp grass in a public park. She couldn't imagine herself doing it here, ever again. Why did she say yes? 'Maybe next time somewhere warmer. And more comfortable.'

He stood up and zipped his jeans. 'Right, yeah. Sorry, my parents aren't really cool about me bringing anyone back.'

'Tried it before then, have you?'

'No it's not that. I just meant they're not cool. Not like Will's mum. She'd be okay with you taking me back there, yeah? You said she lets Belle stay over, right?'

'Yes she does. Doesn't mean I'd do it though. It's freezing. Let's go.'

He pulled her up and picked a leaf out of her hair. 'It's not that bad out here, is it? Adds a bit of a thrill.'

'I don't like it.'

'Right. Well that's that then.' He walked off and she had to run to catch up with him.

They didn't say much on the way to the pub. Marcus was sulking. Let him sulk. There was no way she was going to do it in a park again.

By the time they got inside the pub and she'd thawed out, she was beginning to soften. Maybe she would ask if it was okay for him to stop over. Lucky old Netta was going to Paris with Frank. Marcus could stay then. Kelly didn't think it would be a problem, but that wasn't why she hadn't wanted to ask. It was more to do with Will. She got the impression he didn't like Marcus. Not that he'd said it but the other day, he'd told her to be careful, which was bizarre. When she'd asked him why, he'd just said Marcus had had a lot of girlfriends. Perhaps he was worried about her. There was no need. She knew how to look after herself.

With Marcus having to travel from Sheffield, this was only their third date, but they'd been messaging and Face-Timing a lot and he'd been getting pushy about sex lately. That's why she'd given in tonight. Might as well get it over with. All the same, she changed her mind when he'd dragged her into the park. In fact, now that she thought about it, she didn't know how or why she'd let him talk her round. Never again though.

'Netta's going on a mini break in the Easter holidays. I'll see if you can stay then.'

'Great.' Marcus put his arm on her shoulder. The weight of it knocked her closer. She had to steady herself to make sure she didn't crash into him. 'Not sure I can wait until then to have you again though. Why don't you come to me next weekend?'

She didn't like the idea of him having her. Sounded a bit wrong somehow. On the other hand, he was inviting her to go and stay with him in Sheffield. He must like her. And she liked the idea of going to a new town. It would be an adventure. 'I'll have to check with Neil and Netta. We're doing a farmers' market on Saturday. If they can manage without me, I'll come.'

Friday was finally here. Although Kelly had spent the week making it look like she couldn't be arsed, she was excited to be going to Sheffield. She'd got up early that morning, which was mad because she wasn't going until after foodbank.

She'd never known a foodbank day go so slowly. Typical. Normally, it was gone in a flash but not today. Every time she checked the clock, closing time seemed miles away. So irritating. As soon as they locked the doors, she was off to New Street.

At the station, there were other girls like her on the platform. Well, like her but much cooler. They could be students going home for the weekend. Birmingham had loads of universities, according to Liza. She was pleased to see one girl was wearing a coat like hers. Underneath she wore jeans, a plain black jumper and leather Chelsea boots. It was a good look. Very understated. Very French. Kelly was working towards a look like that herself. So far, she only had the good coat that Netta had given her and some jeans that were probably too skinny and cheap.

She still had her eye on the girl when the train came in. Kelly's heart jumped when she saw her coach roll past. She ran towards the other end of the platform to catch up with it.

Her seat was by the window. It was a table seat but there was no one else in the other three seats. Kelly pushed her backpack into the overhead shelf and then she realised she'd forgotten to get her book out. All the calls she was having with Marcus and Robyn were using up her reading time, so she was looking forward to a good read on the train. She pulled the bag down again and took out *Villette*, a pen, and the new notebook she'd been using to write down words that she'd need to look up. She could have looked them up on her phone, but she preferred Edie's old dictionary. It made her feel like a proper scholar. True, it smelt a bit musty, but that just added to the magic.

As she stretched up to return the bag, she saw the girl from the platform coming down the aisle. Kelly tensed, nervous for some reason. When the girl sat facing her, Kelly's nerves went through the roof. She was trying so hard not to look that her eyes were moving all over the place. She probably looked like a complete nutjob. To calm herself down, she did what she always did in these situations, she thought about what Geraldine would say. Probably that she was just as good and clever as anyone. Probably that she should value herself a bit more. Yes, that was exactly what Geraldine would say. Funny. Before Kelly met Netta and Gez, it was her mum and nan's words that gave her comfort. It was strange how her everyday thoughts had been taken over by the Wilde family.

Strange or not, it was enough to give her the confidence to open the book and start reading. She really wanted to see how *Villette* turned out. Also, she was in a hurry to find another of Edie's postcards. Maybe she'd look for one of her own in Sheffield. It might not be as exotic as Edie's holidays, but it was a start. Kelly was pleased with herself. She was just like Edie, travelling to exciting destinations.

She got so carried away with congratulating herself, she forgot to stop her eyes wandering and they accidentally made contact with the girl she'd been trying to avoid.

The girl pointed to *Villette*. 'I don't know that one. Any good?'

'Er … so far, yes. I've only just started.'

She flashed a book at Kelly. 'I'm bingeing on Jane Austen. I'm on *Sense and Sensibility* at the moment.'

'I haven't read it. I've read *Pride and Prejudice* and *Mansfield Park* though.'

'Me too. Did you like them?'

'Yeah, but they were hard work. The way they're written, I mean.'

'I know. Whenever I read anything like that, I have to really slow myself down. But it's worth it.'

'Yeah, exactly. I got so wrapped up in them, I was completely in that world. It just feels so real.'

'I'm the same,' said the girl. 'Who's your favourite character?'

'Elizabeth Bennet.'

'Good choice. I'm Zoe, by the way.'

'Right, yeah. Kelly. I'm Kelly.'

They talked some more about books. Kelly wrote down the names of some that Zoe recommended. It turned out Zoe was on her way to Edinburgh to see a friend. Kelly had been to see Robyn there a couple of times, so that was something else to talk about. When they pulled into Sheffield, she was almost sorry.

'Have a good weekend, Kelly. It's been really nice talking to a fellow bookworm.'

'Yeah, you too, Zoe. It's been great.'

Kelly walked away from the train grinning her head off. What just happened there? Had she been talking to a complete stranger for the last hour about books? Did that really happen? Fucking hell.

11

POLTERGEISTS AND POSHOS

Someone was moving books around in the study. It wasn't Netta, and Liza was too pre-occupied with art books and coursework. Given Kelly's aversion to all things remotely educational it was highly unlikely that it was her. So if it wasn't Kelly, then who was left? Only Frank. Or a poltergeist. The books in question seemed to be mostly Jane Austen and similar classics, and they weren't really to Frank's taste. So, in the absence of any other evidence, Netta was left to conclude that it was either Kelly, or the ghost of Edie Pinsent. Since she didn't believe in the after-life, it left only one possible candidate. That led to more questions than answers. Why was Kelly shuffling books about? Could it be that she was reading?

Netta would have dismissed that idea straight away, but Kelly was definitely being a bit strange. She must have gone to bed early almost every night for the last month, but her light was always on when Netta turned in. She could be watching something on her phone, but that wasn't some-thing Kelly normally hid herself away to do. It would have been nice to think it was because she'd met someone and was having sweet little FaceTime tête-à-têtes. Sadly, the lack of sound coming from inside the room suggested not.

Kelly's last relationship had been with Craig. If you could call that a relationship. From the outside it looked like something different but it was hard to tell. When Kelly was with him, she only talked about what a waster and a two-timer he was. After she left him, he rarely cropped up in conversation. And neither did any other man. Not in that context anyway.

So if it wasn't a man, what else could it be? Netta had tried to find out but her tentative enquiries got her absolutely nowhere. She'd considered the possibility that Kelly was sinking again, like last year but if anything, she was perkier than usual. So, in the absence of any other plausible explanation, Netta was now beginning to wonder if Kelly was actually reading.

As she was considering this, she was watching Kelly having a strop in the lounge. Will was home for the weekend to meet up with his old school friends and was trying to persuade Kelly to go with him. 'Honestly, they're all right. You already know some of them. They're just normal people.'

'They're poshos.'

'For f… What even is a posho?'

'Take a guess.' Kelly slumped down in the armchair like a sulky child. Sometimes it was easy to forget she was a fully grown adult.

It was always hard to get Kelly out, unless it was with their immediate friends and family. There wasn't a lot of self-confidence below the tough surface level that was usually on display. It might have been easier if Liza was going too, but she'd gone to some climate change thing. Liza was very passionate about environmental issues, and not even the promise of a night out with Will had changed her mind.

The debate was becoming more heated. Netta decided mediation was required. 'Please you two, give it a rest. Will, if Kelly doesn't want to go, she doesn't want to go. Kelly, you really need to stop worrying about what people will think of you and let yourself have a bit of fun.'

Kelly's eyes narrowed. She always reminded Netta of a cat when she did that. Probably because they were green. 'Fine. I'll go. But if they're all snobs, I'm walking straight out.'

Will flung his arms in the air. 'Finally! I mean, it really is not a big deal. We're only going for a drink and a curry.'

'I'll come for a drink. I'll decide about the curry later.'

'Fine,' huffed Will.

'I'll get changed.'

Will pulled out his phone and pressed a button. 'Hey. Kelly's coming. She's just getting ready.'

Netta could hear Belle's voice on the other end of the line but couldn't make out what she was saying.

'I don't know. As soon as she's ready. You'll be all right. Ethan will be there. I'll message him. We won't be long. Yeah, I know. I did say. Okay, see you in a bit.'

Netta watched him tapping out a message on his phone. 'Everything all right?'

'Yeah, all good.'

It reminded her of that day she'd given him a lift back to York, after seeing Kelly close to tears. She'd tried to ask him then if everything was okay between him and Kelly.

He'd shrugged. 'Yeah. Why shouldn't it be?'

'No reason. She just seemed a bit down this morning.'

'She's never great in the morning though, is she?'

'True.'

'What do you think about me doing a Masters?'

That had thrown her. She'd wondered if he'd changed the subject deliberately. If he had, it had worked. They'd spent the rest of the journey talking about course options. Any further talk of Kelly had been closed off.

Back in the present, Will sent another message, then made for the stairs. 'I'll see if she's ready.'

'Okey dokey.' It seemed any further talk of Belle was also closed off.

Kelly had taken an hour to get ready. Judging by the pile of clothes on her bed, she'd gone through her whole wardrobe before settling on a clean pair of jeans and a pretty vintage-style top. She'd made a real effort with her hair and make-up too. She'd looked quite stunning. All that for a drink and a curry with a bunch of poshos.

Netta had taken less time to make herself presentable for her night out. She and Frank were going to the Hope and Anchor. There was a good Thai restaurant not far from it and they were eating there first. They ordered their food and drink and Netta relaxed, putting all thoughts of polter-geists, poshos, and her son's relationships out of her mind.

'I had a good heart to heart with Robyn today,' said Frank. 'She's looking for a new flat. She and Nick are split-ting up. It's amicable, so she's taking her time to find the right place. They've two bedrooms, so they've become temporary flatmates.'

'That's very grown-up.'

'I know. I told her I'll go up and help her move when she's found somewhere. She said they've been growing apart for a while, but she's fine about it. I gather she's been pouring her heart out to Kelly a lot over the last few months. It's helped her a lot.'

To Kelly? Perhaps that was the reason for the early nights. But that still didn't explain the silence in her room, or who was moving the books around.

'Rob's got another friend here in Brum. Archie. They were at school together. Apparently, he's been really good too. He's going up there next week to help her look for somewhere. I bump into him occasionally. I'll have to buy him a pint next time. And Kelly. I must thank her properly. You know, she never fails to surprise me. Just when I think I have the measure of her, she goes and does something quite unexpected,' he said.

'I was thinking the same thing. Now you know what's been going on, are you more or less worried?'

'Less. Now I know Rob's okay.'

'Good, because I was thinking we should talk about your upcoming special event. Would you like me to throw you a surprise sixtieth birthday party?'

'God no. You know what I'd like to do? Go away on a trip, just you and me. What d'ya say?'

'A big trip or a little trip?'

'I thought a long weekend. In Paris.'

'Ooh la la. I like the sound of that. Very romantic.'

Frank kissed her hand across the table. 'I can be when called upon.'

Netta kicked off her shoe and attempted a discreet stroke of his leg with her foot. 'Remind me to call upon you more often.'

He coughed and pretended to straighten his non-existent tie. 'Steady on old girl. I'm nearly sixty, you know. Not sure the ancient ticker can stand that much excitement.'

12

FANNY PRICE WAS A LOSER

Kelly slipped her arm through Will's, hoping it would help her keep up with him. He was walking too fast. The bus had taken ages to come and they were later than he'd wanted to be.

A sharp pain in her side made her stop. 'I've got a stitch. You're going too fast.'

Will pulled up. 'You are so unfit.'

'What are you, the exercise police? I'm not unfit. I cycle loads. I'm just little and you've got gigantic legs.'

'Gigantic legs?'

'Yeah, they're enormous actually.'

Will crouched down with his back to her. 'Jump on. You can give your tiny elf-like legs a rest.'

'God, you're so funny. Look at me laughing so much.'

He got up, a big smirk on his face, and held his arm out for her. She slid hers in. The closeness of him gave her goosebumps, and as they hit Kings Heath High Street, her stitch was replaced by a slight breathlessness. She pictured them walking in some foreign street, like Edie and Roberto, discovering new places together. She let herself pretend that they were a couple, and that they weren't heading to a pub to meet his real girlfriend.

She thought about *Mansfield Park* and Fanny Price, who spent years loving her cousin, Edmund, waiting for him to come to his senses. She'd cried over that book, but she hadn't enjoyed it as much as *Pride and Prejudice*. It was too close to her feelings about Will. Things had worked out in the end for Fanny, but Kelly was glad to finish it and move on to the next one.

There were no more postcards in the other Jane Austen books, so she'd looked for them in the others. One turned up in a book called *Villette*, by Charlotte Brontë. It was from Paris. Edie had been there with her spinster friends in 1965. Kelly had spent a long time looking at that postcard. She'd been meaning to start the book tonight but it would have to wait now.

'Have you ever been to Paris, Will?'

'Yeah, a couple of times. Why d'you ask?'

'I saw something about it on telly. It looked like a good place to visit.'

'It is. If you like museums and fancy food.'

Fancy food. Kelly's heart sank. She hadn't factored that into her sophisticated French dream. 'Is the food very fancy?'

'Pretty much. But I think you can still get a Macky D's there.'

Well at least she could live on Big Macs and Chicken McNuggets if she needed to. That felt like cheating though, and not very sophisticated. If she did want to live the dream, it might necessitate a foray into fancy eating. Necessitate and foray – two more new words she was trying out.

'*Necessitate: Make (something) necessary as a result or consequence; force or compel to do something.*'

'*Foray:* 1. *A sudden attack into enemy territory.* 2. *A brief but spirited attempt to become involved in a new activity.*'

She could occasionally slip necessitate in at work without getting too many funny looks: 'I think this necessitates a bit more sugar,' for example. Foray was a different matter. Not too much room to slide foray into the jam-making business. You couldn't really go on a foray into the stock room, could you? It was hardly enemy territory, unlike her potential attempt to like new food. Unlike tonight. Tonight was definitely a foray, this being enemy territory and most likely a brief but spirited attempt to become involved in a new activity.

Will held the pub door open for her. 'Belle's meeting us inside. I told her you were coming.'

Kelly let go of his arm and put on a fake happy face. 'Great. At least that's one other person I'll know.'

She stiffened as they walked through the doors. The pub was rammed, hot and suffocating. She should take her coat off but she didn't want to. The coat had been Netta's. She'd given it to her after a wardrobe clear out. It was expensive. Not the sort of style Kelly would normally buy, but she loved it. It made her look classy, like an intellectual. Underneath, she was a scrawny, scummy no-hoper but on the outside, she looked stylish and cool.

'I'll get the drinks in.' She jumped in first. She didn't want the awkwardness of having to wait for Will while he was at the bar, or the embarrassment of being spotted by Belle, and being dragged over to talk to a bunch of posh nobs she didn't know and didn't want to know. It was also a good way of avoiding the inevitable – being dragged over by Will to talk to a bunch of posh nobs she didn't know and didn't want to know.

When she got to the bar, she spotted Belle on the other

side, talking to some guy. Kelly could only see the back of him but he was nodding his head as if he was listening really hard. Belle was doing the talking. She looked very sincere. She was probably talking about the disadvantaged. As Geraldine would say, that was her 'talking about the disadvantaged face'. Kelly suspected that Belle saw her as disadvantaged. That rankled her, even though she did feel disadvantaged compared to Belle and her sort.

She handed Will a pint. 'They're round there, in the corner.'

When they got there, she saw that there was a larger group of about fifteen, standing or sitting around a couple of tables. They were chatting, laughing, or messing about. All good in each other's company. It was easy for them. They were school friends. Most of them had grown up together. There might have been a few boyfriends and girlfriends there too. Kelly wouldn't know.

Belle threw her arms around her, like they were proper buds. 'I am so glad you're here. I don't know anyone. I was running out of people to talk to.'

Kelly tried out a friendly smile. She'd forgotten Belle had met Will after he'd left school. Technically, she was an outsider like her. Technically. 'All right, Belle. You seem to be doing okay.'

'Do I? Well they're Will's friends so they're all nice.'

Will put his arm around Belle's waist and kissed her. Kelly looked away. She was starting to melt under the coat. The back of her neck was sweating up.

Belle leaned into her ear. 'I've left my coat on that chair. There's room for yours as well.'

'Right, ta. It is a bit warm in here.'

She must have noticed Kelly was hot. That was nice of her. Belle was a nice person really. Kelly knew that, which was another reason why Will being with her hurt. She draped the coat carefully over Belle's, then pulled the chair far enough away from the table to make it safe from spillages. It was her only good coat and she didn't want it ruined.

The guy sitting next to the chair looked up at her. He was beautiful, no other way to describe him. Except perhaps, fucking beautiful. His hair was thick, black and wavy and he had big, cow eyes and fat, cherry lips. Fucking beautiful.

'All right?' She sounded like she'd have hit him if he'd said no. It hadn't been the look she was going for.

'Sure.' He turned back to his friends.

Kelly went over to Will and Belle. They were talking to the guy she'd seen Belle with earlier. Will said his name was Ethan.

Amazingly, the evening wasn't too bad. Will stayed with her most of the time and Ethan turned out to be normal, in a not too posh and up himself kind of way. When Will asked her if she was coming for a curry, she was surprised how quickly the time had passed.

They walked back along the High Street, to the Rajdoot. It was one of Netta's favourite restaurants. Colin the Prick also went there a lot, but he wasn't here tonight. They sat at a long table. Belle was next to her. Will and Ethan were opposite them.

Someone sat on the other side of Kelly. 'Hello, Coat Girl. Anyone sitting here?' It was Cherry Lips.

'Nah, it's free.' Kelly was hot again. Her face was on fire. Embarrassing.

'Hey Marcus. How's it going?' said Will.

'Good, yeah, good. Thought I'd come and say hi.'

'Cool,' said Will, although he didn't look like it was that cool. 'Ethan said you're doing a Masters now. You're at Sheffield, right?'

'Yep. You're at York aren't you? Do you like it?' said Marcus.

'Yeah, I do. Belle's at Leeds, so we still get to see each other plenty.'

Belle popped her head around Kelly. 'Hi.' She was blushing. She was actually blushing, in front of Will.

Marcus turned to Kelly. 'And what about you, Coat Girl. Who do you belong to?'

Kelly jerked her head backwards. He might be the best-looking guy here but he was a bit of a dick. 'I don't belong to anyone. Check yourself, mate.'

'Sorry, no offence. I meant, have you come with someone? You're not from our usual crowd.'

'Kelly's my friend, Marcus,' said Will.

'I live with Will's mum,' she added.

'Okay. So what do you do then, Kelly?' Marcus's gorgeous cow eyes looked straight into hers.

Kelly poured herself a glass of water. Her mouth was very dry, but she managed to cough out: 'I make jam and pickles.'

Will came to her rescue. 'Kelly is one of my mum's business partners. They have a small jam and pickle company.'

'Wow!' someone at the other end of the table said. 'You're like, what, the same age as us? And you're already running a business.'

If Kelly thought she couldn't go any redder, she found out she was wrong when everybody turned towards her. 'It's only a small business. Anyway, I'm probably a couple of years older than you.'

'No, it's impressive. I'm impressed.' Marcus's cherry lips parted into a sparkling smile, like they were inviting her to lean over and kiss them.

When they left the Rajdoot, Marcus walked back with them to the bus stop. He was asking Kelly about herself. She gave him the edited highlights. She didn't want to scare him off. They'd fallen into a slow walk that made them lose pace with Will and Belle. Marcus gave her another of those smiles. 'Listen, I have to go back to Sheffield tomorrow, but I'll be home again next week. Do you fancy going somewhere?'

'You mean on a date?'

'That was the idea.' He frowned at her and she immediately knew she'd just said something really silly.

She looked ahead to Will and Belle who were strolling along hand in hand and remembered how she felt back in January, when she saw them asleep on the sofa. Fuck it. She wasn't Fanny Price. Fanny Price was a loser. 'Okay.'

The three of them got on the bus and sat on the back seat with Will in the middle. Marcus watched from the pavement as it drove away. The evening hadn't been the disaster Kelly had expected it to be. Will's friends weren't too bad really, and she had a date with Marcus. He was definitely a posho, but she could live with that.

'Glad you came?' Will asked.

'Maybe.' Kelly looked out of the back window. Marcus was still at the bus stop. Even in the dark and getting further away, she could see how amazingly beautiful he was. Just before he disappeared out of sight, Kelly thought of Mr Darcy.

13

COAT GIRL GETS ADVENTUROUS

Kelly was staring at herself in her bedroom mirror with one hand on her hip. The other was holding her phone. 'Jeans and the green top then, yeah?'

'I think so,' said Robyn, on the other end of the line.

'If you say so. I'd better go. Thanks for helping me choose.'

'You're welcome. Are you excited?'

'Not sure. If a million trips to the toilet equals excitement, then I must be.'

Kelly bumped into Liza on the landing. She was going out with her friends from uni and looked amazing. Will looked more like his dad, but Liza was Netta's younger double. If Liza was anything to go by, Netta must have been gorgeous when she was young.

Liza looked Kelly up and down. 'I love that top on you. It makes your eyes look incredible.' Lize was always trying to make Kelly feel good about herself. It was embarrassing sometimes.

'Thanks. That's a great dress. You look fantastic.'

'We both do. Where are you meeting Cherry Lips?' They'd been calling Marcus Cherry Lips since Kelly had told Liza about him.

'Digbeth.'

'How are the first-date nerves?'

Kelly screwed up her nose. 'Hyped.'

'I'm going into town. Shall we get the train together?'

The escalator carried them up from the platform to one of the waiting areas in New Street station.

'If you hate him and need to get away, just message me. I'll tell you where we are so you can meet us, or I'll organise an intervention or something,' said Liza.

'Okay, but I'll be all right. If I hate him, I'll just tell him to do one and go home.'

They were going in opposite directions, so they parted once they'd gone through the barriers. As soon as Liza was out of sight, Kelly slowed down. She was early, and she didn't want to get there before Marcus. She spent ten very long minutes browsing through the rails of a shop that was too expensive for her. Even the sale rail was too much. Then she remembered there was a bookshop on the next floor and wasted more time in there.

In the end she was late. She'd spent too long in the bookshop and then she'd taken two wrong turns in Digbeth. It wasn't a place she went to very often. Neil did. Aside from it being close to the gay village, it was full of places serving craft beers and artisanal coffees and food.

Artisan: skilled worker who makes things by hand. Derivatives – artisanal: relating to a product, especially food or drink, made in a traditional or non-mechanised way.'

Yep, that was Neil. Whereas Kelly was quite happy with a Costa coffee and a bag of chips drowned in curry sauce.

She was a bit jumpy going into the pub. Marcus had messaged to say he was there but she couldn't see him. It was the sort of place her mum would have called an old men's pub, only these days the old men were gone and it was full of twenty and thirty-year-olds wearing overshirts and beanies. They probably drank artisanal coffee in tiny cups, as well as their craft beer. Her mum would've thought it was hilarious if she came in here, which she wouldn't. You probably couldn't have paid her to come into somewhere like this. She liked a bit of sparkle, her mum. A bit of bling. A bit of life. It was the anniversary of her death next month. No wonder Kelly had been thinking about her.

As she got further in, she was relieved to see Marcus on the end of a seat that ran all the way along the back wall. He was reading a paper.

He looked up and his big, brown cow eyes met hers. His cherry lips broke into a smile and he folded the paper. 'Hi.'

All the time he was at the bar waiting to be served, Marcus kept looking over to her. Not shy, sneaky little peeks but full-on, moony gazing. Like he couldn't believe she'd turned up. Like she was the one who was special. It was kind of weird. Nice, but weird.

At last, he brought back the drinks. 'Are you sure you don't want to try one of the craft beers? They're good.'

'Nah, you're fine. It'd be wasted on me anyway. Just plain old lager'll do nicely.'

He gave her another luscious smile. 'Can I sit next to you?'

She moved across to give him room to squeeze in. The

pub was filling up and there was only a small space between him and the next person. Kelly could smell Marcus's woody perfume. His arm brushed against hers and butterflies fluttered around inside her chest. She was twenty-three and she was acting as if she was fifteen. Ridiculous. He was talking to her and she said something back that was probably really stupid, but she was too busy drinking in the beauty of him to think about it. Yeah, she was being ridiculous.

They left the pub after that drink to go for a pizza. Marcus had booked a table somewhere. He didn't say where but Kelly guessed it probably wasn't Pizza Hut. She asked him the name of the place and no, it definitely wasn't Pizza Hut. 'Where's that?'

'The Custard Factory.'

'Ah right. I don't really know it.'

He took her hand. 'I'm sure you'll like it.'

She wondered what it would be like to have sex with him. Generally, she wasn't a massive fan of sex but maybe with him, it might be different. Not tonight though. She didn't want him thinking she was easy.

The streets around the Custard Factory were all lit up. Some of them had strings of lights running from one side to the other. It was pretty. It felt like they were somewhere else and not in Birmingham at all.

The restaurant was artisanal, you might know. Kelly nearly ordered the plainest pizza on the menu but then she remembered she was trying to expand her food tastes, so she went for something that had goat's cheese, caramelised onion and rocket on it. Three new things in one meal. Adventurous or what? As long as it didn't make her puke, she'd be fine.

'Anything to drink?' asked the waiter.

'Do you have any Bordeaux wine?' She was still trying to live the dream.

'Afraid not, but we do have a nice Cabernet Sauvignon from Australia.'

'Oh, okay. I'll have a glass of that then.'

'I didn't realise you liked wine.' Marcus had that frowny look on his face, like the one he did when she asked him if they were going on a date. It made her feel a bit silly again, and she wondered if she'd said the wrong thing. Perhaps you weren't supposed to call it Bordeaux wine.

'I like all sorts of things.'

'Like what?'

Shit! She'd walked into that one. Unable to think of a single thing, she changed the subject. 'My nan and grandad used to work in the Custard Factory. When they made custard here, I mean. She always said they met over a big vat of the stuff.'

'Really? I wonder what they'd make of this place now.'

Kelly didn't answer. She was wondering what her nan would have made of Marcus. She'd never liked Craig but perhaps she'd approve of him.

The waiter brought their drinks over. Marcus picked up his beer and leaned across the table. 'I'm glad we met, Coat Girl. Are you?'

'I think so. We'll see.'

She took a sip of wine. It tasted okay. Marcus was watching her. Those butterflies were back again. She hoped he couldn't see the state she was in.

He clinked his glass against hers. 'Here's to finding out.'

The pizzas were brought over and she checked hers, worried what she might find. Rocket must be all that green stuff. Green stuff was sophisticated, wasn't it?

14

IF ANYONE WAS GOING TO BE HER MR DARCY

Marcus was waiting for Kelly at the station. 'Hey you. You made it. Journey okay?'

'Fine.' She didn't tell him about Zoe. It didn't feel right somehow, and he didn't know she was a bookworm. She stopped herself from laughing out loud. She was a bookworm. In your face, Colin Grey, and all those other doubters out there.

Marcus took her to the house he shared. It was an old terraced house in a street full of the same houses, each one with a 'To Let' sign stuck on the wall. There were streets like this back home in Selly Oak, near the university. They never took the signs down.

There were a couple of other people moving about on the ground floor of the house, but she didn't get to meet them. Marcus took her straight up to his room and virtually ripped her clothes off. He was quieter this time when he came. Maybe it was being out in the open air that made him think it was okay to be so loud.

Afterwards, they went to a place that did Turkish kebabs. She'd never tried proper Turkish kebabs before but they were like the ones Neil made when they had barbecues, so they weren't exactly unknown. She awarded herself half a point on her new food challenge for that one, and a full point for a funny looking mixture that Marcus said was houmous dip. She felt stupid when he told her because she knew what houmous was, although she'd never tried it. It was just that she'd only seen it in a tub before, not dolloped on a plate with red stuff sprinkled over it.

The pub they went in afterwards was busy, but they managed to get a couple of chairs in a corner. Marcus left her there while he went to the bar. He stopped to talk to two guys and a girl while he was there. The girl glanced at Kelly for a few seconds, then turned back to the others. Marcus stayed with them for ages after he'd been served. She was beginning to think he'd forgotten about her, but then he looked over. She did her most pissed-off face. You didn't invite your girlfriend for the weekend and then leave her on her own for fifteen minutes, while you hung around with people you probably saw every day. Not on. Not. Fucking. On.

He took the hint and came back. 'Sorry about that. Couldn't get away.'

When Kelly went to the toilet later, she saw that the people he'd been talking to were part of a bigger crowd. It was funny that he hadn't wanted to sit with them. Perhaps he thought she'd be uncomfortable, being as she didn't know any of them.

When Marcus woke her in the morning, Kelly was still groggy. It was a bit early for her. She liked to come round slowly on a Sunday morning, but he had other ideas. His hands were all over her. He was after sex again. They'd already done it a second time last night. He'd been a bit rough with her and she was feeling sore, so she said no. He went all quiet again, like he'd done when she'd told him she didn't like doing it in the park, so she said okay, if he was gentle.

It was nearly midday by the time they were showered and dressed, and Kelly was starving. 'Got anything to eat?'

'Not really. I haven't been shopping. There's a café I go to that does a great brunch. We could go there.'

For the second time that weekend, Kelly did the pissed-off face. You'd have thought he'd have done some food shopping, knowing she was coming. 'Fuck's sake. Let's go before I keel over.'

Someone called out to Marcus, as they walked into the café. It was the girl he'd been talking to in the pub. The two guys the girl had been with then, were with her now.

Marcus led her over to them. 'Everyone, this is Kelly. Kelly, this is everyone.'

One or two of them said hello. Kelly's stomach clenched at the thought of all these new, clever people taking her in. In an attempt not to sound like a complete idiot, she mumbled a quick: 'Hi.'

Marcus pointed to the only empty chair. 'Kelly, you take that. I'll find another one.'

She sat next to a guy who said his name was Kyle. He sounded like one of their foodbank regulars who came from Newcastle. On Tyne, as the client liked to remind her. 'Not the other one.' Before then she didn't even know there was another one. She'd always taken it for granted that there was only one Newcastle.

Marcus came back without a chair. Apparently they

were all taken. The girl from the pub moved up on the sofa she was sharing and patted the space she'd left. 'Sit here.'

He sat down and gave Kelly a sheepish grin. 'This is my friend, Poppy, by the way.'

Kelly nodded. 'All right?'

'Hi there.' Poppy smiled. The word simpering came to mind. It was one she'd learned ages ago.

'Simper: Smile in an affectedly coquettish, coy or ingratiating manner. Derivatives – simpering, simperingly.'

It was only the second time Kelly had been able to find a use for that word. The first had been when she'd been thinking about Belle.

When they finished eating, Kelly asked Marcus to show her around Sheffield. His friends had been okay, but she wanted to get out and explore this new city.

He took her to a road with lots of vintage and charity shops. Before she'd met Robyn, Kelly had hated shopping. She was clueless about what looked good or bad, and she'd never really had much money anyway. Robyn showed her you could spend very little in places like charity shops and still look good, if you knew what you were looking for.

Marcus didn't seem to mind shopping. He helped pick out things for her to try on and was happy to tell her what he thought of them, but she still sent a selfie to Robyn before buying anything. On Rob's say so, she bought a purple batwing style top with a slash-neck.

When they'd had enough of shopping they went back to the house. Some of his housemates were there, including Kyle, the guy from the café. They chatted for a while, then Marcus took her upstairs. She was dreading him asking for sex again, but luckily he was tired. They lay together like two spoons and fell asleep.

When she was getting ready to go out that evening he told her he'd bought her a present. 'I saw it in the shop while you were trying that top on. You can wear it tonight. We're going to a club.'

It was a slip dress. It was pretty but a bit thin and revealing. Not something she'd normally wear, but she put it on for him.

He insisted on taking a photo of her and made her pose in a stupid, pouty way. 'You're beautiful, you know. Kind of ethereal.'

Ethereal? Sounded weird. She'd have to look that one up.

'You've got that 'heroin chic' thing going on,' he carried on.

'I don't do drugs.'

'I know!' He laughed at her. No. He sneered at her. 'You're so fucking literal sometimes, it's priceless. I'm going to take a shower.'

Kelly dropped down onto the bed, winded. She'd been exposed as a stupid, thick, know-nothing and he'd laughed at her. If he'd hit her, she'd have been less hurt. She wanted to cry, but then she felt a tear on her cheek and saw that she already was. She dried her eyes and checked her make-up. Tears never did any good. They just made you look weak.

She sent another selfie to Robyn to ask about the dress. Rob messaged back to say it could work if she wore it with a jumper or an overshirt, and boots or trainers, or a T-shirt underneath. Kelly had only brought her trainers so that was good. She raided his wardrobe for a shirt. When he got back, she was ready and all traces of tears were gone.

He looked her up and down. 'You look great. But take the bra off. It looks stupid.'

As they left the club that night, Marcus put his arm around her and kissed her. He seemed to have forgotten that he'd belittled her earlier. Maybe he just didn't realise. Or maybe she'd overreacted. She really needed to be less touchy because she might ruin things. They were a proper couple and sometimes you had to compromise. Like tonight for instance. He'd made her take the shirt off in the club so that he could see her properly, and he'd taken more photos of her. She'd been uncomfortable because she had no bra on and was absolutely sure everyone could see her nipples through the dress, but he said she was being ludicrous. She hadn't really liked the area he'd taken her to either. It was loud and lairy. There were too many idiots getting pissed and puking up in the street. It reminded her of Broad Street, back home, which she hated. But in spite of that, she didn't ask to leave because he was enjoying himself. It was all about compromise.

'It's great around here, isn't it?' he said.

'It's not really my kind of place, to be honest.'

He looked a bit irritated. 'I thought you'd like it.'

'Why?'

'I dunno really. I just thought you would. I made a special effort to bring you here for that reason. Well, that's disappointing.'

Kelly cringed. She'd upset him. 'Sorry.'

. . .

The next morning, she asked if she could see his university.

He snorted. 'What do you want to go there for?'

'I'm interested to see what it's like. When I think of you, I can picture you there.'

'That's quite romantic.' He seemed to have got over the upset of last night.

She didn't answer. It wasn't the real reason. The real reason was that she wanted to know if she could picture herself there.

The university didn't look like she'd imagined it would. She'd expected it to be one or two really old buildings with pointed roofs. Definitely pointed roofs, surrounded by cobbled streets. This university was more spread out. Its buildings were a mixture of old and new, and there weren't too many cobbled streets as far as she could see. In that way it was a disappointment. But there was something about it that she liked. She began to think about what it would have been like if she hadn't thrown her education away. She could have gone to a place like this. She could have been so much more.

She changed her mind about looking for a postcard. She didn't want Marcus to laugh at her again.

Marcus stayed with her at the station until her train arrived. She laughed as he blew her a kiss from the platform. He was sweet and cute. If anyone was going to be her Mr Darcy, it was him. Although Mr Darcy was actually a miserable fucker until Elizabeth turned him, so in that respect, Marcus was nothing like Mr Darcy at all.

15

DAGGERS IN THE LIVING ROOM

Kelly still had her eyes closed but she was awake. She didn't rush to open them because she wanted to make the most of the thrill of her and Marcus sharing her bed. Netta had been cool about him staying, so here they were, two lovers snuggled up together in the bed she loved, in the room she loved, in the home she loved. Perfect.

She opened her eyes slowly and tingled with delight when she saw that he was facing her. Kelly watched his eyelids fluttering. Her nan used to say fluttering eyelids meant you were dreaming, like when dogs do that running thing in their sleep. It reminded Kelly of when her mum was alive. Half alive, if she was being factually correct. Not quite dead but not quite living either. In her mum's last few months she'd spent more time asleep than awake. Kelly used to lie in bed with her, watching her mum's eyelids quivering like crazy, wondering what she could be dreaming about. Whenever she asked, her mum always said she was dreaming about her and her brothers. Even at the time, Kelly doubted it could always be about them. More likely, she was just dreaming about release.

Marcus parted his lips and let out a soft whistle. She told herself off for being morbid. Her mum was long dead and nothing could bring her back. She just had to accept it and stop relating everything back to her.

'I know you're looking at me. I can feel your x-ray vision burning into me.' Marcus opened his eyes.

She smiled at him. 'You're a bit full of yourself, aren't yer?'

'So you weren't looking at me then?'

'Maybe I was, maybe I wasn't.'

It had been right to let him stop over. They'd stayed in last night and watched a movie with a takeaway and some beers. Everyone else was out, so it was just them and the three dogs – Frank's dog, Fred, was staying with them while Frank was away. The sex had been better this time, even though they'd both been a bit drunk.

Marcus kissed her on her bare shoulder, then her neck, then her lips. She kissed him, and then he was bending over her. She pushed him back and jumped on top of him. This time she'd show him some of the things Craig taught her.

'Oh shit, that's good. That is so…' His words turned into groans and grunts. They got louder and louder. Why did he have to be so loud? He'd been the same last night, but at least they were alone in the house. Although she could have sworn she'd heard one of the dogs howling in time with him.

At last he was finished and quiet. They lay on their backs. 'I like your ceiling,' he said.

'Liza designed it.'

'Cool. Okay if I take a shower?' He leapt out of bed and already had the door open when Kelly realised he was buck naked.

'Put some clothes on. Liza and Belle might be out there.'

. . .

Kelly pulled on her pyjamas and a jumper. Once she'd made sure Marcus was safely out of the shower and back in her room without flashing his dick at anyone, she went downstairs. Liza, Will, and Belle were already in the kitchen.

She put the kettle on and dropped some bread in the toaster. 'Anyone want any?'

'I'm good,' said Liza.

'Me too,' said Belle.

Will said nothing. Was it just her or was he looking tense?

Marcus came into the kitchen. 'Morning.'

'Hi.' Belle's voice was all squeaky and little. It made Kelly think of that word simpering again.

Will's head did a short, silent nod. Only Liza seemed normal.

'Everything okay?' said Marcus.

'Mmm,' said Belle.

'Do you think you could you keep the noise down in future, maybe?' Will nearly spat it out.

Marcus screwed his eyes up for a second, then grinned. 'Shit, sorry man. Sorry everyone. That was me, wasn't it? I can get carried away, especially with Kelly. She's just so good at it. I can't help myself.'

Fucking. Hell. Kelly wanted to crawl away and die. Will glanced at her. Or was it a glare? Whatever it was, it was telling her that perhaps she should.

'Marcus likes my ceiling, Lize.' She was desperate to change the subject.

Marcus flashed Liza a smile. 'Oh yeah. It's really cool. You're pretty arty.'

Liza shrugged. 'That's why I'm doing an art degree.'

He laughed. 'Funny and talented.'

'That's me.' Liza frowned at him, like she was trying to work out what he was up to. She wasn't the only one.

After breakfast, Kelly took a shower and got dressed. When she came down again, she found Marcus on the living room sofa. Maud was in her armchair, keeping an eye on him.

'Where's everyone gone?'

'Liza's gone out. Will and Belle took the other dogs for a walk. We're alone.' He pulled her onto his lap. 'I could go again. Right here.'

Right here? Images of Will and Belle shagging flooded her brain and made her stomach turn. 'Nah, I don't think so.'

'Upstairs then?'

'I'm not a fucking sex machine, you know.'

Marcus put his hands up. 'Sorry. It was just so good this morning.'

She'd gone too far and been too snappy, but he shouldn't have said that thing. She put her arms around his neck. 'Listen, don't go telling people I'm good at sex, okay? I'd rather keep that sort of stuff between us.'

'It's nothing to be ashamed of.'

'Not if I was a prostitute. But I'm not, so keep it to yourself. Anyway, what d'you wanna do today?'

'I have to go home. It's my dad's birthday. We're going out for a family meal. I can't get out of it. I'll try to come over later.'

She walked with him to the front door. 'If you don't come over, when will I see you again?'

'Not sure. I've got a couple more family things on. I'll call you.'

Kelly watched him go, wondering if he'd have stuck around if she'd let him have sex. With no one but Maud left for company, she went back up to her room to read *Villette*. She still hadn't got very far with it. There'd been too many other things going on, and she always seemed to be either thinking about Marcus, or spending time with him. She lay on her bed and stared up at the ceiling. She remembered what Marcus had said to Liza earlier: 'Funny and talented'. Was she being paranoid or was there something in the way he'd said it? Paranoid probably.

She yawned. She'd forgotten how hard it could be to get a good night's sleep when you were sharing your bed. She opened the book but before she could finish the chapter, she was drifting off.

By the time Kelly woke up, she'd lost half the day. Someone was moving about downstairs and she went to see who it was. She found Will on the sofa watching the football.

'Where's Belle?'

He kept his eyes on the game, but he didn't look like he was watching it. 'She went home.'

'Marcus went as well. He had a family thing on.'

He didn't say anything. Something was bothering him. Surely it wasn't the noisy sex? This was stupid. 'Will, have you got a problem with me?'

This time he looked up at her. 'With you? No. But Marcus.'

'What about Marcus?'

'He's a dickhead.'

'That right? Well you'd know, wouldn't you?'

'What's that supposed to mean?'

'What do you think it means?'

He stood up to face her. 'Are you saying I'm being a dickhead?'

'Spot on, clever boy, spot on. You're acting like a tool, just because I bring someone back.'

'That's got nothing to do with it.'

'No? What is it then? Was it the noise? Too much for your sensitive ears, was it? Too much for poor little Belle? I mean, I know you two think you're being ever so discreet about it, but at least no one has to wash the sofa down after me and Marcus have a fuck.'

Someone scored a goal on the telly. The fans were cheering, the commentator was shouting, but the only two people in the room were speechless. Kelly was silently kicking herself. Will was giving her the daggers. 'I knew it. I fucking knew it.'

And then he stormed out of the room.

16

LIZA SHEDS SOME LIGHT

Paris. The most romantic city in the world, if you believed the hype. Netta wasn't sure she did completely believe it. Personally, she'd have preferred a little taverna on a quiet island. Just her and Frank, eating and drinking with the locals. But it hadn't been her choice. It wasn't her big birthday. It was Frank's, and he seemed very happy with his pick. They'd done the Louvre, the Musée d'Orsay and the Eiffel Tower. They'd strolled along the Seine, hand in hand. They'd eaten in charming little bistros and elegant restaurants, and people watched in busy street cafés. Now, they were huddled over a wobbly table, uncomfortably squeezed between similar couples outside a café, close to the Sacré Coeur. Frank's bottom was spilling over his tiny chair, his buttocks clenching like maniacs to stop themselves slipping off. They'd been waiting forever for their coffees, and now they were being hassled by street vendors and artists, keen to draw their caricatures. Romantic it was not.

Frank sighed. 'Shall we just go?'

'But we've ordered coffees.'

'Over half an hour ago.'

Netta grabbed her bag. 'Okay. Let's make a break for it.'
Frank nodded. 'Now!'

They stood up together and began to take small, quick steps. A waiter came through the door as they passed, with what could have been their long-awaited drinks. Netta grabbed Frank's arm and began to speed up even more. They ran down Montmartre faster than either of them had intended to. The thrill of it made her giggle hysterically. It set Frank off and neither of them could stop running or laughing, all the way down the steep hill. Somehow, when their sides ached too much to go on, they did manage to slow down to a stop.

Netta wiped beads of perspiration from her forehead. She hadn't done that much exercise in ages. 'I can't believe we just did a runner.'

Frank took in a huge gulp of air. 'I think it's only called that if you consume the goods and leave without paying.'

'Don't spoil my fun. I like the idea of being a rebel.'

They collapsed onto a nearby bench. Frank reached his arm across the back and rested it on her shoulder. 'That was the best laugh I've had in ages.'

'Same here. I feel quite naughty now. Shame I can't think of anything else to top it.'

'Will we find somewhere less touristy and have a nice lunch instead?'

'Excellent idea, Mr O'Hare.'

He held his hand out for her and they strolled away from the busy streets. There'd been a time when she'd found simple things like holding hands difficult, but it came easier these days. She put his hand to her mouth and kissed it. Perhaps there was romance in this city after all.

. . .

That lunch had been one of the best they'd had while they'd been in Paris, and they'd gone back to the same bistro for their last meal in the city. They were on the plane home now. Flying over the green belt that surrounded Birmingham.

Rain lashed against the windows as it touched down at the airport. The skies were grey and gloomy and Netta couldn't help feeling she'd rather be back in Paris, even if it meant having to endure minuscule chairs and lackadaisical serving staff.

When they let themselves into her house, Betty and Fred went crazy with excitement. You'd think they'd been away for weeks.

Will came downstairs with a backpack. 'Hey. How was Paris?'

'Great. We'll tell you about it later. Liza and Kelly out?' said Netta.

'Yeah. Liza said she'd be late back.'

'And Kelly?'

Will put his backpack down. 'Dunno. Shall I make you both some tea?'

Frank sat on the sofa and made a fuss of the dogs. Netta followed Will into the kitchen, distractedly scrolling through the messages that had come through on her phone while they'd been driving. There were the usual dozen or so from her mum, and one from Kelly. 'Ah, it looks like Kelly's gone to visit her family after work. She won't be back for dinner. Everything been okay? No problems?'

'No, all good. Belle came over to stay. You're still okay with that, right?'

'Yeah. I really don't mind. It would be a bit hypocritical if I did, seeing as Frank often stays the night, or I'm round at his.'

'I suppose. Just wanted to check we weren't taking liberties.'

'Of course you're not. I like Belle. She's lovely. Did Marcus stay too? I said he could.'

'Yeah, he did.'

'He seems nice enough. I don't really remember him from when you were at school.'

'No, we weren't mates. We just hung with the same crowd.'

'Kelly seems keen on him.'

'Yeah. I'm going to stay at Belle's for a couple of days, before we go back. You don't mind, do you?'

Netta did mind. She would have liked to have spent some time with him herself, but she wasn't going to say that. 'Not at all. Are Belle's parents okay with you staying there then?'

'They're cool with it.'

'Right. I assumed…' She was going to say she assumed Belle's parents didn't like him staying over, since they always stayed here, but she thought the better of it.

'Here's your tea. I'll see you in a few days.' He picked up his backpack and left.

Netta went into the lounge and sat down with Frank. 'And then there were none.'

'Hmm. Was it me or did he sound a bit cagey?'

'I thought the same. I wonder if something's happened.'

Kelly came in an hour later. Netta was relaxing on the sofa with her feet up. Frank had already gone home with Fred. 'How were things at your dad and Carol's?' she asked.

Kelly sat on the other end of the sofa. 'All right. I'm

going back next week. It's my mum's death anniversary. We're going to her memorial plot.'

'That'll be nice. Have you had a good few days with Marcus while I've been away.'

'Yeah. It's been good. Really good.'

'I got you some postcards. I know you only asked for one but I couldn't make up my mind, so I got three.'

Kelly took the cards out of their paper packet, a look of wonder on her face. They could have been treasured artefacts the way she was handling them. 'Thanks. I mean, really, thanks. They're amazing. Tell me about Paris. What did you do? Was it really sophisticated?'

'Yes, parts of it are sophisticated. We went to the Louvre and saw the Mona Lisa. It's a really small painting in a big room, crowded with people fighting to see that one little painting.'

'Honest? I bet it's really special though, isn't it?'

'Yes it is. We saw lots of art while we were there. You couldn't keep Frank away from it. And we went up the Eiffel Tower.'

'That's so brilliant. And did you go to the cafés and stuff? Did you, like, drink coffee and wine at those little tables and watch the people going past.'

Netta thought about Montmartre. She could have told Kelly about Frank's bottom nearly losing its grip on the teeny tiny seat, but she'd save that for another day. She didn't want to bring things down with niggles and practicalities. Besides, Kelly's excitement was infectious. All of a sudden, she was excited about Paris too. More so than when she'd actually been there.

She was curious to know what had sparked Kelly's interest off. 'What made you ask for a postcard?'

'Just a programme I saw. Or it might have been something Geraldine said. I can't remember. It sounded like a nice place to visit.' Kelly picked up the remote and switched on the TV. She was back to the usual Kelly. The shutters had come down.

Netta was annoyed with herself. She should have kept her mouth shut and let Kelly enjoy the moment. There was no point asking her about Will now. She'd clam up completely.

She had to wait until Liza came in to find out what was going on. Kelly had already gone to bed for another early night.

Liza stuck her head around the door. 'Sorry I'm so late. The thing I went to ran over.' She yawned. 'I wanted to get back earlier so I could hear all your Paris stories but I'm too tired now.'

'I'll tell you all about it tomorrow, don't worry.'

'Okay. Have the others gone up?'

'Kelly has. Will's staying at Belle's.'

Liza lowered her voice. 'Does that mean him and Kelly aren't talking?'

Netta lowered hers too. 'I don't know. Will left before Kelly got back. Have they fallen out?'

'Not sure. Daren't ask. They're being really touchy. I think they might have argued over Marcus. But if they did, it was when I was out.'

'Why would they argue over Marcus?'

They were talking in whispers now. Liza closed the door and came closer. 'I don't think Will likes him. Then again, it could have been the sex.'

'The sex?'

'Yeah. Marcus is really loud. We were in the kitchen

having breakfast and all you could hear was him howling. Me and Belle thought it was hilarious, but Will was really pissed off. Don't let Kelly know I've told you. She'd be like, so shamed.'

'What do you mean, loud?' whispered Netta.

'Like, really, really loud. Like, *Hound of the Baskervilles* loud.'

'Howling?'

Liza nodded her head slowly.

Netta's nose instinctively screwed itself up. 'That's a bit—'

'I know.'

17

A CHANGE IN FORTUNE

Kelly walked up the short drive to her dad's house. It had been her house too once, but she hadn't thought of it as home in a long time. Most of the drive was taken up by a skip, so she had to walk on the grass. Her dad and Carol were doing the place up this year instead of going on holiday. The skip had been empty when she'd called round a couple of weeks ago, after her argument with... No. She wasn't going to say his name. She was still fuming.

She distracted herself by having a nose in the skip. Now that it was nearly full, she wanted to see if there was anything in there she recognised. There was, but it was nothing important. Reassured, she rang the doorbell. No one answered it. After a few minutes, she rang it again.

Conor opened the door. He was at least a head taller than her. Broad too. He must have got that from their mum's side. Their dad's family was like Kelly. Small and scrawny. 'It's absolute chaos in there. Escape while you can.'

Kelly laughed. Conor was always coming out with comical lines. He was clever like that. He'd be eighteen soon and was going away to university in September. He'd get on

well there. He made friends easily, unlike Dan. Her brothers
looked alike but that was as far as it went. Dan wasn't the
smartest kid in school but he was good at practical things.
He was an electrician now. Earning good money too. While
Conor was always funny and a bit over the top, Dan was
quiet and steady. He only had a few friends but they'd been
mates since they were little. It was the same with his girlfriend, Shanice. They'd been going out since they were
sixteen. Last year, they bought a house together and now
they were talking about getting married. Conor was going
out in the world. Dan was settled.

Kelly stepped into the house and saw that everything
was as Conor had described. Carol's two boys were arguing
over the PlayStation and Kelly's half-sister, Emily, was in
tears.

Kelly went into the kitchen. Through the back window
she could see her dad messing with a barbecue in the
garden. Dan and Shanice were out there with him.

Carol was chopping cucumber. 'Con, will you do me a
favour, love? Tell Dad to come in and sort that racket out,
otherwise I may have to kill someone.' She turned to Kelly.
'Hello, Kelly. You look lovely. I like your top.'

Kelly was wearing the top she'd bought in Sheffield.
She'd put it on today because she thought her mum would
have liked it. She took a bottle of wine from her bag and put
it down on the worktop. 'Thanks. I brought this. It's from
Bordeaux.'

'Lovely. I didn't know you drank red wine.'

'Yeah. I drink it all the time.' It was only a little lie. She
drank it some of the time. When she was trying to be
sophisticated.

'Very sophisticated.'

Kelly's face went pink. 'Well, you know. Do you want

some help?'

'That'd be great. Do you mind finishing off the salad?'

Her dad came in from the garden. 'All right, bab? You're looking well. Food won't be long, Caz.'

'Good. Do something about that lot in there, will you?' said Carol.

Carol's boys were not happy when the PlayStation was declared a no-go zone. It sounded like there were some major strops going on. But then her dad reappeared with Emily in his arms, followed by the boys. He got them playing football with Dan and Con, and put Emily on his shoulders while he was turning meat on the barbecue.

Kelly watched him, mesmerised. It was only quite recently that they'd been properly getting on. She'd spent such a long time despising him for being weak after her mum died that she'd forgotten how lacking in crapness he could be sometimes.

Carol stood behind her. 'He can be quite sweet occasionally, can't he?'

To her amazement, Kelly was a bit too filled up to give an answer.

Carol picked up the salad bowl. 'Right, I think we're ready. You take this and I'll open the wine.'

Shock News! The barbecue had been lovely. Kelly had really enjoyed herself. Often when she was at her dad's she couldn't wait to get out but today, she'd been pretty chilled. She'd told them she had a new boyfriend and they'd wanted to know all about him. Carol invited him over. Her dad complimented her on the wine. Apparently, he liked Bordeaux. Who knew? She even told Conor that she'd started reading and he didn't take the piss one bit. In fact he was impressed that she'd started with the classics because he'd found them hard to get into.

After they'd eaten, Kelly and her brothers went with their dad to the crem. The four of them were standing in front of the memorial plot. Her dad had brought flowers and he'd just finished putting them in a plastic vase. Dan commented on how well kept the plot was. Her dad said he liked to keep it neat and tidy. Another surprise. Kelly had assumed that when he'd met Carol, he'd be done with her mum. Now she had to admit that there was another thing her dad wasn't crap at.

'I wish I could remember more about her,' said Conor.

'Tell me what you do remember,' said her dad.

'She was fun. We laughed a lot. I have this memory of her tickling me.'

Dan smiled. 'She used to do that a lot. You couldn't be unhappy around Mum for long. She always had a way of making you laugh. Do you remember those silly voices she used to do when she read us a story?'

'Oh yeah. I think I do,' said Conor.

Her dad put his arm around Conor. 'Sounds like you've remembered all the things she'd have wanted you to. What about you Kel, what do you remember?'

There was a lump in Kelly's throat that she was struggling to get rid of. 'Loads.' They all looked at her expectantly, waiting for more. 'Dancing. She liked dancing. And singing. She was always singing.'

Her dad smiled. 'Yes she was. She was a real party animal. But she loved the old Irish songs as well. When you were babies, she'd sing you to sleep with them.'

A scene popped into Kelly's head. Her mum with one of her baby brothers in her arms, singing one of the old songs. 'The one about Carrickfergus.'

'That was one of her favourites,' said her dad.

They stood a while longer, each with their own special memory, until her brothers began to look like they'd run out of memories.

'I guess we should go.' Conor had obviously had enough.

'You boys go on ahead.' Her dad raised his eyebrows in Dan's direction. Dan seemed to know what he was hinting at. They must have talked it over earlier. Kelly had wondered why they'd come in two cars. Now she knew. Her dad wanted a talk. And it had all been going so well.

'Let's sit down.' He pointed to a bench close by.

She went with him, wondering what he wanted to talk about. As far as she could tell, she hadn't done anything to upset Carol which always used to be the reason for their talks. They'd made a lot of ground since Kelly's nan died two years ago. Carol had been good to her then. Last year as well, when Kelly had her wobble, Carol came round to Netta's to cheer her up. So it probably wasn't Carol. Unless her dad had some news to deliver. Oh God, don't let Carol be dying. She couldn't go through that again.

'I'm glad you came today,' he said.

'Me too. It's been nice. I didn't know you came here regular.'

'You don't then?'

She shook her head. It never occurred to her to come. It wasn't like her mum was actually in there, although he seemed to think she was.

'I like to make sure everything's nice for her. She was very special. I er … I loved her … so much.' His voice was breaking. At one time Kelly would have told him to man up but she was a bit more understanding these days.

'You love Carol too though, don't you?'

He looked surprised. 'Yes. Of course. She's a wonderful woman. She put up with you and that wasn't easy.'

'Yeah, thanks for that, Dad.'

'It is possible to love more than one person in a lifetime you know. Your mum was my first love. I thought we'd grow old together, but it wasn't to be. I was broken when she died. You know that more than anyone. Carol put me back together again. I'm a very lucky man to be able to say I've had the love of two incredible women in my life.'

'Dad, is something wrong with Carol?'

He screwed up his face. 'No. What makes you say that?'

'This talk. Oh shit, it's not you, is it?'

'No. I'm absolutely fine and so is Carol. I do want to talk to you, but not about that.'

'What? Is it bad news?'

'No. If you just shut up for a minute, I'll tell you. Not long before your nan died, she left some money in my safe-keeping for you. She didn't leave any for anyone else. Just you. There's a letter explaining why. I can guess why but I've never opened it, so I can't say for certain. The only thing she told me was that I shouldn't give you the money until I was sure you were mature enough not to waste it.'

'Wait, are you saying you didn't think I was mature enough when she died?'

'Kelly, bab, I know you weren't. You were all over the place.'

'But it's been two years.'

'I know. I was going to give it to you last year, but then there was that business—'

'Okay, okay, I get it.'

He gave her an envelope. 'Your nan's letter's in there, along with a cheque for £15,000, plus interest.'

Kelly's jaw dropped. 'How much?'

'£15,000. It might seem like a fortune but it's not really. Spend it wisely.'

When she'd picked herself up off the floor, her dad offered to give her a lift home but he said they needed to go back to his house first. There was something else he wanted her to have. Kelly was too gobsmacked to say anything. She hadn't opened the envelope yet. Part of her was expecting it to be a practical joke. Except her dad didn't do practical jokes. Her mum, yes. Her dad, no.

Her dad looked her in the eye. It wasn't something he did often. 'You know, I look at you sometimes and I see her.'

'What are you talking about?'

'I see your mum in you.'

Now he really was joking. 'Bollocks. I look just like you.'

'You might resemble me physically but sometimes, there's a look you give me and it's Caitlin all over. Anyway, who do you think you get those green eyes from? In case you haven't noticed, mine are blue.'

'Mum's eyes were green?'

'Yes. Did you forget?'

'I must have.'

'That's okay, bab. You can't remember everything. The things I wanted to give you are some bits and pieces that used to be your mum's. I found them when we were sorting through the loft. I'd forgotten I'd put them away for you kids when you were older. You've got a box each. You don't have to have them if you don't want them though.'

'I do. I do want them.' She was hating herself already for forgetting the colour of her mum's eyes.

18

A WORD FROM GLADYS PAYNE

Liza was over at Frank's, painting. Netta had looked in on them an hour ago and they were side by side, each at their own easel in his studio-cum-breakfast room. It filled both purposes. They'd looked so content that she felt like an intruder, but it did her heart good to see them like that. Netta had never asked Liza if she did the same with Colin who had a purpose-built studio in his house. She'd also stopped asking Frank if Liza was a nuisance, after he told her that he used to do the same thing with Robyn before she left home. She realised then that he actually enjoyed it. Perhaps it even kept him from missing his daughter a little bit.

Right now, Netta was in her garden. The sun streaked through the trees on one side of the lawn and Maud was snoozing in their shade. Betty was with Liza, and Netta was on her knees weeding the strawberry patch.

When she'd been married to Colin, the garden had been his domain. Even the plants were determined by him. Actually, the whole property had been his domain. He chose everything – the furniture, the colours on the walls, the soft furnishings. Everything. Her taste wasn't up to scratch apparently.

Of course he hadn't stopped there. Over the years, everything became his domain. Even the clothes she wore. When she'd been young, she'd loved dressing differently. The more outrageous the better. Until he set to work on her. The influence was subtle. A suggestion here, a look there. A remark. A sneer. A sulk. It was gradual and painfully drawn-out. For her anyway. He was happy to take his time moulding her into Annette Grey. Dull and grey by name and nature. Dull, grey and compliant.

The flat she moved to when he forced her out of the family home had a balcony. There was just enough room for a bit of furniture and a few pot plants. It suited her then. She didn't have the confidence to handle anything more.

In contrast, this house had a huge garden that was full of trees, flowers, and fruit. Thanks to her dad, she'd learned which plants were weeds and which were not. Now she really enjoyed a solitary potter. It was one of the little luxuries she allowed herself every now and then. But this time there was a purpose to her pottering. Next weekend was going to be a gardening one. Friends and family would be coming to do a big garden tidy up, and she was trying to get a head start to give them more time for partying afterwards.

Kelly's top half appeared over the gooseberry bushes that separated the strawberry patch from the lawn. 'That's where you are. I've been looking all over the house for you. Fancy a glass of Prosecco?'

Netta pushed herself up. 'Wow! There's an offer that's hard to refuse. Sod the weeding.'

Five minutes later, they were sitting in the garden chairs enjoying a glass of fizz.

'This is nice. Did you stop off on the way home for it?' said Netta.

'Nah. It was a present from Dad and Carol, being as I've got something to celebrate.'

'Ooh. Intriguing. Are you going to tell me what, or are you going to keep me in suspense?'

Kelly took an envelope out of her pocket and gave it to Netta. 'Take a look at that.'

Inside the envelope was a smaller one that looked like it held a letter. There was also a cheque for just over £15,000, made out to Kelly. The signatory was Andrew Payne, Kelly's dad. 'Your dad gave you £15,000?'

'Not exactly. Read the letter.'

Netta opened it and went straight down to the bottom. 'It's from your nan. Are you sure you want me to read it?'

'Absolutely.'

'Okay then. If you're certain.'

'*Dear Kelly,*

If you're reading this then I'm dead. I don't know how long ago I died because I've told Andrew (your dad) not to give it to you until he can be sure you're properly grown-up and sensible. It could be years for all I know, but I hope you didn't suffer too much when I went.

You might be wondering why I've left this money for you. I'll tell you. Of all my grandchildren, you've been the one who's cared for me the most. Sometimes to the point of daftness, but you always were a bit too soft. Just like your dad. And don't you be rolling your eyes, just because I said the two of you have something in common. I know he let you down badly when you needed him the most, but he's trying hard to make it up to you. By the way, that Carol's a nice girl, if you give her a chance.

Anyway, I'm digressing. I've been saving this money up for years.

God knows what for, but you don't miss it when it's just a few pounds a week, do you? You should try it, now that you've got a proper job. You'll be surprised how quickly it mounts up. My little pot of gold turned out to be £15,000. I know that sounds like a lot, but if I split it between all my children and grandchildren, it wouldn't be worth anything to them. So I've decided to give it to the person who deserves it the most. In case you haven't guessed, that's you.

Your dad's quite on board with it. We sorted it all out after I had the stroke, so that the rest of the family didn't know. It's been our little secret for however long it's been until he gave you the money. There's no need to tell the others. They'll only make his life a misery.

So that's it, Kelly. The money's yours now. I won't tell you what to do with it, but I will say this. Make it count. Do something with it that gives you a better start in life. Whatever you do, don't waste it on losers like that Craig, or I'll come back and haunt you.

Oh, and be nice to your dad. He loves you to bits. So do I.
Your loving nan,
Gladys Payne.'

Netta folded the paper up. 'What a wonderful letter.'

'I know. It's just so Nan, as well. I wish I could tell her I've got a proper boyfriend now, and I am getting on all right with Dad and Carol.'

'Maybe she knows. After all, she hasn't been haunting you.'

Kelly narrowed her eyes. 'You don't really believe that, do you?'

'Not really. Do you?'

'Nah. When you're dead, you're dead.'

'She's right though, your nan. You should make it count.'

'I will. I just haven't worked out how yet. Dad gave me a box of things that used to be my mum's.'

'That's nice. What's in there?'

'Dunno. Haven't looked. I'm not in the right frame of mind at the moment.'

'Plenty of time,' said Netta.

'Yeah, I guess.'

Kelly fiddled with her glass. She didn't seem that happy for someone who'd just come into money. It was only natural, Netta supposed. There'd been a lot for her to take in today and Kelly wasn't always as robust as she appeared. On the face of it her life was on the up. She had this Marcus now. According to Kelly that was going well, but it seemed to have driven a wedge between her and Will. They still didn't appear to be speaking to each other. And even Liza seemed reticent to be drawn into conversation with Kelly about Marcus. So while things felt like Kelly should be happy, there were little inklings that maybe she wasn't.

On top of that, Netta was uneasy. There were things going on that she couldn't quite get a grip on. It was like they were there, but hidden. As if they were veiled somehow. And why was it that whenever she heard Marcus's name she thought of Craig, Kelly's vile ex?

19

POPPY HITS A NERVE

The train was getting close to Sheffield. Kelly had caught it straight after foodbank, just like before. This time there was no one to chat to about books, so she got on with reading *Villette*. It was a difficult book, especially as there were a lot of French phrases thrown in. It had put her off at first because she couldn't understand any of it, but then she realised it didn't matter because it didn't stop her enjoying the story.

There was something about the main character, Lucy Snowe, that reminded Kelly of herself. Lucy was about the same age as her, but a lot braver. She'd set off for Belgium on her own with hardly any money, no job to go to, and no family to watch her back. That part wasn't like her, unfortunately. That part was more like Edie. She was the brave heroine who refused to do what was expected of her. No. It was the other side of Lucy that could have been Kelly. The plain, unloved loner. The lonely watcher who didn't fit in. That was her. Even though she had Marcus, it was still her. She could see that now. Lucy had shown her.

She hadn't felt as guilty about coming this weekend

because there weren't any markets booked, but she was missing the big garden tidy up. That was a shame because she liked it when everyone came round to help out. She'd tried to explain that to Marcus, but he kept banging on about not being able to go another week without seeing her. She'd asked him to come to Birmingham instead and you'd have thought she was expecting him to walk to the whole way. In the end it was easier to say she'd come.

He was waiting for her on the platform. He kissed her with his fat cherry lips and hugged her so hard he almost squeezed the life out of her. 'I've missed you.'

That was nice. That's how it was in a proper relationship when you cared about someone. Craig never said stuff like that. She felt about bad about being annoyed with him for making her come. 'Missed you too.'

'Good. You can show me how much when we get to mine.'

They bumped into Kyle when they got to the house.

'Anyone else in?' asked Marcus.

'No, I'm just going to meet them. See you later?'

'Yeah, might do,' said Marcus.

As soon as Kyle closed the door, Marcus pushed her towards the stairs. 'Right, upstairs you.'

Bloody hell. There was eagerness and then there was just plain rudeness. 'Don't I get a drink first?'

'I'll get some beers from the fridge. Go and get your clothes off. I'll be up in a minute.' He slapped her bum hard.

The sting sent shockwaves through her. 'Ow! Don't do that. I don't like that sort of stuff.'

'What sort of stuff?'

'Rough stuff.'

'Rough stuff? You think I'm into S&M? Fucking hell, Coat Girl, you've got a mind like a sewer. It was a joke. Jeez.'

'Sorry. I didn't mean… I'll go up.'

Kelly schlepped up to his room and sat on the edge of the bed. She'd ruined it, killed the moment. Now he was in a sulk and she'd have to be extra nice to get him out of it. She heard his footsteps on the stairs, took her clothes off and got into bed.

He came in with two beers, still in a mood. 'Let's take a look at you then. Or is that too fifty shades for you?'

She threw back the quilt. He pulled her up and stood her in the middle of the room while he walked around her, as if he was inspecting her. He had a hard-on. She unzipped his jeans and put her hand into his pants. 'Sorry. I'll make it up to you.'

Kelly was glad when the sex was over. He'd done that stupid howling thing again, which was so cringe. He must only do it here when he knew the house was empty. Probably worried his mates would laugh at him. She slipped her jeans back on and found a clean T-shirt in her bag.

Marcus came in with two more beers. He was happy again. Until he saw what she was wearing. 'Why aren't you wearing that dress I bought you?'

She pulled her trainers on. 'I didn't bring it with me.'

'Why not? I said to bring it. I thought you liked it?'

'I do. It was dirty and I didn't have time to wash it.' Two lies. She could be good at lying when she had to be.

'Oh. Bring it next time then, yeah?'

'Yeah. Sure.'

. . .

He took her to the same pub as that time he'd left her sitting alone while he talked to his mates at the bar. He didn't get the chance to do that this time because his mates were sitting right by the door.

Kyle caught their attention. 'We've saved you some seats.'

Kelly sat next to him. Marcus went to the bar, then took the seat next to her. On the other side of him was that girl Poppy. She was in full on diva mode, moaning about how awful her senior school had been, making everyone laugh with stories that weren't even funny. Kelly was bored already. Her mind started wandering back to *Villette* and Lucy Snowe. Then she heard her name.

Poppy waved her hand in front of Kelly's face. 'I said, which school did you go to?'

Kelly's mouth was suddenly full of cotton wool. She checked herself and did what she always did on these occasions. She put on the poker face. 'You wouldn't know it.'

'Try me. I'm from Birmingham too.' She rolled her eyes. 'Amazing as that might seem.'

'I went to a few. They were just schools.'

'So secretive.' Poppy's face was so fucking smug, Kelly wanted to shove her fist in it.

'What's the schedule for the pub crawl tomorrow? I've got to work so I'll have to pick it up late,' said Kyle.

Poppy slapped a flyer on the table. 'It's all on here.'

Kelly gave Kyle a sideways glance. He smiled at her and she guessed he'd changed the subject on purpose.

'Why wouldn't you say which school you went to?' asked

Marcus, on the way back to the house. 'Was it really bad? Are you ashamed of it?'

Kelly shrugged. 'I just didn't like the way the conversation was going.'

He put his arm around her. 'Yeah, Poppy can be a bit intimidating.'

Kelly laughed. Intimidated by that snotty bitch? Do her a favour. Craig standing over her, looking like he was about to knock the shit out of her was intimidating. Poppy was nothing. Literally. Nothing.

She was expecting him to drag her straight up to bed when they got in, but they stayed down with the others. She played on the PlayStation with Kyle for a bit. When she let someone else take over, she noticed Marcus had dropped off. She shook him awake. They went to bed and he was asleep straight away. No more sex. Good.

Kelly couldn't sleep though. She was thinking about what had happened in the pub. Poppy had seen she'd hit a nerve. Otherwise, why the smug face? Kelly was annoyed with herself for giving such a crap answer to Poppy's question. It was true, she had been to a few schools. If you could call that middle one a school. They said it was, but then they said a lot of things. Especially about her anger management issues. They were nice enough, but she'd hated being there with all the other misfits. She behaved herself, did everything she needed to get back to a normal school, and made sure she never got sent there again. But even then, it was already too late.

'Stigma: A mark of disgrace associated with a particular circumstance, quality, or person.'

She'd looked it up after she got that cheque from her dad. Only because she'd been considering using it on university fees. She'd been seriously thinking about it, until she thought she might have to tell them she'd been sent to a Pupil Referral Unit for her 'behavioural problems'. There were lots of words that kept coming up when she looked the units up online. The one that stuck in her mind was stigma. Whether anyone meant it to be so, or not, that was exactly how she felt. It was a mark of disgrace, and that was why she'd told no one. Not even Netta or Geraldine. And no way was she going to tell Poppy.

20

KELLY FEW SCHOOLS

Kelly was shopping on the same road that Marcus had taken her to last time. It was the one with all the vintage shops. She made a note of the name this time, Eccleshall Road. Carol's birthday was soon and she wanted to get her something nice. Carol liked little pots and Kelly had seen some good ones when she'd been here before. She'd asked Marcus to come with her but he had this charity pub crawl that Poppy had arranged. Kelly hated that kind of thing, so she'd told him she'd go on her own and they could meet up later. She was surprised and a bit put out that he'd agreed straight away. The way he'd carried on about needing to see her, you'd have thought he wouldn't want to let her out of his sight. Maybe all he really needed was a shag. It occurred to her that all the compromises in this relationship were one way only. She didn't tell him that. Obviously. Perhaps she'd bring it up when she told him about her inheritance. If she could face the fall out.

She was beginning to know her way around Sheffield now. It wasn't that big compared to Birmingham, and the idea of exploring on her own made her feel brave. Like

Lucy Snowe and Edie. She found a hand-crafted bowl she thought Carol would like. You could say it was artisanal. There you go then. She was buying something artisanal. Kelly Payne was going all middle-class.

She didn't want to get to the pub too early so she carried on shopping, looking for things of beauty, as Robyn called them. Rob was a thing of beauty. Inside and out. She took after her mum as far as looks went. God help her if she'd turned out looking like Frank. Knowing Robyn though, she wouldn't have cared if she did. She was like that. So was Netta. They had absolutely no egos. In fact, neither of them had any idea of the effect they had on people just by being in the same room.

Her phone beeped. Robyn was replying to her last message telling her to buy a pretty, pale-green dress she'd found:

'Next time I'm home, let's go to Sheffield. It looks like a cool place xx'

Kelly was quite proud that she'd found somewhere new. It was nice to be the cool one for a change. She checked for messages from Marcus. He'd been sending updates whenever they'd moved on. The last one had been at three o'clock, about an hour ago. She should find him before he got too pissed.

She called at the house to leave her shopping. Kyle let her in. He'd just got back from work. 'You didn't go on the crawl then?'

'Nah, I'm not a big drinker. I had some shopping to do. I'm going to catch them up now.'

'Me neither. We can go together if you like.'

'Yeah, that'd be good. I'll stand more chance of finding them that way. Last message I got was at three. What about you?'

He checked his phone. 'Four-fifteen from The Beehive. Let's go with that.'

When they got to The Beehive, they found the crawl had moved on. Kelly checked her phone to see if Marcus had picked up her last message, telling him she was on her way. He hadn't. She tried calling. It went to voicemail. Memories of that last Christmas Eve with Craig popped into her head. She pushed them away. Marcus was not Craig, and this was nothing like that day in 2017.

Kyle checked the group messages and the flyer Poppy had given him last night. 'Let's try the Frog and Parrot. It's not far.'

They found the crawl when they got to the Frog and Parrot, but they couldn't find Marcus and his friends. Someone told them the crawl had split at The Beehive and the others had gone to another bar that wasn't on the schedule. When they got to that bar there were only a few stragglers left. They took them to another pub. At that pub, another three stragglers took them to another. As they went from one bar to the next, they were picking up stragglers along the way.

Kelly was getting more irritable with each stop. 'We're like a couple of pied fucking pipers.'

Kyle laughed. 'It is like we've started a crawl of our own. Except we haven't had a drink.'

Two pubs later, they caught up with the breakaway group. They'd re-joined the original crawl.

Kelly spotted Poppy in the middle of the crowd. When she saw them, Poppy threw herself on Kyle. Then again, she might have just fallen on him. She didn't seem to be able to stand. 'Kyle, where've you been?'

'Where's Marcus?' shouted Kelly over the noise.

'Oh look, it's Kelly Few Schools. I thought you'd pissed back off to Birmingham.' She did one of those sarcastic, over the top, Brummie accents when she said Birmingham.

'Is Marcus here?' Kelly was trying very hard not to lose it.

'Is Marcus here? Let me think.' Poppy put a finger to her lips, then pointed it to a door on the other side of the room. 'Last I saw of him, he was trying to shag Ellie on a pool table.'

'She doesn't mean it, she's pissed,' said Kyle.

Kelly turned on him. 'Yeah? Well you better get her sobered up before I rip her fuckin' head off then, hadn't you?'

Kelly pushed through the crowd, out to a corridor. To the right were the toilets. To the left was another room with a frosted glass window on its door. It was dark inside but as she went in, she noticed a small bright light near an empty pool table. It was coming from a group of four guys, the only people in there. It lit their faces up, and was brightest on Marcus. It was the light from his phone.

The music that was playing was old stuff from before she was born. It was really loud. Perhaps that's why they didn't hear her come in. Unless they were just too drunk. Or too busy concentrating on what he was showing them. It was one of the photos he'd taken of her in that horrible dress.

'She's so fucking desperate she'll do anything I say. She actually went out like this. Tits on show and everything. I swear, if I'd told her to take her pants off in the middle of the club and bend over for me, she'd have done it. She's such a—'

'Put it away, man. What the hell is wrong with you?'

One of them turned away. Then he saw Kelly. 'Marcus.' He nodded his head in her direction.

Marcus turned around, a big, sneery leer on his face. 'Kelly! Here she is. My little scumbag. My yummy scummy.'

'Give me that phone.' Kelly was angry but not hysterical. That would probably come later.

He held it up, too high for her to reach.

'I said give it to me.'

He tried to put his arms around her. 'C'mon, Coat Girl. It was just a joke, that's all.'

'A joke?'

'Yeah, a joke. A laugh.'

'Yeah? Here's a joke for you.' She swung her arm up hard. It landed in the middle of his face. 'Laugh about that.'

She walked out while he was screaming something about broken noses. As she shot out into the street, she saw Kyle bent over someone who was throwing up in the road. Poppy. Kelly began to run. Kyle called after her, but there was no way she was going to stop. She couldn't face any of them. She carried on, not knowing or caring where she was going. Anywhere was better than the place she'd come from.

21

A STOLEN PAST

Kelly found herself at the train station. She didn't know how she'd got there but that wasn't important. The main thing was it offered a way out. She was just in time for the last train to Birmingham. Home, where there were people who didn't think she was a dirty scumbag. Or if they did, they kept it to themselves.

It wasn't until the train left Sheffield that she let go of the fear. She'd half-expected Marcus to come after her and either hit her back, or say something else that made her feel like a filthy, worthless nothing. Of the two, she'd have preferred the physical pain of a fist. Bruises healed over quickly enough. Words stayed with you forever. Right now, they were stuck in her head, those words he'd said about her. Those horrible, spiteful, disgusting words.

For the first time in weeks, she let herself think about Will. Since that argument, she'd been blocking him out and refusing to allow him space. Had he known what Marcus was like? Was he trying to tell her? She should have listened to him. She should have trusted his word and not her own stupid, idiot brain. Because there was no doubt about it, she was really fucking stupid to think that she'd ever be anything to Marcus, other than a joke and a dirty shag.

The train got into Birmingham just after eleven. New Street station was alive with people piling into the city for a big night out. Young people mainly. The older ones were mostly getting the trains out of town. Their big night out was done. Kelly took an empty seat in the middle of the station's huge atrium and watched them for a while. It wasn't that they were especially interesting to her, it was just that she wasn't sure where to go next. Then it came to her. She'd go to her place. Not to the house she called home, but to the place that had once been her only escape.

She left the station and walked to the bus stop. The air was cool and she was chilly. She'd left her jacket in Sheffield, along with her backpack and her shopping. The book too. Never mind. She wouldn't be reading any more books, and no one would miss one out of the hundreds that were on Netta's shelves.

She got off the bus outside a twenty-four-hour store that she used to come to a lot when she lived around here. Inside, she bought two bottles of cheap white wine. Fuck Bordeaux. This was good enough for her.

She stepped outside the shop. If you took a right and walked for half an hour, you'd come to her dad's house. She took a left, towards the old rec.

The rec had changed a bit since she'd last been here. The old wooden roundabout and half-broken swings were gone and there were newer, more child-friendly things for kids to play on. If Kelly thought she couldn't feel any worse than she already did, she was wrong. Her mum had pushed her on that knackered old roundabout. Her dad had sent her soaring in the air on those swings. When her mum died, she'd hung out here with her mates and, when the so-called mates deserted her, she came alone. Just her and a bottle of the cheapest alcohol she could buy. She came here all the time when her dad brought Carol home. She came here when she needed to get out of Craig's way. This was the place of her escape. At least it had been. This new, cleaner version had stolen her past and she felt the loss of it.

Kelly sat on one of the new swings and opened a bottle. She always made out that she wasn't really a drinker, and she wasn't. Now. But that hadn't always been the case. When things got really bad, drink had been necessary too often. Not that she'd been a teenage alkie or anything. You needed money for that. Unless you were good at nicking stuff. She'd been broke, and she had a conscience, so alcoholism was never going to happen. Self-medication was all it was. Self-medication when the shit got too much to handle. It helped with the 'anger management issues'. It was a lot easier to stop yourself being angry when you were too pissed to care. No wonder they sent her to that unit. 'Kelly Few Schools'. Fucking Poppy.

The wine was sweet and sickly and she winced at the first few mouthfuls. She'd become used to better than this. That was Netta and Frank's doing. Geraldine's too. They'd upgraded her. Gentrified her. Just like this playground. Thing was, the playground was still on a piece of shitty old grass that was worth nothing, and that was the same with her. The best Kelly would ever be was a slightly more cultured chav.

'*Cultured: 1. refined and well educated. 2. (of a pearl) formed round a foreign body inserted into an oyster.*'

Kelly slapped the side of her head. 'Stop fucking doing that!' She was sick of words. Sick of dictionaries. Sick of trying to be something she wasn't. She put the bottle to her mouth, threw back her head and swallowed down the sugary drink. It was horrible but soon she wouldn't care.

The sound of voices made her look through the railings, across the grass to the pavement. Two men bouncing along. Probably on something. One of them was Craig.

She'd had a feeling she might see him here. It was halfway between his flat and his local. In fact, this was where she'd first met him. He'd been walking past on his way home and saw her on the roundabout, drinking alone. There were no railings then, so it was easier to see from the road. He'd come over and asked if she was all right. If ever he saw her after that, he'd stop and talk. Nothing heavy. He'd been quite sweet. Two years later, she moved in with him. She was seventeen and living at her nan's. Her nan wasn't happy about it and neither was her dad, but she ignored them and moved in anyway. Kelly was good at ignoring well-meaning advice. She was boss at it.

When they were far enough ahead not to notice her, she slipped off the swing and followed them to Craig's block where his friend left him. Kelly stood in the shadow of some bushes, invisible. She was shaking. It was colder now and her thin top was nowhere near enough to keep her warm.

Craig didn't go straight into the building. He stayed outside checking his phone. Then he lit up a spliff and looked up at the sky. She'd never known him to be a star gazer. She remembered the way he'd been with her back in those days in the playground, and when they first lived together. He may have been a bastard later, but at least she knew where she stood with him. And when it came down to it, there was no real difference between him and Marcus.

They both only wanted her for one thing. They'd both made it clear in their own way, that was all she was good for.

She had a sudden need to be with Craig. Maybe that was why she'd gone to the rec. Maybe she just wanted to be with someone who was on her level. She could go over to him now. It would be so easy. He'd be surprised, for sure, but maybe he'd be pleased to see her. Kelly stepped out of the shadows.

'Have you been waiting for me?' A woman's voice stopped her from going any further.

Craig killed his spliff. 'I was worried about yer.'

The woman pointed to the spliff. 'Need one of them to calm your nerves, did you?'

'Sorry, babe. I am trying.' Craig looked genuinely sorry. That was new.

The woman laughed. 'Yes you are. Very trying.' She stopped in front of him. They kissed and went inside.

So Craig had moved on. They looked like a proper couple, as well. Vince hadn't mentioned that when she saw him at the foodbank. The tenderness of their kiss was a shock. Craig had never kissed her like that. No one had ever kissed her like that.

She went back to the rec and sat on the swing with her wine. Everything was shit. Everything was always going to be shit.

'Don't tell Andy.'

Kelly was jolted out of her sleep. She'd been dreaming. She couldn't remember anything about the dream, except for those words: 'Don't tell Andy.'

She opened her eyes. The sun was coming up. All around her the grass was dewy and glistening. A fox was standing in front of her, unmoving. It spooked her out at first, but then she moved her hand and saw it flinch, and realised that it was more scared of her than she was of it. If she got up, it would probably run. So she lay very still and watched it, watching her. Netta had a thing about foxes and she never got why, until now. There *was* something special about them. Something mystical.

Kelly waited for the fox to move on before sitting up. She tried to recall how she'd ended up asleep on the grass. The last thing she remembered was sitting on the swings with the wine. She looked around and found the empty bottles. No wonder she couldn't remember anything. She shivered. Her clothes and hair were wet. It was more than dew. She must have slept through rain. Whether she wanted to or not, she needed to go home.

She walked along the canals and streets until she reached her road. It was Sunday morning. The family and friends would be here soon. First to walk the dogs and then to carry on with the garden clear up. Kelly didn't want to see them. If she had anywhere else to go, she'd run away to it. But there was nowhere, and she was so cold and tired.

22

THE GHOST OF KELLY PAYNE

The front door slammed. Netta and Liza heard it from the garden. Since they weren't expecting anyone else for a while, Netta assumed it was Frank. The sound of hurried footsteps on the stairs changed her mind. She went into the hall but whoever it was had already reached the top and was speeding along the landing. A bedroom door closed. It could only be Kelly.

Liza joined her at the bottom of the stairs. 'Do you think something's happened?'

'I'll go up and see.'

Netta tapped on Kelly's door. There was no answer. She tried again, this time adding: 'Kelly, can I come in?'

The door opened slightly. When Netta pushed it further she saw Kelly had moved away to sit on the edge of the bed, her back to the door. Netta went in with Maud and Betty at her heels. Maud jumped onto the bed and leaned against Kelly's side. Betty went round to the front and put her head on Kelly's knees.

'Go away dogs,' Kelly croaked.

Netta sat down on the opposite side to Maud. 'What's happened?'

Those two words brought about an eruption in Kelly. She began to weep, great heart-wrenching sobs that sent her rocking back and forth. Netta took her in her arms. Kelly's hair and clothes were damp, but it wasn't the time to ask why. She held Kelly tight and said: 'It's all right. Everything's going to be all right.' She didn't know if that was true. All she could do was hope that it was.

Some while later, Netta closed the bedroom door, leaving Liza lying next to Kelly on the bed. Earlier, when the sound of Kelly's weeping had been too much to stand, Liza had come into the room, edged around Maud and held on to Kelly. It had been something of a love sandwich, with all points covered by humans and dogs, and had been enough to stop her tears. She told them everything. With her heart fully poured out, she looked exhausted. She said she was cold but her forehead was hot. They helped her into some warm, dry pyjamas and put her to bed. Netta was going down to make her a hot lemon. Liza was watching over her now, just as she'd done so many times last year.

Kelly's breakdown last year had come as a shock to all of them. One minute she was fine and the next she wasn't. It seemed as simple as that on the surface. They'd speculated on what had caused it. They were in the last lockdown at the time and some blame was attached to that. There was an old lady at the same care home as Kelly's nan that she'd grown particularly attached to after her nan had died. The lady died too during that lockdown. Not from Covid but from old age. They'd thought that could have been the trigger. But there were probably a number of factors. The likelihood was that Kelly hadn't got over her nan's death quite as easily as they all thought she had. And even though it had been over ten years, it was also likely that her mum's death was still affecting her.

No one picked up on it until it was too late. Kelly was an expert at hiding her true feelings. It was only after she'd virtually closed herself off that they realised. They'd searched for signs then, and saw there had been some, if they'd looked closely enough. There were the quiet periods, the long bike rides, the increasing lack of communication. The dwindling interest in food was another one, but they'd put that down to Kelly's normal finicky food preferences. When they looked back on it afterwards, it all added up. If Kelly had taken to her bed and stayed there, again, it might have been more obvious. But she didn't. She got up every day. She went to work and to the foodbank. She existed, and that was all it was. She was the ghost of Kelly Payne. Neither here or not here.

It had taken a huge effort on everybody's part to bring Kelly back to the living. Since his course was remote, Will had stayed at home after that Christmas. It helped. Netta, Liza and Frank also took turns on what Liza dubbed 'Kelly Watch'. Netta's mum rang Kelly every day without fail and was a constant visitor, as soon as it was allowed. Kelly's dad and stepmum came too. Carol visited lots of times with little Emily, Kelly's half-sister. Robyn came down from Edinburgh. Between them all, they slowly breathed life back into Kelly. But Netta was always on the lookout for signals now, because it never felt like Kelly was completely back. Her fire was too easily extinguished. Netta had been hoping Marcus might give her back some of that lost confidence. How wrong she'd been. The little shit had knocked the stuffing out of her friend. Rather than pulling Kelly up, he'd destroyed her.

As it was Sunday morning, it wasn't long before the house began to fill up. The Sunday morning walk had been a ritual since Maud's puppies had been rehomed. First to arrive were Netta's parents with Minnie. Then Neil and Chris came with their dog, Buster. Then Frank with Fred. Netta told them what had happened. Not in the detail that Kelly had gone into, it was up to her to decide how much she wanted them to know. Instead she gave it to them high level, but with enough to leave them in no doubt as to what had been going on.

Her mum sighed. 'I had a feeling it wasn't all sunshine and roses. You know how it is when you sense someone's trying too hard to show they're happy. I'll go up and see her.'

Her dad shook his head. 'What a vile little bastard. Pardon my language, but I'm too furious to hold it in.'

'You're only saying what we're all feeling, Arthur,' said Frank.

Neil's eyes were welling up. 'Geraldine's right, you know. Kelly was trying too hard. I don't know how I could have missed it.'

Netta squeezed his arm. 'We all missed it. I suppose we were looking for the wrong thing.'

Deflated, they stood in the kitchen not knowing what to say or do next. It was Chris who broke the silence. 'We need a plan of action. We'll have to draw up a rota. It's Kelly Watch time again, and someone will have to go to Sheffield to get her things.'

'I'll go. I'd like to face that dickhead,' said Neil.

'Same here,' said her dad.

Netta had visions of them beating Marcus to a pulp. Much as she'd like to do the same herself, it would only make matters worse. 'Neither of you know what he looks like. I'll go.'

'I'm coming with you.' Liza was in the doorway, her face hard and serious.

Netta's dad looked alarmed. 'Are you sure, sweetheart?'

'Absolutely.'

'Maybe one of us should come with you. It might get difficult,' he persisted.

'Grandad, this is 2022.'' Liza said. 'We women are quite capable of fighting our own battles. I'll go with Mum. We'll get Kelly's things back and we'll deal with that arrogant shithead in our own way. Won't we, Mum?'

'Yes, we will.' If Netta hadn't been so furious she'd have smiled at her daughter's fierce naivety. Yes, they would go to Sheffield. Yes, they would give Marcus a piece of their minds. Would it make any difference? It probably wouldn't.

23

THE MYSTERY OF THE MISSING DRESS

Kelly was ill. Physically ill. Sleeping outside in the rain must have caused it but there may have been more to it than that. As far as Netta could see, Kelly had no will to fight it and what should have been a cold had turned into something much worse.

Netta's mum and dad had been here every day for the last four days. Her dad was mostly packed off to his allotment and her mum stayed with Kelly. No one could get Kelly out of herself like Netta's mum. It had all come from when she'd had her own breakdown. Kelly had been the one who'd saved her then, and it left very few boundaries between them. Plus, neither her mum nor Kelly were great ones for the polite, beating about the bush tactic that Netta employed. If her mum was 'bad cop', Netta was definitely 'good cop'. The combination worked well.

Netta and Neil had orders to fulfil and market stalls to man, so knowing Kelly was in good hands made it easier for them to carry on working. Unfortunately, she was having to miss the foodbank today, but it was the only day that worked for her and Liza to go to Sheffield. She didn't want to leave it too long: Marcus had sent Kelly several messages, the gist of which were that she'd done his face some serious damage but he was willing to forgive her. Each message dragged Kelly further down, and more coaxing was needed to build her up again. Liza had suggested blocking him but Kelly didn't seem ready to do that yet. It was as if she needed them to validate her self-loathing. Netta understood that feeling. She'd been the same once.

Will rang. She'd called him last night. He'd told her that he and Kelly hadn't spoken since her weekend in Paris. They'd argued over Marcus. Surprise, surprise. He'd been gutted about Netta's news and had decided to come back home to see Kelly, despite being all set to visit Belle that weekend.

'Hi Mum. I just wanted to let you know I've sorted things with Belle. I'll be home tonight.'

'All right, darling. Is Belle okay with that?'

'Yeah. She's coming back too.'

'Oh, okay.' She wasn't sure Kelly would welcome seeing Belle but as usual, honest bluntness was not her forte. 'Well if she thinks she can help.'

'I don't know if Kelly'll speak to me though. I've tried calling and messaging but she won't pick up.'

'I'm sure she'll be happy to see you. You two have a special bond.'

'Maybe we used to.'

She said goodbye to Will and noticed her mum had messaged to say they were on their way. She didn't want to go until they got here. She nipped upstairs to tell Liza, then looked in on Kelly. Kelly was asleep. Netta closed the door softly and crept away.

As she got down to the hall, she saw Frank's outline

through the stained-glass windows and opened the front door for him.

'The lads are here, so we're off.'

Netta walked out to the car with him. Robyn's friend, Archie, and his friend, Obie, were waiting by it. They were going to Edinburgh to help Robyn move into her new flat. Netta hadn't met them before but she recognised the tall white guy with glasses from a recent photo Robyn had sent to Frank. That was Archie. So the slightly smaller, shy-looking black guy had to be Obie.

'I'll call you tonight once I'm in the hotel,' said Frank. Archie and Obie would be sleeping on Robyn's floor, but Frank had taken the sensible middle-aged approach and booked a room. He gave her a goodbye kiss. 'Watch how you go today. If there's any trouble just get out of there. All right?'

'Don't worry, we'll be fine.' She turned to Archie and Obie. 'Look after this old fella, won't you? His back's not what it used to be.'

Archie grinned. 'We'll do the heavy lifting. You can direct proceedings, Mr O.'

Just as they were about to leave, Netta's parents pulled up behind them and her mum jumped out of the car. 'Glad I caught you. I've made you a packed lunch. I wasn't sure if you boys were meat-eaters, vegetarians, or vegans so I've made something for all three.'

Frank gave her mum a peck on the cheek. 'Geraldine, you're an absolute star.'

'I've got one for you as well,' said her mum, as they watched Frank drive off.

Netta smiled. 'I should think so too. Will's coming home tonight. Apparently he and Kelly fell out over Marcus when I was away. She's not talking to him.'

'Hmm. We'll see about that.'

Netta was in no doubt that by the time Will got home, Kelly would be talking to him. Whether she wanted to or not.

Liza opened the car door. 'Right let's do this.' They'd been sitting outside Marcus's house for the last fifteen minutes, talking themselves up. It was time to stop talking and do something.

A young man with a Geordie accent answered the door and confirmed that Marcus was in. The house had that slightly unsavoury, not properly clean smell that took Netta right back to her student days, to the house her first love had lived in. Doogie Chambers had been many things, but he was not what you'd call domesticated. Not back then anyway. He and his mates lived in their year's best party house. Music, drink and occasional drugs occupied their spare time. Cleaning didn't.

The Geordie showed them into a room that just about passed for a lounge and went upstairs to get Marcus. They could hear muffled talking upstairs and then Marcus came down. He jerked his head back and managed to convey surprise, amusement and contempt in a single look. 'Mrs Wilde! Liza!'

A pretty young woman with long, fair hair edged her way out from behind Marcus. She looped her arm around his and gave them a rather disinterested once over. Netta disliked her already. 'And you are?'

'I'm a friend of Marcus's. Who are you?'

Marcus touched the girl's back. 'It's okay, Pop.'

Pop? So she was the infamous Poppy.

Liza had caught on too. She stuck her finger up in Poppy's face. 'Kelly Few Schools sends her regards.'

'That bitch. Have you seen what she did to Marcus?' Poppy pointed to his nose which was only slightly bruised.

Netta snorted. 'Is that it? According to the messages you've been bombarding Kelly with, facial reconstruction was required. What a woeful specimen you are.'

Poppy flashed a peeved glance at Marcus. Perhaps she didn't know he'd been messaging Kelly.

'Look, I don't know what Kelly's told you but honestly, it was nothing. We had a fight. She attacked me. You must know what she's like. She's not good at articulating her anger so she lashes out. And she's jealous of Poppy, because she can't handle her being my friend. I get that.' Marcus gave them a resigned smile.

It was a reasonable argument, delivered with the exact dash of charming 'woe is me' to make it sound almost plausible. Someone more gullible might have believed it. Someone who hadn't lived through the same experience herself. But Netta had been there and bought the T-shirt, as they say, and it was all she could do not to punch him. 'I want those photos you took of Kelly deleted. Give me your phone.'

'Sorry, I can't do that. I have rights you know. I think you'd better leave now, before I have to call my friends.' Marcus smirked at her.

Maybe if he hadn't done that, Netta might have been more reasonable but that smirk was more than she was prepared to put up with. In a flash, she was within an inch of him and had his nose between her fingers. He let out a yelp. She pinched a little harder. 'Listen to me, you appalling little turd, I am just about holding back at least five men at home who are hell bent on beating the shit out of you for what you've done. Now give me your phone before I break your twatting nose right off.'

It did the trick. He reached into his back pocket and put it in her free hand. She passed it over to Liza.

'Code?' said Liza.

'Seven, eight, four, one.'

Netta let go of his nose. Liza tapped out the number and did what she had to do to delete all trace of Kelly. Then she handed the phone back to him. 'We want Kelly's things,'.

Marcus rubbed his nose. 'They're in my room. I'll get them.'

'No. She can go.' Netta pointed to Poppy who'd gone quiet.

Poppy looked to Marcus.

'Do you mind, Pop?' he said.

Poppy huffed, then made for the stairs. When Liza went after her, she stopped in her tracks. 'I'm not going unless I go alone.'

'Wanna bet?' said Liza.

Poppy gave in and stormed upstairs with Liza on her heels.

Netta looked Marcus up and down. He was good looking all right, with a face that should have belonged to a better, kinder person. After Craig, he must have seemed like a dream come true to Kelly. Craig. She'd been wrong to confuse him with Marcus. They had little in common as far as Netta could see. No. The man she should have seen in Marcus was closer to home. It was Colin.

She pointed her finger at him. Alarmed, he stepped backwards. Yes. He was just like Colin. 'You think you've got the right to behave the way you do because you've got a pretty face and a bit of money but one day, you'll get your comeuppance. One day, you'll meet someone who'll make you feel as worthless and low as you made Kelly feel. I just wish I could be there to see it.'

He shifted on his feet and attempted a laugh.

Two young men appeared in the hallway. One of them was the Geordie. The sight of them resurrected Marcus's bravado. 'Help me chuck these mad bitches out, will you?'

The Geordie came into the room. 'I don't think so, Marcus. We're here to make sure these ladies don't come to any harm. Don't worry though, we will be throwing someone out after they've gone.'

Marcus sneered, but Netta could smell the fear coming off him.

Liza came back down with Kelly's backpack and a carrier bag. 'There's a dress missing. Kelly said she bought it on Saturday. It was light green with flowers. Where is it?'

Poppy blushed.

Marcus shrugged. 'Haven't a clue. That was all there was when I woke up on Sunday morning.'

'I'll tell Kelly it's gone missing then, shall I?' said Liza.

'Say what you like.'

Liza reached into her pocket for her phone and took some photos of him. 'I do a lot of life drawing on my course. Sometimes we use live models and sometime we use photos. There's this one photo of a guy with a prick the size of my thumbnail. If any of those pictures of Kelly turn up anywhere, I'm going to photoshop your head onto one of those photos and post it everywhere, so the whole world knows you've got a prick that matches the size of your brain. D'ya get me?'

Marcus snorted. 'Yeah really.'

'Yeah. Really. So you better not have any backed up somewhere.'

'You deleted them all.'

'I better have. Oh, and same applies if you bother Kelly again. Don't message or call her. She never wants to see or hear from you again. Let's go, Mum.'

Netta followed Liza. There was no need to say anything more.

But Liza wasn't quite done. She'd saved the best for last: 'By the way, you're a real creep aren't you? Ugh! I feel dirty just being in the same room.' She did a theatrical shudder and walked out with Netta trailing in her footsteps.

Netta turned the car around the corner and they left Marcus's road. 'Was that true about the guy with the tiny prick?'

'Nah. Anyway, that would be unethical of me. I'd probably get thrown off the course if they found out. Also, I'm crap at Photoshop.'

Netta laughed. 'Well I believed you.'

'Yeah, well you can be very naive sometimes, Mum. Let's hope that creep is too. Grabbing his nose was a master stroke, by the way. It actually made his eyes water.'

Netta chose not to be affronted by being called naive and focussed on Liza being impressed by her spur of the moment nose grab. But it was Liza who'd been the most impressive today. She'd been awesome, in the truest sense of the word. 'You were magnificent in there, darling.'

'Was I? Thanks, Mum. We make a good team.'

'We do. The Wilde girls take on the bad guys.'

Liza pushed her fist in the air. 'Go, Wilde girls. I am still a Wilde girl, aren't I? Even if my name's Grey.'

Netta patted Liza's knee. 'You are most definitely a Wilde girl. Through and through.'

24

GERALDINE RETURNS A FAVOUR

Geraldine came into the room. Kelly knew it was her, even though she had her eyes closed: there was no one else in the house, and Geraldine had been in and out all morning. Kelly made a few breathing noises to make it sound like she was sleeping.

Geraldine sat on the bed. 'I know you're not really asleep. You're a very poor actor.'

Kelly rolled over and opened her eyes. 'Fucking hell, Gez. Can't you just leave me alone to mope and fester.'

'Fester: 1. (Of a wound or sore) become septic, (of food or rubbish) become rotten. 2. (Of a negative feeling or problem) intensify, especially through neglect. 3. Deteriorate physically and mentally in isolated inactivity.'

Fuck's sake, she was doing it again. That dictionary was like a genie in a bottle. Once she'd taken the stopper out, she couldn't get the bastard back in again.

'Ooh good word, fester. I don't recall that coming up in the Jane Austens. Was it your latest book?'

'No. It was just a random pick during one of my dictionary forays.' Kelly was still popping that word into sentences when she could, along with the others she'd learned this year. Except it was an unconscious thing now. She didn't realise until after she'd said a word that she'd dropped it in. It would have pleased her before, because she wanted to be that person. Now, it was just bloody annoying.

'Foray? Very nice.'

Kelly sat up. 'It's like I've got a photographic memory or something. As soon as I learn a new word, I can remember exactly how it is in the dictionary.'

'Well done you. Not many people can do that. You're very lucky. And very clever.' So Geraldine was still banging on about her being clever, in spite of all evidence that she wasn't?

'Gez, I am neither lucky, nor clever.'

Geraldine smirked. 'Listen to you. You sound like a nineteenth century heroine.'

Kelly gave her the death stare. Had the woman no feeling? She'd just gone through the third most awful experience of her life, and all Gez could do was mock her. 'I suppose you think that's funny.'

'Don't you?' Gez wasn't giving up. She had her teasing face on and she was going to make proper use of it.

'No, actually. I don't. I think I preferred you at the beginning of the week, when you were being nice to me. In fact, I think I preferred you when you were a miserable old cow who never had a good word to say to me.'

Geraldine sniffed. 'No you don't. I know things have been terrible for you and if I could, I'd go back in time and make them never happen. But I can't do that. No more than I can stand by and let you fester.'

Gez was right. Kelly didn't really prefer her as she used to be. She loved this version of Geraldine Wilde. All the same, Geraldine had pushed her to read the books and better herself, and what good had that done? 'Anyway, I expect I'll soon forget those words, and there won't be any more forays. Even if I don't forget them, I'm won't be learning any new ones. So you can think of them as a limited edition. No more books either.'

Geraldine picked up Arthur Three from the bedside cupboard and pulled a bit of stray fluff off him. The day Kelly's nan died, she'd gone to Geraldine's. Because they were in lockdown, Gez could only sit at a distance in her garden and watch Kelly falling apart, so after a while, she went into the house and came back with Arthur Two, her old teddy bear. Kelly had held onto that bear for ages. He'd been just what she needed. Geraldine had let her keep him for as long as she wanted. A few months later, Netta bought another bear for Kelly. Arthur Two went home and this new bear took his place. They called him Arthur Three. When Kelly had her wobble, and desolation and emptiness was all she saw, Arthur Three had been her only friend. She'd clung on to that bear more than any other thing in her life. Desolation and emptiness? If nothing else, that bloody dictionary had given her the words to describe how she'd felt before her friends rescued her.

She took Arthur Three from Geraldine and breathed in his scent. He smelt of Yardley English Rose. She sprayed him with her nan's favourite perfume every now and then. She thought about her nan's letter and the money, and her dad waiting for her to be properly grown-up and sensible before he gave it to her. What would they say about the way she'd let Marcus treat her? She'd let them down. She buried her face in Arthur Three. *I'm so sorry, Nan.*

Maud was curled up on the bed by Kelly's feet. She'd hardly left her side all week. She chose that moment to come in between Kelly and Geraldine. Kelly was wrong about Arthur Three being her only friend in those dark days. Maud had been there too.

Geraldine ran her hand along Maud's side. 'She's a beautiful soul, this one. All seeing and all knowing.'

'I know.' For the second time that week, Kelly cried her heart out.

The crying had helped. After Sunday, Kelly thought there was none left, but it must have been building up again without her knowing. It was probably those messages from Marcus getting to her. She was out of bed now, still in her PJs but sitting in the breakfast room with Geraldine, eating a cheese sandwich. It was delicious. Geraldine had a way of making food taste really good. Even something as simple as a cheese sandwich. The only other person who could do that was Neil. Not that she'd ever tell him. His head would swell to massive proportions unbecoming to a gentleman. Whoops. There she was sounding like a nineteenth century heroine again. That simply would not do.

'I gather you and Will had a falling out,' said Geraldine.

'Did he tell you that?'

'No, he told Netta when she spoke to him last night.'

'What did she speak to him about?'

'What do you think?'

Kelly put her sandwich down. All of a sudden it didn't taste so good. 'I wish she hadn't.'

'He'd have found out sooner or later. Now he knows. He's coming home tonight.'

'To gloat I suppose. To laugh at me.'

Geraldine arched her eyebrows. 'To gloat? To laugh at you? We are talking about Will here, aren't we? Not that vicious swine you've been knocking about with for the last few months?' She turned to pour tea from the china pot into their china cups. Gez could be a bit nineteenth century herself sometimes.

'Why else would he come back?' Kelly knew the answer but she needed to hear it.

'Because he cares about you, obviously. If you can't see that, my dear girl, then I despair.'

'Are you talking like an old Jane Austen matron on purpose?'

'Do you like it?'

'No. I've told you, I'm not reading any more books. I'm done with educating myself.'

Geraldine's eyebrows arched again. 'I seem to recall a certain young lady once giving me some invaluable advice. Something about getting better and not letting that bastard win.'

'Yeah, yeah, I get the message. But I am better already, and it was different for you. Much worse.'

'Different yes. Worse maybe. But the effect is similar. I was in a pitiful state until you gave me that advice. Now I'm giving it back to you. If you want to stop reading, that's fine. Just do it for the right reasons. Don't do it because that cretin has made you think you're not good enough. You've got a brilliant mind, Kelly. It's so sharp. You're good and kind, and you're miles above the likes of that Marcus and his snobby friend. If you let them get to you, they'll win. Do you want them to win?'

'No.' It was best not to disagree when Geraldine was this fired up.

'Well then, are you going to stop reading? Because that would suit them down to the ground.'

Kelly didn't answer straight away. She was thinking about Poppy and the way she'd singled her out to ask about her school. It was as if she'd been able to see Kelly's weak point just by looking at her. That sneery expression when she'd asked. That name she'd given her, Kelly Few Schools. Well fuck that. She'd finish that book if she got it back. She'd finish a hundred books if she had to. Then they'd see just how uneducated she was.

'Well?' Geraldine tapped the table impatiently.

'No, I'm going to carry on.'

'I should think so too. Besides, haven't you got more postcards to find?'

The postcards. She'd forgotten about them with all the upset. 'You're going away next week, aren't you?'

'We are. We're going to stay with Arthur's cousin in Nice.'

'Will you bring me a postcard back?'

'Only if you promise to forget all this falling out nonsense with Will and talk to him.'

Kelly tutted. Gez was impossible sometimes. 'All right.'

'In that case, I will bring you a postcard back. Not only that, but I'll go one better. I'll post one to you as well.'

Geraldine took her cup between her thumb and forefinger and put it to her smiling lips. Kelly could not believe she'd once thought Gez was like Mrs Bennet. She was much more like Madame Beck in *Villette*. Madame Beck was a very devious character.

25

NO MAN IN THE WORLD LIKE MR DARCY

Arthur came back from his allotment. He'd been spending a lot of time there this week. Kelly was sure even he must be sick of it by now. When he saw her in the breakfast room, a grin spread across his face. 'Nice to see you up and about.'

'No choice, Art. Gez has been nagging at me all day to stop festering in my pit up there.'

'Take no notice, Arthur. She's all the better for getting up. Come and sit down. You can tell us all the gossip from the allotment.' Geraldine gave him a kiss. Not a peck on the cheek though. A proper mouth-to-mouth, on the lips, kiss. Must have been that earthy smell, heating her up.

Kelly got up and gave him her chair. 'Tempting as you spilling the goss on the allotments is, I'll give it a miss and have one of those hot baths Doctor Geraldine has been prescribing. I'll be at least half an hour in there. Feel free if you want to get down and dirty, you two. I'll cough loudly if I can hear anything.'

Arthur chuckled. 'You cheeky young madam.'

When Kelly got up to the landing, she heard him ask: 'How is she really?'

'On the mend, physically. Not quite there yet on her state of mind. It's really knocked her confidence, poor love. I don't like to leave her really. I wish we weren't going away for another week.'

Kelly lay up to her neck in bubbles. Her body still ached from that flu or whatever it was, but the hot water made it better. The bathroom was full of thick steam. It was the perfect place to do some thinking.

She couldn't believe she'd been stupid enough to fall into the same trap as she'd done with Craig. He'd been good to her in the beginning as well. You'd think she'd have seen through Marcus's sweet talk, because Craig had given her the same shit. She blew a handful of bubbles into the air. She was kidding herself, wasn't she? Because she had seen through it. She knew really that it was all lies, and she knew which way it was going. She was just too desperate to believe it. That's what really got to her about the things Marcus said in that pub. They were true. She was so desperate, she'd have done almost anything he'd asked her to. Maybe not the things he'd said, but maybe not far off. It was the kind of desperation that came from loneliness and hunger. A hunger for someone she couldn't have.

She sank down into the water until her head was underneath it. She had to cure herself of this craving for Will, otherwise she'd go mad again. Gez was worried about her. They were all worried about her. She owed it to them not to slide back down again. She owed it to herself too. It was her turn for happiness. Whatever that was.

As she came up for air, she thought of *Villette*. Lucy Snowe loved someone who couldn't be hers and it was driving her mad too. Kelly needed to know how Lucy's story was going to end. More than that, she needed Lucy to find happiness. Because if she got her happy ending, perhaps Kelly would too. Some day.

She heard Netta's voice on the landing. They must be back from Sheffield. All day, she'd been dreading this moment, frightened of hearing what he might have said to make her look even more stupid, and common, and filthy than she already looked. But Geraldine had said she was brilliant, had a sharp mind, and was good and kind. Kelly had never thought of herself as anything but thick. She'd definitely never thought of herself as being good and kind. It was funny the things other people saw in you.

Kelly got out of the bath, feeling clean and new. It wouldn't last long but she wanted to make the most of it. She put on clean clothes so that she'd look a bit less like a manky scuzzer when Will got home. She chose some jeans and a thin black jumper and checked how they looked in the mirror. They went well together. She searched her memory banks for the right word, and found two – restrained elegance. She was aiming for a look similar to that girl she'd seen on the train to Sheffield. She'd gone out and bought a jumper like hers the week after they'd met. Meeting her had been the best thing to come out the whole Marcus and Sheffield affair. Kelly had felt good about herself after it. Like there were all kinds of possibilities out there, just waiting for her to find them. She'd thought Marcus was the one to help her do that. Or maybe she just thought he was the one. Turned out she was so wrong. All he was interested in was fucking her and telling everybody about it. And demeaning her. He was really interested in that.

'Demean: Cause to suffer a severe loss of dignity or respect.'

Marcus was not her Mr Darcy. But then, Mr Darcy was a fictional character just like all the others. It might have sometimes felt like he existed, but he didn't. He was too noble and too perfect to be real. The truth was, there was no man in the world like Mr Darcy. Not even Will Grey.

Liza knocked the door. She had Kelly's backpack and the bag with the pot Kelly had bought for Carol. 'I couldn't find the dress. Marcus claimed not to know anything about it, but that Poppy looked a bit shamed.'

'She was there then, was she?'

'Yep.'

'She's welcome to him. They suit each other. I suppose he was horrible about me?'

'He tried to make out it was all you. Mum soon shut him up though. I deleted everything I could find about you on his phone and told him what I'd do if he contacts you, or posts any pictures of you.'

'What did you say you'd do?'

'I took some photos of him and said I'd photoshop his head onto a picture of a guy with the tiniest prick in the world, and post it everywhere. Not that there's anything wrong with being small down there.'

Kelly couldn't help laughing. Only Liza could threaten to make a guy look like he had a minuscule dick, and then feel bad about ridiculing minuscule dicks. God love her.

'If you want, I can give you the full deets.'

'Nah, you're all right. I've heard enough. Thanks, Lize. For doing it, I mean.'

'You'd do the same for me.'

'Yeah, I would.'

'We're fam, right?' Liza hugged Kelly.

Kelly held on tight. 'We are.'

'Also, I looked inside your backpack. Sorry, I know it was private, but I was looking for the dress. I saw the book.'

So her secret was out. It wasn't the most awful secret in the history of secrets, but she still didn't know if she was ready to share it. Kelly took the book out and flicked through the pages. She was pleased to see it wasn't damaged and Edie's postcard was still marking the last page she'd been reading. 'I wasn't sure it would still be there. I thought he might bin it, or ruin it in some way.'

'Charlotte Brontë writes some pretty complicated shit. Do you like it?'

'It's a bit heavy on the religion and French but, yeah, I do. I know what you mean about complicated. I thought Jane Austen was hard, but she's easy compared to this.'

'Austen as well! If Nan knew, she'd say you were a glutton for punishment.'

'She does know. She was the one who suggested it.'

'You are kidding me? I thought she liked you.'

The noise of barking dogs interrupted their laughter. Liza listened at the door. 'It's Will.'

'You won't tell anyone about the book, will you?' whispered Kelly.

'No. Let's talk some more when we get the chance though, yeah?'

'Okay.'

Kelly checked herself in the mirror again. Her eyes were sunken and hollow, her face was pasty. She looked like death warmed up. Will's voice floated up from the hall. She wanted to be sick.

Liza took her hand. 'You look great.'

26

EXORCISING A DEMON

Geraldine was dishing the dinner out in the kitchen. Netta was helping her. Arthur and Will were in there too. They'd been talking very quietly until Kelly and Liza came downstairs. Then all of a sudden, they ramped up to normal levels and went on and on about the journey from York as if it was really interesting. Which it wasn't. They were fooling no one.

Will cast her a shy glance, then looked at his feet. Kelly was no better. She couldn't look him in the eye.

'Come and sit down. Dinner's ready,' Geraldine was completely oblivious to what was going on.

They sat at opposite ends of the table, as if they couldn't stand being near each other. It was true as far as Kelly was concerned. She couldn't speak for Will. Everyone talked around them. No one mentioned Marcus or Sheffield, or anything to do with Kelly's state of mind. They found other things to talk about that were only slightly more interesting than the journey from York to Birmingham.

After dinner, Geraldine and Arthur said they were going home. Arthur would be back on Sunday morning to drop

Minnie off before they went to Nice. Other than that, they wouldn't see them again for a couple of weeks. On the way out, Geraldine hugged Kelly and told her she'd message her every day.

Kelly whispered in her ear: 'Liza knows about the books.'

Geraldine nodded. 'Get better soon, sweetheart. I won't forget the postcards.'

When she came to hug Liza, Geraldine whispered something to her. Liza whispered back. It wasn't hard to guess what it was about.

They all walked Geraldine and Arthur out and waved them off. Kelly waited for the car to disappear around the corner and wondered how she was going to cope without Gez. When she turned to go back inside, she saw Liza and Netta had already gone in. She was alone with Will.

'You all right?' His eyes shot down to the ground.

'Yeah, course.' She wasn't really. It wasn't the thing with Marcus, although that was bad enough. It was the thing with him. It was broken, and no matter how hard they tried, she didn't think they'd be able to fix it.

They went back into the kitchen and helped to clear up. Netta took a call from Frank in the study and the rest of them watched TV. In one way, it was all perfectly normal. In another, it was quite surreal.

When Kelly got up in the morning, Netta had already gone out to do the market stall with Neil. Normally she'd have been there with them, but they wouldn't let her go back to work until she was better. It was a nice idea while she had company, but she didn't fancy being alone in the house for hours on end. She guessed Will and Liza were going to be her minders today, but they weren't up. That was good. She and Will hadn't properly spoken yet, and she wanted to put the difficult conversation off for as long as possible.

She went out in the garden with the dogs. It was a nice morning and she was enjoying being out there. It was the beginning of May and the weather was warming up. It would be a good morning for a bike ride. She herded the dogs back into the house, left a note on the kitchen table, and took off on the bike. She'd used it a lot during those lockdowns. She'd used it even more during her wobble phase. She liked that she could just go whenever she needed to, and all she had to concentrate on was the pedalling and the traffic. No empty silences. No bad thoughts.

She hadn't got too far when the tightness in her chest made her realise she wasn't as well as she thought she was. She took it more slowly and pushed on. She didn't want to turn back yet. A few more miles and her head might be clear.

She went past Geraldine and Arthur's and reached her nan's old care home. She'd carried on going with Liza after her nan died because the old folks liked to see them. There was one old lady that Kelly always looked out for. Her name was Queenie, although she only found that out after she died. It was about the same time as the start of Kelly's wobble period that Queenie passed. Kelly stopped going then. She didn't make a conscious decision to stop. It just happened. It was one of many things she stopped doing. She lost interest in everything, especially herself.

Kelly slowed down at the top of the drive and considered turning in. But Queenie was gone. So was her nan, and anyone that was left in there from those days would have forgotten her by now. They'd have moved on, just like Craig.

Her body ached and she felt a bit woozy. She should go home before she made herself bad again.

Kelly put her bike away and let herself in through the kitchen door. Will was in there, eating cereal. 'Are you okay? You look a bit pale.'

She sat down. 'I think I might have overdone it. I'll be all right in a minute.'

'Have you eaten? I'll make you something. Liza's gone to help on the stall for a couple of hours. She said to call if you need her.'

He made tea and toast and talked in awkward bursts, while Kelly responded in the same unnatural way. It was like they'd been taken over by two very different people, or aliens maybe. Like one of those old movies they watched for a laugh sometimes – *Invasion of the Body Snatchers*.

He put down a dinner plate full of buttered toast. Kelly hoped he wasn't expecting her to eat all of that. She picked up a slice and spread some jam over it. Their own jam. Naturally. Once you've tried the best etcetera, etcetera. 'You trying to fatten me up?'

'Some of it's for me.'

She handed him the jammy toast. 'Thank Christ for that. You had me worried for a minute.'

Will laughed. Perhaps now they could be themselves again and stop dancing around each other. They ate a slice each and she began to spread another two.

'I'm sorry.' He kept his eyes on her hand as it pushed jam across the toast.

'Me too.'

'I should have said more.'

'I should have listened.'

'I'd heard rumours. I should have asked around. If I had, I might have sounded more credible. I just sounded like I didn't like him. I don't, but that's not the point.'

'It doesn't matter. I didn't like him either to be honest. I just didn't know it until it was too late.' She handed him more toast. 'Are we friends again, then?'

'We were never not friends. You just didn't know it until it was too late.'

'Ha, fucking ha.' Kelly tried to keep a straight face but she had no control over her mouth and it forced its way into a smile. Maybe they could fix things. Maybe it would be okay.

Liza came home around midday. 'Chris turned up, so I wasn't needed anymore.'

'As you're home, do you mind if I go out for a bit? Only Belle's come back,' said Will.

'No problem,' said Liza.

'Oi, you two. I'm not a fucking relay baton, you know. And I can look after myself,' said Kelly.

Liza and Will stared at her.

She rolled her eyes. 'Okay, okay. Point taken.'

Liza scooched up to Kelly as soon as Will was gone. 'So tell me about the reading.'

'What do you want to know?'

'Everything. Don't leave a single thing out.'

Kelly did leave some things out. She didn't tell Liza it was Colin's snotty attitude that had set her off. Or that she felt like the one thicko in a household of clever people. Liza would have felt bad if she had. But she did tell her how much she was enjoying being a reader, and she did show her Edie's postcards.

Liza was got really excited over the cards. 'Oh my God, these are so amazing. Do you think there are more?'

'I hope so, being as I'm using them to tell me which books to read. If this is it, it's gonna be a short list.'

'We should look for them. Do you want to do that? Would it spoil things if I helped though?'

Kelly didn't know what to say. Lame as it was, finding those postcards gave her a buzz. She didn't know if it came from the cards or doing it in secret, but she didn't want to run the risk of losing it. She also didn't want to hurt Liza's feelings. 'It'd be nice to share it with you, Lize. Do you want to help with something else first though?'

Liza ducked a cobweb in the shed. 'Normally, I wouldn't condone this because it goes against my environmental beliefs. But I'm prepared to sacrifice them on this occasion.'

Kelly grabbed the barbecue lighting fluid from the shelf. 'Thanks, Lize. I appreciate that.'

'We should probably do it in the barbecue.'

'Good call.'

They went to the spot in the garden where the barbecue lived. Kelly opened up the lid and threw in the dress that Marcus had bought her. She poured the fluid over it and tossed in a lighted match. The dress shot up in flames.

Liza pulled her back. 'Woah! Death trap!'

Kelly watched the dress disappear in the mini blaze. 'Goodbye hideous dress.'

Liza put her arm through Kelly's. 'Goodbye hideous man.'

'Yeah. Fuck you, Marcus.' Liza was right. He was a hideous man. Hideous and pathetic. Geraldine was right too. She was too good for him.

The dress was nearly all gone. Not long now before it would be a pile of ashes.

The thought of ashes reminded Kelly of her nan, and then her mum. She hadn't looked at her mum's things yet. It was another task she'd been putting off, along with doing something about that cheque. It wasn't that she didn't want to look in that box. She did. It was just that she was scared to. Up until that day they went to her mum's plot, she'd been absolutely certain that she remembered everything about her. But then her dad asked about her memories and Kelly's mind was blank, until she managed to drag the dancing and singing out from a dark corner. The song about Carrickfergus came out of nowhere and saved her from total shame.

Obviously, she hadn't forgotten everything about her mum. She could remember stupid things like her mum's top words, posho and shitebag, and her love of a bit of sparkle. Or could she? Had she just made them up? She didn't know anymore. What hurt most was that she'd forgotten the colour of her mum's eyes. She'd thought they were blue. It was only later that day when she sat down with Netta, that she realised what she'd done. The blue eyes she'd been seeing on her mum's face were Netta's. She'd got the two mixed up. Now, she was afraid to open that box in case she found that she didn't know her mum at all.

'What are you doing?' Will was coming towards them with Belle.

Liza flicked ash off her top. 'We're exorcising a demon.'

27

THE MAN WHO WAS AFRAID OF DOGS

It had been a fine day and fine days invariably meant more customers. Netta and Neil had managed okay without Kelly, thanks to Liza and Chris. It had been a difficult week without a third pair of hands, but not an impossible one, and they agreed not to rush Kelly back to work until she was better. Although that did pose a problem. With her mum away, there was no one to keep an eye on Kelly while they were working.

'Let's see how things are by tomorrow evening. If she needs someone, we might be able to organise shifts,' said Netta.

They'd taken the remaining stock and equipment back to the office. They called it the office even though it was a kitchen with an extra room, where they did everything else. Everything took so much longer when they were a person down, and it was nearly six by the time they finished.

Frank rang her as she was getting into the car. 'You caught me just in time. Two minutes later and I'd have been driving home. How's the move going?'

'Good. Rob didn't have a lot of furniture. Most of it was

Nick's. But we've done a trip to Ikea and a couple of other stores. Lots of assembling necessary. Good job I brought my toolbox.'

'Spoken like a proper dad.'

'Yes, I've been very much doing an Arthur today. The lads have been great. I'd forgotten what a likeable fella Archie is. Obie's grand too. How's everything back there?'

'Okay, I think. I'll let you know when I get home. I'm still at work. Neil and I have been wondering what to do about Kelly next week. We don't think she's well enough to work but we don't want to leave her alone all day, after last year.'

'I can help when I'm not teaching. Actually, Rob's off for the week. She might like a bit of company, if Kelly fancies a trip up to Scotland. Let me talk to her.'

She spent the drive home thinking about Kelly. Liza had messaged earlier to say things were back to normal with her and Will. Netta was glad she'd suggested leaving them alone for a few hours. It had been a gamble but it sounded like it had paid off. All the same, it would probably be some time before Kelly herself was back to normal. Whatever normal was these days. A trip to Edinburgh might do her good and it would solve the problem of what to do this week. She wouldn't say anything yet though. She'd wait until Frank had spoken to Robyn.

The house was quiet when she got in. Netta assumed they'd taken the dogs out, but then she saw them sitting in the garden. Kelly was smiling. It was a joyous thing to see. Netta opened the fridge and found the beers and wine she'd bought on her last shopping trip were rather depleted. No wonder they were looking so chilled out. She poured herself a glass of white and went out to join them.

There was a spare chair near the barbecue. She sat

down and caught a whiff of something like a bonfire. 'Has someone had an ill-fated attempt at cooking dinner?'

Liza sniggered. 'Not exactly. We have been burning something though.'

'That shitty dress,' said Kelly.

Liza raised her beer bottle. 'Let us unite against the gaslighters of this world and overcome them.'

Kelly did the same. 'Yeah, what she said.'

'Yes, indeed. And have any of you given any thought to tonight's dinner, or have you just been waiting for me to come home and magically whip something up?' said Netta.

'Pretty much.' Kelly's face was deadpan. They all fell about laughing, including Netta.

She pulled off her shoes and stretched out her legs. 'Well I'm too tired to cook tonight. Why don't we have a takeaway or fish and chips?'

Belle coughed. 'Actually, we're going out for a meal.'

'Lovely,' said Netta. 'Anywhere special?'

'That new place in Moseley. We got lucky, they had a cancellation.' Will glanced at Belle. In return, Belle gave him a weary looking smile, but his attention had already moved on and her smile slipped away.

Netta remembered he was supposed to have been going to Leeds this weekend. They must have had something planned. She was about to ask what the occasion was but something distracted her. A look passed between Will and Kelly. It was gone as quickly as it appeared. If she'd blinked, Netta would have missed it, but it was enough to open her eyes. Will was torn. He was being pulled in two different directions. She had no idea why she hadn't picked up on it before, but she could see it now. Then she saw the expression on Belle's face and realised, she could see it too.

·   ·   ·

Netta's dad brought Minnie over early on Sunday. He was wearing light grey flat-front chinos and a pale blue polo shirt. If he'd had parka on, he wouldn't have looked out of place on a scooter. She'd got used to him in his old allotment gear lately. It was quite a shock to see him all scrubbed up.

'I like your outfit. It really suits you,' she said.

'Thanks, sweetheart. It's your mum's doing. I've had to up my game since she became such a glamour puss. Can't run the risk of losing her.'

Netta suppressed her amusement at the idea of her mum being considered a glamour puss. How things had changed. 'I don't think there's any danger of that, Dad.'

'You say that but I've caught a few fellas casting a sly eye over her. I'm on constant alert, ready to fight them off.' He right hooked the air, grinning, and Netta remembered how lucky she and her mum were to have him in their life.

He clapped his hands together. 'Right, I'm off. Take care of my little girl for me, won't you? We'll miss her.'

'Oh, you won't miss the rest of us then?'

He winked. 'Maybe a bit. Look after yourself, Nettie. You spend too much time worrying about everyone else.'

She kissed him. 'I'll try. By the way, you can tell Mum that Kelly and Will are friends again.'

'She already knows. Those messages have been going like the clappers every minute of the day since we left here on Friday. I'll be glad when we get on the plane. Never thought I'd be looking forward to airplane mode.'

When Neil and Chris arrived with Buster, everyone except Kelly and Maud set off for the Sunday morning park walk.

Kelly had been on an ill-advised bike ride yesterday and was feeling the effects today.

Netta walked with Chris and Neil, letting the other three tear around the park with the four dogs. She told them about Frank's idea of asking Robyn to invite Kelly up to Edinburgh.

'That could be ideal. We'll manage all right between us,' said Neil.

'Okay. Frank will be back later. I'll see what he says.'

The order changed about halfway round the park. Chris and Neil went on ahead when Liza dropped back to be with Netta. 'I'm glad Kelly's away from that creep, aren't you?'

'Yes. I'm just sorry she found out what he was like in such a hard way. I wish I'd talked to her about him more. I might have spotted the signs.'

'Because of Dad, you mean?'

Netta carried on walking. 'What do you mean?' She knew exactly what Liza meant but she was playing for time, trying to work out what to say. How much was it right to tell your daughter that her father was a gaslighter too?

Liza kept pace with her. 'It's okay, Mum. I know what Dad did to you.'

Netta's step faltered. 'Has someone said something?'

'No. You all go out of your way not to say anything. I guess you think it's better to keep me in ignorance in case I get upset. I don't need to be told though. I saw it with my own eyes when I was growing up. I might not have understood it then. He might have fooled me into thinking you deserved it, but I see it now. I've been thinking about it for a while, but this shit with Marcus has made it clearer.'

Netta studied her daughter, wandering how best to put it. Honestly. She should put it honestly. 'I won't lie to you, darling. Your dad does have a way of twisting things round to his version of reality. And yes, it did … it did…'

'Destroy you?'

The air was being sucked out of Netta. A button had been pressed. One that hadn't seen the light of day for several years. It wasn't fair. She hadn't expected it. Liza grabbed her before she stumbled. She regained her composure. It was all right. She was loved and valued now, and her life with Colin was no longer important. 'Yes. Very nearly. But I had my friends and family to support me. I grew stronger. And happier. That's why we must look after Kelly.'

'I know, Mum. I know.'

Netta was standing over the hob. Chris and Neil had gone home ages ago and she was preparing dinner for an unspecified number of people. She hadn't been sure how many would be eating and when in doubt, she always plumped for a big pot of spaghetti Bolognese.

'Frank's back,' called Liza from the lounge.

'Okay, can I have some help in here?'

Kelly and Liza came into the kitchen.

'Can one of you stir, and one of you get the table ready?' She rushed into the hall and out through the front door.

Frank and the two young men were already out of the car. She gave him a hasty kiss. 'Welcome back. I've just made dinner if anyone's interested. It's spaghetti Bolognese.'

Archie looked to Obie who gave him a quick nod. 'Sure.'

When they walked back inside, the dogs erupted. Fred was all over Frank. Betty and Minnie were just all over everyone. Maud watched them all regally from her armchair.

Kelly shouted from the kitchen: 'Dinner looks like it's done.'

Will and Belle came down. Frank took Archie and Obie into the kitchen. The young dogs were off the scale in their excitement levels now. Archie seemed to take it all in his stride, but Obie seemed quite alarmed.

Netta took over juggling the pots of spaghetti and sauce. 'Can someone put the dogs in the garden? Everyone else can take a seat.'

Will got the dogs outside and shut the door before they could come back in.

The noise quietened down outside, but the talk inside was lively. From Frank and Archie's corner, anyway. Obie was much quieter.

Netta handed out the food and gave Archie and Obie an apologetic look. 'Sorry about the dogs. They're still young. They get excitable when they're all together.'

'They're great,' said Archie. 'What sort are they?'

'God knows,' said Liza.

'It's a bit of a mystery. Maud's mostly terrier. We know who their father is but we're not quite sure what breed he is, if any. He's big though, in case you hadn't guessed,' explained Netta.

'My parents have a collie,' said Archie.

Netta turned to Obie. 'What about you, Obie?'

Obie looked up from his food. 'No. No dogs in our family. Never had one.'

'Neither had I until I moved in here. I didn't know what I was missing.'

Suddenly, Obie jumped. Everyone stopped eating and stared at him.

'Sorry, something just … on my leg.' He looked down. 'Oh, it's another dog.'

Kelly looked under the table. 'It's only Maud. Fuck's sake, you're not scared of Maud, are yer?'

Obie looked both affronted and humiliated. 'No. It's just that it's leaning against me.'

Oh dear, he'd done it now. Kelly gave him a filthy look. 'She. Not it. Count yourself lucky, mate. Maud don't lean against your leg unless she likes you.'

Archie laughed. 'Maybe she's trying to turn you into a dog lover, bruv.'

Obie eyed Maud warily and kept his mouth shut.

Kelly's phone rang as they were finishing off the meal. 'It's Robyn. I'll see what she wants.' She went off into the lounge. A few minutes later, she was back. 'She just wants a chat. I'll go upstairs.'

Archie and Obie were gone by the time Kelly returned.

'Good chat?' said Frank.

'Yeah. She wants me to go up and stay with her for the week. What do you think, Net?'

'Absolutely. You'll have a great time and you could help Robyn finish the flat off.'

'Yeah, I was thinking the same. But what about work?' said Kelly.

'We'll manage. We weren't expecting you back yet anyway. You should go, shouldn't she Frank?'

'Definitely.' There was an unmistakeable twinkle in Frank's eye.

28

THRILLS AND SPILLS

Oh God, the excitement of getting on a plane. Kelly couldn't remember when she'd ever been this hyped. It didn't matter that it was only little and looked like a toy plane next to the others. It didn't matter that the flight was only an hour and a quarter. She was on a plane. An actual plane!

She'd been to Edinburgh a couple of times, but only on the train. She'd never, in her entire life, been on a plane. When Frank suggested it, she thought he was just messing. Surely only celebs and rich businessman flew to Edinburgh? Surely it would cost like, mega? Turned out it was actually cheaper than the train. When they looked last night, there was still availability for this afternoon. Netta helped her book the tickets. All Kelly had to do was pack. Netta lent her a suitcase for that, as well.

She'd walked to Selly Oak station this morning, pulling her suitcase behind her. Normally, she didn't notice the weather unless it was really hot or cold, but today was different. Today, she'd appreciated the mildness of the breeze. She'd picked out the clouds and followed their slow drift, cutting through the incredible blueness of the sky. She'd be up there with them soon.

A change of trains at New Street took her to Birmingham International and soon after, she was in the airport. All the way here, all the time waiting to board the plane, she'd been convinced someone would stop her and tell her to piss off home because she had no right to be here. But no one did. The lady at the check-in desk had asked her if it was her first time flying and had been really nice, telling her what to expect and giving her a window seat.

Kelly sat in her seat, buzzing. There wasn't much to see through the window but that didn't stop her looking. She didn't want to miss a single thing. A big man in a suit sat next to her. She'd been right about the businessmen after all. She took the booklets out from the pouch in front of her and read them from cover to cover. She noticed one of those drop-down trays in front of her, like they have on trains. She was just checking its lock when the door to the plane closed with a bang. It made her jump and her fingers slipped and lost their grip on the tray. It dropped down with a slap. The suit man flinched.

'Sorry,' she whispered, quietly pushing the tray back up and locking it.

The plane started moving, passing buildings and other planes, until it was out in the open.

The suit man offered her a sweet. 'Helps stop the ears popping when we take off.'

'Right. Thanks.' Kelly took one and held onto it, waiting for him to unwrap his.

'First time?'

'Yeah. Is it that obvious?'

'No, not at all. I think it's time for the sweet. When your

ears start to pop, my advice would be to suck on it like there's no tomorrow.'

When the thrust of the engines got too much for her ears, she did as the suit man said. It worked. She turned to him and gave him a thumbs up. He gave her a funny little salute while his cheeks went in and out, and his Adam's apple bobbed up and down.

They were in the air now and Kelly was drawn to the window again. She saw that the incredible blue sky she'd seen earlier was even more brilliant up close, and the clouds were unbelievable. And they were above them. How freaky that was. It was like the world had been turned upside down. Unreal.

When they arrived at Edinburgh, the suit man stayed with Kelly until she reached Robyn.

Robyn kissed her on both cheeks. 'Made a new friend?'

'He sat next to me. He was nice. Looked after me. He reminded me of your dad, funnily enough.'

'How was the flight?'

'Amazing. Can't wait to go back.'

'Not in too much of a rush, are you? We've got some work to do, and some fun to have.'

The flat Robyn had lived in with Nick had been in an old building with no lifts and a lot of stairs. The flat itself had been big, with high ceilings and tall windows. As they turned into Robyn's road, Kelly could see this new place was going to be nothing like the old one. The road was lined with newish apartment blocks with balconies. It was wide and straight, so it was easy to see from one end to the other. Kelly was looking down it now and she couldn't believe what she was seeing. At the very end of it was a massive ship that looked like it was wedged between the apartment blocks. She knew Robyn had moved close to the port, but she hadn't expected this.

'I know. It's fantastic, isn't it? I keep thinking I'm living abroad,' said Robyn.

The flat was as different to the old one as Kelly had imagined it would be. It was very modern and a lot smaller. It looked cluttered, but that was probably because everything was still in boxes. The cupboards and shelving units were empty. They must have been the ones Frank and those two guys had put together.

'I was living in a furnished house share when I met Nick,' said Robyn. 'Then I moved into his place, so I didn't really have any furniture. I've had to start virtually from scratch. Nearly everything's new or pre-loved. Dad's been great. He's helped me buy the big things.'

Kelly walked out onto the balcony. If she leaned over the side, she could see that ship. 'It's amazing. You're so lucky.'

'I am, aren't I?' Robyn leaned over too and pointed to the ship. 'It has some very quirky features that I love. Obviously. Best thing though, it's my place. I never felt that way with Nick's flat. It's a nice feeling.'

'I bet it is. I'm so jealous.'

'You'll get there. Things'll get better.'

'I hope so.' She wanted to believe they would, but better things seemed a long way off right now.

'Fancy a glass of wine while the sun's still shining? I

haven't got any chairs for the balcony yet but I've got cushions.'

Kelly smiled. 'Sounds brilliant.'

They took the cushions out and chilled with a bottle of wine and a bag of crisps. When Kelly had talked to the others it had helped, but she'd only spoken to them about Marcus. With Rob, nothing was off limits. Sure, they talked about Marcus and how he'd made her feel, but they also talked about that other subject that she never spoke to anyone else about. Her feelings for Will. When she finished unloading and they decided to go out and eat, Kelly felt lighter. Lucky even. Lucky to be here in this moment, and lucky to have a friend like Rob.

They were sharing a pizza in an Italian restaurant near Robyn's flat. Rob tore a slice off. 'Dad said Archie and Obie stayed for dinner last night.'

'Yeah. That Obie guy was scared of the dogs. Even Maud. He nearly crapped himself when she leaned against his leg. Ridiculous.'

'Oh no. What do you think of Archie?'

'He was all right. More cheerful than his mate. Why are you asking me? Oh wait, do you fancy him? I thought you were like, best mates from way back.'

'We are. We did see each other when we were at school. You know, romantically. We stayed friends when we split up and he was really supportive when my mum died. And now. He's been great. I don't fancy him though. But he's such a sweet guy.'

Kelly screwed her eyes up. She wasn't buying that 'sweet guy but I don't fancy him' argument, but she kept her mouth shut and waited for Robyn to spill. She didn't have to wait long.

'Okay, maybe I have been feeling a few tiny tingles whenever he's been around lately. Maybe. But I've just come out of a relationship and I don't want to rush into another one. Plus, he doesn't think of me that way. We're mates and I don't want to spoil that. Plus again, we're three hundred miles apart. How is that gonna work?'

29

THE NEW SPINSTER SOCIETY

It had been the best week of Kelly's life since, she didn't know when. She bloody loved Edinburgh. When she'd visited Robyn before, she'd only stayed for long weekends and they'd hardly had time to do anything. This time they did loads.

They got up early each morning so they could work on the flat before going out. The first morning, they unpacked all the practical stuff so they didn't have to keep washing the same few cups and plates. The next morning they started on Robyn's books and ornaments. That took longer than it should have because they kept stopping to look at the beautiful pictures in Robyn's art and fashion history books. Gradually, the boxes, bags and suitcases were emptied, pictures went up on the walls, and the place began to look more like a home than a storage facility.

Afternoons were spent either shopping, doing touristy things, or both together. Kelly bought a few things for herself, including a postcard, and Robyn got more stuff for the flat. Although she'd lived in Edinburgh for ages, Rob said she'd never done the touristy stuff, so she was enjoying it as much as Kelly. They went to the castle and a couple of museums. They took a walk up Calton Hill. They went to the beach at Portobello. In one of the cafes on Cockburn Street, they sat outside on chairs that managed to stay upright, in spite of the steep hill, and ate delicious chocolate orange cake. Kelly held her cup French style, and told Rob how much she'd like to be doing this in Paris someday.

'You should go. You could use some of the money from your nan to do it,' said Robyn.

'Yeah, but…' She couldn't think of a reason not to, except that she had no one to go with.

'I'll come with you, if you don't want to go alone. Might have to be next year though when I'm solvent again. Plenty of time for you to think it over.'

The next day, they went to the Grassmarket. Kelly watched the waiters zipping in and out of crowded outdoor tables. A busker was playing music, and the sun shone down on them. She could have been in France or Italy. Anywhere in Europe. She bloody loved Edinburgh.

'So, you are not to spend another moment thinking about that gaslighter. Agreed?' said Robyn.

Kelly nodded. 'Agreed.'

'And you should not ever imagine the things he said about you are the tiniest bit true.'

'Okay.'

It was Kelly's last night and they were on the lash again. This time they were in a street called The Shore. The cobbled street that ran along one side of its harbour was all lit up. It was lovely. They were sitting outside one of the bars waiting for Robyn's friends to arrive.

'Also you are definitely not to think about Will as

anything other than a brother from another mother. Ditto, me and Archie. Yeah?'

Kelly laughed. 'Let's see which one of us breaks first.'

Robyn waved a hand. 'Oh that'll be you.'

'Thanks, mate.' She pretended to be outraged but she knew Rob was right. Tonight though, she didn't care. She'd had the greatest week, and no way was she going to ruin it thinking about things that had been, and things that might have been. 'It's nice here.'

'Yeah. I come here with Dad when he visits. He likes it too. It reminds him of Amsterdam.'

'Is it like this then, Amsterdam?'

'I suppose. It has lots of canals like Birmingham, but the streets are a bit like this. Except they have these tall, skinny buildings. It's a great place to walk around. Or cycle. Everyone cycles there. You'd love it. Another one to add to your list of places to visit.'

Kelly made a mental note to look into Amsterdam. Then she made another, to start a list of places she'd like to visit someday. When she had more courage.

Robyn checked her phone. 'They're about ten minutes away.'

Kelly nodded. She was a bit nervous about these friends. She had a horrible feeling they might turn out to be just like that nasty bitch, Poppy.

Robyn frowned at her. 'Are you worried about meeting them?'

'A bit, I suppose.'

'It's okay, they're normal like you and me. They're the only friends I have here that I made by myself. The others were Nick's friends first. You'll like them.'

'It's not whether I'll like them.'

'You're scared they won't like you. Don't be, they'll love you. Like I said, they're just like you and me.'

Robyn smiled and the pressure melted away. At that moment, Kelly got what had made this week so special. It wasn't just that they'd done fun things, or that she'd enjoyed helping Rob put her new home together. It was because Rob didn't see her as someone who needed looking after, or to apologise for. She saw her as a mate. A bestie. A peer.

'Peer: A person of the same age, status, or ability as another specified person.'

Kelly was in no doubt her friends and family in Birmingham cared about her, but sometimes it was like being at a massive pity party, with her as the guest of honour. Rob was the one person that didn't see her as poor, sad little Kelly.

'Here they are.' Robyn stood up and waved at two women who were about the same age as them. They were a little bit dressed up, but nothing over the top. One had a short haircut, similar to Kelly's. She was the first one to speak. 'Bloody buses are so crap. If these shoes weren't killing me already, I'd have walked it. Sorry, I'll shut up now. Oh I should have said, I'm Erin. Hello, Kelly.'

'And I'm Jas,' said the other one.

They kissed Rob on both cheeks and to Kelly's surprise, they did the same to her. Then they started to talk. They asked all about Rob and Kelly's week, then they asked about Kelly, and Birmingham. They were thinking of starting up their own business, so they wanted to know how Kelly and her friends had started theirs. They told Kelly all about themselves. Jas was from Glasgow and Erin was Irish. They were non-stop, and so interesting. Kelly hadn't talked this much before. Not even when she'd spoken to that girl on the train to Sheffield. In fact, she didn't know she had that much talk in her.

· · ·

When she woke up in the morning, Kelly had a massive hangover. They'd really put it away last night. She stumbled into the kitchen to find Robyn making tea. 'Morning, Rob.'

Robyn pushed a packet of paracetamol over to her. 'Morning.'

They sat out on the balcony with their tea. They'd bought a table and chairs for it now, so they didn't have to use the cushions.

'Did you have a good time last night?' said Rob.

'Yeah, it was brilliant. It was nice being with people who are the same age, and not students. I love your friends.'

'They're your friends as well now. Don't you remember inviting them to Birmingham?'

'Did I?'

'Yeah. It'll be fine. Dad's got loads of space and it'll put his mind at rest, if I turn up with them. He thinks I live like a hermit. When you get back, could you do me favour? Archie left his sunglasses here. Could you take them back to him? He has a coffee wagon he runs with Obie at weekends, in Stirchley.'

'A coffee wagon? I thought they'd be, I dunno, doing something a bit more important than that.'

Robyn shrugged. 'They tried that and didn't like it. I guess we have to find what makes us happy, don't we? Are you up for some breakfast? I've managed to blag a couple of extra hours off before I go to work, so I can see you safely on the airport bus.'

They ate croissants on the balcony. The croissants were from Tesco, but Kelly still felt continental. She leaned over to see the ship at the end of the road. Yes, very continental.

She had the postcard with her that she'd bought earlier in the week and was thinking about writing something on the back, like Edie did.

'What are you going to write?' asked Robyn.

'I was thinking about Edie and her friends, and how they brought her back to life after her troubles. They called themselves The Spinster Society. I was thinking you, Jas and Erin are like my Spinster Society.'

'Aww that's sweet. Sorry, didn't mean to sound patronising but I am genuinely touched. You'll have to think of a new name for us.'

'Yeah. I guess calling someone a spinster is a bit offensive these days. I'll have a think about what to put later. I want it to be good if it's going to be there forever.'

'Listen, thanks for coming this week. I was a bit overwhelmed after Dad and the guys left, so having you here's really helped. I've been really down lately. I wouldn't have got through it without my extremely long calls to you. So thanks for being my friend.'

'Same here.' Kelly was filling up. 'Shit. Now look what you've done.'

Robyn gave her a sloppy kiss. She was crying too. Then they both started laughing. The tears ran down their faces, but they were good tears. Happy tears.

The farewell was emotional. Kelly didn't want to leave after Rob had said that to her but she had a plane to catch, and Rob had work to go to. She didn't get her book out on the bus. Instead she took in the last of Edinburgh. She'd read in the airport while she was waiting for the plane. If she was lucky again, she might get a window seat and she'd gaze at the upside-down world outside and think about how her self-respect had been turned upside-down too. A week ago, it had been whittled away to nothing. Today, it was as high as the sky itself. Robyn had made it clear she was a valued friend, and so had Geraldine. Kelly was a good person. A kind and decent person. She just needed to remember that.

30

A CALL FROM CARRICKFERGUS

There weren't many houses in their road, so it was easy to see who was in, and who was out. Frank's car wasn't on his drive or outside his house. Netta's wasn't either, but it was too early on a Monday afternoon for Netta to be home. She and Neil would be working for another two hours yet. By rights Kelly should be there with them. She felt bad about letting them down lately. She'd have to work extra hard to make up for it.

She turned the key in the lock and saw two big, hairy shapes scuttering into the hall, through the glass. Like excitable kids, Betty and Minnie couldn't wait to say hello. Kelly bent down and let them lick her face. She wiped the slobber off. 'Hello, you pair of pains.' Behind them, Maud waited for her turn. Kelly scooped the little dog up and squeezed her. 'I've missed you, Maudie. Not so sure about you two mentalists though.'

She dumped her bag in the hall and went into the kitchen. Betty and Minnie went too, running around her legs and nearly tripping her up. She gave them doggie treats, then took them out into the garden. After a couple of circuits, they quietened down and flopped onto the grass. Kelly sat on a chair and Maud lay by her feet. She stroked Maud, all the while thinking about the jobs she had to do.

The first was easy. She blocked Marcus from every possible place he could access her. Then she deleted his messages. He hadn't sent anything since Liza had threatened him. She must have scared the shit out of him.

She needed to find a new book but she'd promised Liza they'd do it together, so she'd have to wait. She'd finished *Villette* at the airport, and to say she'd been disappointed with the ending, was an understatement. She felt cheated by its ambiguity.

'Ambiguity: The quality of being ambiguous or open to more than one interpretation.'

She'd put so much time and emotion into that book, only to find that she didn't know at the end whether Lucy Snowe had lived happily ever after or not. What a cop out. It was a good job she was in a better place now, otherwise she'd have been totally wrecked. Hopefully the next book would be a bit more cheerful.

The most immediate job was the one she'd been putting off for a while. She needed to go through her mum's things. She'd tried to do it on the Sunday morning before her holiday, while everyone was at the park, but she'd chickened out and had spent the rest of the day in a bad mood because of it. She was ready now though. Ready for anything it might throw at her.

On her way back through the hall, she noticed Geraldine's postcard next to the phone. It was a painting rather than a photo, of a woman on a balcony that overlooked a road with palm trees down the middle. Beyond that was the beach and the sea. The cars on the road were really old ones. The woman on the balcony and the people on the pavement below, looked like they were in the 1920s. She'd seen something like it in one of Robyn's books. Kelly read the back:

'Dear Kelly,

I chose this one because I know how much you like vintage. It's from an old holiday poster. I hope it'll do. We're having a smashing time. See you soon.

Love,

Geraldine.'

Kelly looked at the picture again. It was beautiful. Truly beautiful. Too good to hide away. She'd get a frame for it and put it next to her bed, and she'd add Nice to her new list. She sent Geraldine a thank you message, then went upstairs to face the box.

The box was in front of her on the bed. It only a shoe box. It shouldn't be that hard to open and look inside. She'd been here before though, and she knew it was very bloody hard. But she'd talked this through with Robyn. There could be things in there she might want to see. Things that might fill the memory gaps. Things that might help her. She breathed in, and took off the lid.

Two black velvet boxes sat on the top of everything else. The first held two gold rings. One was a wedding ring. The other must have been her mum's engagement ring. Kelly tried them on. They were too big. She put them back in the box and opened the other one. Inside was a Saint Christopher on a chain, and a small bangle with a tiny cross attached to it. Both were silver. Something was engraved on the inside of the bangle. Kelly brought it closer and saw that it was a name: *'Caitlin Donohue'*. She realised then that it was her mum's Communion bangle. Her finger traced the Celtic pattern on the outside and a fresh memory came alive. Nanny Donohue, her Irish granny, having a go at her dad because her mum hadn't had a Catholic funeral. Then came another. Kelly asking her mum why she couldn't have a Communion like her Irish cousins. 'Because it's all shite, my gorgeous girl. That's why,' was the answer she got. Even when she was dying, her mum never went back to the church.

The front of the Saint Christopher was no different to any other, but the back had the tiniest inscription that she had to screw up her eyes to read:

'God protect her as she travels by air, land, or sea. Keep her safe and guide her, wherever she may be.'

Kelly fixed it around her neck. The cold metal stuck to her warm skin. It was comforting. Like she was carrying a piece of her mum with her.

She looked through a packet of photos. There were a few of her, at different ages, with her mum, and some of her mum as a kid, a teenager and a young woman. One in particular stood out. Her mum, about twentyish, sitting cross-legged under a tree on a beach. She was wearing a red bikini that showed off her lovely curvy figure, and she was holding something in her hand that was as red as the bikini, a food of some sort.

Aside from the photos, there were some drawings that Kelly had done when she was little. It would have been nice to have had something her mum had written, but there was nothing like that. She'd had a letter once. Her mum had written one each to Kelly and her brothers when she was still well enough to write. Kelly had carried that letter every-where. She read it so many times, the folds had frayed. Then she made the mistake of leaving it lying around in Craig's flat. The stupid twat used it to light a spliff. Puff. Gone. Just like that.

The last thing in the box was a memory stick. She didn't have a computer herself, but Netta's laptop was in the study and she didn't mind her using it. Kelly's dad had warned her about the stick, and she'd deliberately saved it to the end.

Kelly clicked on the only folder in the drive. It was called 'Cait'. There were four files in it, all videos. The first was her mum singing karaoke on a stage. It was 'Wonderwall', one of Kelly's dad's favourites. It wasn't the best picture. Her dad had said they were taken on his video camera. It was what people used to film things before mobiles did everything. Her mum sounded drunk but she was belting it out and having a good time.

The next two were of her mum with Kelly and her brothers when they were little. In one, Kelly was on a dance floor with her mum, busting the moves to 'Macarena'. Kelly remembered it was at a holiday camp. They'd danced to that tune every night. She'd been obsessed with it. After-wards, her mum bought it for her and played it all the time, until Kelly had got bored with it.

Kelly recognised the living room in her dad's house as soon as the last film began to play. The camera was aimed at a little woman in one of the armchairs. Nanny Donohue glanced at the camera, and then turned towards the settee where Kelly's mum was sitting with her arms around Dan and Conor. The room was quiet, and then her mum began to sing: 'I wish I was in Carrickfergus…'

For a while the camera stayed on her mum, then it moved to the other chair. There was Nanny Payne with Kelly on the arm, next to her. You couldn't see her mum then, but her voice was clear. It was the saddest thing Kelly had ever heard. As the camera panned out she saw that her grandmothers were both silently crying.

Kelly recalled that day. Part of it anyway. She'd have been eleven. It was probably the last time her mum sang like that. Not long after, she got sick.

'Don't tell Andy.'

A first she thought that had come from the video, but it had come from inside her head. Just like that morning on the rec. She didn't know what it meant or why she was hearing it, but she knew whose voice it was now. It was her mum's, and it had something to do with that day. Something that may or may not have been good. That word again. Ambiguity.

Kelly clicked play again. It was just like her mum was singing directly to her, calling her to Carrickfergus. Kelly's throat hurt. Oh fuck.

When Netta came in, the film was still playing on a loop. Kelly had stopped crying and it was more of a sniffing backing track to her mum's singing.

Netta looked anxious. 'What is it?'

'I've remembered. I thought I'd forgotten her but it was all in here, waiting for a trigger.' She tapped her head.

'That's good, isn't it?' Netta came over to look at the screen. 'What a wonderful voice. Is that your mum? It must be. She looks like you.'

'Do you think so? Really? You're not just saying that?'

'You can't mistake those eyes.'

Kelly froze the film on a frame with her mum in. It was true, she had inherited her mum's eyes. Her dad had said that too. All this time she'd been thinking she was exactly like him and she was wrong. There was something of her mum in her too. She was her mother's daughter.

31

TREASURES FROM ANOTHER TIME

So this was the woman who'd been haunting Kelly for so long. Netta watched her, this ghost from Kelly's past, singing 'Wonderwall'. She could certainly hold a tune. She was a beauty too. More than that, there was a sparkle about her. Stardust. No wonder she had left such a gaping hole when she died. No wonder Kelly's dad had fallen apart.

Kelly had shown her each of the videos, with a running commentary on all but the one in which her mum sang 'Carrickfergus'. There was nothing to do on that one but watch it, transfixed. Netta had heard the song before. Frank sometimes played it. She'd never heard it sung like that though. Maybe it was Caitlin Payne's heart-breaking voice. Maybe it was knowing that Caitlin died a year later. Whatever the reason, it was devastating to hear, and equally devastating to watch.

'She must have been very special.' Netta heard her own voice faltering.

'She was. I thought I'd forgotten her though. I thought I wouldn't recognise her. But I do. It's coming back to me now.'

She put her arm around Kelly. 'Of course you hadn't forgotten her. It's just that after a while, the memories go deeper. They become part of you. They're in the things you say and do. Sometimes I'll say something without thinking and then realise my gran used to say it.'

'I do that too.'

'There you go then. I love that one of you and your mum dancing. You should show it to Liza. She used to like dancing.'

As if she'd been waiting in the wings, Liza chose that exact moment to come in. Kelly waved her over. 'Come and have a look at this, Lize.'

Netta moved out of the way so she could get in. 'I'll let Frank know we're back.'

She went into the breakfast room and messaged Frank. She could have done it in there but she needed a few minutes alone. The girls were giggling over the 'Macarena'. It sounded like they were trying to follow the moves. It was good to hear them enjoying themselves. Ordinarily, she'd have been more over the moon about it, but she was in a melancholy mood. It wasn't just that unforgettable song that had set her off, it was the sight of Kelly and her mum dancing together and the realisation that she envied Caitlin Payne. She'd blithely said that Liza had liked dancing, as if it was the most natural thing in the world. But the truth was Netta hadn't been party to Liza's interests when she was small. Mostly, that was because Colin had seen to it that she was shut out of those little day-to-day things that made a mother and child relationship. But it wasn't entirely Colin's fault. There were times during her dark period when she'd voluntarily stepped away. A few years ago she'd accepted that part of herself but occasionally, she was blindsided by a flash of grief and guilt. Watching Kelly dancing with her mum was one of those occasions.

She went back into the study. The girls were still dancing. Liza called her over to have a go. She joined them in a line, falling over her own feet trying to keep up with the steps and hand movements. She giggled with them at their lack of coordination, and her melancholy lifted. She might not be able to go back to the past, but she was damn well determined to enjoy the present.

Frank was cooking dinner, which was just as well since two hours had easily drifted. Some of it was taken up by learning the dance steps. The rest was down to Kelly telling them about Edinburgh. She was so animated that Netta's mood lifted even higher. She suddenly remembered the card from Nice. 'Oh, did you find Mum's postcard?'

'Yes thanks. I asked her to get it. I've been collecting them,' said Kelly.

'That's why you wanted one from Paris. Do you have many?'

'A few.' Kelly looked down at her hands and then at Liza. 'I could show you them.'

'Lovely.' Netta was intrigued. There was something about Kelly's new hobby that was making her self-conscious, and Liza clearly knew why. But it would have to wait. Frank was messaging to say dinner was ready.

Over dinner, Kelly put Frank's mind at rest about Robyn. Last week, he'd confided in Netta that he suspected Nick had been over-protective to the point of being controlling, and Robyn's self-confidence was shot.

'Sounds like you two had a great week,' he said when Kelly had finished.

Kelly nodded enthusiastically. 'We did. And there's no need to worry that she doesn't have anyone up there. Jas and Erin are so nice. They're coming down when we can arrange it. Rob says you've got room to put them up.'

Frank smiled. 'Of course. I'll call her later.'

'And her flat's looking really nice. She's all settled in now. Lize, she said you should come next time. You'd love it.'

Liza looked thrilled. 'Cool.'

Netta stood up. 'Shall we clear up and let Frank call her?'

They went back to Netta's lounge and settled down on the sofa. Liza reached for the remote. The programme that came up was some kind of holiday show, two celebrities gadding about France in a motorhome. It reminded Netta of her mum's card. 'How about showing me that postcard collection, Kelly?'

'Okay.' Kelly chewed on her lip. 'Before I do though, I need to tell you something.'

Aha! The big confession. The secret that pair had obviously been keeping from her.

'The thing is…' Kelly glanced over at Liza. 'I've been reading some of Edie's books.'

So it was Kelly moving the books around. That explained it. Although it still didn't explain how reading a couple of books had turned her into a collector of postcards. 'Right. And?'

'I started with *Pride and Prejudice* and found a card in there. Then I found one in *Mansfield Park*, so I decided to read only the books with postcards in. The next one was *Villette*.'

'Okay, so you've read three books. Good going, by the way. You didn't start with the easy ones.'

'Thanks. That was Geraldine's doing. She said I should read proper books. She suggested *Pride and Prejudice* because of Mr Darcy.'

So her mum was in on it as well, was she? Netta might have known. Bloody hell. Was she the only one in the dark here?

'But now I'm following Edie's trail.'

'Edie's trail?'

Kelly gave Netta a look that questioned whether she'd been listening to her at all. 'The postcards were Edie's.'

'Edie's? Oh my goodness. Edie's? How do you know?'

'She's written on them. I'll get them.'

While Kelly went to retrieve the cards, Liza whispered: 'I didn't know about this until we went to Sheffield and I saw a book in Kelly's bag.'

Kelly came back before Liza could say anymore. 'Here they are. Look, she says on the back when she went and who she went with.'

They were lovely old things, treasures from another time. And on the back of each one was Edie's handwriting. Netta had spent weeks poring over that handwriting when she read Edie's diaries, but lately, she'd hardly given Edie a thought. Yet here she was, coming back into their lives. Just like Caitlin Payne. 'I wonder if there are more.'

'I said we should look through the books for them,' said Liza.

'Yes let's. That would be marvellous,' said Netta.

Kelly stood up. 'Let's do it.'

They rushed into the study, full of enthusiasm.

'We should take it steady. Remember these are old books,' cautioned Netta.

'Also, it kind of spoils the moment if you go too fast.' Kelly took a single book off the shelf. Her fingers almost caressed it as they flicked through the pages. It was like watching something close to a religious experience.

After a while, Liza held a book aloft. 'Here's one. *Middlemarch*. Ooh I've read that. It's good.'

They came together to look at the postcard. It was a black and white photo of Amsterdam. A canal side view bordered by tall, wonky houses. According to Edie, she went there with The Spinster Society in 1966.

Kelly's eyes widened. 'So that's what Amsterdam looks like.'

A few minutes later, Kelly found another one hidden between the pages of *Little Women*. On the front was a photo of a cable car trundling up a steep hill. Behind it was the sea. The writing on the back read:

'San Francisco, 1968 – The spinsters, Janis, and dearest Lulu.'

The next half hour's search proved fruitless and Netta sensed the girls were lagging. 'Wine! We need wine to keep up our spirits.'

She went to the kitchen and came back with a bottle and three glasses. That would help, but there was one more thing that would keep them in the mood. She opened up Spotify and found 'Macarena'.

'Right, let's get this party started.' She danced towards the bookcase. It looked more like she was doing a sand dance but who cared? They were having fun again.

A bottle of wine later, there were twelve books on Kelly's reading pile and an assortment of postcards from around the world. They spread the cards out on the desk. Kelly added the three Netta had brought from Paris, the one from Nice, and one she'd bought in Edinburgh.

'Edie was a real adventurer, wasn't she?' said Liza.

'Yeah,' said Netta and Kelly together.

32

OBIE, MAN OF MISERY

All week, Kelly had been working hard to make up for her time away. On top of that she'd been extra pleasant to everyone at work and the foodbank. They probably wondered what had come over her, but that didn't bother her. Nothing bothered her at the moment.

She'd stopped thinking about how Marcus had made her feel. Mostly anyway. If it did cross her mind, she checked herself and thought happy thoughts. If you didn't count those few negative times, she was feeling pretty good about herself. She put that down to four things. The Edinburgh effect was definitely a factor. Telling Netta about the books and postcards was another. She could read anywhere in the house now that it was out in the open. It was liberating.

'Liberate: Set free, especially from imprisonment or oppression.'

The third factor was rediscovering her mum. That was a liberation too. Because although she'd found her mum again, she also found she was able to let her go. Not that Kelly wanted to let her go completely. Like Netta said, her mum was still with her. She was a part of her, but Kelly no

longer needed to carry her mum around with her like a
massive Mum banner, to prove how much she loved her. It
was enough to know it.

The fourth factor was that little girl dancing the
Macarena. Kelly hadn't recognised her. She'd spent ages
looking at herself in the mirror afterwards. An older version
of that kid had stared back at her, but this one had all the
life sucked out of it. It had been well depressing, but Netta
and Liza and that mad postcard hunt had given her a lift.
So instead of breaking down, she'd made herself look long
and hard, and consider the facts. It wasn't all Marcus's
doing. It was Craig's too. And yes, her dad had let her down
badly when she'd needed him most, but seeing her mum
again had given her reason to forgive him. Her mum was
the brightest star in his sky and when she died, he'd wanted
to go with her. She couldn't blame him for that because
she'd wanted to go too. She might not have realised it until
now, but it was true. She'd wanted to go with her mum.
She'd wanted to go with her dad too. The dad he'd been
before her mum died.

The problem was her dad had got over his death wish
well before Kelly did. He'd had Carol to help him with that.
Kelly had no one. Perhaps that was why she'd made so
many bad choices and been so desperate for someone to
love and take care of her. Not someone like her mum. Her
nan, and then Netta had helped with that. It was her dad.
She'd been looking for someone to replace him, even
though he'd been there all along, trying to reach out to her.
She just couldn't see it. She'd been too angry.

Somewhere in her busy week, Kelly had found the time
to set up her first bank account, and with Neil and Netta's
help, she'd deposited the cheque. She spent the rest of the
week mulling stuff over. By Friday, she'd reached a conclu-

sion. You could only spend so long blaming other people for the decisions you make. At some point, you have to woman up and be responsible for yourself. She'd reached that point. She wasn't sure what that meant yet, but there were three things she was certain of. One. She would carry on educating herself. Not because she had anything to prove, but because she liked it. Two. It was time to properly forgive her dad and Carol. She sort of had already, but something was stopping her going all the way. She needed to find out what it was and do something about it. Three. It was time to start liking herself.

It was Saturday afternoon. Geraldine and Arthur were due back tomorrow. Kelly couldn't wait to see Gez and give her a full debrief on all that had happened to her in the last fortnight. It would be just like their debrief sessions when Geraldine was having therapy, only the other way round. Gez would be doing the listening this time. But that was tomorrow. Today, Kelly had a favour to do.

They'd been at Kings Heath market that morning and had just finished their review of the morning's trade. She left Neil and Netta to drive the van back to the office, and set off for Stirchley to deliver Archie's sunglasses.

It only took her about forty minutes to walk to the place where Archie's coffee wagon was. Well, it was half Archie's. The other half belonged to that miserable, wimpy mate of his. What was his name again? Obie. That was it. Archie had offered to come and pick them up at the house but she'd told him she was in the area anyway. Forty minutes wasn't exactly in the area, but she was curious about this coffee wagon. Robyn had told her Archie and his mate had both gone to Birmingham University. Kelly still couldn't get her head around the idea that they'd wasted their education and become baristas.

The place she was looking for was called The Factory. It was an old factory or warehouse that had been converted into a craft brewery and bar. Cue, inward eye rolling. The coffee wagon wasn't in the building itself. That was just the brewery, a bar, and tables with benches for customers. The wagon was in the yard next to it, along with some food stalls.

She couldn't see Archie in the wagon. Misery guts Obie was there though, looking miserable. Especially when he saw her. She thought about going to the stall next to it and pretending she'd come for chicken wings, but she had the glasses to deliver, so she took a deep breath and went to the wagon.

Obie folded his arms. 'Yeah?'

'All right? Archie around?'

'No.' There was a bit of a tumbleweed moment while misery guts looked over her shoulder and stared into the void. 'He'll be back soon. Do you want coffee?'

Did she want coffee? She wasn't sure.

Misery guts sighed, like, the heaviest sigh in the world. 'I've got customers waiting.'

'All right, stay cool. I'll have a cappuccino.'

He didn't say anything, but he didn't need to. His narrowed eyes and flared nostrils said it all.

Kelly was trying to work out whether he recognised her, and was still annoyed over that stupid dog incident, or whether he was genuinely this rude to all of his customers. There was only one way to find out. 'Do you remember me?'

'Yeah I do.' Still annoyed then. 'Anything else?'

Kelly shook her head. He tapped his fingers on the card

machine and held it out to her. Wait, was that a scowl? Was that a fucking scowl he threw at her?

She slapped the card against the machine and grabbed her coffee. 'You wanna try cracking a fucking smile with it, bruv.'

Fucking men. All the fucking same. Except for Arthur and Frank, of course. And Neil and Chris. And Will. All right, not all men. But some men. Some men were definitely all the same. She'd been feeling really positive until that miserable shit burst her bubble. Fucking … some men. Kelly had been fuming for half an hour now and still no sign of Archie. If he didn't come soon, she was going to have to speak to that shitebag again, and she could really do without that. And he was still scowling at her. The cheek of him.

She sent Robyn a message to tell her she was trying to deliver Archie's glasses but his so-called mate was not being helpful. When she looked up, she saw Archie by the wagon with Obie, the man of misery. They were talking about her. She could tell that because the man of misery was pointing at her.

Archie took out his phone, read something and smiled. Then he came over and sat down at her table. 'Hi Kelly. Thanks for bringing my sunglasses. They're my only prescription ones, so I've missed them.'

'No problem.' Kelly's anger melted just a tiny bit. Archie was lovely. No wonder Rob had a soft spot for him. Then she saw Obie, still throwing shade at her. 'Your mate's a bit rude.'

Archie smirked. 'Well, you did belittle him in front of everyone that one time.'

'It was so not belittling. If that's all he's got to be angry about, he's lucky.'

'He's not angry.'

'Miserable then.'

'He's not miserable either. He's … troubled.'

'Why is he troubled?'

Archie winked at her. 'Gotta go. It's Obie's break. Thanks again for bringing the glasses.'

He went back to the wagon. Obie patted him on the back, stepped out into the yard, and walked past Kelly without looking at her.

Kelly tutted. 'Troubled in the head, if you ask me.'

33

THE BOOK GROUP

'Don't know if you're interested, but there's a book group starting up in the other place Archie works at,' said Robyn.

Kelly was on a rug in the garden, pulling out daisies while talking on the phone. 'He's got two jobs?'

'Sort of. They have a pop-up coffee stall in this new café in Moseley. The Pit Stop? Not sure how it works with the other gig but I think they're helping a friend to get it off the ground. The book group is one of the ideas they've had to get people through the door. I'll send you a link.'

'Did you tell him about me reading then?'

'No, the book group came up in a long conversation. I just said I might know someone who was interested.'

'You two are having a lot of long conversations lately.'

Robyn's laughter tinkled down the phone. 'We're just good friends. Honest.'

'Okay I believe you. I'll think about the book group.'

'I won't say anything to Archie but he'll be there, if you're feeling nervous about it. So will Obie. They do everything together. Well, nearly everything. They've got this bromance thing going on.'

The dogs started barking inside the house. 'I'm gonna have to go, Rob. Geraldine and Arthur are here. Sorry.'

'That's okay. The girls are coming over for a wee flat-warming drinkie in a bit. I have nibbles to take out of the packet. They said to say hi to you, by the way. Also, they're mad for a trip down south. Are there any dates when you're not free?'

'Let me check my diary. Oh look at that. I have absolutely no engagements whatsoever between now and er, forever. Get them down here quick.'

'I'll talk to them about it. But if you want somewhere to go, there's always the book group.'

Geraldine and Arthur looked suntanned and healthy. Nice sounded great and was definitely going on Kelly's list of places to visit. When they'd finished telling everyone about their holiday, Geraldine went upstairs to see Kelly's latest postcard collection and the books they'd come with. While they were there, Kelly told her about her own fortnight.

'You've had quite an eventful time,' said Geraldine.

'Yeah. I'm not sure about this book group though.'

'What is it that bothers you?'

'I suppose I'm scared of looking stupid.'

'Stupid?'

'Thick.'

Geraldine huffed. 'What have I said about that inferiority complex?'

'Er, don't have one?'

Another huff, along with a raised eyebrow. 'We both know this is not a joke, Kelly. Pretending it is, will do you no good whatsoever. Let me remind you again. You are not thick. You're quite the opposite, in fact. You should go.'

'I won't know anyone there. Anyway, they'll be a bunch of poshos. Poshos and know-it-alls.'

'I expect you thought Netta, Liza and Will were poshos when you first met them, but that didn't stop you becoming best friends, did it? And if I remember rightly, you thought I was a nasty old woman, but look at us now.'

'You're still a nasty old woman. Making me do things I don't want to do.'

'Hah! I tell you what, I'll come with you. It's been years since I did anything like that.'

Kelly rolled her eyes. 'You do know you'll probably be the oldest one there. They'll think I'm your carer, or something.'

'Oh I didn't realise there was age bar to culture. I'd better let Arthur know we're only allowed talk about vegetables and daytime TV, now that we're heading towards senility. That's settled it then. I'm definitely going, whether you do or not.'

Geraldine was getting a bit cross now. You always knew when Gez was getting tetchy because she folded her arms under her chest and if she was sitting down, she sat so upright, she might as well be standing. If Kelly had learned one thing about Geraldine by now, it was this. When the arms were folded, it was best not to argue.

'All right, I'll go with you. But if it's full of stuck-up poshos, I won't go again.' Kelly was frowning. On the outside anyway. Inside she couldn't help smiling. Gez was a bit of a bully in her own way.

The Pit Stop café was at the Balsall Heath end of Moseley. From the outside, it looked like it had been a garage once. Inside, it looked like someone had been shopping in one of those second-hand furniture shops. None of it matched. There was a word to describe it on the tip of Kelly's tongue. Eclectic.

'Eclectic: Deriving ideas or style from a broad and diverse range of sources.'

It was so big, it had two counters. One served hot food and sandwiches. The other served coffee, cake and mostly sweet things. Archie and Obie, the man of misery, were serving a queue of customers at this one. Kelly and Geraldine joined the queue.

Luckily, it was Archie that served them. Man of Misery was making the coffees, which was a relief. Kelly didn't want to subject Geraldine to his all round, general miserableness.

'All right, Archie. We're here for the book group.'

'Cool. They're over there.' He pointed to six people sitting around two tables that were pushed together. They were a mixture of ages and they looked as eclectic as their surroundings.

'Hello again. We'll take two cappuccinos with us,' said Geraldine.

Archie nodded. 'Hello again, Mrs Wilde. Thanks for that food you made for our drive to Edinburgh. It kept us going all the way. Two cappuccinos, Obes.'

MoM looked up and caught Kelly's eye with a stony stare. Still angry with her then? For no reason at all, in her humble opinion. What an arsehole. He put the coffees on the counter and turned away. Idiot.

Geraldine was talking to Archie about what the café had been, back in the day. He seemed really interested and in no particular hurry to take any payment. Kelly wondered if they made any money at all. She flashed her card. 'I'll get these, Gez.'

Obie grabbed the card reader before Archie could get to it. 'It's okay, I'll take it.'

He held it out at arm's length and made a face at her, like he was daring her to do the same thing she'd done last time. Kelly decided this time she would exercise a little more decorum. Gez would only tell her off if she didn't. She tapped the card gently and gave him a smile, laced with a hint of sarcasm. That would teach him. Ignorant fecker.

Geraldine interrupted the stareathon. 'Shall we go over?'

Gez had her hand on Kelly's arm. Kelly was glad of it because she was suddenly terrified of approaching those two tables. She felt insanely sick.

Geraldine whispered in her ear: 'They look like perfectly nice, normal people.'

Yes they did. Not poshos at all. Kelly nodded, but she still wanted to throw up.

'Remember my breathing exercises? Do them with me,' Geraldine said quietly.

They took some slow breaths, the way Geraldine's therapist had taught her. Kelly used to help Gez practise those exercises so she knew them well. The sickness went away and she managed to walk to the tables without making a total fool of herself.

'We're here for the book club.' said Geraldine.

Kelly thought her knees were going to buckle but one thing kept her going. Although he was behind her, she had this feeling Obie was watching her. She couldn't let him see how scared she was. He'd enjoy it too much.

A woman stood up and smiled at them. She was old but not quite as old as Gez. 'Welcome. Have a seat. We're just about to introduce ourselves.'

A guy about the same age as Kelly fetched some chairs.

The girl at his side looked like she was with him. She seemed familiar.

The woman carried on: 'I'll start, shall I? I'm Nina. I like to read all sorts. I live alone with my dog, so I do read a lot. I also work here three days a week. It's a new place with lots of friendly people but what it was missing was a book group. Until now. Thank you all for coming.'

They went round and each person said a few words about themselves. Some said more, you couldn't shut them up. Others said enough to get through the torture of speaking about themselves. Geraldine was brilliant. Before therapy, she wouldn't have said a word, but not now. She was confident and funny, and they all loved her. Kelly's turn was more like the torture side of things. She mumbled and stuttered her way through a couple of lines about only recently taking up reading, so not to expect too much from her.

When the girl who looked familiar spoke, Kelly realised where she knew her from.

'I'm Zoe. Like everyone here, I love reading. I'm really into the classics at the moment so I might bore you with my ravings. If I do, just tell me to shut up.' She focused in on Kelly. 'I know you. Didn't we meet on the train to Edinburgh? You got off at Sheffield. We had an amazing conversation about Jane Austen.'

'I thought I recognised you,' was about all Kelly could manage. An amazing conversation? How cool was that?

After the introductions, Nina suggested talking about books they were reading at the moment, or that they'd read and loved. Kelly didn't say anything but there were enough people who were happy to talk. She was fine listening to what they had to say, and she wrote down a couple she liked the sound of that were also on Edie's pile of books.

They took a break halfway through. Geraldine went up to get more coffee. Kelly watched her chatting away, not just to Archie but to MoM as well. In fact, MoM seemed quite happy. He even smiled. She needn't have worried about him being miserable to Gez. He obviously saved that for her alone.

She was pulled away from the goings on at the counter by Zoe who dropped into Geraldine's seat. 'I can't believe I've met you again. After you got off the train, I was kicking myself for not getting your number. It would have been great to meet up and talk some more. It must be fate.'

'I suppose so.' Kelly hadn't meant to sound like she couldn't give a toss. It was just that she was always waiting for the punchline. Something spiteful, aimed at sticking her back in her box. She had Marcus and Poppy to thank for that, she supposed. Then again, that defence mechanism had been there well before she met Marcus.

She remembered she'd decided to start liking herself. To do that she had to sometimes allow it that other people might genuinely like her. They might even find her interesting and want to talk to her about books. And if Robyn's friends had liked her, Zoe might do too. It was time to let the barriers down. Slowly though. That way if something shit happened, the effect was controllable. She smiled at Zoe. 'At least we can talk here now.'

'I know. It's all right, isn't it? I was a bit worried about coming, to be honest. That's why I dragged Max along.' Zoe nodded to the guy who'd got the chairs for them. He was talking to another guy. 'He's found someone else who likes sci-fi. I expect I'll get the full lowdown tomorrow. We work together.'

'Oh, so you're not—'

'Together? No, just mates. His girlfriend doesn't mind

me borrowing him sometimes, if I need a plus one or a confidence booster. She's good like that.'

Kelly nodded at Geraldine who was on her way back with a tray. 'She's my confidence booster.'

'I can see how that would work. She's pretty fabulous.'

'Yes she is.'

Kelly eyed two chocolate brownies on the tray. 'Cakes, Gez? You shouldn't have.'

Geraldine sat down. 'Compliments of the house. I was going to buy them but that lovely young man insisted.'

'Archie, you mean.'

'No, the other one. Obie.'

'Obie? Gerroff!'

'Gerroff yourself. He's nice. Very polite and pleasant. I asked about his name. It's short for Obiefune.'

'Say again?'

'Obi-few-ni. It's Nigerian.'

Kelly laughed. 'Only you, Gez.'

'What's that supposed to mean?'

'Only you could find the most bad-tempered person in history, pleasant.'

Gez dug her fork into her brownie. 'Funny. He said the same about you.'

34

KELLY GOES ALL FRENCH

Kelly opened the door to the Pit Stop. Geraldine was going somewhere else before book group, so she'd had to come on her own. She'd given herself extra time to allow for bus changes and traffic, but it wasn't needed and she was early. She hadn't had time for dinner after work, so she went over to Nina's counter first.

Kelly was considering something called a croque-monsieur. She was still trying to get the hang of foreign food. In theory, Edie's postcard stash made her keener. In practice, she wasn't quite so keen on actually eating the stuff. Nina told her croque-monsieur was just a fancy cheese and ham toastie, so she risked it.

'I'll bring it over to you. Do you want a drink with it?' said Nina.

'I was going to get a coffee from Archie.'

'You can order it here.'

'Oh. Right. I'll have a cappuccino then.'

Feeling a bit let down, she found a table and took *Middlemarch* out of her bag. Nina went over to the coffee counter. Archie waved at her and Kelly gave him a little wave back.

Then she saw Obie, giving her the evil eye again. She opened her book and stuck her nose in. Fuck him. He could shove his free brownies.

She was trying to read and fume at the same time when a cup landed on the table in front of her. She looked up, expecting Archie to be there. But no. It was him. The mardy fucker.

'Thank you?' He said it in such a sarky way that she immediately fumed even more.

'Thank you for what? For the coffee I paid you for, or for the shitty service?'

Obie puffed out his cheeks. Although, how he could do that while he was grinding his teeth, she didn't know. 'Shitty service?'

'Yeah, on account of you being so fucking surly.'

He ground his teeth a bit more. If he carried on, he'd probably run out of teeth soon. But he didn't carry on. He just nodded and walked away.

'Wanker,' Kelly muttered under her breath. 'Surly fucking wanker.'

'Surly: Bad-tempered and unfriendly.'

On the plus side, she'd been able to use another new word. Someone at the foodbank had called her surly once. When she checked its meaning last week, she'd been insulted. But then she thought, fair enough. They're not wrong. She'd been known to be both bad-tempered and unfriendly occasionally. She'd looked it up because she was trying to find a way of describing Obie, Man of Misery. Not that she spent much time thinking about him. He just popped up now and then. Hardly at all, in fact.

She noticed there was a heart shaped swirl on the top of her coffee. A heart? Hilarious, or what?

Suddenly, a plate holding something that looked like a

fancy cheese and ham toastie skidded across the table at her. She had to catch it to make sure it didn't shoot into the air like a flying saucer. Surly fucker was back. 'You know, you're rude.'

'Oh really? What kind of rude? Rude as in bad-mannered, or rude as in a bit dirty?'

'Not dirty. Of course not dirty.'

'Just bad-mannered then. That's all right. I can live with that. Because that makes two of us.'

She allowed herself a little smirk as she bit into her croque-monsieur and watched him storm back to his counter, spit out some words at Archie, and bounce out the café door.

'Touché. Ooh, I've gone all French.' She picked up a spoon and stirred the coffee until that stupid heart disappeared.

Obie was back by the time Geraldine arrived. 'Obie's a bit quiet.'

'We had a disagreement.'

Geraldine sighed. 'Honestly. Why you have to go out of your way to wind people up, I have no idea.'

'Because he's an ignorant pig, Gez. That's why.'

'Well I haven't seen that side of him. And behaving like that doesn't show you in a very good light.'

Kelly didn't think she cared whether MoM saw her in a good light or not, but Geraldine was folding her arms again. Best not argue.

Zoe pulled up a chair on the other side of Kelly and said hello. Her mate, Max, sat by his sci-fi loving friend. Kelly had been thinking about her since the last meeting. Or more accurately, she'd been thinking about what she'd said about

Max giving her a confidence boost. To look at Zoe, you wouldn't have thought she needed one. But there you go. Perhaps Zoe and her weren't that different, after all.

Nina opened the meeting before they could talk more. 'Hello everyone. I'm glad you all decided to come back. I thought we'd start by going round the table again and reminding everyone of our names. If you've read anything in the last two weeks, you might want to say something about it. If you haven't then that's absolutely fine. Kelly, would you like to start?'

Kelly's heart began thumping super loud. Geraldine touched her arm and she felt a bit calmer. She started to speak, although she couldn't tell if she was whispering or shouting, what with the noisy heartbeat drowning everything else out: 'I'm Kelly. I've been reading *Middlemarch*. It's about this young woman who has the worst idea ever of marrying a man who's old enough to be her dad. I thought I'd made some bad choices in men, but Dorothea takes it to a whole new level.'

She froze as she heard a few titters. But when she looked around, she could see they were laughing with her. They liked the jokey way she'd described the book.

'We've all been there,' chuckled Nina. 'I haven't read that book yet. I think I might have to now. Great start, Kelly. Max, would you like to go next?'

Geraldine gave Kelly a sneaky little squeeze. Kelly listened to the others with a big grin on her face. She probably looked dead stupid, but it was okay.

Geraldine went up for drinks during the break. 'Can't have you upsetting that nice young man again tonight.'

Kelly stayed with the others and listened to Max talking

about his holiday in Rome. Dorothea went there on her honeymoon, and Kelly had found that postcard of Rome in *Pride and Prejudice*, so she was already interested in it. Hearing Max describe all the wonderful things you could see made it even more real.

Gez was soon back with the coffees and two brownies. 'I had to pay for them this time. We've fallen out of favour. Surprise, Surprise.'

'Good brownies though. Chocolate orange.' Kelly was a brownie expert, being as that was the only cake she ever had in cafés.

'Oh, there is something about Obic you like then?'

'Eh?'

'His baking. He makes them.'

Kelly nearly choked on her brownie.

Nina clapped her hands together. 'Right, shall we carry on? I was wondering what you all thought about having one book a month that we read and discuss.'

'I er … I might have a problem with that. I mean, I might have a problem reading the book if it's not on my list,' said Kelly.

Nina frowned. 'Your list?'

'Yeah. Actually, it's not my list. It's Edie's. I can't read anything else until I've read them all. I'm fine with everyone else reading a book, obviously. It's just that I've got to follow the list.'

'Kelly, love. I think you'd better explain Edie's list. I'm sure they'd all like to hear,' said Geraldine.

There were lots of nods, so Kelly told them about Geraldine's challenge and finding the first postcard, then the second, and on she went until she finished with searching for the others while dancing the Macarena with Netta and Liza. 'So you see, I need to read them all before I can try anything else. But I am writing a new list from the ones you all talk about. I'll start that when I'm done with Edie's.'

'That's a lovely story.' Nina looked like she was about to cry.

Max put up his hand. 'Here's an idea. Why don't we all follow Edie's list and discuss one of the books each month.'

'It's really old authors.' Kelly couldn't picture Max curling up with Jane Austen and Charlotte Brontë somehow.

He shrugged. 'I'm good with that.'

'I like the idea too. Shall we put it to the vote?' said Nina. Everyone's hand went up. 'Looks like it's unanimous. Can you bring the list with you next time, Kelly? We'll take a vote on which one to start with.'

'How about bringing the postcards as well? I'd like to see them,' said Max.

'Erm, yeah. No problem.' Kelly thought maybe she was in shock and hadn't understood correctly. She turned to Geraldine to make sure she had.

Geraldine beamed at her. 'That went well, didn't it?'

35

A CURIOUS STATEMENT ABOUT SPACE

Netta was literally quite stunned by Kelly's excitement.

'I couldn't believe it. They were all up for following Edie's reading list. I've got to take it to the next meeting. They want to see the postcards as well.' Kelly sat on the sofa, but bounced straight back up again and paced the room. She couldn't even stand still. 'They were really interested in all of it.'

'That's wonderful. And you were okay telling them about it were you?' She was surprised Kelly had suddenly gained the confidence to share her secret.

'I didn't really have a choice after Nina asked us to read the same books. I said I couldn't because of my list. Then Geraldine said I needed to explain the list, so I did and it was all right.'

Ah, that was it then. The Geraldine factor. That explained everything. 'Sounds as if the book group's going well. Glad you made the decision to go?'

'Yeah. It wasn't really my decision though. Gez kind of pushed me into it. You know what she's like when she decides something's for your own good.'

Netta put her finger on her chin. 'Hmm, let me think. Do I know what that's like? I think I do.'

They both laughed. Netta thought about times in the past when her mum had made it clear what she thought of Colin. She'd pulled Netta up for her behaviour sometimes as well. Her mum had been different then, more angry and bitter. Her sharp criticisms had been things to avoid. Mainly because they were always spot on and that was a hard thing to take when they were aimed at you. Even if they were meant for your own good. But these days, the words were delivered more softly. The funny thing was, they carried more punch.

'On a different subject, I spoke to Will. He'll be home for the summer in a few days. Did he message you? He said he was going to.'

Kelly checked her phone. 'Looks like he sent it while I was at book group. Guess I must have been too wrapped up to notice. I'll drop him a message. He'll only say I'm ignoring him if I don't. Is Lize in?'

'No, she's gone for a drink with Colin.'

'Colin? What's that about then?'

Netta shrugged. 'Not sure. Perhaps he's decided to make more of an effort.'

A while later, Netta was sitting in the garden on her own. Frank was out with the Hope and Anchor darts team. Kelly was in the study, reading, and the dogs were keeping her company. It was a reasonably warm June evening. Perfect for watching the light fade, and for contemplation.

She'd been thinking about Edie and those postcards. In the past, Edie's words had guided Netta. Now they were doing the same for Kelly. It was as if Edie was saying: 'I'm still here. Don't forget me.' As if she were there in the background, watching over them. It was both strange and comforting, and it was funny to think there may be more Edie treasures buried in this house, waiting to be discovered.

She was also wondering how things were going to turn out with Kelly, and just how badly she'd been scarred by that awful Marcus. The trip to Edinburgh and this book group seemed to have given her a boost, but there was one thing looming on the horizon that had the potential to wipe all of that out. Will was coming home.

The last time he'd been home was that weekend after she and Liza went to Sheffield to get Kelly's things back. Netta recalled the look that had passed between him and Kelly. She still wasn't sure what it meant, except that there may have been more than friendship on Will's mind. What Kelly had meant by it was a mystery. Short of asking her, it would remain a mystery. Unless… Unless there was someone else who may have more of a clue than her.

'Hey, Mum.' Liza strolled across the grass. She had a pretty summer dress on and she'd curled her hair into long, loose waves. She looked gorgeous. Netta's heart lurched. Her daughter was a beautiful young woman. Astonishing that she'd only just noticed it.

Liza took the chair next to her. 'What are you doing sitting out here in the dark?'

'Is it dark? I hadn't noticed. How did it go with your dad?'

'Okay I guess. You know Dad. Always complaining about how hard his life is when it really isn't. He's been offered a summer teaching job at an art retreat in Italy. He's asked if I want to go with them.'

'That's nice. Are you going?'

'Dunno. I definitely wouldn't go all summer. They'd

drive me mental. Maybe for a few weeks, if I could take a friend. I could ask Jade if she wants to come.'

'Good idea. I'm sure you'd have a great time.'

'You wouldn't mind if I went?'

'Of course not. Why should I mind?'

Liza looked towards the house. 'In case Kelly gets down again.'

So that was it. Liza was worried about Kelly. 'She'll be okay. And if she does get a bit down, we'll manage. You mustn't let that stop you having a holiday. Kelly wouldn't want that, and neither do I.'

'You want me to go then?'

'Only if you want to. I'm just saying don't refuse to go because you're worried about Kelly. Or me, for that matter.'

'I guess it'll give you two a bit of space.'

'Hardly. Will's coming home in a few days. I expect Belle will move in for the summer too. Space might be a bit tight.'

Liza rolled her eyes. 'In that case, maybe I will say yes. I'll call Jade. You coming in?'

'In a minute.'

Liza went back indoors. That had been a curious thing to say about giving her and Kelly more space. Where had that come from? Perhaps Colin had said something. Up to his old tricks again, no doubt. Netta cursed herself for not exploring it further.

When the light went on in the kitchen, she could see just how dark it had become outside. She shivered. It had gone cold too. She picked up her things and went in.

36

THE GERALDINE FACTOR

Saturdays were reserved for the various farmers' markets across the Midlands. On this particular Saturday, they were at the Moseley market. The nice weather they'd had earlier in the week had given way to showers that occasionally moved rapidly to downpours. Consequently, it was a quiet morning and out of boredom, they'd very nearly drunk the equivalent of their combined bodyweights in coffee. Netta was already feeling the caffeine overload.

'Sun's coming out,' said Neil. 'Not sure if that'll save the day though.'

Kelly tapped her on the back. 'Well if you thought things couldn't get any worse, your ex is over there.'

'Where?' said Netta and Neil in unison.

Kelly's head jerked back. 'What do you mean where, Neil? Do you even have an ex?'

Neil looked quite insulted. 'Er, yes, I have an ex. A couple, if you must know. I did have another life before Chris, you know.'

Kelly snorted. 'Okay. Chill, Mister.

Neil shook his head but he was grinning.

Meanwhile, Colin was making a poor show of pretending to browse the stalls. If he was here at all, it could be for only one thing. Sure enough, he wound his way over to them. 'Hello, Netta.'

'Colin. This is a surprise. I didn't know you were a market shopper.'

'I'm not really.'

'You don't say,' said Kelly.

He forced something like a smile out, obviously afraid anything else might get back to Liza. Unfortunately for him, Kelly had no such concern. 'What can we do for you on this rare visit, Colin? Got a jam emergency have you? Need some urgent pickle for your cheese sandwich?'

Netta sucked her cheeks in to stop herself from smirking. Kelly was on form today.

Colin gave a polite laugh. He deserved a few Brownie points for trying to take it in good part. 'Actually, I wondered if you had time for a coffee, Netta?'

The thought of yet another coffee that morning was bad enough, but with him? Definitely not. 'I'm working, Colin.'

'I can see that, but you don't look too busy at the moment.'

Netta sighed. She wasn't going to get out of it that easily.

She took him to the café they usually went to after the Moseley market. It was a nice enough place. Reasonably priced, but probably the least artisanal café in Moseley village. She chose it for that reason, knowing it was the kind of place he'd turn his nose up at. That was a petty of her but so what? Although it had been months since she last saw him, she was still annoyed by the things he'd said about Kelly.

She added a touch of milk to a cup of tea – coffee was

out of the question – and stirred it in. 'What do you want, Colin?'

'I wanted to talk to you about Liza. Have you said something to her?'

'About what?'

'About us.'

'Us? There is no us.'

He flashed her a look, and she was immediately reminded of the time, long ago, when he found out she'd been unfaithful to him. His expression changed. The look was gone. Although it wasn't really gone. Just hidden.

'I was talking about the past. Liza seems to have got it into her head that I was a complete and utter bastard to you.'

Netta sucked her cheeks in again. A smirk was tempting, but definitely not called for. 'I think she worked that one out for herself without the need for my help.'

'So you have said something to her then?'

'Not exactly. She really did work it out for herself. We had a conversation around six weeks ago. She asked me if what she was thinking was correct and rather than lie, I told her it was.'

'You always did have a knack of turning everything round to your way of thinking.' His expression changed again and the old, malevolent Colin was back. He really was something of a chameleon.

Netta pushed her untouched tea to the middle of the table. There was no point arguing. She'd been here before and it never ended well. 'So did you. I'm going.' She stood up.

He grabbed her hand. 'Don't go. Please. I know I treated you badly, but it wasn't all me.'

She pulled her hand out of his. 'Let's not do this. It really isn't worth the effort.'

He pushed the tea back over to her. 'I do want to talk about Liza. I'm worried about her. Will you hear me out?'

She sat back down wearily. 'Tell me.'

'Let me just say first of all, I'm not having a poke at you or anyone else, but I'm worried that Liza thinks she's not as important in your eyes as Kelly. I know you're both very close to Kelly. I get that. But did you know, when I asked Liza to come to Italy, her first answer was that you might need her to take care of Kelly?'

'She mentioned something like that to me, yes. I told her she's not responsible for Kelly and should go.'

'Good. She needs a holiday. She's been working very hard with her coursework.'

'I know that, Colin. I'm quite up to speed on Liza these days.'

He gave her the slyest of his chameleon smiles. 'I'm sure you are. These days. In which case, like me, you're probably wondering why she doesn't have any boyfriends. You'd think a lovely girl like her would be fighting them off, wouldn't you?'

Netta cleared her throat. No she wasn't wondering. Because she hadn't actually noticed. 'That's her business. Not ours. She's not a child anymore.'

'If you say so. She's not gay, by the way. Arianne asked her.'

'She asked her? How dare she? Who the hell do you people think you are? Liza's sexual orientation is her business, unless she chooses to share it with us. And as to this boyfriend or no boyfriend nonsense, you wouldn't be happy either way. If she had lots of them you'd be telling me she was as slutty as her mother, and if she had one, you'd be treating him as competition.'

'You're overreacting.'

Netta stood up again, her hands well out of grabbing distance. 'You know, I was really trying not to say this to you again, but I can't help myself. Fuck off, Colin.'

She walked away, leaving him to nurse his coffee.

Netta couldn't go straight back to the stall after that. She was too het up. She'd let him get to her again. She knew it, and so did he. But that wasn't the reason she was upset. She could live with Colin thinking he'd got one over on her. What got to her was the fear that there might be some truth in what he'd said about Liza. That thing she'd said the other night was beginning to take on a new significance. She shook the fear off. She was just falling prey to Colin's manipulations again.

Her phone rang. It was her mum. 'Hello, love, just calling to ask what time you're expecting Will back. It is today, isn't it?'

'No, tomorrow.'

'What's the matter?' As usual, it was pointless trying to sound normal. Geraldine Eagle Ears picked up on the slightest thing.

'Can I come and see you later? I could do with a chat.'

Her mum had the front door open before Netta reached the gate. 'Kettle's on. I've sent your dad and Minnie off to the allotment.'

They went into the lounge. Her mum made herself comfortable in one armchair. Netta perched on the edge of the other one and explained what had happened in the café that morning.

Her mum tutted. 'I might have known he'd have something to do with it. He's never happier than when he's upsetting you.'

'I know that, Mum, but I can't help wondering if there's any truth in it.'

'Which bit?'

'I don't know. All of it. Liza said something to me the other night about giving me and Kelly some space if she went away. I thought it was a bit odd then, but it makes sense after what Colin said.'

'I see. The trouble is though, you don't know if Colin's been feeding her lines to make her think that. Has she said anything like it before?'

'I don't think so, but I'm now going back over all of our conversations looking for clues.'

Her mum clasped her hands together and placed them on her knees. 'Let's forget about Colin for a minute and try to look at it objectively. Is there any possibility Liza might think Kelly's welfare is more important to you than hers?'

'I've never thought that.'

'That's not what I asked.'

'Bloody hell, Mum. Stop getting all therapist on me.'

'I'm trying to help.'

Netta sighed. It was her turn for a touch of the Geraldine factor now. 'Possibly. What do you think?'

'I think it is possible that in the last year or so, Liza may have thought she was less important than Kelly. I think we've all been guilty of putting Kelly first, for all the right reasons. I include Liza in that too. She's been so caring. Perhaps too caring. Possibly, she's stopped valuing herself as highly as she should, and we haven't noticed because we've all been looking in the opposite direction.'

Netta stared at her mother, open-mouthed. That was quite profound. If anyone thought Geraldine Wilde had nothing left to say, they were very wrong.

'You'd better close that mouth before you catch a fly in it,' said her mum. 'Drink your tea. We've got some thinking to do. We need to work out ways to show Liza how important she is to us, without neglecting Kelly. As for her having no boyfriends, I wouldn't worry about it. I expect Colin's put her off. She'll get one when she's ready.'

'She might prefer girls.'

'She might, but I don't think so. I've heard her and Jade talking. They sound very heterosexual to me. Now then, I think our best plan would be small actions that make our feelings clear. Let's not go all out straight away, otherwise she'll get suspicious and then we won't look genuine. See how that goes. And don't make too much of a fuss over Will either. Sometimes it comes across as him being your favourite.'

'Do I do that? I hadn't realised. Shit. I don't have a favourite. Really, I don't.'

'I know. But sometimes little things we do can be misconstrued.'

Netta stuck her head in her hands and wondered if there would ever be a day when her parenting skills would be adequate. First of all there was this new Liza issue, and now it seemed she was fussing too much over Will. Was there anything she could do right? And don't even start on the worry over Kelly and Will.

'Mum, while you're in therapist mode, I'm a bit concerned about Will. I think he might have feelings for Kelly.'

'What kind of feelings?'

'Feelings, feelings.'

'Oh. Well I suppose it's been bubbling under for a good while. Is he still with Belle?'

'I think so. I suppose we'll find out soon enough. I get the impression he's struggling to work out his feelings for both. I'm not sure about Kelly though.'

Her mum batted Netta's words away. 'Oh, Kelly's had those kind of feelings for a couple of years at least.'

'Has she? You've talked about it then?'

'No. Don't need to. It's obvious.'

'Is it?'

'Yes love, it is. But then you've never been quick on the uptake with that sort of thing, have you?'

Netta inwardly winced. It could still sometimes be painful to be on the receiving end of the Geraldine factor.

37

OPENING A DOOR

Will was coming home today. Kelly's emotions were all over the place. One half of her was excited to be seeing him again and the other was a bit irritated by it, for some inexplicable reason. It was all a bit weird, and she was glad she wasn't going to be there when he got back.

She was at her dad's. It was his birthday and he was having another barbecue. As well as the immediate family, Kelly's aunts and uncles and their kids were here, along with some of her dad's friends. They were in full on party mode. Her mum would have loved it.

The smaller kids were tearing around the garden. Just looking at them was wearing Kelly out. In fairness though, that was probably because she hadn't slept well last night. She'd got off okay but then she'd been woken by those same few words: 'Don't tell Andy.' She hadn't been able to sleep properly after that.

She stretched out on the sun lounger she'd managed to grab before anyone else and watched her dad expertly flipping burgers while sipping on a beer. He was wearing a band T-shirt – Blur – and was doing a funny dance at the same time while trying to sing: 'All the people,' in a stupid cockney accent. Who knew he could multi-task?

Kelly was fighting to keep her eyes open. As they flickered to closed, she found herself drifting towards another party. Another barbecue like this one. Her dad was flipping burgers, and out of the four or five kids running around, she could see Conor and Dan. Somehow, she knew her mum and nans were there, even though they weren't in the garden. She knew that was because her mum had been drunk and shouty, and the nans had taken her inside to sober up.

Kelly went indoors to find them. Her mum and nans were upstairs. She went up and sat on the top stair. Except it wasn't her now. It was her eleven-year-old self.

Someone was throwing up in the bathroom. Nanny Donohue was telling her mum off for getting in such a state. Her mum screamed something in reply, but Kelly couldn't work it out. She knew it was something important. Something she must keep secret but it was too muffled, like she was wearing ear plugs. What was it? She had to know. Had to remember. She retuned her ears, and then she heard her mum's slurred voice: 'Fuck off, you old witch. I'm dying. If you can't get drunk when you're dying, when can you?'

There was silence, then Nanny Donohue's irritated voice: 'Don't exaggerate, Caitlin. You're just ill because you've had too much to drink.'

Her mum made a noise that was too frightening and crazed to be called a laugh. 'No, Mammy. I really am dying. Cancer. Happy now?'

Another silence. Then Nanny Donohue was flying out of the bathroom, pushing past Kelly on the stairs, running down, and out into the street.

The sound of spewing again made Kelly go to the bathroom door. She could see Nanny Payne wiping her mum's mouth. She could see her mum falling into Nanny Payne's arms and sobbing. 'Don't tell Andy. He doesn't know yet.'

They both turned and saw Kelly.

Kelly jolted upright. She'd known about her mum's illness before her dad! She'd forgotten that. No, not forgotten. She'd kept it a secret because her mum had told her to, and she always did what her mum told her to do. She'd buried it deep inside until it was as good as forgotten, but now she remembered it all. There was one more thing too. That film she'd watched. The one with her mum singing Carrickfergus. The one with her two nans in tears. It was taken later that day.

Kelly rubbed her eyes and looked around. Her dad was still at the barbecue, having a laugh with his brothers and mates. Carol was smiling at her from across the garden. She was back in the real world. That was good, wasn't it? She got up and went inside the house.

The bathroom was different now. She was glad they'd changed it this year. She didn't want to be reminded of that day every time she came in here. She locked the door and sat on the edge of the new bath. Her eyes were sore. It was the tears. They wouldn't stop. She'd thought she was at peace with her mum now, but she was wrong. There'd be more to come. More memories to unlock. This was just the start.

Someone tried the door. The noise made her jump. She saw her eleven-year-old self in the doorway looking back at her, so small and frightened. Too young to be carrying so much on her shoulders. If only she could reach back in time and help her through it.

'Kelly, it's Carol. Are you all right?'

'Yeah. I'm just…'

'Do you want to talk?'

Talk? Talk might be good. Kelly unlocked the door.

Carol relocked it and sat beside her. 'What's the matter?' She was so soft, so tender, so, not her mum that it brought Kelly's tears back again. Carol put her arm around her. 'It's all right. Let it all out.'

Kelly sniffed. 'It was just a bad memory. Something I remembered about Mum. Sometimes, she could be quite selfish. I'd forgotten that.'

'She loved you though, Kelly. Your dad's always telling me that. And we can all be a bit selfish sometimes.'

Kelly wiped her eyes. 'Sorry, Carol, but I can't imagine you ever being selfish. You seem to be one of life's angels.'

'I have my moments. Are you ready to go back down? I was about to take the cake out.'

She looked at herself in the mirror. Her face was a mess. 'Can you give me a minute to have a wash. I've ruined my make-up.'

'You don't need make-up, my love. You're pretty enough without it.'

Kelly washed her face while Carol went down to get the cake ready. She patted her skin dry and checked the mirror again. Her eyes were red and puffy but she didn't look too bad. Carol said she was pretty. Mind you, mums always said things like that. Maybe stepmums did too, if you gave them a chance.

Carol was putting candles on the cake when Kelly got to the

kitchen. 'All done. Do you want to carry it out? It would mean a lot to him.'

Kelly picked up the cake with its candles blazing and stepped out into the garden. Her dad was waiting for her, his eyes glistening. Emily danced up and down, begging to help blow the candles out. Her dad called Kelly, her brothers and Carol's two boys in. 'I want all my kids to help blow them out. Hurry up, before they melt the cake.'

The kids and stepkids crowded round. Her dad took Emily's hand and held the other one out for Kelly. 'Let's have my oldest and youngest either side, and the rest of you rabble somewhere in the middle. Ready? Three, two, one, go.'

Naturally everyone blew when her dad reached one, except for Emily who started at three. It still took a few attempts to blow them all out. It was hilarious, and no one cared that it was a complete fiasco.

Conor giggled. 'We are so ridiculous. We can't even blow some candles out properly.'

Kelly laughed. 'Harsh.' They might be ridiculous but they were her family, even if she'd only just realised it.

The party began to fade out by teatime. Dan and Shanice were the first to go, followed by the aunts and uncles. Her dad's friends looked like they were there for the rest of the night though.

Kelly announced that she was leaving. She had a bus to catch, and the Sunday service had never been great around there. Her dad wanted to pay for a taxi but she refused. She wanted to think things over and a talkative taxi driver was the last thing she wanted. The invisibility of a quiet bus would suit her. She'd had a few more flashbacks that afternoon. They were mostly of her mum, drunk or arguing. Just as she'd expected, the memory of that scene in the bathroom had opened a door.

Her dad followed her out. 'I'll walk you to the stop.'

'You don't need to.'

'I want to.'

Carol gave her a hug. 'Come again soon.'

'I will.' For once, she thought she might actually mean it.

They walked up the road, past the shop where she'd bought that disgusting wine the night she'd run away from Sheffield.

'I thought you might bring your boyfriend. Marcus, is it?' Her dad looked straight ahead. Neither of them was much good at face-to-face talking.

'He's not my boyfriend anymore.'

'Sorry, bab. Me and my big mouth.'

'Nah, you're all right.' She was about to tell him he was a posho shitebag but stopped herself. She didn't want him thinking she'd made another bad choice, even if it was true. Besides, she had other things she wanted to talk about. 'Dad, was Mum horrible?'

'No. What makes you say that?'

'It's just that I've been getting these flashbacks. She doesn't look like a nice person in them.'

'Carol said you were a bit upset earlier. Is that why?'

'Yeah. I remembered her shouting at the nans in the bathroom. She was drunk. She told them she was dying. She didn't know I was there.'

'I didn't know about that.'

'She wanted to keep it a secret. She hadn't told you yet. I think she used to drink a lot.'

'Your mum was a beautiful soul, Kel. It's true she liked a drink, and she could get a bit loud when she'd had too much, but she was never horrible. Never. She was a rebel, is what she was. She found it hard sometimes to fit in. Her way of coping with that was the odd drink, but it never got out of hand.'

A rebel? Just like Edie. Edie was definitely a rebel. Kelly liked the idea of her mum being one too. 'The box of things you gave me, there was a photo of her on a beach. Somewhere foreign. Do you know where it was?'

'Not sure. Send me a picture of it and I'll see if it triggers anything. It might have been when we went away before you were born, or it might have been from when she was travelling.'

'Mum went travelling?'

'Before I met her. She left Ireland with nothing but a backpack, in search of adventure. She travelled all over the world. I told you she was a rebel. I'm sure we mentioned it before. That's how we met. I was in Thailand for the summer. She was selling drinks on the beach. Couldn't take my eyes off her. Spent the rest of the summer following her around like a lost puppy. When it was time for me to go home, I gave her my address and phone number, but I didn't expect to hear from her again. Two months later, she turned up on the doorstep. "How are yer, Andy?" We were inseparable after that. Until…'

'Until you weren't.'

'Exactly. Have you thought about what you're going to do with your nan's money?'

'Not really. My friend, Robyn, thinks I should use some of it to go on holiday. Paris, maybe.'

'Good idea.'

'You don't think Nan would mind? I thought she'd prefer me to put it to good use.'

'That sounds like a good use to me. She'd like the idea of you broadening your horizons.'

They reached the bus stop. Kelly checked the timetable. Another ten minutes.

'This Marcus. Did he behave badly?'

She screwed up her nose. 'A bit.'

'Want me to sort him out for you?'

Kelly snorted. 'You? Mr Wimp?'

He grinned. 'I'll take your uncles with me.'

'Nah, you're all right. Netta and Liza already did it.'

'Now I do feel bad.'

She laughed. He could be quite funny sometimes. Another thing she just remembered. 'Do you think if Mum hadn't died you'd still be together.'

'Yes.' He said it without hesitating.

'But you wouldn't have Carol or Emily.'

'I know. Which is why I never think about that sort of thing. What is, is.'

'Carol's lovely though, Dad.'

'Emily, not so much?' He winked at her.

'Stop it. You know what I mean. Carol's just … lovely.'

He put his arm around her. 'Yes she is. And so are you, gorgeous girl.'

'Mum used to call me that.'

'I know. Who do you think she got it from?'

He pulled Kelly towards him and squeezed her tight. He smelt a bit of sweat and stale beer but she didn't mind. She heard him sniff and when she pulled away she saw his eyes were wet. 'Wimp.'

'Wimp, yourself.' He gave her a soft push and pulled out a couple of paper napkins from his pocket. They both blew their noses.

'Here's your bus.' He hugged her again. 'Bye, gorgeous girl.'

'Bye, Dad.'

He waited for Kelly to find a seat. She got one by a window, on the pavement side and waved to him. He took his hand out of his pocket and held it up. He'd started crying again. She mouthed: 'Wimp' at him. He held both his hands out as if to say, so what? God. She loved her dad so much. She should have told him. Why did they never tell each other?

As the bus pulled away, he blew her a kiss, and then she realised, sometimes words weren't needed.

38

MOVING ON

The thing about secrets was the longer you kept them, the deeper they got buried. So deep they became untraceable. Until something forced them back up to the surface. Kelly didn't know what exactly had made hers return. There'd been so many shit traumas for her to pick from lately. But they were here now and she was going to have to deal with them. It was two in the morning and she hadn't slept yet. She probably wouldn't sleep at all tonight, unless she faced them.

She sat in the breakfast room, the dictionary open on the table. Netta liked to sit in here on the nights she couldn't sleep. She'd told Kelly once, it helped her to relax if she sat in the dark and watched the garden. Sometimes, she got lucky and saw a fox passing through. Kelly was sitting in the dark now with Maud on her lap. She must have been here for an hour, thinking about one word. Accomplice.

'Accomplice: A person who helps another commit a crime.'

She'd known the word already but wanted to check the specific meaning. If she was honest, it wasn't a factually correct description because her mum hadn't committed an actual crime, but she couldn't think of a better word for it. Accomplice it was then. Kelly was an accomplice. At least, she had been, for the first twelve years of her life.

It was the secrets. The secrets her mum had made her keep. The ones Kelly had buried inside, along with the hurt. The biggest one of all was the one she'd heard coming from the bathroom that day of the party. The others were small compared to that. If you took them individually. But if you lumped them together it looked very different. If you thought about the bigger picture, you could see it was pretty fucking huge. Her dad had told Kelly her mum wasn't horrible. That may have been true, but one thing was certain. She wasn't right in the head.

There was the drinking, the afternoon tipples they needed to keep secret because Daddy wouldn't understand. There were the trips into town to buy things that got hidden away until they could pretend they'd had them for ages; the days of living on toast and jam, or crisp sandwiches because she'd spent the dinner money on those other things. Of course, there was always a proper dinner for her dad when he got home. She'd tell him they'd eaten earlier so he wouldn't notice the rest of them were being fed crap.

The duvet and park days were another thing to hide. Those were the days her mum decided they needed some fun, and gorgeous girls didn't have fun at school. Then Kelly remembered the man who used to hang around with them sometimes. She never knew his name. When he turned up, she was sent away with the boys. Who the fuck was he?

Kelly stroked Maud's wiry fur. It always helped. Secrets. All secrets. Except, were they? Was that why Nanny Donohue was always there, on her mum's case? Perhaps that was the reason she moved over here. Nanny Payne must have known something was up too. For the last two years of her mum's life, there was hardly a day when one of the nans wasn't at the house. They were probably taking it in turns. Minding things on a rota basis. And if they knew, what about her dad? What did he know?

Theories were shooting around Kelly's brain like fireworks. Her dad, the wimp. The sweet and loving wimp. And yet he hadn't always been like that. Now that the past was sliding into place, she remembered him as stronger. The kind of man who would have easily sorted Marcus out singlehanded. Craig too. He was no fool either. Kelly couldn't believe he was so deluded that he didn't see through the lies, or that the nans wouldn't have told him. But maybe he really didn't know, until… Oh God. Was that why he fell apart after she died? Was that when the truth came out about everything, including the mystery man? Kelly put her fist in her mouth. 'Oh Dad.'

There was a creak on the stairs. If she sat still and quiet, whoever it was might not realise she was there. But it was too late. Someone was in the room. She had her back to them but she knew they were there.

'Oh shit!' It was Netta.

Kelly turned. 'Net.'

'It's you. Sorry, I thought it was E… Never mind.'

'What? A ghost? Did you think I was Edie's ghost?'

'Yes all right, I thought you were Edie. That sounds quite stupid now I've said it out loud.'

'It's those postcards. She's probably on your mind.'

'I expect so. What about you? Something on your mind too?'

'I've been remembering stuff about my mum.'

'That's nice.'

'Maybe. Maybe not.'

'Ah. Why don't I make us a nice hot chocolate.'

They closed the kitchen door to keep the noise down and while Netta made the chocolate, Kelly told her about the flashbacks. When the drinks were ready, they went back into the breakfast room and sat in the dark.

'Will you talk to your dad about them?' said Netta.

'I don't think so. We're in a good place now. I don't want to spoil things. Anyway, I'm not sure how much he already knows. If he knew about everything, it would be bad enough dredging it all back up, but just think what it would do to him if he didn't. I don't want him hurt.'

Kelly took a sip of her drink. Why was it so much easier to talk when there was chocolate in the area? 'Huh. I just realised something. I used to get so mad at everyone because they were always trying to protect him, and now I'm doing the same thing.'

'You've moved on.'

'I think I have.'

'How do you feel about your mum now?'

'I don't know yet. It's all come back so quick. I'll think it over for a few days and if I'm still not sure, I might talk to Geraldine about it. It explains a few things though, doesn't it?'

'How do you mean?'

'Well, it's hardly any wonder I'm always turning my nose up at proper food. Next time Neil has a go at me for not fancying his latest concoction, I can tell him it's all my mum's fault. That'll shut him up. Seriously though, I can see why I went off the rails. I was probably already on the way before Mum got ill. I mean, she was hardly gonna to win prizes for her parenting skills, was she?'

'I'm not the one to ask about parenting. I've always been a bit clueless to be honest. But I do know there's no such thing as the perfect parent. We all have our flaws, and we all have a little bit of crapness in us. The best we can hope for is that it doesn't ruin our kids' lives.'

'Yeah. I think my mum probably had a lot of crapness in her though, Net. Otherwise she wouldn't have made me her accomplice. It was like she needed someone to shoulder the guilt for her. It shouldn't have been me.'

'No it shouldn't. Did she have any friends?'

'Not that I can remember, except for that bloke who was probably her lover. Or he could have been her dealer, I suppose. I'm guessing lover. I think I'd have known if she was doing drugs. I think even Dad would have spotted that.'

'Sounds like she could have done with a good friend.'

'Dad said she didn't fit in. I suppose that means she was an outsider. He also said she was a rebel. I thought that was cool when he said it, but I'm rapidly reassessing that opinion, in the light of this new evidence. Do you think I'm an outsider?'

Netta was quiet for a few minutes. That didn't look good. 'I think you were when we first met. I think we both were. I expect that's why we became friends. But I think we've both moved away from that in the last few years. We still have our moments but generally, I'd say we've lost our outsider status.'

'Good. I don't want to be an outsider anymore.' Kelly yawned. At last she was beginning to feel sleepy.

Netta yawned as well. 'We are going to be so useless in the morning. We'll have to make Neil do all the work. Shall we go up?'

Kelly yawned again. 'You go. I won't be long. I need a few more minutes to get my head settled.'

Netta pointed outside. 'Our fox is here. She has new babies.'

Kelly peered out of the French windows and just caught

the back of the fox and two cubs going into Frank's garden. It reminded her of the night she'd spent in the old rec. Thank God Craig's girlfriend turned up before she made a fool of herself. 'How do you know it's the same fox?'

'I just know. And the fact that she's lost the tip of her right ear helps. Every year I think this will be her last, but she keeps coming back with new cubs. The circle of life's a wonderful thing.'

Kelly saw a third cub appear from behind the bushes and trot off towards the others. She nudged Netta. 'That must be the rebel in the family.'

'Ah, Kelly, there's a rebel in all of us if we let it out. We just have to be brave enough to do it.'

Kelly was back on her own with Maud. Netta had gone up fifteen minutes ago. She was really tired now.

Maud followed her upstairs. They stopped outside Will's door. Kelly listened for the sound of him sleeping. Belle wasn't here tonight. It was only his first night back. It would probably be a day or two before she stayed over. That was their usual pattern.

She'd hardly given him a thought since the party. Her mind had been on the secrets. When she got in from the barbecue, she'd given Will a hug and it was nice. Comforting. None of the usual sparks. Still, give it a few days for all this Mum stuff to process and she'd probably be filled with raging lust for him again. Or whatever it was.

39

NOT GETTING CARRIED AWAY

'Right, girlie, get your party dress ironed. The Edinburgh Ladies are coming to town on Friday,' said Robyn.

'Not sure if I've got a party dress, seeing as I burned that disgusting effort Marcus bought me, and the other one I got in Sheffield went mysteriously missing,' said Kelly.

'We'll have to do something about that when we come then. I've promised the ladies a day of shopping. Until then, party top and jeans?'

'I can manage that.'

'Have you heard of a club called the Night Owl? Archie's suggested it instead of the usual places. They play a lot of old music there.'

'I think Netta and Frank might go there sometimes.'

'You are joking me. Dad goes there? I am seriously beginning to wonder about Archie. Old school or old fash-ioned? It's a fine line. Do you mind if he comes along too, by the way? Can't really not invite him as it was his idea, and the ladies love him. Obie will probably come too, though. Bromance alert. Sorry. I know you don't like him.'

'Man of Misery? He doesn't like me either, but I'm sure he'll stay out of my way.'

Robyn burst out laughing. 'Man of Misery? That's so funny, although a little cruel, so I shouldn't laugh. I don't think you'll need to worry about him. Jas will keep him busy. She so fancies him. See if Liza wants to come too. Gotta go. My break's finished.'

Kelly put her phone in her pocket. She was on a break too. She flicked the kettle on. So Jas was hot for MoM, was she? Fine by her. Although what she saw in that gloomy fucker was beyond her.

'Was that Robyn?' Kelly hadn't noticed Netta come into the rest room while she was on the phone.

'Yeah. She's coming on Friday with her friends. We're going to a place called the Night Owl.'

'Really? I love that place. They play some great music. Northern soul, Motown. That sort of stuff.'

'Brilliant.' Kelly had no idea what Netta was talking about, but it did sound like the Night Owl was a place where oldies went. That was okay. She was often more comfortable with oldies than people of her own age.

Neil came in from the kitchen. 'Coffee ready? I've got some new treats for you to try.' He put a plastic tub on the table.

Netta lifted the lid. 'Ooh is that cannoli?'

'It is. I've been experimenting for our end of summer party. I know it's a way off yet but I like to plan early.'

Kelly gave the tub a suspicious once over. 'What's cannoli?'

'It's a sweet Italian pastry. Try one.' Neil had the usual anxious and slightly cross expression that always appeared when he was challenging Kelly with new food. He needn't have worried this time. He had her at sweet and Italian.

She bit into it. The creamy filling oozed out and she had to shove the rest in her mouth before it made a mess. Oh but it was good. 'That is delicious, Neil.'

Netta licked her fingers. 'It is actually.'

'Marvellous. That's going on the list, then. Well done, Kelly, for not making a fuss.'

'Er, patronising.' Kelly put her head to one side. She always found that to be the best head position when delivering a snappy retort. It got Neil every time.

'Retort: Say something sharp, angry, or witty in answer to a remark or accusation.'

She'd been going for sharp and witty, with a hint of anger with that one.

Neil's bubble was very much burst. 'Sorry, I didn't mean to sound patronising.'

Ordinarily she'd have been pleased with that outcome but today she felt a bit guilty. She must be going soft. 'I'm only joking, mate. I appreciate your efforts to expand my culinary tastes. Maybe it's working. I've been trying loads of new foods lately. I guess it's Edie's postcards inspiring me to try new things.'

'Excellent. I'll bring in more new dishes for our lunches then.'

'Great.' Kelly tried to sound enthusiastic at the thought of the overflow of foreign foods she was about to be subjected to. Could be she'd gone too far in her encouragement.

Kelly went to the Pit Stop straight from work. She'd asked Geraldine to come an hour earlier than book group to give them time to talk. The Mum flashbacks had stabilised now.

There were no more new ones. Just the same memories getting a bit clearer each time.

Gez was already there. Kelly went to order a coffee. Her stomach was rumbling, but it would have to wait. At some point, she'd get one of those croque-monsieur toastie thingies but she didn't want to be tricked by Nina, like the last time. She wanted to say hello to Archie. She was beginning to think of him as a friend. A friend with a poor choice in besties, where Obie was concerned anyway.

Archie was serving but a girl who was usually on the other counter was making the coffees. There was no heart shaped swirl on the top of Kelly's cappuccino this time. Just a few chocolate sprinkles.

'Where's your happy mate today?' Damn. She hadn't meant to say that. She hadn't meant to say anything about MoM at all, but it just came out.

Archie frowned. 'He's actually a really great guy.'

'I'm sure he is. With other people.'

He shook his head and gave her a smile that, if asked, Kelly would have said was mocking. 'He's having a day off.'

'Oh right.'

'There are only so many insults he can take.'

Kelly did the head-on-one side thing, but this time she had nothing to say. She gave Archie a hard stare instead. Just to let him know he was this close to getting a mouthful from her, and it was only her love for Robyn that saved him. Then she went over to Geraldine.

'Obie's had the day off then? Had enough of your gobbyness, has he?' were the first words Geraldine said to her.

Kelly threw herself down in an armchair. 'Don't you start. I'm having an emotional crisis over here, and all people keep banging on about is how I've upset the king of gloom.'

'Okay, I'll shut up about him. Although, it wouldn't hurt to treat him how you'd like to be treated yourself. You might be surprised at the results. Come on then, tell me about your emotional crisis.'

'I don't know where to start. There's so much of it.'

'That can be tricky. How about when you noticed the first signs?'

Kelly closed her eyes. She was making a journey back in time. Not way back, just a little bit. 'The morning after I ran away from Sheffield, I remembered something but I didn't understand what it was. So I think it was when I looked at my mum's things that I started to notice it properly. The videos. It's different to looking at a photo, isn't it? It's like they're alive and they're with you. I think it was seeing her like that. Seeing myself as a kid as well. I started getting flashes from the past.'

'The ones you told me about on the phone?'

'Yeah. Just bits, until my dad's birthday party. They've been coming in waves since then. They've made me realise a few things about my mum. She wasn't that great. She was a bit of a lush, to be honest. Maybe not a full on alckie, but she did have a drink problem. She didn't look after us properly either. Especially me. She treated me like a mate when she should have been treating me like a daughter. All these years since she died, I was convinced I had to look after my brothers because Dad fell apart, but I was already doing it before because she couldn't cope. She used to make me bunk off school all the time because she didn't want to be on her own. She was like a really needy kid.'

'Well, that explains a lot,' said Geraldine.

'That's what I said to Net. Everything's falling into

place. All the behavioural problems I had after she died, the anger and everything. It was a backlash. When I was fourteen, I was excluded from school. They sent me to a special unit.'

'I didn't realise. What was it like?'

'The teachers were nice enough. Very patient, considering the shit they had to put up with, but I hated it. I did what I needed to get back to a normal school. Then I just kept my head down until I was sixteen.'

Geraldine squeezed Kelly's arm. 'You know, you could have told me this before. I wouldn't have judged you.'

'I know, but I don't tell people because I'm ashamed. Even telling you now fills me with shame.'

Geraldine nodded. She was good at keeping quiet and listening when it was needed. That was why Kelly wanted to speak to her. She loved Netta with all her heart, but it was Geraldine who really understood her. Geraldine knew her like no one else could.

'I've realised something lately. This probably sounds crazy but all this time, it's like I've been trapped behind a glass door. Seeing those videos made it open up a tiny bit, and the memories came out and opened it a bit more. Now it's open wide and it's like I'm out there, seeing and feeling things the way I should be. It does sound crazy, doesn't it?'

'No, my darling, it doesn't. It sounds perfectly reasonable to me. I think I went through the same process when you saved me. The question is, what are you going to do with this new-found freedom?'

Freedom? Kelly hadn't thought of it like that. What was she going to do? 'I have no idea. Any suggestions?'

'I wouldn't rush into anything if I were you. It might be nice to enjoy rediscovering being your dad's daughter.'

'Good one, Gez. I'm on board with that. I'm seeing him

in a new light these days. Carol, as well. I properly like her now.'

'Oh my goodness. Shock horror. Whatever next?'

'Hilarious.'

Geraldine giggled. 'Sorry. I'm genuinely pleased that you're getting on well with them. Maybe it's also a good time to start thinking about other things you might want to change. Your other relationships, for example. Or your future. Your world's opening up, Kelly. It's a good time to see what it has to offer you.'

The café door swung open and Zoe walked in. There was a relationship she could make more of.

'It wouldn't hurt to have another friend your own age,' said Geraldine, in her ear. 'You two get on well, and she's a bit closer than Robyn.'

The rest of the book groupers came in one by one and Nina called them all together. Edie's cards and list took up the first half of the meeting. Nina was quite well-travelled and could remember places at the same time as some of the later cards. Some of the others shared their travel memories too. It really brought them to life.

The book they chose from the list was *A Room with a View* by E. M. Forster. It was the first male author Kelly had read. Although she had thought George Eliot was a bloke, until Gez put her right. They had a month to read it. That would have been a problem once, but she was getting quicker now. She'd probably manage two books in that time.

When the group ended, they began to drift away in ones and twos. Zoe slung her bag over her shoulder. 'See you in a couple of weeks.'

'Yeah. Unless you want to meet up for coffee or a drink sometime.'

'That would be great. Let's exchange numbers.'

When Kelly left Zoe, she looked around for Geraldine and found her talking to Nina. As she reached them, she heard Nina say: 'See you Saturday then.'

'Lovely. Looking forward to it,' said Geraldine.

'What was all that about?'

'I'm practising what I preach. I've decided I could do with a friend my own age closer to home too. Nina and I are going out for a dog walk on Saturday.'

'That's great. I've got Zoe's number. I'm going to meet up with her soon.'

'Good. Glad you've been listening. Maybe next time you'll listen to me and be nicer to him.' Geraldine nodded at the coffee counter. They were closing up. Archie was wiping down and Obie was putting away the unsold cakes. So he hadn't taken the whole day off then.

Obie looked up and caught her watching him. His head did a tight little nod. He had a whole army of different nods up his sleeve. This one wasn't the impatient nod he usually gave her. Nor was it the friendly, welcoming one he treated Geraldine to. It was measured. Like he was telling her: 'This is me saying hello, but let's not get too carried away, shall we?'

Kelly nodded back, sending her own message. 'Yeah, let's not get too carried away.'

40

THE EDINBURGH LADIES HIT TOWN

It was rare for the whole household to go out together. Or should that be both households? Netta normally included Frank in hers, but Robyn was home with her friends and suddenly the household was very different. Not that it mattered really. The main thing was, they were all going out together and she was looking forward to it.

The Edinburgh Ladies, or ELs as Kelly was now calling them, arrived sometime in the afternoon. Frank picked them up from the airport and by the time Netta and Kelly had got home, he was already looking elated and more than a little overawed. Elated to find Robyn had two lively, chatty friends and overawed for probably the same reason. They were absolutely lovely girls but possibly a bit of a shock for a man who happily spent hours painting, with only a large, shaggy dog for company.

They'd booked a table at the Rajdoot. Just as well because there were eleven of them altogether, including Belle and Liza's friend, Jade. The restaurant would have struggled to fit them in without notice. They were on a long table at the back, presumably so they weren't too loud for the other diners.

The ELs sat at one end of the table with Kelly in the middle of them. She was positively glowing. She'd found her tribe. Netta had had one of those once, before she met Colin.

Liza was sitting to the side of the ELs with Jade. She had to lean in to pick up the conversation but since the talk was mostly about Kelly's trip to Edinburgh, she wasn't saying a lot. Much as they tried to include her, Liza was not one of the in crowd. Netta's insides were churning. Where was Liza's tribe? Besides Jade and Kelly, who were her friends? She never brought anyone else home. When she'd been younger, Liza had had lots of friends. Okay, they were mostly over-privileged, spoilt and a tad shallow, but they were her friends. Netta couldn't recall the last time she'd seen Liza with any of them. Jesus Christ, how could she not know these things?

Liza gave her a quizzical look. 'You okay, Mum?'

'Yes I'm fine, darling. Just miles away. Are you having a good time?'

'Yeah. It's brilliant all this, isn't it?'

'Yes it is.' She studied Liza's face and couldn't find a trace of unhappiness. She was being melodramatic. Bloody Colin was getting her all fired up again, the malicious shit. There was no denying, his 'concerns' about Liza had been troubling her. Particularly after speaking to her mum. Since then, she'd been making more of an effort to take an obvious interest in Liza's life. Not that it was easy. Her daughter wasn't the most forthcoming. Not secretive exactly, but not exactly brimming over with information either.

Talking of the devil himself, Colin walked in with his

partner, Arianne. They took a table at the front. As soon as he noticed them he made a beeline for them, leaving sour faced Arianne minding the table. Netta wondered if he'd seen Will. Surely he wouldn't be coming over if he had? Unless that was the reason for him coming.

Before Colin reached them, Frank announced his arrival: 'Hello there, Colin. I thought it was you.'

Will was sitting opposite Netta. He carried on eating and didn't look up. Belle put down her fork and slid a hand on his knee. A few seats away, Kelly glared at Colin.

Colin held his hand up. 'Hi there. We just got here and spotted you. Quite a party.'

'Family get-together. It doesn't happen too often,' said Frank.

'I suppose not. Anyway, I thought I'd come over and say hello. Rude not to.'

'Indeed. Hello, Colin,' said Netta.

'Hi, Dad,' said Liza.

'Hello, and hi.' Colin did a couple of comical little waves. 'Hello, Will.'

Will gave him a nod that Netta would have said was curt, if she was being generous.

Liza stood up. 'While you're here, Dad, Jade and me have a couple of questions about Italy.'

His face lit up. 'Great. Right. Well?'

Liza took his arm. 'We'll come over to your table.'

Jade jumped up and took his other arm. 'Thanks for letting me come along, Mr Grey. I'm so excited.'

'Call me Colin.'

They led him back to the front of the restaurant and away from Will.

Belle picked up her fork again. 'Disaster averted. You

might want to thank Liza later.' Unless Netta imagined it, there was a sharpness in her tone that was most unlike Belle. Nonetheless, she was right. Liza had saved the day again.

Afterwards, they went to a nearby pub. Frank and Netta found a table. The others stood around in groups. They'd only been there five minutes when Robyn's friends, Archie and Obie, appeared. The ELs seemed very keen on them. Obie was especially popular. He seemed more relaxed than the last time Netta had seen him, and he was clearly enjoying the attention. Archie, on the other hand, was only one person's territory. He and Robyn were locked in conversation and neither seemed to have an interest in anyone, or anything else. There was a glow about them. A kind of aura that wasn't there until they came together.

'What do you think?' said Frank, quietly.

Netta followed his gaze to Robyn and Archie. 'I've never seen her looking so beautiful.'

'I thought the same.'

'Did you say they used to go out together?'

'A while back. I'm wondering if there's something still there though.'

'I think there might very well be. How do you feel about that?'

Frank shrugged. 'If she's happy, I'm happy.'

'Wait and see then.'

'I guess. You okay? Not too bothered by Colin turning up?'

'No, but I have been thinking about what he said about Liza. I do need to give her more attention. And I'm worried she might not have many friends.'

'Why would you be thinking that?'

'She only ever brings Jade home, and she never talks about anyone else.'

'She does.'

'Does she? When?'

'When we're painting. She's got quite a circle of friends.'

'But why doesn't she bring them home? Why doesn't she talk to me about them?'

Frank shrugged again. 'I think she talks to fill the quiet spaces when we're painting. Probably because I'm a boring old git. Maybe there aren't enough of those spaces between the two of you.'

'So you're saying I'm too interesting? Frank, that is the kindest way of telling me I'm unapproachable.'

Frank laughed. 'You're not unapproachable. But maybe you are very busy with things, and other people.'

'With Kelly, you mean?'

'Not just Kelly. You're the hub of everything, Net. It's an amazing thing that you shouldn't change. Particularly because your kids love that about you.'

'They do?'

'Yes, they do. All I'm saying is, it's okay to take a few days out from being the centre of everyone's world and just make someone else the centre of your world.' He nodded towards Liza. 'She's fine, by the way. You really don't need to worry about her.'

Netta squeezed his knee. 'Thank you. For the advice, and for all the dad stuff you've been doing lately.'

'You're welcome. I don't mind the dad stuff. I miss it.'

She leaned over and kissed him on the cheek. 'I forgot to say, I love you, Mr O'Hare.'

'And I love you, Ms Wilde.'

They kissed. Properly this time.

When they pulled away, they saw Liza and Jade grinning at them. Not Will and Belle though. He was looking at Kelly, and Belle was just looking peeved. Kelly was oblivious to it all. She was watching the ELs, who were still talking to Obie.

41

MOVE CLOSER

Well someone was popular. Someone was very fucking popular. Kelly could not believe it. She honestly could not believe it. The ELs were mobbing Obie like he was some kind of reality TV star. Literally hanging on his every word. And he was lapping it up, smiling and laughing. Yes! Smiling and laughing. Like they were having the funniest conversation. Unbelievable!

She was standing with Liza, Will and Belle. Some of Will's friends had turned up. Not Marcus, thank God. Not that she was expecting him to. Belle had caught up with her in the toilets and said they'd warned him off. Generally her and Belle didn't talk directly, but Belle had followed her into the toilets to tell her and put her mind at ease. That was nice of her. It made Kelly feel a bit guilty for disliking her. Still, it wasn't the first time she'd hated someone who was nice. That guilty feeling would go soon enough. Anyway, she didn't have time to think about that now. She had other things on her mind.

She wanted to join the ELs. She'd had a brilliant time in the Rajdoot with them. She couldn't go over there though.

Not with Obie, Man of Misery there. Although he didn't look so shitting miserable now. He looked extra happy. And gloaty. Very gloaty. He kept looking over at her, and he was definitely gloating. Like she was the one missing out, which she was, but only because he was stopping her from having a good time with her friends. She was absolutely not missing out on him. No way.

She would have talked to Rob and Archie, but they were so steamy, it was 'get a room' time. She didn't know it was possible to have sex with someone without even touching them, until now. Rob and Archie were absolutely having brain sex in the middle of the pub, right now.

Jade nudged her and made her jump. 'Do you know that guy your friends are talking to, Kel?'

'Yeah, his name's Obie.'

'Obie. Is that a nickname or something?'

'It's short for Obiefune.'

'Obi what?'

'Obi-few-ni. It's Nigerian.'

'Cool. You tight with him then?'

'Nah. Geraldine asked him.'

Kelly wasn't going to tell Jade she had another name for him, being as Jade was obviously as hot for him as the others. And she wasn't going to say she knew Obie well enough to upset him, but not well enough to make him smile. Apparently. And she definitely wasn't going to mention that she'd spent ages looking for his full name online, which would have been a lot easier if she'd known how to spell it. If she'd said any of those things it would have given the impression that she gave a fuck, which she didn't. She was just interested in his name because it was unusual. Like another new word. That's all.

'*Obiefune: Name of Igbo, Nigerian origin, meaning do not lose hope.*'

Liza came back from the bar with their drinks. 'Who are we checking out now?'

Jade nodded at Obie.

Liza turned to get a better look. 'Oh yeah, he's cute.'

They sipped their beers and watched Obie. He must have felt their eyes on him, because he looked over and smiled. Fucking smiled! Jade smiled back and Liza waved. Kelly turned round to talk to Will, but he'd moved away. Him and Belle were squashed into a corner, away from everyone. Belle was doing a lot of talking and pointing. Or maybe it was jabbing.

Geraldine stood in for Kelly on the market stall so she could spend Saturday in town with the ELs. Liza, who knew where the best shops were, came with them. Being an eco-warrior, she hardly ever bought anything new, but she still knew a lot more about that stuff than Kelly. They had a great day shopping, and Robyn helped Kelly find a nice dress in a vintage store in Digbeth. Apparently, it was a shift dress. It was just a plain black sleeveless dress that was short-ish, but not too short. It came up to her neck and was absolutely not see-through. It was cool and sophisticated. Kelly liked it a lot.

After a few hours at home to get ready, they were back in Digbeth on their way to the Night Owl. They passed the place Marcus had taken her to on their first date. She'd been looking out for him. Not because she wanted to see him. She never wanted to see him again ever, which was why she was keeping an eye out for him. Apart from that, she was having a good time.

Liza and Jade had come too. Not Will though. He and Belle were out somewhere else. Not Netta and Frank either. They'd asked them but they said they didn't want to cramp everyone's style. Kelly reckoned the real reason was the other way round. It must be hard to let your hair down when your kids are watching you and laughing at your parent dancing.

Kelly was thinking about her mum and dad. She'd spoken to her dad yesterday. He'd told her they used to spend a lot of time at the Irish Centre in Digbeth. The video of her mum singing 'Wonderwall' was taken there. It would have been nice to go there and see it, but it was pulled down a few years ago. The Irish Centre was in Kings Heath now, but that wasn't the same. No connection. She'd lost that Irish part of her when her mum died. Nanny Donohue left for Ireland not long after, and never came back. For a few years, she sent cards for Christmas and birthdays and then she was gone. Just like Kelly's mum.

Robyn looped her arm in Kelly's. 'You're quiet.'

'Am I? Just thinking about my family.'

'Bad stuff?'

'No, just vaguely Irish stuff.'

'I do that sometimes. Dad doesn't say a lot about his Irish roots. The only time it comes up is if the Irish rellies come over to visit. We don't really go over there anymore.'

'I went there once when I was a kid. It'd be nice to go again.'

'You need to start that list of places to visit.'

'I already have. It's mostly Edie's list though. I'll add Ireland.'

'So you're not mad at me for ignoring you a bit last night?'

'Don't be daft. You weren't ignoring me.'

Robyn made a face. 'I was a bit in the Archie zone. I didn't realise till later. Sorry.'

'It's fine. You two really need to sort yourselves out though. You're so into each other.'

'Really? Do you think he's into me?'

'Seriously? I mean the pair of you last night. There was steam coming off you.'

Robyn slapped her hand over her mouth. 'Oh shit. Cringe. I'll have to cool it. What about Obie though? Not so miserable now, eh?'

'Yeah, I did notice. It must just be me he has the grumps with.'

'Hmm, I wonder why that is. Look, there they are.'

Obie and Archie were waiting outside the club for them. They'd brought mates with them. Reinforcements probably, to give Obie a break from all this female attention.

Kelly stayed at the back of their group when they reached them. There were others at the front who were much keener on getting up close and personal with Obie than her. She let them get on with it.

Unfortunately, her foolproof plan backfired when the men moved out of the way to let the women go first. She ended up practically face to face with him when Erin held the line up because she couldn't find her purse. Kelly tried looking the other way but he was staring straight at her. She had a choice. She could either say something, or carry on looking like a dickhead. She chose not to look like a dickhead. 'All right?'

'Yeah, I'm good. You?'

'Yeah me too.'

'Good. They're waiting for us to go in.' He smiled at her. He actually smiled. At her.

Whoosh. Kelly's entire body was on fire. Her face was so

hot, it was literally throbbing. She was amazed the fire service hadn't been called to put her out. Shit and double shit. Now that was cringe.

The music that was playing was from the 1950s through to the 1990s. Kelly recognised some of it though. Mostly from Geraldine and Arthur. They loved their old music. Kelly could imagine them dancing to this stuff when they were younger. They were a bit too ancient now.

She went to dance with the other girls. Straight away, Archie was at Robyn's side. He so wanted her. You could tell from a mile off. Robyn caught her eye. Kelly winked at her and Rob threw back her head and laughed. Kelly absolutely bloody loved Robyn O'Hare.

There was no sign of Obie. Kelly hadn't seen him since they'd got here about an hour ago. The club wasn't massive but there was an outside part to it as well. She assumed he was out there, until she saw him dancing with a girl. They were really going for it, doing proper sort of dancing. At least it looked like proper dancing to Kelly.

After a while, they all headed outside into the warm night air to cool off. It was as crowded out there as it was indoors but it was cooler. Obie came out to them. He was on his own.

Jas perched her bum on the edge of a table and kicked off her shoes. 'This place is so fun. Obie, what was that dance you were doing? You're really good at it.'

Obie screwed up his nose and shrugged. 'I think it's called Northern Soul. I only learned the moves when I started coming here, so I'm not really sure.'

'That your dance teacher, was it?' Kelly could have smacked herself over the head. She hadn't meant to say that. She'd been thinking it, but it wasn't supposed to have come out. It was too late now. Everyone heard her. Including Obie, who looked a bit stunned.

'In a way I guess,' he said.

Jas put her shoes back on. 'Right, I'm going in for more. Anyone else coming?'

They all traipsed back in. Kelly wasn't quite ready to dance again, but she was too mortified to stick around.

'*Mortify: Cause to feel very embarrassed or ashamed.*'

She'd been looking for an excuse to use that one. Shame it had to be now.

They squeezed into a space inside. Obie stayed with them this time, dancing next to Jas. Kelly sneaked a glance at him every now and then. He was a good dancer and he wasn't too bad looking, she supposed. When he cracked his face anyway.

The DJ put another one of those Northern Soul tunes on and Obie started doing his moves. The rest of them tried to follow him and Archie, who was pretty good too. Kelly was trying to match Archie's steps but it was all too quick.

'Like this,' a voice said in her ear. She didn't need to look up. She knew it was Obie.

She stumbled. 'I'm not very good at dancing.'

'You look pretty good from what I've seen.'

'Yeah? You must be short-sighted then, mate.'

He laughed. 'Follow me.'

It was hard to concentrate with him so near to her. Each word of encouragement from him made her body temperature skyrocket, and whenever he smiled or laughed, she faltered. But after three or four songs, she was close to getting it. Then the music changed and something slower on came on. It was the excuse Archie and Robyn were waiting for and they came together. The others began to make for the bar or outside. Kelly went to follow them, but Obie stood in front of her. 'Do you want to dance?'

Whoosh! She was on fire again. She nodded because she didn't trust herself to speak.

He took her hand. Kelly stepped towards him. Close enough to dance, far enough to keep some distance. He put his free hand on her back and let it rest there. They began to sway in time to the music. She looked up at him and he smiled again. She couldn't stop herself smiling back. The singer was telling her to move closer, so she did. His body was next to hers now. His arms around her. His heat made her sweat. They moved in time with the music and each other like one single body. They didn't speak, but their eyes were locked on each other. His were the deepest, darkest brown. Almost black. Nothing like Marcus's soft, velvety cow-eyes. Obie's were intense. There was danger in them. Something frightening.

42

HELLO LONDON

Kelly was reeling. What happened? What the actual fuck happened? One minute she absolutely hated Obie, and the next… What did happen next? It wasn't like they even kissed. But that dance. That dance. That dance was … explosive. She literally nearly exploded. Stars. There were definitely stars. Or maybe it was just the spotlights shining in her eyes. Because explosions and stars, and all that shit didn't happen in real life, did they?

She hadn't realised until after the music stopped that she'd been dancing with Obie for a lot longer than one song. She hadn't noticed it changing.

Someone had grabbed her. It was Liza. 'The taxi's here. You coming?'

'Yeah.' But she couldn't move, couldn't take her eyes off him.

She was being pulled backwards. Obie was still on the dance floor but he was getting further away, until she was out of the door, in the street, and in the taxi. On the way home and all through the next day, her head was full of him and that dance.

It was Wednesday now and it was still all she could think of. The ELs had gone home on Sunday. They'd had a good time and Jas wasn't bothered that she hadn't got off with Obie, and Kelly had. If you could count that dance as getting off. Purists would probably say not because there was no kiss or sex involved, but Kelly thought otherwise.

She would have called Robyn by now but Rob was super busy at work, getting ready for the Edinburgh Festival Fringe. So Kelly had to stew in her own turmoil and confusion. There was no one else around to help her. Liza and Netta had gone to London, and Geraldine was too tied up with her social calendar to meet.

By the time she finished work, she'd had enough. She'd been useless all day, and had nearly spoiled a batch of apricot jam. There was only one way to put an end to this stupidness. She had to face Obie. She left Neil to lock up, got on her bike and cycled to the Pit Stop.

Outside the café, Kelly was having trouble locking the bike because her hands were shaking. God she was pathetic. It was just a dance and he was just a bloke. Not even a nice one most of the time. When she finally sorted it, she gulped down the nauseous feeling and went inside.

Her heart sank when she saw he wasn't there. Archie was though. He leaned over the counter, frowning. 'It's not book group week, is it?'

Kelly put on an innocent face. It wasn't her most convincing face at the best of times. 'No, I was just on my way home and fancied a proper coffee. We only have instant at work.'

'I get it. Sometimes only a proper one will do. Cappuccino?'

'Yes please.'

Archie held out the card reader. 'Did you have a good time at the weekend?'

She blushed. 'Yeah. It was great seeing everyone again. You?'

'It was brilliant. And Rob? Did she enjoy herself?'

Kelly's blush started to cool. Archie's pumping had nothing to do with Obie and everything to do with Robyn. 'She had an amazing time. She always has an amazing time when you're around.'

Now it was his turn to blush. 'Did she say that?'

'She doesn't need to, mate.'

He grinned. She'd made his day. Even if Obie wasn't here, some good had come out of her stop-off.

'Take a seat. We'll bring it over.'

Kelly went over to her usual table at the back of the room. Archie had said: 'We'll bring it over.' Perhaps Obie was here.

She pulled her book out. She'd started *A Room with a View* now. As she did with the other books, she was using the postcard that came with it as a bookmark. This one was from 1973, The Spinster Society again. It was from Sam Lord's Beach, Saint Phillip, Barbados. The picture was of a long beach that ended with a cliff in the distance. The sand was silvery white and there were palm trees that looked like they were swaying in the breeze. The sea was bluer than the sky and the waves were rolling in. How incredible to walk along that beach and swim in that sea back in 1973. How incredible to do that now.

She was just wondering whether the ELs would be up for a holiday, like Edie and her spinsters, when she heard a door swing behind her. It was the one that led to the kitchen area. Kelly opened her book and pretended to read. With her head down, she thought she could see Obie's feet pass by. Archie said something but it was too quiet to hear, then the feet were coming towards her. She didn't dare look up until a hand put down a tray with two coffees and a brownie.

'Hi, Kelly.' It was him.

She put the book down. 'You do know my name then?'

He frowned. 'Of course. One cappuccino. Plus one brownie on the house.'

She coughed to clear the quiver that she knew was going to be in her voice. 'You're never gonna get rich if you keep giving your products away.'

He sat down opposite her. 'I know. It's not all about making money though, is it?'

'I dunno. Isn't it? How do you pay your bills if you don't make any money?'

'We're doing okay, and our overheads are low.'

'Really? You must live in a right shithole then.'

'Nah, we're good.' He grinned at her. It was kind of lopsided, like a half-grin, like someone who wasn't sure if he should be happy. It was the most beautiful grin ever.

Kelly opened her mouth to deliver another put-down, but she couldn't think of any. Eventually she managed: 'You should smile more often. It makes you look almost human.' There, that would do.

'Hmm. Coming from you, I guess that's a compliment. Nice picture.' He tapped the postcard.

'It's from 1973. Barbados.'

'Really? Can I have a look?'

'Sure.' She liked that he'd asked first. Most people would have just taken it.

'Nina told us about your old lady's collection. Is it from that?'

'Yeah. Funny thing to talk about.'

He shrugged. 'It can get boring here sometimes. We talk about all sorts of shit then.'

'Cheers, mate.'

He grinned again. He was quite sweet really. She could get to like him.

'Do you mind if I take a photo of it?'

'Go for it. Didn't think it'd be your thing though.'

'It's for my grandparents. They're from Barbados originally.'

'Really? I thought your family was from Nigeria.'

'My dad is. How did you know that?'

'Geraldine told me. It can get boring here sometimes. We talk about all sorts of shit then.'

'Ouch. I left myself wide open for that one, didn't I?'

He had a funny way of speaking. When he said the letter i, he dragged it out. So when he said wide, it sounded like it really was wide instead of a short piddly word. She'd heard people speak a bit like it before – some rappers – but she wasn't sure where they were from. London, most likely. She knew a few people from London through the foodbank. They talked a bit like him in some ways and nothing like him in others. She should ask. 'Where you from?'

'London. Peckham.'

'Do they all talk as funny as you in Peckham, then?'

Obie slapped his chest. 'Wait. You think I talk funny? Oh my days.' He was laughing again.

'All right, London. I get it. We both talk funny.'

'You speak for yourself, Birmingham. I sound just fine.'

Kelly pointed to the coffee counter. 'You're getting busy over there.'

He jumped up. 'Oh shit. I'd better go.'

'Me too. I'm supposed to be helping Will cook dinner tonight.'

'Will? That's the guy you were with on Friday night?'

'Yeah. Well, not with. We're not together or anything. We're just mates. He's got a girlfriend. Belle. Long blonde hair, very pretty. You must have noticed her. She was standing on the other side of him.'

Obie pressed his lips together and frowned, then shook his head. 'I wasn't really looking to the other side of him. But she's his girlfriend? Cool. I'll see you next Wednesday?'

'Yeah, I guess. Although ... we're doing a market in Stirchley on Saturday. We usually go for something to eat after. Maybe I'll suggest your place.'

'Yeah?'

'Yeah.'

'Okay. Good. Well. Might see you on Saturday.'

'Yeah. See ya, London.'

'See ya, Birmingham.'

Kelly watched him go back to the counter. He hadn't even noticed the lovely Belle because he wasn't looking to the other side of Will. He'd been looking at her though. She remembered that because she'd thought he was gloating. Oh! Maybe he wasn't gloating at all. Maybe he was checking her out. Well, well.

43

SWEET REVENGE AND SWEET NOTHINGS

Kelly found a table close to the coffee wagon. Obie held his hand up to let her know he'd seen her and she waved at him.

Geraldine waved too. 'I don't suppose that was meant for me, now you two are best friends.'

Neil glanced over at the wagon. 'Is it the one doing the serving, or the one making the coffee?'

'Neil! You'll make him think there's more to it than there is,' hissed Kelly.

Geraldine rolled her eyes. 'It sounds like there's already plenty to it. It's the one doing the serving, Neil.'

Neil made a really poor attempt to act like he was just looking around the place and not looking at Obie at all. 'Nice.'

'What do you mean, nice? Stop looking at him. You're showing me up.' She didn't know why she was whispering. It wasn't like he could hear her.

'Keep your hair on, Kel. I was talking about the set up here. Shall I get some food?'

'Just get me something you think I'll like, Neil. I trust your judgement,' said Geraldine. She'd been helping out on the stall again today, while Netta was away.

'Me too. Something a bit foreign but not too spicy,' said Kelly.

Neil grinned. 'Not your usual suspect bag of chicken-flavoured crisps then?'

Kelly tutted. 'Fuck off, Neil. You know I eat more than crisps these days.'

He smirked at her. 'Oh yes, I forgot. I expect you'll be getting the coffees, will you?'

'She will. Give him my love,' said Geraldine.

Kelly tutted once again and went off to the wagon.

Obie glanced up as she got closer and treated her to another of his cute grins. 'All right, Birmingham? Two cappuccinos and?'

'An americano please.'

'Please? You feeling okay?'

'Fuck off, London. I'm trying to be polite here.'

'I know, and you were doing really well until you swore at me. How was the market?'

'Good. We always do well when Geraldine helps out. She's our secret weapon. We can only allow her on the stall for so many days a year, in case we decimate the opposition.'

'Wow. She's that potent?'

'Yep. She says hello, by the way.'

'That's nice. I'll come over when it quietens down.'

She reached their table about the same time as Neil. He'd gone safe with a burger and fries for Kelly.

'I said foreign,' she grumbled.

'America's foreign.'

'Oh yeah.'

. . .

Neil had to go after they'd done their post-market debrief. He was giving Geraldine a lift home and offered to drop Kelly back too, but she wasn't ready to leave yet. Obie had been too busy to come over and she didn't want to leave until they'd spoken again. It was pathetic, but the next book group wasn't until Wednesday. That seemed a long way off.

'I can stay if you want me to,' said Geraldine.

'You're all right, Gez. I'll read for a bit, then I'll get the train or walk home.'

'Good idea. I'll just go and say goodbye to the boys.'

Geraldine went up to the coffee wagon and came back with another cappuccino. 'To keep you company. It's quietening down a bit over there now.'

'Cheers. See you both in the morning.' Kelly smiled at the swirly heart on top of the froth and opened her book.

A Room with a View wasn't as hard to read as the others. It made it easy to ignore the noise around her. It was only when she heard a familiar voice that she looked up and saw some people filling up a nearby table. Two of them, she recognised. Once they'd claimed their table, they went to look at the food and drink stalls. They saw her then, Marcus and Poppy. He had his arm around her.

Poppy was facing Kelly. She had the same expression she'd had when she asked Kelly about her school, as if Kelly was some kind of lowlife. She was wearing a pale green tea dress with pretty little flowers. It was too tight for her, but then it wasn't meant for someone of her size.

Marcus sneered at Kelly, the way he did that time he'd made her stand in front of him, naked, while he inspected her like a piece of meat. It had made her feel dirty then.

Now, it made her angry. She put down her book and walked up to them.

'Kelly. Wasn't expecting to see you here.' The creepy sneer was still on his face.

She ignored him and kept her attention on Poppy. 'Nice dress.'

Poppy looked down her nose at her. 'It's vintage.'

'I know. I bought it.'

Poppy shot a look at Marcus. If he was embarrassed, he didn't show it.

This time it was Kelly's turn to sneer. 'If I'd known you were that keen on my clothes, I'd have saved you the dress that Marcus bought for me. Unfortunately, it was so disgusting I had to burn it. Might have been perfect for you though.'

Poppy's mouth clamped shut. Another girl who was with them sniggered. Somebody obviously found it funny. Kelly stayed where she was and stared them out.

Marcus began to look uncomfortable. 'We're just here for a drink.' His voice came out all squeaky. Spineless fucker.

Kelly raised herself up. 'Yeah? Me too.' Then she went back to her seat, picked up her book again, and started to read. She could have walked out but that would have meant they'd won, and she couldn't have that.

Reading was impossible. Obviously. Her eyes may have been following the words on the page, but they weren't taking them in. She just hoped she looked like she was read-ing, and that she didn't look up.

She was working so hard at it that she didn't notice straight away someone had sat next to her. It was the near-ness of him that broke her concentration. The sudden heat of him that brought back the memory of Saturday night. She sensed him there but she couldn't move her eyes off the book.

'Are you okay, Birmingham?'

'Uh huh.'

'Do you want a hug?'

'Yes please.' She was whispering again, but this time it was because it was too hard to speak.

Obie put his arm around her and pulled her into his warm body. She leaned in against him. He pulled her closer. 'Is it okay if I kiss you?'

She nodded.

His mouth touched her forehead and she felt the gentlest, softest of kisses. Kelly looked into his eyes and put her lips on his. Suddenly there was no one else around. It was just her and Obie, and no one else existed.

He was the first to break from the kiss. He smiled at her and then suddenly looked worried. 'Did you mind me kissing you? I wasn't trying to take advantage. I thought you needed a hug, and then it just happened.'

'I think I kissed you.' Kelly was worried too, although probably not for the same reasons.

'I kissed you first.' He looked so serious and loveable, she could have kissed him again.

'Technically. But that was only a pity kiss 'cos you felt sorry for me.'

His mouth dropped open. 'It was not a pity kiss. Maybe the hug was technically a pity hug, but the kiss was definitely not.'

'Oh really?'

'Yes really. You are very annoying, you know. I've wanted to kiss you for a while actually.'

'Why?'

'Isn't it obvious?'

'No.'

'Because I like you. No idea why, because you're always taking the piss out of me or swearing at me. But if I've gone too far and you don't like me in the same way – thinking about it, I'm not sure if you like me at all – but if I've gone too far, then I'm sorry.'

'Obie, shut up. I like you, okay? I like you in that way.'

'You do?'

'Yes, you clown. Listen though, I might not seem it but I'm like a delicate flower at the moment. I can't be with anyone who treats me badly. You get that, don't you?'

'I get that, and I'm not that kind of man.'

'Good. Because if you did... Well, let's not go there.'

'Fair enough. I guess I'd better get back to work. Looks like those two have gone now anyway.'

She turned to where Marcus and his friends had been sitting. 'Oh yeah. When did they go?'

'No idea. I've been busy.'

'Funny. I'll go and leave you to work.'

They stood up at the same time.

'I'll see you soon then?' said Kelly.

He pushed his hands into his pockets. 'Yeah. About that. Do you wanna go out sometime?'

Something did a tap dance straight across Kelly's heart. She was a bit woozy. 'Okay. When?'

'Tomorrow?'

Kelly skipped all the way to the station. That's what it felt like anyway. She now understood what walking on air actually meant. Obie had kissed her again before she left. Tomorrow, they were going on a date. She had a new man in her life, and this time it would be different. She was absolutely certain of it. Never mind walking on air, she was flying. Nothing could touch her now.

She was almost there when she heard her name being called. She turned around and saw Marcus running after her. Fucking Marcus, spoiling her happy moment. She carried on walking but he caught up with her and grabbed her arm.

She spun around, ready to hit out. 'What?'

He took a step backwards and put his hands up. 'Whoa! I just wanted to apologise for those things I said, that's all. I was drunk and stoned. I didn't know what I was saying.'

Ah, the old drunk and stoned excuse. Kelly had heard it so many times before from Craig. 'Yeah you did. Just do me a favour and fuck off, Marcus. I'm not interested.'

He winced. 'I thought you and me had something special. The things we did. The sex. You enjoyed it as much as I did. It was amazing, wasn't it?'

His cherry lips curled upwards into a smile. He was gorgeous and charming. And full of shite. 'Nah. There was nothing special about you and me. We were just two people who went out for a while. That's all. And that amazing sex didn't happen. It was just plain old sex, and it wasn't even good. One more thing. If you think me going down on you, or us trying out a few different positions is kinky or dirty, then there's something seriously wrong with you. I'd recommend therapy.'

'I didn't give her that dress,' he blurted out. He sounded feeble and whiny. Perhaps he'd always sounded like that.

'One final take-away point for you, Marcus. That

howling thing you do when you're coming. That actually isn't normal. It's ridiculous. Get help.'

Kelly didn't look back until she reached the station steps. Marcus was still in the same spot but he wasn't looking at her. He was looking at the ground. Searching for his lost ego maybe.

44

THE LIZA CAMPAIGN PAYS OFF

'Oh my God! Kelly's going on a date with Obie.' Liza looked up from her phone, her eyes nearly popping out of her head.

Netta unlocked the door to the flat they were staying in. 'Obie? Didn't she say she didn't like him?'

'She did, but you should have seen them dancing on Saturday night. So hot. I've gotta call Jade.' She went straight to her bedroom, presumably for some serious Face-Time action.

Netta flopped down on the sofa. After a full day of doing touristy stuff, she was done in. She'd booked this trip to London so they could have some time together before Liza went to Italy. It was part of her 'getting to know her daughter better' strategy. Her Liza campaign.

They'd never been away together, just the two of them. The curse of Liza being the youngest child, she supposed. Netta hadn't known how it was going to go and had been more than a little worried they might not have enough to say to each other. She needn't have been. Frank's advice about giving Liza space in her busy schedule had worked. That week, they'd talked about all sorts of things. The art they saw, fashion, climate change, family history. All sorts. Except friends. They'd hardly touched on that subject. Liza had dropped a few names here and there, but it wasn't enough to satisfy Netta that her daughter was okay.

Tonight was their last night. They were eating out at a French restaurant. A good one with awards. She was pulling out all the stops to get Liza in the mood for talking. The only thing that might knock her plan off whack was this latest news about Kelly. Liza might be too full of that to discuss her other friendships. And who could blame her? It was rather surprising news. Or was it? When she'd seen Kelly watching the ELs with Obie last Friday night, she'd wondered if there was more to it, but she'd dismissed it because of that thing going on with Will. Unless she really had imagined the thing with Will. No, she couldn't have. Or rather, her mum couldn't have. Netta could quite easily have misread the situation, but her mum? Never. And then there was Belle. Her behaviour that night had been very different. Normally she was quite passive but there'd been a couple of glimpses of a different side to her that night. It was all extremely perplexing.

The restaurant was quite intimate and a little overpriced. She'd chosen the second cheapest bottle of wine, which still cost the earth, and they were now eating their expensive starters.

'So, I spoke to Kelly after Jade. She'll give us the full deets tomorrow, but she saw Marcus today. And – newsflash – that Poppy was with him, and she was wearing the missing dress. Newsflash number two, Kelly totally roasted the pair of them.' Liza put her cutlery down with a satisfied flourish.

'Oh I wish I could have been there. I'd have loved to have seen that cretin taken down a peg or two.'

'And me. I guess my Photoshop skills won't be needed after all. He was a real creep though, wasn't he? With men like him and Dad, you wonder if there are any decent ones around these days.'

'There are plenty of decent men, darling. Look at Grandad and Frank.'

'Both old.'

Netta considered pointing out Frank was only a few years older than Colin so she was hardly comparing apples with pears, but it wasn't worth the effort. 'Will, then.'

Liza waved her away dismissively. 'Brother. Anyway I wonder about him sometimes. He's not the golden boy you think he is.'

'What do you mean?'

'The way he treats Belle sometimes. It's a bit question-able. Don't tell me you haven't noticed. Honestly, Mum, do you go around with your eyes shut?'

Netta was mildly hurt but overwhelmingly curious. 'Clearly I do. You'd better enlighten me.'

'Have you never noticed how he always puts Kelly before Belle? You know that weekend we went to Sheffield, when he came back to see her? It was a special anniversary for him and Belle. They were supposed to be going some-where. She had it all booked and everything, but he made her cancel it.'

'How do you know this?'

'I heard them arguing about it. I think Belle's really fed up with him. Can't say I blame her.'

'Ah, now that I have noticed. I suppose Will was worried

about Kelly. After the last time.'

'Maybe. But I told him we had it under control. He could have left it another week, if he really cared about Belle, but he chose Kelly. Don't tell Kelly will you? She doesn't know.'

Netta wanted to ask if Liza knew how Kelly felt about Will, but she didn't want to put ideas in Liza's head. Besides, this wasn't supposed to be about Kelly. Or Will either, for that matter. 'I don't think Will's a golden boy. He's–'

Before she could say another word, a waiter swooped in to clear the plates. Netta paused and smiled politely. She waited for him to move away then opened her mouth to speak again, but someone else swooped in with an amuse bouche that had to be introduced. By the time all that was finished, she couldn't remember what she was going to say about her alleged golden boy. She tried a different tack: 'I know there have been a couple of exceptions, but most men are decent. You mustn't let them put you off.'

'I don't. I just tell them up front I won't take any shit from them. If it scares them off, they're obviously not worth it.'

'Very true. Are you seeing anyone at the moment?' That was clumsy. Not quite how she'd wanted to ask.

Liza licked the last of her amuse bouche off her spoon. 'Has Dad said something to you?'

'No. Maybe. Actually, yes.'

'Mum. You really shouldn't let him get to you. He wins every time you do. Are you eating that?'

Netta handed over her amuse bouche. 'I know, I'm sorry. It's just that it made me realise I don't know enough about you.'

Liza let out a world-weary sigh. 'Okay. What do you want to know?'

'Who your friends are. What you do with them. Do you have someone special? That kind of thing.'

'That's very mumsy of you.' There was an ever-so-slightly sarcastic twinkle in Liza's eye.

'Well I am your mum.'

'Did Madame not care for the amuse bouche?' The waiter was back again. This was getting tedious.

Liza pulled a face. 'She's amusing enough already.'

'I'm saving myself for my main course,' said Netta.

The waiter tipped his head curtly. They started sniggering the minute his back was turned.

Liza leaned in a little. 'In answer to your many questions, I'm not seeing anyone at the moment. No one serious anyway. I like men, in case you were wondering. You already know my two besties, Jade and Kelly. I've got other friends at uni who I go out with sometimes. I go to climate change workshops and rallies with some of them, and I have other friends that I know through my action groups. Is that enough?'

'Yes. For now anyway.'

'Is that what this week's been about then?'

'Yes. Although I feel a bit silly admitting it. We've had fun though, haven't we?'

Liza picked up the wine bottle and topped up their glasses before the waiter could do it. 'Mum, it's been the best. You really need to stop tearing yourself apart over me though. I'm fine.'

'I'll try. About Will. He's not my golden boy. I love you both equally.'

Liza's eyes rolled a touch dramatically. 'I know you do. Don't get me wrong, I love Will. He just needs to sort himself out. Maybe if things work out with Kelly and Obie, it'll make him wake up.'

45

SOMETHING WAS HAPPENING

Kelly's phone said it was a minute away from six o'clock. He was going to be late. Crap. At least it was a nice day and there was plenty going on around her. People were hanging around on Pigeon Park's benches and grass. The sound of hymn singing leaked out from the cathedral and mingled with a nearby drum and bass beat and the general people noises. She sat on a bench and tried to look like she wasn't that bothered.

The park was a graveyard really, not a park at all. Geraldine told her people came here to hang out when she was young, though it wasn't known as Pigeon Park then. But Netta said it was called that when she was a teenager. It was funny to think of all those generations of young people coming here for the same reason. And now she was here. Not chilling with friends, but waiting for Obie.

It was after six now. He was definitely late. Unless he wasn't coming. That was a strong possibility, being as he hadn't messaged her to say he was on his way. He hadn't messaged at all, even though she'd given him her number. They'd made the arrangements before she left him yesterday. He might have forgotten. Or he might have been playing a joke on her. A big, spiteful joke. Bastard. Right, that was it. Two more minutes and she was going home.

Two minutes passed more slowly than she was expecting, but the time was finally up. He definitely wasn't coming. Kelly got up to leave. Then she saw him on the other side of the railings, out of breath and holding onto his side. She tapped out a message:

'*Been running the marathon?*'

Obie took his phone out and looked at it, then scanned the area until he saw her. He put his arms up in the air and walked over to her, looking shamed. 'Sorry. The traffic was terrible, man. I had to get off the bus at Digbeth and run the rest of the way.'

'You could have just messaged me. That's why we modern people have phones these days.'

'I know, I know. I thought I could make it. I am so out of condition. Can we just pretend I got here on time and start again?'

'Go on then.'

Obie kissed her on the cheek. 'Hello, Kelly. You look nice.'

Kelly's eyebrows shot up. 'Is that the best you can do?'

'Give me a chance. I'm just warming up.' He did that funny little lop-sided grin again. It was quite sexy, in a sweet kind of way.

'I'd say you were warm enough already, Mr Sweaty. Where are we going?'

He wiped his forehead with his sleeve. 'Perhaps we should go see a movie. That way I get to sit with you for a couple of hours without having to endure your insults.'

'What's on?'

'Dunno.'

This was nothing like her first date with Marcus. He'd had everything planned. Kelly liked that it was the complete opposite. 'You're not very good at this, are you?'

'No. Shall we just start with a walk and see where we go from there?'

'Yeah, why not? I'll try not to insult you too much.'

'Sounds good.'

He took her hand and did that cute grin again, and Kelly felt like she could walk for hours, as long as it was with him.

They strolled along Colmore Row and through to Broad Street where they got onto the canal towpath and followed it down to the university. Even though she didn't live far away from it, Kelly had never been there before. Obie gave her a tour and pointed out the buildings, explaining what they were. It was different to the one she'd seen in Sheffield. More like how she imagined a university would be.

For a one-time miserable fucker, Obie Kalu was a good talker. That was his surname, and yes, it was Nigerian. He told her how he and Archie had met on their course and discovered they both loved old-school music. That explained the Night Owl then. They became best mates and when Covid happened, they ended up moving into Archie's grandad's house.

'Did his grandad die?' said Kelly.

'No, he's alive and well. He lives with Archie's mum and dad. It was only supposed to be while the pandemic was on, so they could make sure he was okay, but it's become permanent. Archie and me look after the house for him. It's rent free, so it's a bonus for us. We can afford to give brownies away to our favourite customers without worrying about the money. He'll sell it eventually, I suppose.'

From the university they returned to the canal and headed back into town, then out again, ending up at a pub in the Jewellery Quarter. Kelly asked him about London. He was shocked she'd never been there and said there was nowhere else like it. It sounded like he missed it and she couldn't help wondering why he was still in Birmingham. 'So when did you leave university?'

'2019.'

'How come you stayed here and didn't go back to London?'

'It's complicated.'

He obviously didn't want to talk about it, so Kelly changed the subject: 'What was your degree in?'

'Medicine.'

'Medicine? So you're a doctor?' A doctor who sells coffee, she thought.

'No. I was a medical student, but I dropped out and the end of my third year. So did Archie.'

'I didn't know you could do that.'

'You can, but it doesn't go down well.'

'I guess not. So you're a couple of med-school dropouts. Like Frenchie, in Grease. Only she was a beauty-school dropout.'

'That's us. You like that film?'

'Yeah. Me and Liza watched it so many times in lockdown. Is that why you sell coffee now?'

'Yeah. That was thanks to Archie's grandad as well. It used to be his food wagon. He moved on to a café, but he kept the wagon for old times' sake. We did it up and scraped together enough money to buy the equipment. What about you and the jam business?'

'Ah well that's a long story of bad things happening, until I met someone who showed me what a proper friend was.'

'Robyn?'

She shook her head. 'Netta. She was the first. Robyn and the other good things came later.'

When it was time to catch the last train home, he stayed with her until it came. The barriers were up, so he was able to come down to the platform until the last minute. She didn't want to go. She could have easily gone back to Pigeon Park and stayed there all night with him, amongst the stoners and the homeless people.

She stood just inside the open doors while he stayed just outside of them on the edge of the platform. The doors closed when the whistle blew. Kelly put her hand on the window. Obie put his on the other side so that only the glass separated them. The train chugged into life. He took his hand away and it began to roll towards the tunnel.

When she came out of the tunnel, a message pinged on her phone:

'Forgot to say, I don't work Monday nights. Want to meet tomorrow?'

She tapped out a reply before he had a chance to change his mind:

'Yes please. That's me being polite btw.'

He beeped back with a time and place. A second later, another message came through.

'I had a great time tonight. See you tomorrow x'

Oh God, he'd put a kiss on the end. She was tingling. She was dizzy. She was… What? Something was happening to her, and she had no idea what it was.

46

ARTHUR THREE'S IMPORTANT MISSION

'I'm going to see Nina. I'll let you get the coffees.' Geraldine was on the way to Nina's counter before Kelly could argue otherwise. Not that she was going to argue. Even though she'd seen Obie on Monday, the anticipation of seeing him at book group had been building up all day. Right now, she was on max exploding point.

He was making a drink and had his back to her. She slowed down so she could time her arrival to happen just as he turned to the counter. It worked. He did it at the exact same moment she reached him.

He smiled. 'Hi.'

'Hi.' Her insides burst into flames again.

'Two cappuccinos?'

'Uh huh.' Cappuccino. One of the loveliest words in the dictionary. Was it even in the dictionary? Whatever. It was now. She was vaguely aware of Archie aiming a card reader at her. She waved her card at it without taking her eyes off Obie.

He leaned over the counter until they were nearly close enough to kiss. 'Shall I bring it over to you?'

'No, I'll wait.' Any excuse to stand and watch him.

'I'll make it now then, shall I?'

'Uh huh.'

When he finished, he put the cups down in front of her. One of them had a leaf shaped into the froth and the other, a heart.

Kelly pointed to the heart. 'Is that one mine?'

'Uh huh. This too.' He put two brownies on plates. 'You like the chocolate orange ones, yeah?' Oh Jesus. He was so fucking adorable.

'To think you go on about me and Arthur being all lovey-dovey,' said Geraldine.

'Okay, Gez. I know I've gone a bit crazy but I can't help it. I've lost control. You don't think he can tell, do you?'

'I wouldn't worry about that, sweetheart. Look at him. He's no better. I don't think I've heard him singing before.'

Obie was singing along to the background music. He copped Kelly watching him and his face lit up. She so wanted to throw her arms around him and kiss every inch of him. It was mental. Absolutely mental. 'I'm gonna have to move so I can't see him, otherwise I won't be able to concentrate.'

Zoe arrived. They'd been for a drink yesterday, for the first time. They'd mostly talked about books, and Obie. Kelly couldn't keep her mouth shut when it came to him these days.

She sat next to Kelly. 'Obie's looking happy.'

'Isn't he though?' Kelly couldn't believe she once thought he was the most miserable man on the planet.

· · ·

When they went around the group this time, they were asked to talk about a book they'd struggled with. Kelly told them about *Villette*. 'I loved the book and I could really identify with Lucy Snowe. I wanted her so much to be happy, but the ending was a massive disappointment. I didn't know whether the man she loved had lived or died. It's like she says he might have died, but if you want a happy ending then let's say he didn't. It really messed me up. I couldn't get it out of my head.'

'Isn't that the sign of a good book? Not being able to get it out of your head,' said Max.

Nina nodded in agreement. 'I think Max is right. It can be good to have your perceptions challenged. Life isn't always that clear cut, is it?'

Kelly wasn't buying it. 'I think being dead or alive is pretty clear cut.'

'Maybe it's not such a bad thing to allow you to choose your own ending, rather than having it handed to you on a plate,' said Geraldine.

'I hadn't thought of it like that,' said Kelly. 'I guess it could be a good thing to decide whether you want a happy ending or a real life one.'

'They can be both at the same time,' said Geraldine. 'The two aren't mutually exclusive.'

Weren't they?

Kelly rushed back home after the market on Saturday. Obie was coming over straight from The Factory but could only stay a couple of hours because he was going back to work. This time at a restaurant in Moseley. Was that three jobs he had? He seemed to work a lot. Especially for someone with low overheads.

The house was empty, as she'd known it would be. Will and Belle were away with their university friends, and Liza and Netta had gone out with Geraldine. It was a perfect time for Obie to meet Maud and Betty properly. She'd invited him over for that reason. It was important to her that he liked her four-legged friends and they liked him.

While she was waiting, she took the opportunity to give Betty a pep talk which basically consisted of telling her she'd better behave herself if she didn't want her biscuit rations cut.

Obie messaged to say he was on the platform at Bournville station. She flew out the door to meet him. Betty looked disappointed not to be going with her, but Kelly was worried it would make her too hyper which would freak him out. She'd take Betty out later.

She got to Selly Oak station at the same time as the train. He met her on the stairs and held out his hand. 'Hello, Birmingham.'

She took it and pulled him closer. 'All right, London.'

On the way back to the house, she pointed out the obvious landmarks to him. The name of the pub they sometimes went to, the best fish and chip shop, the Chinese supermarkets. She couldn't believe what an idiot she sounded. She'd gone all gushy, and it was phenomenal.

'*Phenomenal: Remarkable or exceptional. In particular, exceptionally good.*'

Kelly opened the front door. 'Don't let Betty's size put you off. She's actually really gentle.'

Obie followed her in. 'I'm not scared of dogs. I just haven't had much to do with them. We didn't have pets at home, and it was just a bad time when I came here before. I had stuff going on.'

'Like what?'

He shoved his hands into his back pockets. 'It doesn't matter. It's over now.'

'A girlfriend?'

'No, nothing like that. Family stuff.'

Betty trotted into the hall and he froze. Kelly tried not to smirk. *Not scared, my arse.* Betty stood in front of them and pushed her soft, damp nose into Kelly's hand. Kelly knelt down and let the dog lick her face.

'That's not very hygienic you know,' he said.

'Yeah all right, med-school dropout. Do I look like I care?'

Obie laughed. 'Ooh nasty.' He touched Betty's back and whipped his hand away, nearly as quickly. 'See. Not scared at all.'

Betty licked his hand. He looked completely grossed out. Kelly could tell what he was thinking. 'Don't you dare wash your hands.'

'But it's all drooly and everything.'

'She's telling you she likes you. I swear, if you go and wash your hands now, that's you and me done.'

'Bit harsh. Okay, I won't but I will have to scrub them clean before I go to work though?'

They went into the living room. Maud was snoozing in her chair.

Kelly crouched down in front her. 'Hello, Maudie. I've brought a friend to meet you again. But this time, he's going to be a good boy and not squeal like a baby if you go near him. Can you keep an eye on him while I get him a beer?'

Obie followed her towards the hall. 'As I've already said, there were extenuating circumstances.'

Kelly pointed to the sofa. 'Sit.'

Obie and Betty both sat down at exactly the same time.

Him on the sofa. Her on the floor next to the sofa. Satisfied, Kelly went into the kitchen.

When she came back she found Obie still in the same place. Betty and Maud had moved though. Betty was on the sofa, next to Obie, and Maud was on his lap. He was being love-bombed by his worst nightmare.

'The little one jumped on me, and then the other one did the same.' He looked and sounded a bit panicky.

'They must really like you. Maud never sits on just anybody's lap. You have to be pretty special to get attention from her.'

'I don't feel that special. I'm feeling a bit hemmed in, if I'm honest.'

It was strange. Maud had only seen Obie twice and both times, she'd attached herself to him. She only did that with a certain kind of person. Her nan used to call them lost souls. Maud had been there for Kelly when her soul had been lost. Maud was always there, even if Kelly didn't need her as much these days. Obie though. She didn't have him down as a lost soul. Although there was that thing Archie had said about him being troubled.

Kelly sat on Maud's armchair. 'She must think you need some love. Just relax and go with it. You'll be okay.'

'Fine.' He sounded irritated, but he did loosen up and let his back sink into the cushions. Maud snuggled in closer and his shoulders dropped. Whatever it was Maud was up to, it seemed to be working. She lay her head against his chest and let out a little groan, and a miracle happened. A tear escaped from Obie's eye and ran down his cheek.

He wiped it away, but another one came, and then another. He sniffed. 'Bollocks.'

Kelly moved to the sofa and put her arms around him. 'Maud knows. She always knows.'

He wiped his eyes with the back of his hand. 'What does she know?'

'She knows when you need her.'

'Shit. This is mad.'

'Do you want to talk about it?'

He shook his head, so Kelly just held him. It was heart-breaking, listening to him trying to force back the tears. It was pretty wonderful too, in a strange way. She'd never felt as close to anyone as she did with him, right now. And something else, she was beginning to feel strong. Like there was nothing she couldn't face. Was it just being with Obie that did this to her, or was it a combination of everything coming together at once?

The time for him to go came too quick. He'd stopped crying and the dogs had moved off the sofa so that Kelly could sit with him. They'd sat for an hour, holding hands and hardly speaking. Then he said he had to go to work.

While he was in the bathroom, Kelly went up to her room to get something. She met him on the landing.

'Sorry about all of that. I don't know what happened,' he said.

'You don't need to apologise. Here. This is for you to borrow.'

'It's a teddy bear.'

'His name's Arthur Three. When my nan died, his predecessor really helped me. When you get home tonight, go somewhere private. Hold onto him and think about the things upsetting you. It'll help. Trust me.'

'Kelly, I'm a grown man.'

She kissed him. 'I know. Try it though. I won't tell anyone.'

He sighed. 'Okay, but I want you to know I'm only doing this for you.'

Late that night, the ping of Kelly's phone woke her. She stuck her head out from under the duvet and saw a message from Obie. Two words:

'It worked.'

Kelly smiled. She reached for Arthur Three and then remembered he was on an important mission. She'd have to make do with her pillow. She pushed her face into it and imagined it was Obie.

47

OBIE, MAN OF MANY SURPRISES

Kelly screwed her eyes up. 'The Staffordshire what?'

Obie checked the information board again. 'Hoard.'

'Hoard? Right. Only I thought you said whore. I wouldn't have come if I'd known it was just a load of old manky jewellery.'

He stuck his hands in his pockets and frowned. Then the right-hand corner of his mouth turned up. It was the grin that made her face crack.

He shook his head. 'Hilarious.'

'I thought so.'

'So you don't hate it here then?'

Kelly put her arm around his waist and kissed him. 'I love it. It was a great idea.'

'It was Geraldine's. She said you'd like it.'

She might have known. Bloody Gez, trying to educate her again. She was right though. Who'd have thought looking at Anglo-Saxon relics would be interesting.

As far as Kelly could remember, she hadn't been to the Birmingham Museum and Art Gallery before. It wasn't the sort of place her mum and dad went to. It was actually pretty cool. When they'd arrived, she and Obie had walked up the big white staircase into a round room that just blew her away. She couldn't believe that people were wandering through it without stopping to look at the beautiful glass roof and the paintings that filled the walls. True, some of them were a bit boring – fields and trees, or a boat on the sea – but some of them were fucking incredible.

They left the Staffordshire Hoard and wandered through the other exhibitions. She especially liked the Pre-Raphaelite paintings. The women in them made her think of Robyn. She had that same look about her.

When they got back to the round room, Kelly was pulled into a painting of a man and woman sitting on a boat. There was a baby under the woman's shawl. You could just about see its head. The couple were staring straight ahead, like they were concentrating on watching something. It was called *The Last of England*.

'I guess my grandparents were like that when they left Barbados. Must have been frightening leaving everything behind,' said Obie.

'Exciting as well. I think my mum would have been excited to leave Ireland.'

They moved on to look at another painting. A young woman, sitting by a sea wall with her head in her hands was being comforted by an old woman. *Never Morning Wore to Evening but Some Heart Did Break*. Kelly read the title out and repeated it a couple times to get her head around it. There was something about it that broke her own heart.

Obie put his arm around her. 'Are you okay?'

She nodded. 'It's just so sad.'

'I know. It makes me want to cry as well.'

He wiped her cheek and then she understood how he knew. She sniffed. 'We are so soft.'

He hugged her. 'That's a good thing.'

Kelly wrapped her arms around him. Not in her experience. In her experience softness only brought trouble and pain.

Obie let her go. 'Wait here. I'll be back in five.'

He was probably longer than five, but she didn't mind. She liked being on her own in this room with her thoughts. That last painting had triggered another memory of her mum, not long before she died: 'You'll have to be the strong one when I'm gone, gorgeous girl. Your dad's too soft.' That was a hell of a burden to put on a twelve-year-old kid.

Obie came back with a small bag for her. 'Present.'

She looked inside and found two postcards of the pictures they'd been looking at. 'Aww, they're beautiful. Thank you.'

He shrugged. 'I was looking for posters but they only have cards.'

'Cards are perfect.' She could add them to her collection. When she got home she'd write on the back, the way Edie did. She'd done that on her Edinburgh card now and she already knew what she was going to put on this one:

'Birmingham, 2022 – With Obie, man of many surprises.'

They left the museum and sat on the steps of Chamberlain Square. Obie leaned back and soaked up the sun. 'Do you want to come to mine tomorrow for dinner? It'll be just you and me. Archie's going to Edinburgh.'

Robyn had already told her about Archie's trip. He'd asked if he could go up for a 'talk' apparently.

'I didn't ask you because he's away though. I'd like to cook for you, that's all. I'm not expecting anything in return. I don't want you to think–'

'Okay, I get it. I would love to come.' She put on her sunglasses, hoping to hide her disappointment.

. . .

Kelly checked the directions on her phone and took a left into Obie's road. Nearly there. Her heart was thumping and her mouth was dry. She could easily have drunk the bottle of wine she was carrying and still been thirsty. She'd been seeing Obie for almost a month now, but this was the first time she'd been to his house and she was nervous.

It wasn't going to the house that was doing her nerves in. It was what it meant and also, what might happen while she was there. He'd said he wanted to cook for her. That was a new experience. When she'd lived with Craig, they'd existed on microwave meals and takeaways, and Marcus had never given the impression he wanted to do anything other than shag her. Talking of which, Obie hadn't made any moves in that direction yet. That was another reason why her insides were pumping. What was going to happen after they'd eaten? Or even before, if he was anything like Marcus? God, she hoped he didn't howl.

So maybe she had been a bit disappointed that he didn't mention sex when he invited her. But that was only because she wasn't sure he actually fancied her, and she really wanted him to fancy her. Another part of her didn't really want sex, because what if it was shit? What if it was as crap as it had been with Marcus? What if sex with Craig was as good as it would ever get? That was depressing, because it had only ever been slightly better than shit with Craig. Netta had told her once that she'd probably enjoy it more if she had an attentive lover. She hoped that was Obie, because there was nothing more likely to put her off a man than bad sex. And howling.

She thought about Will and that time she'd heard him and Belle doing it on the sofa. Belle had sounded like she'd been enjoying it. Unless she was faking it. She didn't sound like she was faking it though, so if she was, she was a lot better at it than Kelly. No. Will was probably a really attentive lover. Lucky Belle. Lucky, lucky Belle.

She reached Obie's front door. It was a terraced house, like Neil and Chris's. In fact it wasn't that far away from where they lived. She rang the bell and ignored images of Will loving her attentively. He belonged to someone else and she was with Obie now.

Obie opened the door. 'Hello, Birmingham.' His skin was gleaming. It must have been the heat from the kitchen. She could smell the cooking on him when he kissed her.

They went down the narrow hall to the kitchen at the back of the house. 'I brought red wine. It's French,' she said.

He looked at the label. 'Cool. It's a good one.'

'Netta and Frank's favourite. Do you know about wine then?'

'I'm learning. Ready for when we open our restaurant.'

'You and Archie?'

He already had a bottle open and poured out two glasses from it. 'That's the plan. Long term anyway. Other things to do first.'

'Like what?'

'I have debts to pay off.'

'Student loans, you mean?'

He shook his head. 'Not exactly. I'm trying to make enough to pay my parents back the money they invested in me.'

Invested seemed like a funny word to use when you were talking about your parents, unless they were bunging you a few quid to help you start a business, but she didn't think that was what he meant. 'Because you dropped out?'

'Uh huh. Food's ready.' He put bowls of food out on a candle-lit table. It looked and smelled scarily spicy.

Obie caught Kelly biting her lip. 'What?'

'I should have said, I'm not very adventurous with food.'

'I know. Geraldine told me. I've toned the spice down for you.'

'Is there anything else Geraldine's told you about me that I should know?'

'Not that I can remember. Try the plantain.' He put some kind of vegetable on her plate that looked nothing like any she'd tried before.

She had a wary nibble. 'That's nice. What did you say it was?'

'Plantain. It's related to the banana.'

'No way.'

Obie laughed. 'Girl, you've got a lot to learn.'

Kelly lay on her back on the floor in the living room. Her stomach was hurting.

Obie came in with more wine and sat down next to her. 'Feeling any better?'

'I think so. I don't normally eat that much. It's your fault. You're too good a cook.'

He lay down on his back. 'Glad you think so. Anyway, a few big meals will do you good. Speaking as a med-school dropout, a couple of extra pounds wouldn't kill you.'

'You think I'm too thin?'

He rolled onto his side to face her. 'Nah. I think you're perfect.'

Kelly sat up. If anybody was perfect it was him. She kissed him and put her hand on the bulge in his pants.

He put his hand over hers. 'Are you sure? I don't want to rush, after–'

'Yes.' She lay back and put his hand on her boobs. It had to happen sooner or later. Better that it was now, in a nice house, when they were alone.

Obie kissed her. It was gentle and tender. That was a good start. She undid his shirt buttons. Please, she thought, don't let this be another bad sex day.

48

THE ENIGMA AND THE WALRUS OF LOVE

Oh my God that was good sex. Netta had been right all along. All it took was an attentive lover. So this is what she'd been missing out on?

Kelly pulled the duvet up around her. The bed felt empty without Obie, but he'd be back in a minute. He'd only gone downstairs to make tea because they'd been so dry after all that wine. While she waited, she cast her eyes around the room to see what else she could find out about him. In the last month, as she'd got to know him better, Kelly had told him plenty about her life. She'd opened up about her mum and dad, her problems growing up, her nan dying, and her inheritance. She'd even told him about wanting to educate herself and her new found love of books. She'd given him the headlines on Craig and Marcus too, but not the full deets. She'd wasted too much time on them already.

Obie had talked a lot too, but not about his family or his life before he came to Birmingham, and he still hadn't explained that afternoon when Maud got him crying. Geraldine said he was an enigma.

'Enigma: A mysterious or puzzling person or thing'

Kelly had looked it up and decided Gez was quite correct. Obie was definitely an enigma.

The room was quite tidy. There was some old furniture that probably belonged to Archie's grandad and a newish desk with a laptop on it. Next to it was one of those retro stereos and a pile of vinyls. There was another one downstairs that was proper old, not fake old, along with more vinyls. That might have been Archie's grandad's as well.

Arthur Three was sitting on top of a chest of drawers. She was glad Obie hadn't hidden him away somewhere. Next to Arthur three were two framed photos. One of Obie, a bit younger than he was now, with a middle-aged couple. Probably his parents. The other was of him with a really attractive girl. Kelly hoped she was his sister.

Obie came in with the tea. Except for a pair of boxers, he was naked. He had a nice body. Kind of strong, but not too muscly. She liked that he had a little belly that overlapped the top of his pants slightly. It showed he wasn't one of those blokes who obsessed over themselves. She nodded at the photos. 'Is that your Mum and Dad?'

He climbed back into bed. 'Yeah. It was taken when I started uni.'

'What about the other one?'

'That's me with my sister, Gini.'

That was a relief. 'You must be really close to keep photos of them like that.'

He gave her a funny look. 'We were. Not now though.'

'Were they upset about you dropping out?'

'My dad was. He won't speak to me.'

'Shit, that's a bit heavy.'

'Yeah well, that's my dad. That first time I went to your house, he'd just had a heart attack and he refused to see me.'

So that was his extenuating circumstances. No wonder Archie had said he was troubled. And she'd been a real bitch to him. Fuck, fuck, fuckity fuck. She was riding the guilt train now.

'I can see his point though,' said Obie. 'Everyone else in my family works in medicine. He's a gynaecologist. Mum's a midwife. Gini's a doctor. I'm the only one that couldn't hack it. I let them down. But I've got a plan to make things better. If I can save enough to pay them back, he might forgive me.'

'That's why you've got so many jobs. I get it now. But won't it be years before you make enough to pay them back?'

'Probably, but it's something I have to do.'

Kelly sipped on her tea. She didn't want to say it was an impossible task or that it was going to dictate his life for years. There was no need. He probably already knew that. 'You can always talk to me about it, you know. I do understand.'

'I know. I'm not great at sharing stuff. At least I've got my boy Arthur Three to talk to though. He's a very good listener.'

'He is. Well if you don't want to talk, we could always do something else.' She slid her hand into his boxers. Jesus, what had come over her? She was actually asking for sex now.

Obie lifted her hand back out. 'I don't want it to be a pity shag.'

'Fuck off. For one I don't do pity shags. For another, I don't pity you. Plus, I am having trouble keeping my hands off you.'

'Oh. That's good. So you want my body, eh?'

Kelly giggled. 'Get over yourself, Obiefune. You're not

that hot. Lucky for you, I happen to like a man with a less than perfect body. Also, you are pretty good at it. You're a very attentive lover.'

'Say again?'

'An attentive lover. Don't let it go to your head or anything though.'

Obie shook his head. 'Nuh uh. I'll tell you what I am. I am the Walrus of Love.'

'The what?'

'Wait, don't tell me you've never heard of Barry White, the actual honest to God, Walrus of Love?'

'Nope, sorry.'

He jumped out of bed and picked a record out from the stack of vinyls. 'My grandma got me into him. She's a major fan.'

He put the record on the turntable and a big, booming voice started singing about not getting enough of someone's love. Obie started to dance. He was properly smiling now. He held out his arms for her.

A memory of Marcus making her stand in the middle of the room while he assessed her flashed across Kelly's mind. 'No, I've got no clothes on.'

'So what? Neither have I.'

'You've got your pants on.'

He took his pants off and threw them at her. 'Not anymore.'

Kelly squealed and put her hands over her eyes. When she peeked out between her fingers, she saw him dancing around the room, his butt gyrating, his bits dangling. He was funny, joyful and unbelievably sexy. She watched him, until she couldn't resist his call. She danced in his arms to the Walrus of Love, and she wasn't even the tiniest bit shamed.

· · ·

Aside from popping home a few times, Kelly stayed at Obie's for the rest of that week. He'd cooked all the meals except one. The only time she'd cooked, he'd eaten her pasta and complimented her on it, even though it was crap compared to his cooking. It was another thing she liked about him.

It was their last night before Archie returned. She'd be able to come and stay anytime she wanted, but it wouldn't be the same as this week. This week they'd been like a proper couple. She hadn't realised how being with someone special could make the most simple things seem cool. Even cooking food together was amazing.

Obie had become less of an enigma this week. He'd said more about his life in London, and how he'd come to realise he couldn't be a doctor. It sounded to her like his dad was a bit controlling, but she didn't think Obie could see that. She wasn't going to point it out though. You had to realise these things yourself.

Tonight she was sharing again. She laid out her postcard collection on the floor. The latest was from Liza and Jade, in Italy. She added the photo of her mum on that beach. Her dad told her it was taken in Thailand. Obie arranged them into the different continents. Most were in Europe, but there were some others from different parts of the world.

'It must have been quite something to travel so far and wide in Edie's time,' he said.

'Yeah. She was a pioneer really. She lost so many of the people she loved but she didn't let it hold her back. I wish I could be as brave as she was.'

'What would you do, if you were?'

Kelly thought for a minute. 'I'd travel, like my mum did. I'd go to all these places across the world and collect my own postcards.'

'That sounds like an adventure and an education.'

'I suppose so. What would you do?'

'I guess I'd forget about trying to make it up with my dad and go with you.'

Her and Obie travelling the world. She could hardly believe something like that was possible. It made sense though. They were great together.

'Except I'm not brave,' he said.

'I don't know about that. You were brave enough to walk away from your dad's expectations when you'd had enough.'

'That was just once. And I was kind of pushed into it because I knew I was going to fail the course. It's easier to be brave when you've run out of options. Anyway, I couldn't let Archie down. He's my bud, and we've got those restaurant plans.'

49

A SURPRISING ANNOUNCEMENT

It had been a funny week. Liza was still in Italy and Kelly had been staying at Obie's. Netta had seen Kelly at work and the food bank, but that had pretty much been it. The house was much too empty without them and she was strangely anxious about both her girls, for different reasons.

The anxiety over Kelly was easy to pinpoint. It was Obie. Kelly had completely fallen for him. It was lovely to see her so happy but it was also a worry. Since Marcus, she'd been waiting for Kelly to break all over again. That hadn't happened so far. But this thing with Obie, there was an intensity about it that could only have one explanation. Kelly was in love. Obie seemed like a really nice guy, but Marcus had seemed nice at first, and Kelly's track record with men wasn't the best. If Obie went the same way as Craig and Marcus, she doubted Kelly would recover easily.

Her anxiety about Liza wasn't as simple to nail down. The week in London had been the best time she'd ever had with her daughter. It embarrassed her to admit that, even to herself, because it made her realise how much she'd been neglecting their relationship. It brought back the same old doubts that had dogged her for most of Liza's life. Doubts about her capacity to be a good mother. She'd thought she'd consigned all that stupidity to history after she'd reconciled with her children, but no. That sort of stuff never goes away completely.

The London trip had gone some way to making her less worried about it, but Liza was away with Colin, and there lay another of her fears. What if Colin was doing his worst? What if Liza returned from that holiday hating her? It was all nonsense, of course. She was being irrational, but that didn't stop her thinking it. She needed to get a grip. It was just because the kids weren't around. Although Will was at home, she'd hardly seen him. He and Belle seemed to be flitting about from one place to the next and when they were here, they spent most of the time in his room. He may as well be at uni. She was losing him. Another thing to be anxious about.

Netta needed to talk to someone with more sense than her, and the only person she could think of was her mum. She made a call.

'Hello, love. Everything all right?'

'Hi Mum. I just wondered if I could come over a chat.'

'Okay. When?'

'Now?'

'I'll get the kettle on.'

Her mum let her in. 'Your dad's at the allotment with Minnie, so we've got the house to ourselves.'

'He hasn't gone on my account, has he?'

Her mum gave her a scornful look. 'Of course not. I

can't keep him away from the place. He'll be back soon. Do you want to try my lemon drizzle cake? It's the first time I've made it. I got the recipe from a friend.'

'A friend? Is that Neil?'

'No. I have more than one friend who bakes, you know. This one's from Nina. She's a new friend from the book group.'

A new friend? Her mum certainly was branching out.

They sat out in the garden. It was looking particularly delightful in the late afternoon sun. The scent of roses hung in the air, bees darted around a nearby lavender bush, and butterflies danced over their heads.

Netta settled into a chair. 'It's lovely out here.'

'Yes, it is. Your dad works hard on it. He's added a few new plants to encourage the bees and butterflies. That's Liza's doing. They talk a lot about the environment.'

'I didn't know that.' She tried not to be too peeved at the growing realisation that Liza 'talked a lot' to anyone but her.

'Come on then. What's all this about? Something's bothering you, otherwise you wouldn't be ringing me up for an urgent chat.'

'All sorts of stuff. Most of which is probably stupid. For a start off, I'm concerned about Kelly. She's head over heels for Obie, and I'm worried it's going to go badly and it'll knock her back.'

'Why do you think it's going to go badly?'

'Because of Marcus and Craig, I suppose. And because the feelings she has for Obie seem so extreme. One minute she hates him and the next, boom!'

'She's mad for him. Sounds a bit like you and your first serious boyfriend. Weren't you exactly the same with Doogie?'

'I suppose so. But look how that ended. Very badly.'

'Surely it ended badly because you took up with Colin, and he manipulated and controlled you?' Ouch. The Geraldine factor struck again, and this time the blow was a heavy one.

'Well, yes, but I wouldn't have gone out with Colin in the first place if Doogie hadn't been sleeping with someone else.'

'Would you rather have never met Doogie then?'

Would she rather that? Of course not. She loved Frank now, but Doogie had been the absolute love of her life. Even all these years later, they still had a connection. An unbreakable bond. 'No. I'm glad we met. I'm glad we fell in love.'

'There you go then.'

'But Kelly's not me. And what if Obie's like the other two?'

'No she isn't, and you'd do well to remember that. Have you seen her and Obie together?'

'Not recently.'

'Wait until you see them before you make a judgement. And Obie's nothing like the other two.'

'But she might still get hurt.'

Her mum shrugged. 'That's all part of life's cycle, Netta. She'll get over it. Look, love, I know Kelly's had a tough time but the pieces are beginning to slot together for her now. She's coming to terms with everything to do with her mum. She's back on a firm footing with her dad, and she's accepted Carol. She's making new friends, and she's really beginning to flower. She's not the same girl that we had to rescue last year. She doesn't need us to prop her up anymore. If we keep trying to protect her, we'll just hold her back.'

'I suppose you're right.'

'Yes, I suppose I am. Try the lemon drizzle.'

Netta took a bite. 'Very nice. A new friend, you said?'

'Yes. She works at the café where we have the book group. She runs the group really. We walk our dogs together. She has a cockapoo. Minnie loves him. Nina runs a ladies coffee morning as well. I'm going to it next week. I'm ready to widen my circle of friends now, Nettie. It's been lovely becoming friends with your friends but I'm going independent. I'm finding my own. Anyway, enough of me prattling on. What else is bothering you?'

'Oh it's Liza. I've only had a couple of messages from her while she's been away, and I've got all sorts of silly stuff churning over about being a bad mother to her, and Colin filling her with hate for me.'

'Now that is daft. For one, you're not a bad mother. You've made some mistakes, but we've all done that. For another, Liza is a very clever girl. She sees straight through Colin. But you already know that. You're just being paranoid because you haven't seen her for a while. She'll be home soon though. There's a climate change protest she wants to go to in London.'

'How do you know that?'

'She messaged your dad. He's going with her.'

'Dad's going to a protest?'

'Yes. Don't look so surprised. I told you they talk a lot about the environment. It's just a march. They're not chaining themselves to anything. I might go too. I'll see if Nina wants to come. We could make a day of it.'

Kelly was in the lounge when Netta got back. She looked up

from her book. 'Frank said to tell you he's making dinner. It's probably just us three. Not sure where Will is.'

'He hasn't been around much this week. We've been working on the basis that we cook for whoever's here. Are you stopping then?'

'Yeah, Archie's back now. I could stay there, but I don't want to be a pain. I'll see Obie tomorrow night.'

'How's it going?'

'Good. Really good. Guess what, I'm enjoying the sex. Can you believe it?'

'Oh good. That's great.'

Sex wasn't a topic of conversation that came up much between her and Kelly but when it did, it usually ended with Netta reassuring her that she'd eventually find someone she enjoyed doing it with. It looked like Obie was that someone. That was promising. And at least Kelly hadn't asked her if Frank was an attentive lover again, which is what normally happened. She remembered what her mum had said about seeing them together. She must have sensed a chemistry between them. Netta was curious to know if she could see it too. 'I was just thinking, would you like to bring Obie to dinner one evening?'

Kelly looked surprised. Well, shocked was probably the best way to describe it. 'Really? You wouldn't mind?'

'I wouldn't ask if I minded. I'd like to meet him properly. The last time was rushed, and he was a bit put off by the dogs.'

'He's okay with them now. I'll have to check when he has a night off. He works at three different places because he's trying to save some money.'

'For anything in particular.'

'His mum and dad stumped up a ton of money for him to go to university but he dropped out. He wants to pay them back. Oh, Frank's messaged to say dinner's ready. We'd better go.'

Frank put some warmed naan breads on the table. 'I hope this isn't too spicy for you, Kelly. I'd already added the heat before I knew you were here.'

Kelly ripped a piece of naan and dipped it into her curry. 'You're all right, Frank. I've been eating loads more spicy stuff this week. Obie's been educating me. I've tried all sorts of new food. He cooks dishes from all over the world. He's really good. Him and Archie want their own restaurant someday.'

Frank raised his eyebrows in a suitably approving manner. 'Impressive.'

Kelly grinned. There was a pride in her that was new. She was proud of Obie. It was clear as day. 'Yeah. Don't worry though, Net. He's not snobbish about food. He said he liked my pasta, so you don't need to worry about cooking for him.'

'Thanks. I think. I've invited him to dinner,' she explained to Frank.

'That reminds me. I've thought of something I'm going to spend my inheritance on. I want to go travelling.'

Netta nearly choked on her curry. 'Right. Okay. On your own, or with somebody?'

'Well, I'd like to go with Obie but he's tied up with working and saving. Plus, he doesn't want to let Archie down about the restaurant. So I don't know.'

'On your own then?' There was a knot in Netta's stomach. That anxiety was back. Kelly on her own in a foreign country? It didn't bear thinking about.

'Maybe. I haven't given up on Obie yet.'

'Where are you thinking of going?' asked Frank.

'All over the world. I want to go to the same places Edie went to, and a few more.'

'Good for you.' Frank glanced at Netta as he said it. It looked like she wasn't the only one who thought it was a bad idea.

50

THINGS SAID OUT LOUD

Well that went better than expected. Netta and Frank looked like they'd been slapped, but other than that, they'd taken Kelly's announcement about travelling well. They probably didn't think she was serious. But she was. Kind of, anyway.

It had been on her mind for a while. Edie had started it with her postcards, but then came the other littles nudges – going to Edinburgh, talking about Paris with Robyn, the postcards from Geraldine and Liza, and that photo of her mum in Thailand. The photo wasn't so much a nudge, as a shove. The memories that had flooded back lately had made a big difference to the way Kelly saw her parents. They'd brought her closer to her dad, which was a good thing. But there was a negative side to them too. The light they'd shed on her mum had left Kelly with an uncomfortable feeling that was she was in danger of hating her. There were only two things that stopped her. One was the belief that her dad wouldn't have loved her mum so completely if she'd been a bad person. The other was that photo. The young woman in it was different to the person Kelly remembered. She was happy. Eyes wide open and full of spirit. That was the real

Caitlin Donohue. That was the one she would have liked to have known. Unfortunately she only knew the needy one. But maybe there was a way to feel closer to that Caitlin, if Kelly was brave enough to go out into the world like she did.

But Kelly wasn't brave enough. Mouthy, yes. Truly brave, no. That was why she'd taken her card collection to Obie. She was hoping he'd be up for it too. For a while, she thought he was, but then he'd backed down. And why wouldn't he? They'd only been together for a short time. She'd been mad to think he'd suddenly drop everything for her. The trouble was, now that she'd said it out loud she couldn't let it lie. She hadn't mentioned it to him again, but she'd made herself tell Netta and Frank. So it was out in the open. Whether she was brave enough or not, she'd taken the first steps towards the biggest adventure of her life.

Kelly left Netta over at Frank's and went up to her room to call Robyn. It was the first chance they'd had for a proper gossip since before Archie had gone up to Edinburgh. Naturally, Robyn spilled the full deets on Archie's visit. Cutting a long story short, they were thinking very hard about how a long-distance relationship could work.

With the Archie discussion over, and after more spilling on Kelly's week with Obie, she decided to drop the bombshell about her travelling.

'Wow! Big step. Cool though,' said Robyn.

'It's just an idea at the moment. I've gotta be honest, I'm a bit scared of it. It wouldn't be so bad if someone was with me.'

'I know. I wish I could go with you, but I'm not at that point in my life right now. We could still do the Paris trip though. I could meet you there. Oh wait, I've just thought of something. You could arrange to meet different friends in different places, so you wouldn't be on your own all the time.'

'That might work. You don't think I'm being stupid then?'

'Of course not. As long as you're careful. There are plenty of girls who travel on their own. You'll learn a lot about other cultures, maybe pick up a few languages. Have you told your dad yet?'

'No, but I think he'll be cool with it.'

Kelly finished her call with Robyn and noticed Liza had messaged to say she was coming home on Friday. Down stairs, Netta was back from Frank's and was on the phone.

When Kelly got down, Netta was still talking in the living room: 'Okay, send me the flight details and I'll pick you up from the airport. Yes, it'll be lovely to see you too, darling. I've really missed you.'

It must be Liza. Kelly put the kettle on and threw two teabags in the pot. Will came in just as she was adding milk to the cups. 'You want tea?'

'Er, yeah okay.' He glanced at her and she noticed how tired he looked.

Netta finished her call. 'That was Liza. She's coming home.'

'Yeah, she messaged me.' Kelly and Will spoke the same words together. Kelly giggled. Will didn't.

'She's going to a climate change protest in London on Saturday. Grandad's going with her,' said Netta.

Will's eyebrows shot up. 'Grandad?'

Netta looked like she couldn't quite believe it herself. 'Yes. Nan too. Along with a friend of hers. Nina?'

'Nina from book group? Wow. Go, oldies.' Kelly had to hand it to Geraldine, she was full of surprises.

Will did a little half-smile. At least it had cheered him up a bit. 'Cool. I might go with them if it's not too late. I'll speak to Grandad.'

Netta nodded. 'That'll be nice. Will Belle want to go too?'

He picked up his tea. 'Doubt it. Any biscuits?'

'In the tin.' Netta was watching him. Like, really watching him. Like she was trying to work him out. Kelly could have told her not to bother. She'd given up trying to understand Will ages ago.

The whole family was at Netta's for Sunday night's dinner. Frank and Netta, Geraldine and Arthur, Liza and Will. No Belle though. Kelly hadn't seen her since before she spent the week at Obie's. Geraldine had invited herself and Arthur along because Obie was coming to dinner. Her excuse was Obie knew her well, so it would put him at ease. Kelly couldn't help thinking there was an ulterior motive though.

The dogs were going mental, as usual. Kelly had messaged Obie to prepare him but whether anything could prepare him for this lot was anybody's guess. The younger dogs began to bark when Obie knocked the front door. Kelly opened it up, half-expecting to see him legging it up the path, but he was still there. She gave him a pained look. 'Sorry. We've got the dogs from hell here again.'

He smiled. Or was it a grimace? Probably a grimace. 'I brought some wine.'

Geraldine called out from the kitchen: 'Hello, Obie. Come in and meet Arthur.'

Kelly kissed him as he stepped in. 'Gez and Arthur are cooking tonight. Some fancy French recipe they picked up in Nice. Don't worry though, Gez is an excellent cook. Can't speak for Arthur, mind you. I think he's still on his provisional cooking licence.'

She took him into the kitchen where Geraldine, Arthur and Netta were getting everything ready. The dogs were in there too. Amazingly, they'd decided to behave. 'What's come over that lot?'

Arthur was stirring something on the hob. 'Maud's doing some parental crowd control. Hello Obie. Nice to meet you. Gee, I think this sauce is ready.'

Geraldine dipped a teaspoon in and tried it. 'It's perfect. But it's a jus, Arthur. Not a sauce. Try to remember that.'

Arthur kissed Geraldine's cheek. 'Okay, Nigella. I'll do my best.'

Geraldine laughed and gave him a peck.

Kelly put her hand over Obie's eyes. 'Get a room you two. There are people and dogs watching.'

'I know, they're disgustingly happy, aren't they,' laughed Netta. 'What can I get you to drink, Obie?'

Obie's shoulders relaxed. Kelly's did too. It was going to be all right.

Liza, Arthur and Geraldine were keeping the dinner party going with stories from their big day out in London yesterday. Will hadn't gone on the protest in the end because he'd been doing something with Belle.

Liza was telling them how Nina and Geraldine had told a policeman off for having a go at some of the younger

protesters. 'I was sure he was going to arrest them. I seriously thought me and Grandad were gonna to have to bail
them out.'

Geraldine raised her fist. 'We'd have gone down fighting
if he'd tried.'

Obie laughed out loud. He seemed to be really enjoying
himself. 'I didn't realise Nina was such a rebel.'

'Never mind Nina, I didn't know my wife was such a
rebel,' said Arthur.

'Oh no I could tell Geraldine was. She's got a very
mischievous streak,' said Obie.

Arthur chuckled. 'I know what you mean. Now you
mention it, I should have seen it coming.'

'We have more protests in the pipeline,' said Liza. 'You
can all come if you want to. It might not be until after
you're back in York though, Will.'

'Maybe you could come to one near there? It's about
time you came up to visit me again.' Will was talking to Liza
but he was looking at Kelly.

'Yeah, we'll have to sort something out.' Kelly turned
towards Obie and saw he was looking at Will.

'Kelly was telling us about your record collection, Obie.
You like the old soul records?' said Netta.

'He likes Barry White. Anyone else heard of him?' Kelly
jumped in before he could answer himself. She hadn't
meant to, she was just feeling a bit unnerved by Obie and
Will being a bit strange.

Geraldine's eyes lit up. 'Barry White? We used like a
boogie to him ourselves, didn't we Arthur?'

'That's dancing in old people's talk.' Kelly informed
Obie. She wondered if Geraldine and Arthur danced naked
to Barry White too. Knowing that pair, she wouldn't put it
past them.

.   .   .

When the night was over, Kelly went with Obie to the bus stop. He held her hand as they walked along. 'I had a really good time tonight.'

'Yeah, me too.'

'Did you say Will had a girlfriend?' They'd been going for a while before he'd come out with it. After what happened earlier, Kelly had been half expecting something like it.

'Yeah, Belle.'

'But you're friends, you and Will, right? Good friends.'

'Yeah. Why, what's up?'

'Nothing. It's just that … well … he didn't take his eyes off you all night.'

Kelly snorted. 'How do you know? You'd have had to be watching him the whole night to know that.'

'Okay, maybe not all night. But every time I looked at him.'

She stopped and faced him. 'Is this you being possessive? Because I don't like that shit.'

'No, I'm just saying. It's a bit weird. If he's just a friend.'

'He is just a friend. More like a brother. We're tight, that's all. He worries about me. Because of Marcus, and that wobble I had after my nan died. Anyway, why shouldn't he look at me? Fucking hell.'

'I'm sorry, I'm sorry. You're right. I'm being stupidly jealous and possessive, and it's ridiculous.'

At least he realised he was being unreasonable. She put her arm in his to show she didn't hold it against him. 'Yes it is.'

They carried on walking and she waited with him at the stop. He pulled her to him as the bus arrived. 'Sorry again.'

Kelly tutted, then kissed him. 'Goodnight, idiot. I forgive you.'

But he'd said it now, and she couldn't get it out of her head.

51

THE SHOCKS ROLL IN

Kelly slept through the alarm and was woken by Netta banging on her door. She'd had a restless night. It was that stuff Obie had said about Will. It had unsettled her. She couldn't be doing with jealousy. Craig used to lay that on her and it was a nightmare. She might have put up with it back when she knew no better, but she wasn't going to put up with it now.

The other thing that had stopped her sleeping was that every time she'd closed her eyes, scenes from that family meal kept replaying in her head. She hadn't admitted it to Obie but Will had spent a lot of that meal watching her. She'd seen it with her own eyes. But he'd also been watching Obie – or rather, her and Obie – and not in that usual sociable way that people normally did to follow a conversation. He was watching them even when neither of them was talking. What was going on with him? And another thing. Where was Belle? Any other time, Belle was stuck to him like glue. Something was definitely not right.

She didn't mention anything to Netta on the way into work. She just told her Obie had enjoyed the meal.

'He's nice. I like him,' said Netta.

'Yeah he is. Nothing like those other shits I've been out with in the past, eh?'

Netta laughed. 'Quite.'

As usual, Neil was already in when they reached the office and they got straight on with their daily meeting. They had one every morning to discuss the day's work and who was doing what. They were making chutneys today which meant a lot of peeling and chopping. Kelly didn't mind peeling and chopping. Neil had taught her how to do it like a pro, so she was super-fast. Unlike when they'd first started out. It took her hours then to do a few apples. She could get through a ton of them now, no problem. Except for onions. She hated dealing with onions. Today, Neil was on onions. She was on tomatoes, and Netta was on apples.

In the middle of the kitchen was a big, high table with enough room for them to work without getting in each other's way. It was good because it still allowed them to talk while they worked. It was also a good way to get difficult things said, because the others were so busy keeping an eye on what they were doing, they didn't have time to think about what you'd just brought up. This was handy because today, Kelly had something difficult to bring up.

'Neil, has Net mentioned that I'm thinking of going travelling?'

Neil carried on chopping. 'She did say you'd floated the idea, yes.'

Floated the idea? That was a fancy way of putting it. She'd have to remember that one. 'Right. Well it's still floating up the ideas canal, but I might be promoting it into more of a plan. How do you both feel about that?'

Netta and Neil exchanged looks. Netta even put her knife down. 'How long are you thinking of going for?'

'Not sure. As long as it takes. I won't really know until I go. I might hate it and want to come straight back, or I might love it and decide to stay longer.'

This time Neil stopped. 'Kelly, I don't have a problem with you going. Speaking as your friend, it's an amazing opportunity and I don't blame you for wanting to do it. As long as you're careful, that is. Speaking as your business partner, it will be difficult with you not being here. There's too much work for me and Netta to cover between us, so we'd either have to bring someone else in or work full-time.'

'You mean no more volunteering at the foodbank?' said Kelly.

Neil nodded. 'Exactly. Neither of us want to do that, so we'd have to bring someone else in. That's fine. We can pay them with the money you would have been paid. But we'd have to give them an indication as to how long we'd be employing them for.'

'So we'd need some idea of time. At least, a minimum time,' said Netta.

'So I need to say if it's going to be no less than six months, for example?'

'Exactly,' said Neil.

'And if I could do that, you'd be cool about me going?'

'Yes, we would. Although that doesn't mean we wouldn't be worried about you going on your own.' Neil did actually look genuinely worried.

'I know. But I'm hoping I won't have to go on my own.'

Kelly finished the tomatoes and washed her hands. Now all she had to do was tell her other friends, and her dad. And Obie. If she was going to convince him to come with her, it was important he knew as soon as possible.

. . .

'I've decided to go travelling,' said Kelly. She and Obie had gone to a pub in Moseley after work.

'Okay.'

'Yeah. Your fault really for putting the idea into my head.' She said it in a jokey way to disguise her jitters.

'Oh, okay.'

'What do you think?'

'I don't know. Good for you I guess. If it's what you want, you should do it. Definitely.' Obie was saying the right words. Well, sort of. They were in the area anyway, but his face was blank. It was difficult to read him.

'Will you come with me?'

He took a swig of his pint and put it back on the table. 'I'd really like to but I can't. I have my obligations.'

She slid her fingers through the gaps in his. 'They'll still be here when we get back. And if it's money you're worried about, I've got plenty.'

He shook his head. 'I don't want your money, Birmingham.'

Of course he didn't. She already knew that. If it had been Craig, he'd have had the money off her as soon as he could. Obie wasn't that kind of man. He wasn't like Marcus either. Marcus would probably have just laughed at her and said it was chicken feed. He probably had more than that in a trust fund, or whatever it was posh people set up for their kids. No. Obie was nothing like either of them. That was one of the many good things about him. It was also one of the more irritating things about him, because she couldn't work out how to handle him. She'd had plenty of experience dealing with shit boyfriends. But Obie was too honourable, too decent. Her expertise didn't stretch that far. Stubborn too. He was bloody stubborn.

'This thing of yours about paying your parents back. Are you sure it's gonna work?'

Obie picked up his glass and rested it in his hands. 'No. But I can't think of any other way to make my dad forgive me.'

'You shouldn't have to make him forgive you. I thought parents were supposed to love their kids whatever. End of.' There she'd said it. It had been on the tip of her tongue for a while now but she'd held back.

'He does love me. It's just not that simple.'

'It should be. Look, you might hate me for saying this but I'm gonna say it anyway. The things you've told me about your dad. They remind me of Netta's ex and he's a manipulative bastard. I'm not saying your dad's like that, but it does sound as if he likes to get his own way. Sorry. I've said too much.'

Obie put his pint back on the table, untouched. He was swallowing hard. Kelly couldn't tell whether he was upset or angry. 'I still can't go with you.'

'I know. I wasn't saying it for that reason. Would you wait for me if I went though?'

He frowned at her. 'On your own?'

'Of course on my own. Who else would I go with?'

He grinned in that beautiful, lopsided way of his. 'I guess no one else would put up with you. I'll be here when you get back. If you want to come back.'

She didn't know what he meant by that, but at least he hadn't walked out. Maybe it was better to leave it for now and change the subject: 'Do you want to meet some of my biological family?'

'As opposed to…?'

'As opposed to my adopted family. You've already met them.'

'Ah right. Sure. That'd be nice' He was all smiles. He was fine again.

It had taken a couple of weeks for Kelly's dad to find a window to see her. With six kids of varying ages between him and Carol, everything had to be planned ahead.

It was Sunday afternoon so they were meeting at The Factory. Kelly got there early. She was stupidly nervous. Her dad and Carol were already there. They brought little Emily with them. That was good. She was a sweet kid and might help if there was any tension. That said, Kelly had no idea how Obie was with kids. For all she knew, he could be as bad with them as he was with dogs. Shit. She began to panic.

Her dad stood up to kiss her when she reached their table. 'All right, Kel? You're looking well.'

'No she doesn't. She looks absolutely lovely. Men!' Carol got up and kissed her too.

Kelly laughed. 'It's probably Obie's cooking. I'm eating a lot more healthily than I used to.'

Her dad looked around the yard. 'Where is he then?'

She pointed at the coffee wagon. 'You wait here, I'll go and get us some drinks. Do want to come and help, Em?'

Emily skipped along with Kelly to the wagon. Archie was serving. He leaned over the counter to Emily. 'Hello. Who are you?'

The little girl frowned. 'Emily. Are you Kelly's boyfriend?'

'No. That's him over there.' He pointed to Obie who was making an espresso.

Obie put the espresso on the counter and came round to the other side. He crouched down in front of Emily.

'Hello Emily. I'm Obie.' He shook her hand and made her giggle. That settled it then. He was better with kids than dogs.

'He's good with kids,' said her dad, when they got back to the table.

Kelly watched Obie preparing the drinks. 'Yeah. Don't get any ideas though, Dad.'

He laughed. 'Noted.'

Obie brought over a tray of drinks and cakes.

'Obie. This is my dad and my stepmum.' This calling Carol her actual stepmum was a new thing. In fact, it was the first time she'd said it to Carol's face. Kelly figured it was long overdue. Carol looked over the moon and a bit emotional. That was nice.

Obie shook her dad's hand. 'How do you do, Mr Payne?' Then he did the same to Carol. 'Pleased to meet you, Mrs Payne.' He was amazingly polite. Kelly was gobsmacked.

'Pleased to meet you, Obie. Andy and Carol will do though, mate.' Her dad gave her a satisfied sideways look. He obviously approved.

Obie sat down next to Kelly. She squeezed his knee under the table. Emily moved round and sat on the other side of him. 'Hello again, Emily. One cookie and one not-too-hot chocolate, as requested.'

Emily beamed at him. 'Thank you, Obie.'

Her dad and Carol laughed.

'Kelly, he's so nice,' said Carol, after Obie had gone back to work. 'Isn't he, Andy?'

'Certainly seems it. Looks like you've got yourself a good one there, bab.'

'Thanks. Glad you like him. I'm trying to persuade him to come travelling with me.'

Her dad took his elbows off the table and sat up. 'Travelling? Didn't know you were thinking of doing that.'

'Only recently decided. Do you think it would be all right to use Nan's money for it?' She held her breath and waited for his reply.

He leaned forward again. 'I don't see why not.'

'Caitlin did that, didn't she?' said Carol.

'She did,' said her dad.

Kelly breathed again. 'How long was she away for?'

'About two years I think. I met her right near the end of it. Your nan would know.'

'Nanny Donohue? Isn't she dead?'

Her dad snorted. 'Of course she isn't dead. Not last time I heard anyway. She just cut us off after your mum died. But I still keep in touch with Teresa, your mum's younger sister. Your nan lives with her now.'

'In Ireland?'

'No, London. I can speak to Teresa. See if the old girl will talk to you. If that's what you want.'

Kelly stepped out of Selly Oak station and turned towards home. What a shock afternoon that was. Shock number one, Obie Kalu was a child charmer. Shock number two, he was also the most polite person ever. Shock number three, and she'd saved the best till last, Nanny Donohue was still alive. Not that her dad had ever said she was dead. Kelly had just assumed it. Just went to show, you should check your facts before making wild assumptions.

She walked up the front path. There was music coming from the back garden. Instead of going through the door, she took the side gate. Liza and Jade were lying on the grass, topping up their Italian tans. Liza called her over. As soon as Kelly reached them, Liza pulled her down so she was crouching between them. 'Flash news,' she whispered. 'Will and Belle have split up.'

Kelly fell backwards onto her bum. Shock number four.

52

THE BOOGIE MAN

Neil put a box of strawberry jams on the table and ticked it off his list. They were preparing a delivery for their biggest customer who ran a small chain of delis in the Birmingham area. 'Are you bringing Obie to the party?'

Kelly looked up from the jars she was labelling. She'd heard him talking but hadn't been listening. Her mind had been on Will and the news that he'd broken up with Belle. She hadn't seen Will herself, so she couldn't ask him if it was true. He'd gone straight off to stay with a mate after he'd told Liza and Netta.

'Our party on Saturday. Are you bringing Obie?'

'Yeah. He'll have to come in the evening when he's finished work, but I'll come in the afternoon with everyone else.'

'Okay. Is Will coming, Net?'

'I'm not sure if he'll be back, or even if he'll be in the mood. Can you put him down as a maybe? said Netta.

Neil put another box on the table. 'Sure, no problem. How is he?'

'I don't know. He hasn't been in touch. Has he said anything to you, Kelly.'

'No. I haven't heard from him.' It was unusual for Will not to have messaged her at least once, but she then hadn't messaged him either. For some reason she couldn't face it and if she was honest, she didn't actually want him to be here for the party. Although, once again, she didn't know why.

Neil and Chris's parties took a lot of prep, so Neil had Saturday morning off and Netta and Kelly managed the stall with Liza's help. Will was back when they got home. He seemed okay. On the surface anyway. But they were in a rush to get ready for the party, so there was no time to talk to him.

Kelly was getting ready in her room. She was wearing the shift dress she'd worn to the Night Owl. She always felt great in it and Obie liked it. She wanted him to see what he'd be missing if she went away without him. She hadn't given up on trying to persuade him to go with her yet. Talking of which, she just about had time to give him a quick call.

He took ages to answer. She was amazed it didn't push her to voicemail. 'Sorry, it was on charge. I didn't hear it.'

One thing she'd learned about Obie Kalu quite early on, was that he was useless at keeping his phone charged. She'd told him so many times he needed a system, but did he listen to her? The realisation that she was beginning to sound like Geraldine stopped her from reminding him about her foolproof phone-charging system. 'Just checking you're still coming tonight.'

'Yeah.' He said it in a 'how dare you even think I wasn't'

kind of way. 'I'll be wearing my boogie pants, baby.' Boogie was his new favourite word for dancing, since Geraldine had told them she boogied to the Walrus of Love.

'Okay boogie man. The minibus is here. I'd better go.'

Will came out of his room just as she left hers and she nearly crashed into him. He glanced at her dress. 'You look nice.'

'Ta. You all right?'

'Yeah.'

She was going to say he didn't look it but Netta shouted up the stairs that the taxi was waiting. They ran down and out to the minibus. Will scooched up next to her. Kelly could smell his aftershave which she knew for a fact Belle had bought him for Christmas. Belle wasn't gone completely then.

They heard the music pumping when they got out of the minibus. Squeezing through the people inside, they followed the sound of Chris's deep voice until they saw his head over the crowd. He always stood out because he was a big guy but when he was in full-on entertaining mode he stood out even more. Kelly spied the kitchen worktops piled high with food. Chris's mum and aunties always brought a load to go with the mountain that Neil made. Their Caribbean food had always been too spicy for her, but that was before Obie. She wished he was here now to see the spread before everybody laid into it. He'd be having his own little tasting festival and she'd be by his side, trying it all with him, like it was the first time. She decided to eat as little as possible for now so they could enjoy it together when he got here.

Geraldine and Arthur were here. Arthur was with Chris's dad and uncles, talking about the old times and music probably. That's what they normally talked about. Geraldine was with Paula, and some of the others from the foodbank.

Will came up beside Kelly. 'Everyone's here.'

'Nearly everyone. Obie's coming later.'

'Oh yes, of course. I meant all the usual people.'

'Belle's not here either. I hear you broke up.'

'Yeah. I've been meaning to tell you.'

Kelly shrugged. 'You don't owe me any special favours.'

He looked straight into her eyes. 'Don't I?'

Her mouth opened slightly. It stayed that way, waiting for some words to come out but Liza saved her from having to think of any by dragging her away to dance. Will followed them. They moved around to the music but their eyes were on each other. It was all getting a bit weird.

She spent the afternoon dancing, drinking and trying to avoid Will. For the first time since she'd known him, she was scared to be alone with him. If only Obie was here. She checked her phone for the hundredth time. It was nearly seven and still no word from him. That didn't mean anything, being as he was so useless with phones. No need to call him yet. Her stomach rumbled. She was starving. Maybe she could grab a few crisps to keep her going. She went to walk over to the food but the room suddenly began to shift. She needed air.

Kelly found a low wall at the back of the garden. She'd been stupid not to eat, especially when she was drinking. She'd be all right though, if she closed her eyes and sat here quietly.

'Are you okay?' She opened her eyes and saw Will.

'Had too much to drink. Just taking time out.'

He sat next to her. 'Lightweight.'

'I know. What about you?'

'Oh I've had too much to drink, for sure.'

'Drowning your sorrows?'

He didn't answer. She closed her eyes again and for a moment, the world stopped spinning.

'You know why we broke up, me and Belle? It was because of you. Sorry, not you exactly. I'm not trying to make this your fault. We broke up because Belle thinks I care more about you than her.'

Kelly's eyes shot open again. Her head was pounding and now, her heart was too. 'Do you?'

'I … I think so.'

She looked up to the sky. This couldn't be happening now. Not after all this time of wanting and yearning. But it was. He was here, and he was saying he cared more about her than Belle. At last.

He looked right into her, just as he'd done earlier. 'Do you feel the same about me?'

She turned to face him. *Say no. Say no. You can't. Not now.* 'You idiot. I've felt the same about you since forever.'

He leaned over and kissed her, and before she knew it she was kissing him back. She couldn't stop herself. She'd waited so long for it. She'd watched him and Belle from the side-lines, wishing she was the one he was with, and now the chance was hers to take. And why shouldn't she take it? Will loved her and she loved him. Didn't she? She had feelings for Obie but they were different to the feelings she had for Will. Obie! He could be here any minute. Kelly pulled back.

'What is it?' said Will.

'Obie. He'll be here soon.'

'Shit. Sorry. I forgot about him.'

She went back inside, searching the nooks and crannies

for Obie. Still no sign. It was after eight now. He should be here. She went out to the front garden and rang him. It went straight to voicemail. She tried again with the same result so she messaged him:

'Where are you?'

He'd read the message straight away so she waited for a reply. After ten minutes she gave up and tried calling him once more. Voicemail again.

Back inside the house, she saw Will with Paula. He raised his eyebrows at her. She shook her head. It was best to stay away from him in case Obie turned up. He'd be able to tell straight away. She found Geraldine. Safe ground.

'Obie not here yet?' said Geraldine.

'Nah. Shouldn't be long though.'

They piled into the minibus in the early hours of the morning. Obie hadn't come. She'd given up on calling him, but she'd sent three more messages. He hadn't read them. She had a terrible feeling something bad had happened to him, and that bad thing had everything to do with her.

Will sat next to her again. In the darkness, he slipped his hand into hers. She looked around to check if anyone could see. Netta was looking out of the window. She turned her head and caught Kelly's eye. Netta smiled, but she seemed sad. Or maybe she was just tired. Kelly looked away and wondered what Obie was doing now.

The first thing she did when she woke up in the morning was call Obie again. It was a waste of time.

Downstairs, the house was quiet. The Sunday morning dog walk had been moved to the afternoon, to give everyone time to recover. Netta was the only other person up. 'I've just made tea.'

Kelly poured herself a cup.

'Did you enjoy the party?' said Netta.

'Yeah. Except Obie didn't turn up and I can't get hold of him. I'm gonna get dressed and go over to The Factory. See if I can find out what happened.'

Netta coughed. She was looking over Kelly's shoulder. 'Actually, he was there last night, but he left.'

'He left?'

'Yes. He was looking for you. I'm afraid he found you in the garden. With Will.'

53

NETTA SEEKS ADVICE

'I'm afraid he found you in the garden. With Will.' Netta had been up since dawn wondering how she was going to tell Kelly and now that she'd said it, she wasn't sure it had come out as kindly as she'd hoped it would.

She'd seen them too. Not until it was too late, unfortunately. If she had, she wouldn't have sent Obie out there. She'd have steered him in the wrong direction, or got Liza or her mum to distract him while she rescued the situation. But she hadn't. She'd sent him to the garden.

Instinct had made her follow him shortly after. Instinct that had been sadly lacking a few minutes earlier. Obie was standing with his back to her. It was only as Netta got closer that she saw he was watching Kelly and Will. They were locked in each other's arms, completely oblivious to him.

Obie must have sensed she was there. He looked over his shoulder at her and Netta saw the extent of the damage written across his face. Devastation didn't come close. She wanted to say something, but no words would have made it better.

Within seconds he was gone. Netta left the party too, in

time to see him turning the corner towards the main road. She'd taken the same route, but he'd disappeared when she reached the corner and anyway, the necessary words still hadn't come to her.

She'd been expecting something since Will's announcement about Belle. But not that. Not when she'd witnessed the strength of Obie and Kelly's feelings for each other which, as her mum had said, were obvious when you saw them together. But Will had come between them. Perhaps Will was the one Kelly really loved. If that was the case then, tragic as it was for Obie, Netta should be happy for them. The trouble was, she had this nagging sense of déjà vu. Yes, she knew Kelly and Obie were nothing like her and Doogie, the boy she'd loved all those years ago. Just as she knew that Will was no Colin. And yet…

'When you say he saw me and Will…'

Netta was pulled back to her senses. 'I followed him out, a few minutes later. I saw what he saw.'

'You saw us?'

'Yes. You were … together. Kissing. Obie was watching you when I got there.'

Kelly's face went completely colourless. 'How did he seem?'

'Upset.' She checked herself. This wasn't the time to sweeten it. There was no icing to be had on this cake. 'Distraught. Kelly, whatever you choose to do is fine with me. I want you to know, whatever happens between you and Will won't affect my love for either of you.'

'Thanks, Net. I appreciate that. I'm sorry if I've fucked things up. I need to see Obie.' Kelly stood up. 'You've always been a good friend to me.'

'I still am.'

. . .

Netta knocked the door of her parents' house. Her mum was still in her dressing gown when she answered. She had nothing on underneath it.

'Had a lie in?'

'Yes. Dad's in the shower. I'll just go and let him know you're here.'

Netta waited in the hall, listening to the whisperings upstairs. When her mum returned she'd slipped a nightie on under the dressing gown. That's when she realised, they hadn't just had an after-party lie in. They'd had sex.

Her mum ushered her into the kitchen. 'What's so urgent it couldn't wait until this afternoon?'

'It's all gone a bit tits-up with the Kelly-Obie-Will situation. I didn't think we'd be able to talk about it later with everyone else there.'

Her mum arched an eyebrow. She wasn't keen on swearing, or what she labelled as swearing. It was a wonder she put up with it from Kelly. 'What do you mean?'

Netta filled her in on the party goings on, and this morning's conversation with Kelly.

Her dad appeared just as Netta finished. He looked squeaky clean and was, thankfully, fully clothed. 'Hello, sweetheart. This is a surprise.'

'It's all gone a bit tits-up with the Kelly-Obie-Will situation, love,' said her mum. Clearly she wasn't averse to a bit of fruity language herself when it was called for.

Netta suppressed a smile. Despite the circumstances, her mum had lifted her spirits a tiny bit. 'Last night, I saw Kelly and Will kissing. Obie saw them too.'

'Oh dear. Poor Obie. I suppose it comes as no great surprise with Kelly and Will.' So her dad knew too.

'I've been keeping him up-to-date,' her mum explained.

'She has,' he added.

'I see. So what do we do?' said Netta.

Her mum put the kettle on. 'Do? Nothing. If they want our advice, they'll ask. They'll work it through on their own.'

Her dad looked sceptical. 'You seem very sure of that, love.'

'Yes I am,' said her mum. 'Anyone want breakfast?'

The first thing Netta did when she got home was go over to Frank's. He was in his breakfast room studio, getting ready for a morning's painting. He was a lot more surprised than her dad had been. Unlike her mum, Netta hadn't been keeping him up-to-date. She added that failing to the list of things her mum did better. Top of that list was having sex more often than her.

'So we do nothing unless they ask for our help?' said Frank.

'So says Guru Geraldine.'

'She's probably right. It's none of our business anyway.'

'I suppose not. You know, I think that's why Will and Belle split up. I think Belle knew something was going on.'

'Looks like he's up.'

She followed Frank's pointer and saw Will in her garden with the dogs. 'I'd better go and speak to him.'

'Okay. Remember, Net. Nothing.'

She went through the gate between the two gardens and called out: 'Morning,' in her cheeriest manner.

It startled Will who'd had his back to her. 'Hey. You haven't seen Kelly, have you?'

'Yes. She went to see Obie. Is Liza still in bed?'

'No. She's gone to Jade's.'

'Just you and me then. Are you coming in?'

'Actually, I might take Betty for a walk.'

Netta had assumed Will would be happy about last night but he didn't look it. She reminded herself, her son was nothing like his father. Will had a conscience.

54

DO THE RIGHT THING

It was too early for The Factory to be open, but Obie and Archie always got there a couple of hours before. One of the entrance doors was slightly ajar and Kelly squeezed through. The wagon's shutters were still down but she saw Archie talking to another stallholder. She couldn't see Obie, until he came out of the main building. He noticed her and picked up his speed towards the wagon.

She ran after him. 'Obie. Obie, please. I need to talk to you.'

He refused to look at her and kept on walking. 'I don't wanna hear it.'

'What you saw. It was–'

He stopped suddenly. 'It was what? You kissing the guy you insisted was just a friend? Actually no, it was more than that. You were all over each other. So no, I don't wanna hear what you have to say, because there's nothing you can say to make that go away. Leave me be.' And with that he stepped up into the wagon and closed the door behind him.

Archie touched her arm. 'Now's not a good time. You should go.'

'But I–'

'It won't do any good right now. Trust me.'

Kelly nodded. 'Tell him I'll come round to the house tomorrow night, yeah? I'll explain. Tell him I'll explain everything.'

'Sure.'

She left the yard and walked back to the station. The platform was empty. She sat down on a bench. The next train was five minutes away. She got up and walked from one end of the platform to the other, then back again, and again. Archie was right. She needed to give Obie a bit of breathing space. She'd see him tomorrow when he'd calmed down. She'd tell him. She'd– What would she tell him? She had no idea.

She saw she'd had a message from Will. She tapped back a reply and paced some more.

Will was waiting at the station, as she'd asked. He had Betty with him. He put his arms around her and kissed her on the mouth. It felt as strange as it had done last night. Not as she'd imagined it would feel.

'Hey you. How'd it go?' he said.

'Not great. He's not speaking to me.'

'Does he know?'

She nodded. 'He saw us. Netta told me this morning. She saw us too.'

'Right. Do you want to walk?'

He held her hand on the way to the park. 'Do you remember those long walks we used to go on when we were training Betty?'

'Yeah. I used to like them walks. You, me, and baby Betty,' she said.

'Me too. Why did we stop doing them?'

'You met Belle, I guess. Then you went to uni.'

He smiled and they walked on together. For a few minutes she let herself believe everything was normal. Just like those long walks with him, her and baby Betty. But he broke the happy silence: 'What will you do about Obie?'

'I'm going to see him again tomorrow.'

'What will you say?'

She shook her head. 'I don't know.'

Kelly turned into Obie's road. She'd already turned into it and back out again five times. It was getting stupid. This was definitely the last attempt.

She knocked the door and willed it not to be Archie that answered. The way the door was wrenched open, she knew it was going to be Obie, before she'd seen who was behind it.

He stood in the doorway, giving her evils. 'Are you gonna invite me in?' she said.

He moved back about ten paces so she could step in, but was still out of reach. 'That's far enough.'

'You don't think you're being a bit childish?'

He folded his arms. 'No.'

'Well, I think you're being a bit childish.'

'Well, I think you're being a bit loose.'

She slammed the door behind her and moved closer. 'A bit loose? A bit fucking loose? I am the most unloose woman on the planet, mate. Some might even say I'm close to frigid.' She had her finger practically up his nose by now. This was not going well.

'And what does Will say? Does he think you're frigid?'

'I wouldn't know. I haven't asked him. And I haven't slept with him either.'

'Huh. Is that so?'

'Yeah. That's so.'

'Only a matter of time though, don't you think?'

'Well that might depend on how this conversation pans out.'

Obie's mouth hung open. Kelly's did too. Had she just said that? Had she really just said that? What an absolute prick she was.

'Well at least you've got options. Unfortunately I haven't. I had all my feelings in one pot, but it seems I've been a fool.'

Kelly stretched out for his hand. 'I'm sorry, I didn't mean that. I was just angry.'

He moved further back. 'You've got nothing to be angry about. Goodbye, Kelly.'

'I'll come again. When you've had more time.'

'I don't want you to.'

She searched his eyes for a glimmer of something that she might be able to reach, but there was nothing. She opened the door and let the early evening light flood the hallway.

'Just a minute.'

Had he taken pity on her? Perhaps he could see how cut up she was. She turned around and saw he was holding a carrier bag. A bit of fur poked through a small hole. That's when she knew, all was lost. She snatched it off him. 'You know what you are, Obie Kalu? A stubborn bastard.'

'And do you know what you are?'

She shoved her finger in his chest. 'Don't you dare tell me I'm a loose woman. Don't you fucking dare.'

She ran out into the street. This wasn't fair. It wasn't fucking fair.

Kelly rang Geraldine's doorbell. Arthur opened it. 'We've got a visitor, Gee. I suppose I'll have to make myself scarce for a couple of hours.'

Kelly wiped her eyes and sniffed. 'Sorry. I didn't know where else to go. You don't need to leave.'

'It's okay, sweetheart. Good excuse for me to have a pint. I'll leave you both to it.'

Geraldine took her into the living room and switched off the TV. 'I take it you've been to see Obie?'

'Yes,' was as much as she could manage.

'Can I also assume it didn't go as well as you'd hoped?'

Kelly nodded and sniffed at the same time.

Geraldine passed her a box of tissues. 'Sorry to hear that.'

'He's dumped me, Gez. He's even given me Arthur Three back.'

'I beg to differ, lovie, but didn't you dump him? After all, you're the one who was playing away.'

Kelly blew her nose. 'I wasn't playing away. We just kissed.'

'Yes, Netta told me.'

'Well I guessed it wasn't Will.'

'No. He's been very tight lipped. What are you going to do?'

'I don't know. I was hoping you'd tell me.'

'It's not for me to tell you what to do, Kelly. You must decide that for yourself.' Geraldine was doing her therapist face. Pleasant and approachable without giving the impression she was enjoying herself.

'Couldn't you just give me a hint?'

'I'll tell you what I'd do, if it were me. I'd make my mind up who I wanted. Then I'd let the other one down as gently as I could.'

Kelly reached for another tissue as the tears started again. 'What if it's too late for that?'

Geraldine put her arm around her. 'It's never too late to do the right thing, my darling.'

55

PENANCES AND HOME TRUTHS

Kelly was in hiding. For the last few days she'd been to work and the foodbank, but she'd stayed at Arthur and Geraldine's. She was sleeping in Netta's old room. She liked that it made her feel closer to her friend. She missed her, and Liza too. She was beginning to doubt that she'd have the guts to leave them and go travelling. It would have been all right if Obie had gone with her, but she'd messed up that particular opportunity.

Obie. She wondered if he was lying on his bed, thinking about her, like she was thinking about him right now. That was all she did these days. Before that party, it had been the best thing ever to spend all her waking hours thinking about Obie Kalu. Now it hurt. It really hurt. But it was a penance she had to do. She rolled over and picked up the dictionary off the floor.

'*Penance: Punishment inflicted on oneself as an outward expression of repentance for wrongdoing*'.

There was other stuff in there about religion and the church, but that wasn't what she meant. She'd done him wrong, and her penance was not only thinking about him, but also thinking about how much she'd lost. Because she could see now, she'd lost everything.

She'd told Will on Sunday, she needed time. He'd been okay about it, but now he was asking to see her. They needed to talk, he said. Obviously they did. They couldn't go on like this forever.

She was beginning to understand the feelings she had for Will. She loved him with all her heart, but she'd mistaken that love for something else. The kind of something else she'd had with Obie. She only realised it when they kissed at the party. All this time she'd been imagining that first kiss, imagining the sensation. But then it happened and she knew. It was wrong. It was so wrong. She was not in love with Will Grey. She'd confused sisterly love with the real thing. Maybe she'd have carried on thinking she was in love with him and it would have been all right, if Obie hadn't shown her the difference. But he had, and no amount of pretending was going to make it work with Will. Just as Geraldine had told her, she needed to let him down as gently as she could, because if she didn't make things right with him, she'd regret it forever.

They met at the entrance of Kings Heath Park. A pub seemed inappropriate. It was Wednesday evening. Kelly should have been at book group, but she couldn't face going there knowing Obie would be hating her.

They found a bench that was in a fairly quiet spot. Will held her hand. 'It's good that we've had this space to think everything over.'

'You might change your mind when I tell you what I've been thinking.'

'Is it that you made a mistake?'

Kelly looked at him. She wanted him to be the one, so, so badly. It would all be so much easier if he was. 'I, er...' Oh God. She was crying. 'I love you, Will.'

'I love you too.'

This was so hard. 'It's just that–'

'You don't love me in that way.'

It was too much. The tears were flowing properly now.

Will gave her a hug. 'Hey, it's all right. I understand.'

'I'm sorry. I'm really sorry. I thought I did. I thought I wanted you more than anything else in the entire universe, but now I know. I don't.'

'Me too.' His voice was breaking. He looked like he was about to burst into tears as well.

'You don't? You don't want me either? You're not just saying that to make me feel better?'

He shook his head. 'No. It's Belle I want. I want to be with Belle.'

'I want to be with Obie.'

'Shit. I've ruined everything.'

Kelly pulled a pack of tissues from her pocket and gave him one. 'We both have.'

He blew his nose. 'We're such idiots.'

Arthur was on his way out to pick Geraldine up from book group when Kelly reached the house, so she had to wait for them to get back before telling them the news.

'It's good that you've worked things out and stayed friends.' said Geraldine. 'Are you going back to Netta's now?'

'Can I stay for a couple more days? I still have some things I want to think over.'

Gez patted her knee. 'Stay as long as you like.'

'How was book group?'

'Not the same without you.'

'Was Obie there?'

'He was. But he didn't speak to me. I think he was avoiding me.'

Kelly's phone rang. It was her dad. 'I've heard back from Teresa, your mum's sister. She'd be happy to see you. I'll send you her number and the details. Sounds like this Sunday would be good for her, if you can make it.'

'Yeah, why not.' It would be something to do that didn't involve moping around thinking about Obie. And while she was at it, she'd see if someone else would agree to see her.

Kelly walked into the bar. She'd suggested one in town that was up in the business district. They were less likely to bump into anyone they knew there. Belle was scrolling through her phone. Kelly hovered in front of her. 'Hello, Belle.'

Belle's hand shot to the cocktail in front of her. 'Hello.'

'Can I get you another one?' This was awkward, but then Kelly hadn't expected anything else.

'No thank you.'

'I'll just get myself one then.' She bought a glass of wine and sat down opposite Belle. 'Thanks for agreeing to meet me.'

'It's not like I've got a diary full of appointments at the moment. What is it you want?'

Kelly cleared her throat. 'I wanted to apologise.'

'For?'

'For everything.'

'Can you be more specific?' She made it sound like they were discussing a scientific experiment. This new coldness of hers was unnerving.

'For being horrible to you. And for being the person Will thought he wanted, wrongly as it happens.'

Belle drank some more of her cocktail. 'Let's just reel back a bit, shall we? Yes, you were horrible to me. I don't know why. I did all I could to be a friend to you, but you treated me like shit.'

'I was jealous of you.' Bollocks. When she'd rehearsed it earlier, it had come out a lot better. 'I suppose I saw you as a threat.' That sounded calmer, but a bit sad and cliched, if she was honest.

'Because you wanted Will for yourself?'

Ouch. 'I thought I did. As it turned out, we both thought we wanted each other, but we were wrong. I thought I loved Will. I mean, I do, but not in that way. I realised it as soon as we kissed, and so did he.'

'You kissed?' Belle emptied her glass.

'Are you sure I can't get you—'

'No! You kissed?'

'Yes. I'm not gonna lie because it'll come out anyway. We kissed at Neil's party. But after we talked it through, we realised the feelings we had for each other were more like really good mates.' Kelly sounded so lame she was even making herself cringe.

'Really good mates who want to jump into bed with each other.'

'No. No we don't. We didn't do anything like that. Just a bit of kissing. The thing is, Belle, you're the one he loves, not me. He's so miserable without you.'

'Oh poor Will. My heart is, literally, bleeding for him. At least it would be if he hadn't been behaving as if I was an inconvenience for the past year. Do you know how many times I've had to stay at your house because we couldn't possibly leave poor Kelly on her own? Fucking hundreds.

You think I wanted to be there every fucking minute of the day and night? You think I didn't know you and Liza made jokes about me? And that shit Marcus. He made a pass at me, but do you think Will was bothered by it? Absolutely fucking not. Why? Because he was too angry about you having noisy sex, with said shit.'

'Oh. I didn't realise.'

Belle narrowed her eyes. 'No, I don't suppose you did. Seeing things from other people's point of view isn't exactly on the top of your priority list, is it?'

'I'm sorry, Belle. I really am so sorry. I fucked everything up.'

'No. Will has. Don't make excuses for him. He really doesn't deserve it.'

'I think he knows that.'

Belle crossed her legs and folded her arms. 'I'll have that drink now.'

Kelly got two more drinks from the bar. Belle immediately swallowed a mouthful of hers. 'How is he?'

'Pretty bad. He knows he's blown it with you. Has he blown it with you?'

Belle shrugged. 'I don't know. Probably. It depends. It's all so...'

'Crap?'

'I was going to say humiliating.'

'Ah. Yes that's a better word. I know how that feels. I'm sorry. I may not have done the things Will did, but I've treated you badly. I wish I'd been a better friend.'

'Just being a friend might have helped.'

'Point taken.'

Kelly let herself into Netta's house. She was still reeling

from the verbal battering she'd had from Belle. Her nan used to say the truth often hurts. Kelly was definitely stung. Her penance list was getting longer.

Will was on the sofa watching TV. 'Been to the pub?'

'Yeah. With Zoe from book group.'

'Wanna watch a movie?'

She sat down next to him. They were back to being two really good mates again. 'Sure. How you doing anyway?'

He shrugged and flicked through the channels.

'You tried Belle lately?'

'No. You tried Obie?'

'No. I might do again though. It'd be stupid to give up on them too easily, wouldn't it?' She was lying. She'd already given up on Obie speaking to her again, but Will didn't need to know that.

56

THE REAL CAITLIN DONOHUE

Kelly played with her mum's Saint Christopher. She'd been wearing it lately. She tucked it under her T-shirt and rang the bell. The woman who answered the door was very nearly the image of her mum. If she'd remembered Teresa, she might have expected it, but she didn't. As far as Kelly knew, Teresa hadn't been around much when her mum was alive, and she hadn't been around at all after. None of the Donohues had.

Teresa was grinning from ear to ear. 'Kelly. God. The last time I saw you, you were what, twelve?'

Twelve? She must have been at the funeral then. Kelly didn't remember.

'Mam's in the living room. She's been looking forward to seeing you.'

If the old woman in the living room had been looking forward to seeing Kelly, she wasn't showing it. There was no smile, just a sour face and this: 'You look like him.'

'Cheers. You look like her,' said Kelly.

Nanny Donohue's mouth pulled into a pinched little

smirk. 'You always were a cheeky wee devil. I suppose I should be grateful there's something of her in you.'

'Fucking hell.' Kelly muttered it under her breath, but the old cow's hearing was still good.

'Language is it? If you'd been my child, I'd have knocked that out of you.'

'Really? Mum could have taught swearing as a second language, so you didn't do that good a job, did yer?'

Her nan folded her bony hands into each other and glared. Swallowed by the soft, comfy armchair, she looked smaller and thinner than Kelly remembered. A lot older too. But Kelly didn't remember her being this nasty. 'Look, I can go. I only came because I thought you wanted to see me.'

Teresa saved her from another insult by swinging through the door with a tray. 'Coffee for me and Kelly. Tea for you, Mammy. Won't you sit down, Kelly?'

Kelly sat on the sofa, closest to Teresa and furthest away from her nan.

Teresa offered her a plate of cakes. 'Would you have a cake? Your dad said you like brownies.'

Brownies? Shit. Brownies were Obie cakes. Brownies were sadness. She would have preferred something different, but her aunt had gone out of her way to find out what her favourite cakes were. It would be rude not to take one. She picked one out. *Please don't let it be chocolate orange.*

'I got chocolate orange. Your dad said you like those best.'

Her hand froze in mid-air. It was too late to put it back now. Teresa was waiting for her to take a bite. She took one and as soon as it hit her mouth, she wanted to throw up.

'They're nice, aren't they? The bakery up the road makes them fresh each morning.'

'Delicious.' She took a mouthful of coffee to wash it away.

'Andy said you wanted to hear a bit more about your mum's travelling years. I've sorted out some old photos for you. She used to send postcards. I kept them all but they've been lost, unfortunately. I expect they got binned in a clear up. But the photos. I have the photos.'

'I've got some postcards that belonged to an old lady who used to live in my friend's house. I've been collecting them.'

'That's nice. We've something in common then. Let me get those photos.' Teresa grabbed an envelope from the top of the sideboard and gave it to her.

Kelly took the photos out and looked longingly at the exotic places her mum had travelled to. There was one that was similar to the photo she had at home. 'I think I've got one from the same place. Dad gave it to me. She looks about the same age as me.'

'She was,' said Teresa. 'She left home just before her twenty-first, so very close to you in age.'

Nanny Donohue shuffled in her armchair. 'She should never have gone. It was the ruination of her.'

'No, Mammy it wasn't.' Teresa sighed. 'Sorry, it's just that we've had this argument so many times. Mam insists the travelling and your dad gave Caity the cancer.'

'And so it did,' shouted the old woman.

'Mother, for Christ's sake, will you listen to yourself? You sound like some mad old bat, which you are not. Kelly hasn't come all this way to hear your crazy conspiracy theories. She wants to hear nice things.'

'I want to hear truthful things,' said Kelly.

Teresa frowned. 'They're one and the same when it

comes to your mum. Caity was special. She was the kindest, funniest big sister I could have wished for.'

Nanny Donohue snorted. 'She was wild. And she drank too much. And she was terrible with money. I lost count of the number of times me and Gladys had to rescue her.'

Kelly swivelled round to look at the old woman. 'Nanny Payne?'

'Gladys Payne, yes. I moved in with her for a while so we could keep an eye on Caity.'

'I bet that went down a treat,' said Kelly.

Teresa laughed. 'Like a lead balloon, I should imagine.'

Kelly looked through the photos again. 'She looks so happy.'

'She was always happy. Right up till the...' Nanny Donohue sniffed. 'Take some if you want them.'

'Are you sure you don't mind?' said Kelly.

'They're no good to me. I'll be dead soon anyway.'

Kelly glanced at Teresa. Her aunt rolled her eyes. 'Take no notice of her. She's been saying that for years. I'm sure she only says it to get my hopes up.'

The old woman made a noise that sounded almost like a laugh. 'You're a wicked girl, Teresa. Don't be taking any lessons in empathy from this one, Kelly. She's a real dunce at it.'

'What time is your train back?' said Teresa.

'Four. I've got a couple of hours yet.'

'How about if I take you to lunch then. Do you like Turkish? There's a lot of it around here.'

'Yeah, sure.'

'You coming, Mammy?'

'I wouldn't be seen dead in one of those places. You two go. I'm tired. You can tell Kelly all about your wonderful sister.'

'Right you are then. I'll see Kelly to the station afterwards. Unless you want to come?'

Her nan shook her head. 'I won't. Come here, Kelly.'

Kelly crouched down in front of her nan and the Saint Christopher fell out from beneath her T-shirt. The old woman gasped. 'Where did you get that?'

'Dad gave it to me. It was Mum's.'

'I know. I gave it to her. It was supposed to keep her safe.'

'Do you want it back?'

Her nan wiped her watery eyes. 'No, love. You have it. Maybe God will look more kindly on you than He did your mother.' She pulled out a purse that was stuffed down the side of the chair and took out a couple of notes. 'Buy yourself something nice.'

Kelly shook her head. 'It's all right, I don't need your money.'

Her nan put the notes into Kelly's hand and closed it up. 'Take it. I want you to have it. I'm sorry. Sorry I didn't do more.'

Kelly slipped the money into her jeans pocket. 'Dan and Conor look like her. I thought you'd want to know.'

The old woman took a deep breath. 'Tell them not to come then. I couldn't bear it.'

In the restaurant, Kelly let Teresa order the food. She picked lots of small plates of different dishes. Apparently, it was called a meze in places like Turkey and Greece. 'Something for you to remember if you get there. Andy said you're going to travel too.'

'I'm thinking about it. I've already ordered my passport.

I was hoping someone would go with me but that fell through.'

Teresa dabbed her bread in one of the dips. 'The boyfriend?'

'Dad told you about him as well, did he?'

'He mentioned that he really liked him.'

'It didn't work out. Don't tell Dad though. I don't want him worrying about me.'

'I won't. Sorry about Mam. She really did want to see you. She still hasn't got over Caity.'

'I can understand that.'

'She did love Caity. It's just that she finds it hard to show her feelings. And she's a crabby old biddy at the best of times.'

'Did mum love her?'

Teresa thought for a minute. 'Difficult to say. Mam was strictest with her. She was the oldest girl, so she ended up taking a lot of the load with housework and looking after us younger ones. It was like that in those days. No such thing as equality back then. That's why she left. She needed to get away from all that responsibility.'

'So she wasn't wild?'

'Not when she was at home. But maybe a bit when she left. Perhaps the freedom went to her head. I'll tell you what though. She was an inspiration to me. When I was old enough, I took off too. I went to all the places she went to, and a few she didn't. And maybe I went a bit wild too, but it was the best time of my life.'

For the next hour or so, Teresa did most of the talking. Kelly was happy to hear more about her mum and what she was really like. But there was something she needed to ask that she hoped Teresa might know the answer to. 'Mum used to have a friend. I don't know his name, but he always seemed to be hanging around. Did she ever say anything about him.'

'There was one fella. I met him once. I don't remember his name but he was real shifty looking. I told her so too. She knew him from when she was travelling. He was a bit obsessed with her and I think she let him hang around because he reminded her of the travelling days. It was nothing more than that though. She only had eyes for your dad, so don't you be thinking there was more to it.'

Teresa walked her to Dalston station. They stopped by the barriers. 'I have something else for you. I found one card that I'd kept. It's a letter card. Caity sent it to me just before she stopped travelling. There's stuff in there about your dad. About her feelings for him. I've kept it long enough. Let me know if you go. I'd love to meet up with you somewhere foreign.'

'What about Nan? Would she manage without you?'

'Of course. She's not an invalid. Just chronically miserable. Besides, she can always go and stay with one of my useless brothers.' She hugged Kelly. 'I'm glad you came. Goodbye, gorgeous girl.'

Kelly held on tight. It could have been her mum she was holding onto. It could so easily have been her mum.

She got to Euston early, so she spent some time wandering around the area. She didn't like it very much. It was big and busy, and ugly. Was this Obie's London? He came from somewhere called Peckham. She had no idea where that was.

In the end she nearly missed her train and she had to

run to catch it. She found her seat and settled herself, then she took out the lettercard and read it:

'Hello gorgeous girl,

I've decided to call you this from now on. My new man calls me it, because he says I am the most gorgeous, fantastic woman he's ever met in his entire life. Is that a lot to live up to, or what?

I'm not calling you that for the same reason. I'm doing it because it's cute, and you are my cute little sister and I miss you.

Anyway, about this new man. His name is Andy Payne and he is so unbelievably beautiful. Teresa, you would not believe how beautiful he is. No kidding. He has the cheekbones of a god. The look of him just melts me. But that's not all. He's a darling. So sweet and gentle and loveable. I am so in love with him. He says he loves me too, and this is absolutely not a holiday romance.

Here comes the crunch. He went back home to Birmingham last month. I'm lost without him, Teresa. It's crazy, but I feel completely empty. It's like I don't exist without him. I've tried going out with other guys, but I'm just thinking about him ALL THE FECKING TIME.

He gave me his home address and phone number, so I think he wants me to call or write. But you know me, it's not my style. I might just go to his house. Just turn up like. Is that a bit mad? He could have given me a false address and then I'd look like a total eejit. I don't think so though. I really think he loves me.

To be honest, I'm scared he'll want to settle down and I'll say yes because I love him so much. You know me, Teresa. I'm bad at being normal. But maybe it's what I need. I'm about done with travelling anyway. The last six months, I've taken everything a bit too far, if you know what I mean. Only Andy can save me now – ha ha.

Don't say anything to Mammy, by the way. You know what an old cow she is. She'll only try to ruin it for me.

Love you to bits, baby sister. A million kisses coming your way.

Caity xxxx'

Kelly glanced at the pictures on the other side of the letter card as she folded it up. They were of different places in Thailand. On any other day, she'd have given them a closer look. But today, she didn't care. Today, she'd found the real Caitlin Donohue. The person she never really knew. And today, she finally understood her mum and dad's relationship.

She looked out of the window, past her own reflection at the houses rolling by. Her dad was beautiful, with the cheekbones of a god, according to her mum. It was news to her. Although he was good looking, she supposed. She reeled her eyes in and stared at herself in the glass. She looked like him. Maybe she was beautiful too. Hadn't Obie called her perfect?

She opened the letter up again and read the line her mum had written about missing her dad: *'It's like I don't exist without him.'* She knew what that was like.

57

THE LOST ART OF LETTER WRITING

Kelly's passport had arrived yesterday. Netta didn't know she'd sent off for one. But why wouldn't she have when she'd been talking about going for so long? She must have been waiting for it to come before making her announcement. She was leaving, as soon as they could find someone to fill in for her at work, and she wouldn't be back for a year.

The morning had been rather a solemn one. It was like someone had died, but no one wanted to acknowledge it. The conversation was strained and none of them wanted to bring up the fact that Kelly would soon be far away from here. The market was quiet which made matters worse. Netta was glad to pack up.

They went to their usual Moseley café. It was sad to think this might be their last visit here as a threesome. For a year, anyway.

Neil rested his arms on the table and looked at her and Kelly. 'So.'

'So,' said Netta, resigned to having the talk.

Kelly sighed. 'So. How soon do you think we'll be able to find someone?'

'Chris thinks he might have a potential candidate,' said Neil. 'The mum of one of the kids he teaches. We can interview her this week.'

'I thought you might wait till next year now, with it being the end of summer,' said Netta.

Kelly shook her head. 'I can't, Net. I need to go. I'm sorry. I know this isn't fair on either of you. It's just that I need to get away.'

Neil sighed. 'But a whole year, Kel. Are you sure you'll be able to go it alone for that long?'

'I'll make myself. I won't be alone all that time anyway. I'm hoping some of my friends and family will meet up with me. I've got a couple of volunteers already.'

'You can count me and Chris in,' he said.

'Me and Frank too,' said Netta.

Kelly smiled. 'You two are great, you know. I'm really gonna miss you.'

'We'll miss you too.' Netta was trying to fight back the tears. Then she looked over at Neil and saw that he was as bad as her. 'Is this an appropriate moment for a group hug, do you think?'

Kelly held out her arms. 'Let's do it.'

Afterwards they went round to Netta's parent's house. Her dad was at his allotment. Netta assumed he was there of his own free will, and hadn't been banished so they could have another of their chats.

Her mum looked a little teary-eyed herself. 'You're really going then?'

'Yes, I am,' said Kelly.

'Because you want to travel, or because of Obie?'

'Both, since you ask.'

'That bad, is it?'

'Pretty much. I can't stay, knowing he's here. It's too…' Kelly looked down at her hands.

Netta's mum put her arm around Kelly. 'You poor love. If it's any consolation, he looks just as miserable as you.'

Kelly shook her head. 'Not really, Gez. But thanks for trying.'

'But if he's miserable too, that must give you some hope. Have you tried talking to him lately?'

'I've tried calling him but he doesn't pick up. It's a lost cause and it's my own fault. I've really hurt him.'

'You could try writing to him. Couldn't she, Nettie?'

'It's worth a try,' said Netta.

Kelly frowned. 'What, like an email?'

'I was thinking more of an actual letter,' said Netta's mum.

Kelly screwed up her face. 'On paper?'

'Yes. It's old-fashioned, I know, but seeing the words written down can mean a lot more. Wouldn't you say Netta?'

Kelly face was blank. It was a generational thing of course. The concept of pen and paper communication was quite alien to young people. A lost art. But Netta knew Kelly had had at least one letter that had meant a lot to her. 'Didn't you once tell me you used to have a letter your mum had written to you? Do you remember how it felt to read her words, and see them in her own handwriting?'

'Yes. But that was different. She was dead. I'll think about it though.'

Netta's mum patted Kelly's knee. 'You do that. How's Will?'

Netta pulled a face. 'Quiet. He hasn't said a lot. He doesn't talk to me much these days.'

'He's ashamed. Plus, he's still hurting about losing Belle,' said Kelly. 'I went to see her. Belle. To apologise. Will doesn't know that though. Don't tell him.'

'And how is she?' said Netta.

Kelly blew threw her lips. 'Angry and upset, but I think she might be willing to listen to him, if he tried.'

Netta stopped herself from saying poor Belle. No need to rub salt in the wound. 'I'll see if I can get him to talk to me on the way up to York tomorrow.'

Kelly nodded. 'Belle told me I don't like to see things from other people's point of view.'

'Empathy. Have you looked that one up?' said her mum.

'Yeah. My Irish nan mentioned the word when I went to see her. It's true, isn't it?'

Netta and her mum exchanged glances. Her mum beat her to the answer: 'Sometimes. But not with me. With me, you had empathy by the truckload, right when I needed it.'

Kelly nodded. 'You were easy, Gez.'

Will was up early the next morning. Netta was driving him back to York to start his masters. He didn't want to wait for the others to get up before they left. He knocked on their doors and said a quick goodbye instead.

It wasn't until they left Birmingham behind that he began to look slightly less tense. She got the feeling he was glad to see the back of it. Nonetheless, they'd been driving for over an hour before Netta managed to get anything meaningful out of him. It wasn't that he was being sullen or anything. He was just distant. Eventually, she decided to take the plunge and just go for it. 'Things back on track between you and Kelly now?'

He looked up from his phone. 'Yeah, we're good.'

'And Belle. How are things with her?'

'Not so good.'

'You've given up on her then?'

'I think she's given up on me, Mum. Not that I blame her.'

'Oh Will. I'm so sorry.'

He put his hand up. 'Don't. I know you mean well, but please don't feel sorry for me. I've been a complete prick. I've ruined two relationships and I didn't even realise how selfish I was being until Liza spelt it out to me. That's how far up myself I am. Fucking hell.'

'Liza's said something?'

'Liza's said a lot. She's told me exactly how badly I've treated Belle, how I've been stringing Kelly along, and how I've trampled over Obie's feelings.'

'She didn't hold back then?' Not for the first time did Netta marvel at her daughter.

Will smirked. 'You can always rely on Lize for some hard-hitting honesty. She's right though. But you know what the worst of it is? I'm just like him. It's just the kind of thing he would do, and I hate myself for it.'

Oh no, Netta wasn't having this. The motorway services were just up ahead. It was time to put her darling boy right. She moved over to the slip road. 'We need to stop.'

She pulled up in a parking space and turned off the engine. 'Let's get this straight, Will. You are nothing like your dad.'

He looked her in the eye. 'I am though, aren't I?'

'No, you're not. I try to keep my opinions of him to myself, but I'm making an exception today because you need to see the difference. For reasons I've never under-stood, Colin enjoys controlling people. He seems to get some kind of validation from it. That is not you. It's true you've been an idiot and from the sounds of it, not covered yourself in glory with Belle, but you are nothing like your dad. Quite the opposite if anything.'

'Okay. You were quite fierce there, Mum.'

Netta shrugged. 'I get worked up sometimes. Listen, you should try speaking to Belle again.'

He shook his head. 'It's too late for that now.'

'Try one last time, Will. For the sake of my happiness if not your own. She's going back to Leeds, isn't she? Why don't you write her a letter? Open your heart to her. Tell her you recognise how badly you've treated her. Ask for her forgiveness.'

'I suppose I could try mailing her.'

What was it about kids and their aversion to pen and paper? 'Or you could write an actual letter.'

'She changed addresses over the holidays. I don't know the new one.'

'Email it is then.'

On the way back from York, Netta found somewhere to stop and ring her mum. 'We had a good talk. I did the letter speech.'

'Ooh, well done you. Did it work?'

'Not sure. He doesn't know her new address, but he's considering emailing her.'

'Fingers crossed then. I've persuaded Kelly to come to the book group for one last meeting. We'll see how that goes.'

58

THE REDISCOVERED ART OF LETTER WRITING

Kelly reminded herself to breathe before she opened the café door. Geraldine wasn't there yet, but Zoe was. She gave Kelly a sympathetic smile. 'Shall I get you a drink?

'No, I'll do it.' If she was going to have any chance of staying for the meeting, she had to face Obie.

He was pretending to wipe down the counter. She could tell it was pretence because he was wiping the same spot, over and over.

Archie looked flustered. 'Hi, Kelly. Cappuccino?' He waited for a few seconds after she'd said yes. Maybe he was expecting Obie to make it, but Obie wasn't moving, apart from the wiping. 'Right then. One cappuccino coming up.'

Kelly waited in front of Obie. The counter was the only thing between them. The closeness of him sent her heart racing even faster. She wanted to touch him, but the fear of his reaction stopped her. 'Can we talk?'

His eyes were blinking like crazy but he kept them glued to the spot he was still wiping. 'No. I don't think so.'

So this was it then? The last thing he said to her. What a

fucking let down. She'd been mad to think it would be anything else. Kelly's eyes were beginning to sting. She walked out, before she made even more of a fool of herself.

She hadn't got far when she heard Zoe calling her. 'I can't go back in. Tell Gez I'm sorry.' She left Zoe in the street and ran away.

Oh God it hurt. It hurt so much. But she only had herself to blame. If she hadn't told Will she loved him, if she hadn't kissed him, none of this would have happened. She would have said she was weak like her mum, but at least her mum had the self-awareness to know what she was like. At least her mum knew real love when she saw it.

Kelly was on her bed with the dogs and Arthur Three. She was grateful that Liza and Netta were out at Pilates, because she wouldn't have wanted them to see the state she'd been in when she got home. Geraldine had called her. Zoe would have told her what happened. Kelly hadn't answered but she'd sent a message to say she was fine, although it was unlikely Gez would believe her.

She rested her head in her hands but all she could see was Obie and those intense black-brown eyes of his. She remembered thinking how much more dangerous than Marcus's they seemed. It must have been one of those premonitions, because Obie had been the dangerous one. Marcus was nothing. He'd just chipped away at her ego. But Obie had broken her heart. She heard Geraldine's voice in her head telling her that technically, she'd been the heart breaker, not Obie, and she wondered how long it would take him to get over her, if he hadn't already.

She scrolled to her favourite picture of him on her

phone, one where he was gazing at her like he really adored her. Perhaps he did. Perhaps that's why she'd hurt him so badly. She should delete the photos and get rid of all trace of him. But if she did, she'd have nothing left to torture herself with, and she needed to torture herself. That penance thing again. She needed to pay for what she'd done to him, and to herself.

A message popped up on her phone. Gez. Of course it was:

'Write to him.'

'Fuck's sake, Geraldine. Give it up.' Betty and Maud's heads shot up. Kelly patted their backs. 'Pardon me, ladies.'

Her phone pinged again:

'One last try.'

'Fucking interfering old…' She was seriously considering blocking Geraldine. It wasn't as if she even had any writing paper. Maud made a low growling noise. Kelly eyeballed her. 'Don't you start. You're supposed to be my friend.'

Another growl, followed by a whine. Betty looked from Maud to Kelly, like she hadn't got a clue. But Maud knew. Maud always knew.

'All right. But if this ends badly, Maud Pinsent, I'm blaming you.'

She found some proper writing paper in the study. It was pale blue and had the address printed at the top. It must have been Edie's. She would have been a letter writer, for sure. She sat down, ready to write.

Half an hour later, she had two screwed up pieces of paper and one very blank page. She counted the remaining sheets. Twenty left. If these were Edie's, they were precious. She couldn't waste them. That would be unforgivable. She remembered the things Edie wrote in her diaries. Edie was a good writer. She should try to say it the way she might have said it. Kelly concentrated. What would Edie say? She chewed on her pen while she channelled her inner Edie, and then the words came:

'*Dear Obie,*

Geraldine said I should write to you. She seems to think you might read it, even if you won't speak to me. I hope so.

You have every right to be angry with me. I did a bad thing to you. Believe me, we did only kiss, but I know it was more than the kissing I told you there was nothing going on between me and Will, and I lied. When I first met Will, I didn't like him that much, but we got closer when he moved in with us. Somehow, it turned into love. But it was all in my head, Obie. There was never anything physical until Neil's party. What I didn't know until we kissed was that I'd confused that love with something else. I know I shouldn't have kissed him in the first place. I know I should have thought of you, but I was too weak and selfish to stop myself.

I love Will like a brother. Maybe even more than my actual broth-ers. But I don't want to be with him. I don't love him in that way. I finally get it. He's not the one. It's you, Obie. It will always be you.

I thought I knew what loneliness was until I lost you. Now I really do know. Loneliness is not having you near me. It's you not cooking for me because you like cooking for me. It's you not calling me Birmingham because you think I have a funny accent. It's not dancing naked with you to some fat old bloke who sounds a bit pervy. And it's knowing I'll never be with you again.

I'm so much more sorry than I can ever say. I betrayed you. We had something and I broke it, and I don't blame you for hating me. I hate myself too.

I can't stand not being with you in this city, Obie. It's killing me.

So I'm going away. I've told everyone it's for a year, but I don't know if I'll ever be able to come back.

I'm going to London first. I want to explore the place you come from. I don't know why. I should just give up on you, but that's where my head is right now. It's like I can't get enough of beating myself up over you. After London, I've got a list of places and a sketchy plan that starts with France.

You can still come with me. I know you have your own plans and your commitments, and you probably don't want to be with me. But I want to be with you, and I promise, I'll never hurt you again.

I've bought two train tickets for Sunday morning. The train leaves at eleven. I'll send you the e-ticket. If I don't see you or hear from you by then, I'll know we're done.

Kelly x'

Kelly turned into Obie's road on her bike. She was going to put the letter through his door so she'd know he had it. No excuses about it getting lost in the post.

She hadn't planned on running into Archie, but he was just coming through the gate as she reached it. 'Obie's not here. He's gone away for a couple of days.'

'Do you know when he'll be back?'

'Saturday.'

She gave him the letter. 'Could you make sure he gets this? It's important. Only, I'm going away myself on Sunday. Travelling. I'd like him to read it before.'

'Sure. He's due back by lunchtime.'

'Thanks, Arch.' She'd send that ticket to him on Saturday evening. If she did it before he had a chance to read the letter, he might delete the mail.

Archie put the letter in his pocket. 'I'm sorry it hasn't

worked out for you two. You were good together. He's been really happy.'

'Until I ruined it, you mean. Look after Robyn. She deserves someone nice.'

Archie smiled. 'So do you.'

59

RETREAT TO PECKHAM

Obie Kalu was feeling a bit wounded, if he was honest. Things had been tough lately. It was bad enough finding out that the only woman he'd ever felt something for, had a secret thing going on with another guy. But all that stuff yesterday. It was wounding. That's what it was.

He hadn't expected Kelly to turn up like that. In hindsight, that was a bit short-sighted of him, given that it was a book group night. She was bound to come back eventually. The thing was, he'd been thinking about her at the very moment she turned up. Again in hindsight, not too much of a coincidence because he was nearly always thinking about her. But he'd been thinking about her and that guy, Will, at the time, because he was trying look again at what he'd seen. Maybe he'd misread the situation. Maybe they weren't really locked in some kind of Romeo and Juliet style tryst. It didn't matter which way he looked at it though, they were so locked.

So there he was, about to throw himself into a pit of despair and desolation again, when he saw her with Zoe. Then she was in front of him, watching him clean the same spot on the counter, over and over, because he didn't know what else to do. So yeah, he was on edge, and yeah, he reacted badly. He didn't need anyone else to tell him. But just in case he hadn't realised, Zoe came back in from running after Kelly and said one word that summed up her feelings perfectly: 'Nob.'

And then Geraldine came along. 'I hear you've upset Kelly.'

Obie wasn't taking that one lying down. 'I think you'll find Kelly's upset me.'

'I know, love.' Geraldine looked at him like she really felt his pain, but then she delivered the killer blow. 'It's no wonder you despise her.'

Despise her? Nooo! That wasn't it at all. 'I don't. It's just that...' He'd wanted to say he was hurt and bereft, and the only one who'd lost everything. Because at least those two had each other. Except that poor Belle. He didn't say that though. Instead he muttered: 'I've been wronged.' It was a bit feeble now that he thought about it.

He'd thought Geraldine was going to laugh in his face for a minute, but she'd managed to contain herself. 'I can see that, sweetheart. So can Kelly. On the bright side, that silly incident at the party has helped both of them realise they made a mistake.' Then she patted his hand and, just when he'd thought she was on his side, she added: 'I hope you don't make one too. I'll take a cappuccino and leave you to consider my words. Just don't take too long considering them. Time is not on your side.' He was just wondering what she meant by that bit about time not being on his side when she suddenly said: 'Wronged, you say. Do you read much Jane Austen at all?'

So there he was, hurt, bereft and now nonplussed, when Archie, his best bud, his wing man, chipped in: 'She's got a point, mate. Would it kill you to listen to what Kelly has to say?'

Yes it fucking would actually. Not that he'd say that to Arch. So instead, he'd said: 'Do you think you could manage without me for a couple of days? I need to go home.'

Obie dragged his wounded ass out of Peckham Rye station, along Rye Lane. As soon as he reached the High Street, he was hit by familiar sights and smells. The stores brimming with yam, cassava, plantain and so many more. The fishmonger and butcher his grandma went to. The familiar accents – African, Caribbean and London – all mixed up together. He was born in Peckham. His grandparents lived here and so did his sister. Many of his old school friends had stayed in the area. His parents had moved them a bit further out to East Dulwich when he was eleven, but he'd still spent most of his time in Peckham before he left for uni. It had been nearly three years, but he was home. Except that he wasn't. Peckham wasn't home anymore. It was too busy, too loud, too everything that wasn't Birmingham. Or was it just everything that wasn't where Kelly was? He couldn't tell the difference these days.

He'd only been walking for fifteen minutes and already he'd had to stop and say hello to three 'aunties'. They'd be round at the house telling his dad that he was here before the sun went down. That was the other thing about Peckham. It was too close. Suffocating. He remembered then how he couldn't wait to get away. His dad hadn't wanted him to leave London. Birmingham was different, he'd said. Foreign. It won't do you any good to live there.

He'd hated it at first, until he met Archie and started making more friends. Then he began to think for himself.

Perhaps that's why his dad didn't want him to leave home. What he really meant was Birmingham was too far away for him to keep control. Kelly had picked up on that and even if he hadn't agreed with her at the time, it had switched a light on in Obie's head. Kelly could read people even when she hadn't met them. She was clever like that. Mind you, if he hadn't gone to Birmingham, he wouldn't be numb with grief. So maybe his dad was right after all.

Gini grabbed her coat. 'Mum's on her way up. Sorry I can't stay.'

Obie held his sister in his arms until her muffled voice said: 'Obes, I'll be late for work.'

'Sorry.' He didn't want to let her go. Two days wasn't enough to cover three years of missing her. They'd had phone calls, but it wasn't the same.

Gini opened the door to her flat. 'Come back soon, yeah? And sort yourself out, Mister. Hey, Mum. Can't stop. Bye.'

His mum opened her mouth wide. 'She's like a human whirlwind. Hello, baby.' She kissed him and filled the gap in his arms that Gini had left. He clung to her soft, Mum body. Her perfume filled his nostrils, and Peckham finally felt like home again.

She pulled away and looked him over. 'It's so good to see you. Are you okay getting a later train? Someone was ill, so I had to do an extra shift.'

'Yeah, it's an open ticket. So long as I get back sometime today, it'll be fine.'

She sat down on Gini's sofa. 'Have you been sleeping on this? It's not very comfortable.'

'It was okay,' he lied. The sofa was small and hard, and he'd barely slept.

'So, Gini tells me you're nursing a broken heart. Want to talk about it?'

She probably already knew it all. Gini would have told her every single detail as soon as she got the chance, and she'd dragged a lot of detail out of him over the last two days. Still, it had helped talking to Gini. 'Her name's Kelly. I thought she really felt something for me, but then I caught her with this guy who's supposed to be her friend. They were kissing, which was bad enough, but the way they looked at each other, there was more to it than that.'

'I see. What did she have to say about it?'

'We haven't spoken about it properly, just argued. I want to talk but I can't. Every time I try to call her, I just freeze.'

His mum squeezed him into a cuddle and all of a sudden he was a kid again, needing to hear it was going to be all right. Except this time it wasn't.

'Tell me about her. What she's like.'

'She's a nightmare. I'm better off without her.' An image of Kelly telling him to crack a fucking smile slipped into his head and lo and behold, he cracked one, despite himself. 'Also, she's smart and funny. Sometimes she seems really vulnerable and other times she's so feisty and tough, it's scary. She's like really petite, with this cute little pointed chin that sticks out when she smiles. And incredible green eyes.' He saw Kelly's face in front of him, that sweet chin, her amazing cheekbones and those eyes, the kind you can't look away from. The kind that make you do stupid things, like pouring a heart into her coffee, in the hope she'll realise how much you like her. The kind that make you clean a single spot on the counter because you know if you look into them and see that she doesn't want you anymore, you won't be able to get through the day. Shit. That girl. That girl was a nightmare.

His mum held onto him and kissed his head. 'Oh baby, you've got it bad.'

He wiped his eyes. If it had been anyone but his mum, he'd have been embarrassed. 'You think?'

'So why are you walking away without fighting for her?'

His mum walked with him to the station. They'd had a long talk about Kelly and also about his life in Birmingham. She'd told him she was glad he'd found something and somewhere he could be himself. He hadn't realised he wasn't being himself when he was in London, so that came as a surprise. He'd have to think that one through and maybe they'd talk about it some more next time he came.

He was on the alert all the way to the station in case they bumped into his dad. His mum had said there was no chance of that but it didn't stop his uneasiness. 'Aren't you worried someone will see us and tell Dad?'

She frowned and smirked at the same time. 'He's not the boss of me. Anyway, I already told him.'

'What did he say?'

'Nothing. He went off for a sulk, just as he always does, even though he knows it's a childish way to behave.'

'I've been working hard to pay you back. I've got nearly five thousand saved.'

'Obie, you must have been working all hours to save that. Why are you doing it?'

'So that I'll be forgiven.'

She stopped walking and looked him squarely in the eye. 'Baby, it's not about the money. As far as I'm concerned there's nothing to forgive. Your dad's just angry because he thinks you let him believe it was what you wanted. And because he wanted you to follow the family tradition. His pride's been hurt, that's all. He already knows he's behaving like an idiot. I've told him the longer it goes on, the more he'll have to regret. It's just that ridiculous stubborn pride again. He'll come round eventually.'

'But I've worked so hard to get it.'

'And I'm proud of you for doing that. But we don't want it. Keep it, and please stop working so hard.'

It was taking ages to get back to Birmingham. There'd been some kind of incident on the line, and when the trains finally got running again they were packed. Obie hadn't noticed until he'd reached Euston that his phone had run out of charge. He hadn't checked it since that morning. He'd hoped to find a seat with a charging point, but there were no seats at all and he had to stand in the corridor by the toilet. With nothing to look at but the opening and closing toilet door, he let his mind wander and saw Kelly lying on the floor, rubbing her non-existent belly because she'd eaten too much. Kelly making love to him. Kelly dancing with him. Kelly mocking him, Kelly laughing, Kelly smiling. Kelly pleading with him. Kelly. He wanted so much to talk to her, and he wanted to listen but he was scared of what he might hear. His mum's words rang in his ears: 'Why are you walking away without fighting for her?' He didn't have an answer for her then, but he had one for himself now. Because he wasn't brave enough.

Obie let himself into the house. It was late and the place was in darkness. Archie was either in bed or still out. He left the lights off and crept upstairs in case his friend was asleep. He stuck his phone on charge and muted it. After two nights on his sister's sofa and having to stand for the entire journey, he was shattered. He didn't want anything disturbing him. He'd think about what he was going to do in the morning. Everything was so much easier to work out when you weren't exhausted. As soon as he lay his head down, he drifted off.

60

OH, BUT WAIT THOUGH...

Kelly rubbed the Saint Christopher for luck and tucked it under her jumper. Her mum's rings were being left with Netta for safekeeping. She closed up her new backpack. The bloody thing was nearly as big as her. Her passport, papers, cards, and money were in a small travel bag. She kept her phone in her pocket, just in case he called or messaged. You never know.

Over the past few days, she'd said goodbye to her friends and her families. For now, anyway. She'd see some of them again on her travels.

She took a last look around her room. *Little Women* was still by her bed. She'd finished it this week. Jo had been her favourite, naturally, but she'd cried buckets when Beth died. When she got to America, Kelly was going to make a point of checking out Massachusetts, as well as New York. Yesterday, she'd watched *Pride and Prejudice*, the TV show, with Geraldine. It seemed right, being as that was the book she'd started with and also, she wanted to know what all the fuss was about that wet shirt scene. The Mr Darcy on screen wasn't like she'd imagined he'd be but then, the way she'd imagined him had changed two or three times this year.

There was still a pile of books that she hadn't got through, but that was okay. She could read them when she came back. If she came back. Carol and her dad had given her an iPad, and she was going to use it to carry on reading while she was away. It had been an early birthday present. Her birthday was two weeks away. She'd be twenty-four. Unless a miracle happened, she'd be spending it on her own, along with Christmas.

Liza came to the open door. 'Nan and Grandad are here. Ready?'

Kelly put the postcards Obie had bought her in the travel bag. The others were in the backpack, but she wanted his close to her. 'Ready. Listen, Lize. Have this room. Yours is really poky and I won't be needing it for a while.'

'You are coming back though, aren't you?'

'Yeah but, you know. It's a waste of a good room and a beautiful ceiling. And it's about time you got the best.'

'If that's what you want. You haven't been talking to Mum, have you?'

'Not about you. I've just been having a go at empathising. Somebody told me recently, I wasn't great at it.'

She hauled the backpack onto her shoulders. It nearly toppled her. She'd get used to it. After one last look, she closed the bedroom door and went downstairs where the others were waiting for her.

'All set? Let me take that bag so you can say goodbye to the dogs,' said Arthur.

Kelly put her arms around Maud and Betty. 'Bye you two. Take care of each other while I'm away.'

Frank was waiting by the car. She hugged him. 'Thanks for everything, Frank. Sorry for winding you up all the time.'

He kissed the top of her head. 'Go on with yer. Remember to be careful, and remember to enjoy it.'

Maud and Betty were watching through the window. Kelly got in the car before she ran back down the path, and they drove away from the place she'd called home for the last four years.

Arthur dropped them off at New Street. After they'd waved Kelly off, Liza was going on another climate change protest and she was taking Netta and Geraldine with her. 'Don't forget your gubbins, ladies,' he said. 'One whistle each. I've also got one old football rattle and a megaphone.' It was his turn for a hug before he got moved on, and then they were walking into the station.

Kelly checked her phone yet again.

'No word?' said Geraldine.

She shook her head.

'I'm sorry, love.'

She put on a positive face. 'I'll get over it.'

'Looks like you're on platform eight. Have you got everything? Is there anything you need?' Netta was trying to be all business-like and efficient, but her shaky voice gave her away.

The board said it was twenty-five to eleven. He wasn't coming now. That was it. They were done. 'I have everything I need. I'll go down. You go to the march.'

Geraldine threw her arms around her. 'I'll see you in Nice.'

'Me too. Or another location, yet to be decided,' said Liza, when it was her turn.

Kelly saved the hardest to the last. 'Love you, Net.'

'Love you too. If you need me, don't be afraid to call.' Netta's bottom lip was trembling now.

'Stop worrying about me. I'm as hard as nails.' She kissed them all again, then she turned away and went through the barriers.

A trainload of people with banners and placards were crowding around the escalators. Her train had been delayed by five minutes so there was plenty of time to wait for them to clear. Her friends were watching her anxiously from the other side of the barriers. She wondered how she'd get on without them and what this next year would bring. One thing was sure. It would be a year of education, just like this last one had been. She was a little bit scared but it would be okay. She'd be like Lucy Snowe. She'd have her own adventure, with or without Obie. She'd write her own ending.

Netta watched Kelly going through the barriers. She looked so small with that huge backpack. So fragile. Like the only thing holding her down was the bag itself. Kelly had said she was hard as nails. They both knew that wasn't true. But this last year had proved one thing. Kelly was a survivor. When Netta had first known her, Kelly had been a girl who'd clung to anyone who showed some interest or affection. She'd had her wobbles but that girl was an incredibly brave young woman now who could do anything she chose to. Kelly had come of age, and she had flourished.

'If only Obie had come,' said Liza.

Netta put her arm around her daughter. It was time for her to focus on another remarkable young woman now, and it was way overdue. 'She'll find a way to live without him.'

Liza seized Netta's coat. 'Oh, but wait though…'

61

OBIE THE NOB

Obie Kalu tore through New Street Station as if his life depended on it, which it did of course. It was quarter to eleven. He was going to miss her.

Less than an hour ago he'd been woken by banging on his door. He'd opened it to Archie looking panic-stricken. 'Fuck, man. Where have you been? You were supposed to come back yesterday afternoon. I told her you'd be back to read it.'

'I had to hang on so I could see my mum. She was doing a double shift. Wait. You told who? Read what?'

'The letter.'

Obie was still half-asleep. Perhaps that's why he was having trouble understanding. 'I don't know what you're talking about.'

'Didn't you get my messages? I've been calling and messaging you since I realised you weren't coming back on time. Kelly's left you a letter. I promised I'd get you to read it yesterday. She's going away, Obes. Today.'

Today? No, no, no. She couldn't. She just couldn't. 'Where is it?'

'I left it down in the hall for you. Didn't you see it last night? I messaged you–'

'My phone. The charge. It was late. Never mind.'

Archie handed him a blue envelope. 'I came up as soon as I realised.'

Obie took out the thick blue sheets. They were quality paper. Not the kind he'd have expected from Kelly. A torn off page of A4 was more her style. He read her words. They were beautiful. Poetic. He would have liked to have spent more time drinking them in but there wasn't time. Instead his eyes lingered on the three most important lines of his life: *'He's not the one. It's you, Obie. It will always be you.'* She loved him. She hadn't said it exactly, but that's what she meant.

He read down to the bottom. *'If I don't see you or hear from you by then, I'll know we're done.'*

'What time is it?'

'Nearly ten.'

'Shit! I have to get to New Street. She's leaving at eleven.' Dressed. He needed to get dressed. Passport. Where was his passport? In the drawer. Which drawer? Where were his clothes?

Archie was all over the place too. 'What can I do, what can I do?'

Obie pulled on his jeans. 'Passport. Check those drawers. Just empty them out. This is an emergency.'

Archie wrenched open the drawers and emptied the contents onto the floor while Obie threw the rest of his clothes on. He held the passport in the air. 'Got it. I'll drop you in.'

They bolted downstairs and into his old Fiesta. Archie shot through the lights on Moseley Road just before they turned to red. 'We'll make it, we've still got time.'

'I'll call her.' Obie reached into his pocket for his phone, but it wasn't there. He tried the others, then his bag. Then he remembered. It was still on charge in his room. He put his head in his hands. What had Zoe called him? A nob. Yep. That was about right. 'I've left my phone at home.'

'We can't go back now. Use mine.'

'I don't know her number.'

Archie gave him a sideways look and the word nob sprung to mind again. Obie held out his hands. 'That's what contacts are for. So's you don't have to remember these things.'

Archie pulled his phone out of his back pocket and threw it at him. 'Robyn. Call Robyn. Tell her to call Kelly.'

The call went to Robyn's voicemail. 'Robyn, it's Obie. No time to explain. Can you call Kelly now and tell her I'm on the way. Tell her not to get on that train without me.'

Archie dodged another red light with seconds to spare. 'Message her as well. She might see that first.'

Obie tapped out the same message and waited for the ticks to go blue. 'I'm sorry, Arch. About our plans, I mean. We were gonna do so much.'

'We can still do them when you get back. We're just having a time out.'

'What will you do?'

'Not sure. I think maybe I'll spend some time up in Edinburgh, if Rob'll have me. See where it goes from there.'

'Good plan. You should go anyway. Even if I don't get back with Kelly. I know I don't say it much, but–'

'I know. Me too, bruv. It might be quicker to get out now. Must be the Sunday morning shoppers.'

Obie grabbed his bag and ran along Smallbrook Queensway. He was sweating and out of breath. His sides ached and he wanted to throw up. He was running on pure adrenalin now.

The station was busy for a Sunday morning. Really busy. Not just the usual shoppers, but groups of people with placards. Obie pushed through them and glanced up at the departures board. The train was leaving from platform eight. She was probably already down there and he had no way of getting through the barriers, unless he could get a ticket. Ticket machine. Where were the ticket machines? And then he saw them through the placards and banners. Geraldine, Liza and Netta, jumping up and down and waving at him.

'She's there. She's over there,' screamed Liza.

Obie followed her direction and saw Kelly walking towards the escalator, loaded up with one of those travelling backpacks. 'I can't get in.'

They rushed at him. 'Get her attention. I'll ring her,' said Netta.

Liza and Geraldine started blowing through the whistles that were hanging around their necks. Liza rattled one of those football clackers. Geraldine called to Kelly though a megaphone, but her voice was too small to be heard over the noise.

'I can't get through,' said Netta.

'Give me that thing.' Obie grabbed the megaphone and ran to the barriers. He saw Kelly stop at the top of escalator and move aside to answer her phone. There was still a chance. He put the megaphone to his mouth and shouted at the top of his voice: 'Kelly. Kelly Payne. Wait! I'm coming with you.'

62

COME AND GET ME

Kelly was about to go down to the platform when she heard her phone ringing. It was a wonder she could hear anything with all the noise. It sounded as if some of those demonstrators had started the protest inside the station. She took out her phone, hoping for that last minute miracle. But miracles only happen in books. Just like Mr Darcy, they weren't real. And Obie Kalu wasn't calling her. It was Robyn. 'You're not on the train yet, are you?'

'No it's been delayed. Just going down to the platform.'

'Don't get on it. Obie's on his way. He's coming for you. He asked me to give you this message…'

Kelly didn't hear the message. Something else drowned it out. It was Obie's voice, coming through loud and clear: 'Kelly Payne. Wait! I'm coming with you.'

She scanned the station until she saw him, pressed up against one of the barriers with Arthur's megaphone. Netta, Geraldine and Liza were behind him, whistling, rattling and screaming. Everyone in the station was looking at them.

'I love you. I love you, Kelly Payne. Please come and get me.'

There was whooping and cheering. People had their phones out filming him. Someone let him through the barrier and the cheering got louder. So fucking embarrassing. She was so gonna kill him.

And then she ran. She ran, as fast as that stupidly heavy bag would allow her, into the arms of Obie Kalu.

A WORD FROM THE AUTHOR

Hello

I hope you enjoyed reading Kelly's story. If you did, would you mind leaving a review?

Your reviews are important. They help me to reach more readers and they help other readers to decide whether this book is for them.

You can leave a review at your local Amazon store .

To find out more about other stories written by me, read on…

READ NETTA'S COMPANION STORY, BEING DOOGIE CHAMBERS

If this book leaves you wanting to know more about the world of Netta Wilde and her friends, you can join Hazel's **Readers' Club** and get **Being Doogie Chambers,** a free book available exclusively to members of the club.

https://hazelwardauthor.com/readers-club/

MORE BOOKS IN THE NETTA WILDE SERIES.

MINDING FRANK O'HARE

It's nearly time to hear Frank's story.

Keep an eye on his Amazon page for more details on the next book in the Netta Wilde series.

You can **pre-order** it now – out no later than 1st April 2024.

BEING NETTA WILDE

A lonely woman. A single decision. A second chance at happiness.

★★★★★ 'One of my books of the year'
★★★★★ 'A riveting book that l didn't want to finish.'
★★★★★ 'A beautiful story about personal growth, love, loss and friendships.'

FINDING EDITH PINSENT

Two women. Two timelines. One heart-wrenching story.

★★★★★ 'Outstanding!! Wow. Just wow.'
★★★★★ 'A rollercoaster ride and feelgood heart-warming experience.'
★★★★★ 'Edie is so realistic, you will fall in love with her.'

SAVING GERALDINE CORCORAN

One shameful secret. One hidden letter. Two unlikely guardian angels.

★★★★★ 'A truly powerful story told brilliantly.'
★★★★★ 'Sadness, love, humour, surprise. You name it I felt it.'
★★★★★ 'Superbly written and well worth reading, but be prepared to cry and laugh and cry again!'

BEING DOOGIE CHAMBERS

A free novella, exclusive to members of Hazel Ward's Readers' Club.

Doogie Chambers is in love with Netta Wilde. He thinks she's Debbie Harry crossed with Siouxsie Sioux. She thinks he's Heathcliff.

Be the first to know about Hazel's latest news and the general goings on in her life. You can follow her in all the usual places or join her **Readers' Club** and get regular monthly newsletters, a free novella and the occasional free story.

https://hazelwardauthor.com

Printed in Great Britain
by Amazon

41503631R00229